To MIKE & CONNIE SMITH,
LIFE IS AN ADVENTURE AND
JESUS CHRIST IS IN CONTROL.
I'VE LISTENED TO SOME OF YOUR
SERMONS ON CD. POWERFUL. GOD
BLESS YOU.
— Johnny
I CORINTHIANS 15:57-58

1·904·338·3378

Lifespring

JOHNNY EARL JONES

Poise Publishing, Inc.

To Jobi Jones and Chezney Jones,
my wife and daughter,
who are my joy and laughter,
and who have encouraged me through this journey

Acknowledgements

Plans succeed through good counsel.
Proverbs 21:18a, NLT

Each of these people offered either wisdom, encouragement, inspiration, or practical and professional help in the creation of *Lifespring.*

Jobi Jones
Chezney Jones
John Perry
Holly Bebernitz
Annette Dammer
Carl Hernandez
Chad Starling
Ben Vernon
John Hartley
Susan Bray

About the Author

Johnny Earl Jones is a writer who believes every great story begins with fantastic characters. Unashamed of his faith in Christ, he believes life is an incredible adventure, and that every step of the way we should encourage others and point them to their only hope, Jesus the Savior.

Johnny has a Bachelor of Arts degree in Literature from the University of North Florida, with a minor in Journalism. He currently lives in Jacksonville, Florida. His wife is Jobi Jones, a woman of incredible beauty and wisdom, and his teenage daughter is Chezney Jones, a bundle of energy and fun. He teaches the Single Adult Sunday school class called Rock Solid Foundation, and sings in the Sanctuary Choir at North Jacksonville Baptist Church, pastored by the dynamic Dr. Herb Reavis, Jr., which is aired nationwide on the Sky Angel Network.

* 1 *
TROUBLE IN PARADISE

"Save me!" a voice screamed from the forest's night shadows.

Navarro Silvinton turned his white charger in the direction of the desperate cry. He rarely traveled the woods when dark but knew traversing this wide forest would shave a dozen miles from his journey. What he didn't anticipate was trouble. Feral roars, the ringing of weapons, and threats of death directed toward him assaulted his ears. Everything was happening so fast in the deep darkness. Almost faster than he could comprehend.

He was being ambushed.

But Navarro, a stately warrior, wore his leather armor this night, and his sword leapt into his hand as he sprung from his horse. He peered into the thick fog, and located a maimed man a dozen yards away.

"Help!" the figure cried. "I'm going to die!"

The pounding of footsteps turned Navarro before he could get to the man, and he spotted three burly shapes charging him from the hazy darkness.

"Goblins!" he recognized immediately, disgusted when the moonlight broke through the trees' canopy and revealed their ugly, tusked faces. "You have no right here, you wicked creatures!"

"You die, warmblood," the lead goblin spat in his crude language, his jagged sword chopping down diagonally at Navarro. "How dare you disturb our feast. Curses on you!"

Navarro's blade sliced across viciously, knocking away the goblin's sword and sending the brute stumbling off to the side.

"I can't be cursed, evil one. The blood of Jesus has defeated every curse that could ever fall on me. You're the cursed one!"

Navarro pursued the monster but was forced to duck quickly as the second goblin's battle axe sliced across at his head. The momentum of the missed attack sent that one charging by harmlessly, but in came the third goblin with his curved scimitar. The brute chopped at him, and Navarro easily parried away the attack, but the monster's blade reversed angles and came in low for his knees. He started to block this elementary attack when he sensed danger behind him. The axe wielder! When he swiftly glanced behind, he saw the axe blade coming in high for his back. With no chance to parry both attacks, alert Navarro dove forward and over the low-cutting scimitar and out of range from the arcing battle axe. Touching down firmly on his tucked shoulder, he rolled with his momentum and came to his feet, away from the two monsters, but right in front of the goblin with the jagged sword.

"Death awaits, God-fearer!" the brute promised, his sword hacking down swiftly.

"Not tonight!" Navarro retorted, his blade whipping across with such velocity it sent the brute's severed sword-arm spinning away into the darkness before the wicked creature had time to scream. Navarro's fist slammed into the brute's gut, doubling him over. His knee bolted up, smashing the creature's face and propelling the goblin from his feet. The warrior's blade dove down and ended the goblin's evil life forever.

Hearing shrieking behind him, Navarro turned to the charging goblin with the scimitar, the monster's blade raised overhead to impale him.

"Show me what you've got!" he challenged the ugly, scar-faced monster.

Grinning wickedly and with eager saliva streaming from between his tusks, the goblin drove in, his scimitar plunging for the warrior's heart.

Navarro's foot snapped out in a side kick which slammed hard against the brute's solar plexus, stealing his breath and halting his momentum. Navarro charged in and front-kicked the stunned goblin's chest, sending the creature stumbling backward.

"This one is yours, Celemonte," he called to his war horse who snorted and rose up on his hind legs, pounding the monster to the ground with his front hooves. The goblin tried to drive his blade into the horse, but battle-hardened Celemonte stomped the wicked creature again and again until the light left the goblin's eyes.

The battle axe came in at a sharp angle, and Navarro barely got away, escaping with a slight gash on the midsection of his leather armor. Adroit Navarro quickly found his footing and dove in behind the momentum of that attack, his fist snapping out and finding his target, pounding the brute in the side of the head, stunning him. Navarro's blade dove in to seal the victory.

"Thank you, Lord," Navarro praised through labored breaths and walked toward his trusted charger. He looked back to the corpses strewn across the ground, stepping over one dead brute and snatching a dagger from its hilt, slipping it under his own belt. Patting Celemonte on the neck, he slid his sword back into his scabbard and glanced around the dark forest, sure there were no more monsters about.

Navarro started in the direction of the downed man, Celemonte in tow, and swiftly, he made his way to the groaning man's side. The damage was severe, the young man bled profusely from several bite and weapon wounds. He was still conscious.

"What's your name, son?" Navarro asked, his expression soft and sympathetic.

"Tarile," he replied. "Sir, do I have a chance? Am I going to die?"

Navarro knew the boy couldn't be more than 15 years old. He reached down and put his hand on Tarile's shoulder. "I'm here, and I won't let death take you."

"I fear for my friend," Tarile exclaimed. "A different group of goblins dragged him away deeper into the forest."

"I'll be after them in just a moment. First, you must be mended."

"But your armor is soft leather. You can't bind up my wounds with that. What good will that do to stop my blood loss?"

"There'll be no need for bandages."

"How will you keep me from bleeding to death?"

"Do you believe in Christ, the Son of God?" Navarro asked.

"I've heard of him."

"It's through His power you'll be healed."

Navarro gripped the young man's shoulders with both hands and bowed his head to pray. "Father, in the mighty name of Jesus, I ask You pour Your healing virtue through me. The wicked have inflicted harm. You alone can make Tarile whole. Heal him, Lord."

Navarro felt power, like rivers of water, flow down his arm, to his fingers, and into Jule's mangled frame. He held on tightly and praised God. If he'd not found this boy when he did, he likely would have perished. Only seconds passed before the sensation of flowing water stopped. Before Navarro even opened his eyes to peer at Tatile, the young man shouted joyfully and danced about.

"I feel better than I ever have! What's your name,sir?"

"Navarro Silvinton."

"You healed me!"

"Son, you have been healed by the power of Jesus Christ. I'll tell you of the Good News of Christ, the plan of salvation, later, but first we must go after your friend."

"They took him that direction." Tarile said, pointing into the deeper darkness of the forest.

"Are you a warrior?" Navarro asked, but when he saw the boy's small travelers' club, a weapon used primarily to ward off bandits, he already guessed the answer. "Tarile, what were you doing in these woods?"

"Bonnek and I were emissaries from Sheliavon to Avundar's Council of Rulers. We were traveling back to the kingdom, and passing through the Dolunar Forest as a short cut. I didn't think monsters existed in the our lands since the Great War. But the goblins swarmed us."

"This is so strange. No monsters have ever been this close to the Republic of Avundar. Tarile, you'll need protection as I pursue your friend." Navarro gently stroked his warhorse's thick neck. "Celemonte, stay with Tarile and help him find his horse. I must penetrate the night, save his friend, and put an end to these invaders."

The horse pawed the ground in protest.

"You must stay with him. Right now, the boy needs your prowess more than I do. Keep him safe," he said, patting the horse playfully on his face. Celemonte feigned a bite at Navarro's hand then pressed his head against the warrior's shoulder.

"I know you want to stay by my side as I confront these wicked ones. I fear with the arrival of these goblins will come ample opportunities for us to fight together. But for now, I assign the boy as your responsibility."

With barely a whisper of noise, Navarro dashed off the path and into the woods, racing from the cover of one tree to the next, keeping a mental compass of the direction Tarile had shown him.

His blade held securely in his hand, Navarro scanned the forest shadows as he sprinted through the trees, the cool night breeze blowing his blonde mane from his face.

This is the Republic of Avundar, he reminded himself as he tried to reason how a party of monsters could venture into this land without drawing any alarm. Never in recorded history have the forces of evil invaded this land. How could they be so bold now?

All senses on alert, he listened and heard only silence. No crickets chirped. No dragonflies buzzed about, and no woodland creatures skittered here and there. Tonight, the darkness seemed so eerie.

Collecting his thoughts, Navarro turned his eyes heavenward, calling out to the only one who could give him answers.

"Lord Jesus, the coldness of evil looms near. How could it have risen up in this goodly land? I've faced goblins in far away kingdoms, on distant battlefields, but never have I seen them here in Avundar until tonight. Strengthen me for whatever it is that I'm about to encounter."

Navarro slowed, trying to gain his bearings. Anxiously twirling his sword in one hand, he continued to search the darkness with his eyes while reaching into his memory for the words of warning he'd received from a trio of strange men the night before. The oval ruby embedded in the sword's hilt glowed fiercely, and he wasn't surprised.

A throaty growl echoed from somewhere in the woods, shattering the silence and turning him in that direction.

"Lord, You've guided me to victory after victory in many a perilous adventure," he prayed softly, and the acknowledgment of God raised a knowing smile on his concerned face. "In times like these, You grant me wisdom and boldness. I'm relying on Your promise of strength again, Lord, in this hour of danger."

Several roars, followed by a terrified yell, sounded in the still air just beyond a natural hedge of bushes directly ahead of Navarro, and he pulled up close behind the foliage. Carefully pushing apart several leafy branches, he peered through the opening into a small grove. What he saw made his stomach churn. Three more burly shapes pummeled their victim, beating him to the ground.

"The goblins!" he said quietly, enraged. "And they're pounding on Bonnek!"

Rapidly, Navarro formulated a strategy to eliminate the goblins without Bonnek perishing in the process. His mulling was disrupted a moment later when the goblins stopped their bludgeoning frenzy and frantically glanced about, sniffing the air suspiciously. Bonnek lay motionless on the ground. Two of the brutes grabbed their spears and began poking the bushes and checking the perimeters.

The goblins are spooked, he surmised. They sense that a believer in the Lord is near to oppose them.

After several unfruitful moments of beating the bushes, the two turned to the third, whom Navarro guessed to be their leader, and shrugged dumbly.

"Away we goes now!" the leader barked in its gruff language, waving the others forward.

"Are you stupids," one spear wielder argued, pointing to the boy. "This is whats we come for. I not leavin'. He struck me in the face. I eatin' him."

The Boss-Goblin stalked over and slapped the spear wielder hard on the back of the head. "This isses not why we came."

The other goblin shoved back. "It isses the reason I came."

"If you got issues, take 'em up with The Master. But I say we goes now." To emphasize his point the Boss-Goblin yanked his spiked mace from his belt and roared at the rebellious spear wielder. He pointed to the opening out of the grove and ordered again, "We goes now. I senses somethin' watchin' us."

This time both lesser brutes pressed forward.

Understanding their base dialect enough to piece together the conversation left more questions in Navarro's mind than answers. *What are they doing here?* Navarro wondered from his concealed position. *Never have I heard as much as one tale by the most educated historians or profuse storytellers about encounters with monsters here in Avundar, not even from ages past. The sudden appearance of these goblins is incongruous,like pollution in paradise.*

Patiently, Navarro waited for the goblins to amble out of the grove. He'd overtake them soon enough. He moved around the bushes and knelt over the bleeding boy.

"Bonnek," he whispered, shaking him gently. The teen curled up defensively into a fetal position. "You're safe now."

"The monsters," the boy said in a weak voice. "Watch out for the monsters!"

"They're gone."

Bonnek leaned and peered with swollen eyes at Navarro.

"What about Tarile?"

"He's safe. I destroyed his adversaries. He's awaiting your return. You boys have had a rough night."

"I don't think I can move. I fought the goblins as best as I could, but they ganged up on me, and I couldn't fend off all of them. I did get in some good hits though," he said smiling, but a gurgling cough stole his mirth. "I think my ribs and my leg are broken."

"You're a brave young man," Navarro encouraged. "Your tenacity held the monsters back long enough for me to find you before they finished you.

"I think it's about time you and Tarile get home. Your friend is finding your horses as we speak. Welcome the comfort and safety of your parents' protection back in Sheliavon."

"I have only my mother," the boy said sadly. "My dad died in the Great War in Sheliavon over five years ago."

Navarro's expression turned sympathetic. He had fought in that conflict. A tremendous horde of giants and goblins had torn through that kingdom. As a result of the horrible attack, many of Sheliavon's fighting men died.

"You'll be home tonight," Navarro promised.

"How?" the boy questioned, looking to his beaten frame before coughing violently.

"Have faith in God," Navarro said simply, then bowed and prayed. Once again, the Lord's healing power cascaded through his arms and fingers. Seconds later, it was over, and Bonnek was on his knees and embraced him thankfully.

"How can I ever repay you?" the teen asked, his face astonished and beaming.

"Get home safely. But more importantly, trust Christ as your Savior and ask him to forgive your sins. Call on the name of the Lord, and you shall be saved."

"Yes sir. We're going to church first thing in the morning."

"Good.

"On your way back to your horse your path is safe. The other goblins have been eliminated. I must leave you now and pursue the other brutes. God speed, young man. I'll see you again someday."

Navarro dashed quietly into the darkness, leaving Bonnek behind.

His pace propelled him swiftly within sight of the marching brutes. They appeared determined to arrive at a specific destination somewhere ahead. But where? And to meet who?

They did mention a master, Navarro recalled. Something must be directing these creatures.

He straightened suddenly, his mind jolted by a stunning recollection. "The warning!" he remembered, his thoughts drifting back to the events which led to last evening's strange encounter.

Yesterday at sunset, the schooner he and Celemonte rode on had finally pulled back into harbor after a week-long sail from the Telitarian Islands. His God-given responsibilities had led him to that tiny island nation. But once he had helped the islanders claim victory over a swarm of monsters, driving the brutes back into their caves, he'd been eager to get back to Avundar.

Although Avundar was not his homeland, being born and raised on the southern island chain of the Subrosas, he had grown enamored with the Republic's kind people and particularly with the gamboling elves whose secretive lifestyle intrigued him.

Having seen many a scarred battlefield on foreign lands, he admired the unmarred, pristine landscape of Avundar. Its variety of terrain ranged from the rocky Lomonis Mountains to the rich woodlands of the Maribowam Forest and the Verdant Wood to the vast Ormantict Plains. Only the Garden of Eden could have rivaled this land.

Once the ship had moored, he thanked the crew for their hospitality, paid the captain a handsome reward, and departed to follow the coast. Not far up the dark shoreline, though, he spotted a blazing bonfire on the lonely beach and three individuals seated around it.

Unusual, he considered, and unsafe. Although no monsters have ever plagued these beaches, I have heard of Northern barbarians occasionally sailing this far south to steal people from the shorelines to use as slaves. If there was the rare chance of the barbarians being off the coast, these three were providing a beacon with their huge fire. He headed in their direction to investigate and warn them.

"Good evening," he saluted once he got into earshot of the men.

"Not so good, paladin," rebutted one of the men, turning to face him.

Navarro stopped suddenly, taken aback by the man's unusual appearance, his face etched with deep wrinkles and his blinded eyes scarred. Looking to the other men, Navarro noticed they bore similar wounds. But what truly concerned him was how this sightless man knew he was a holy warrior.

"Who are you?" he asked them.

"Hanulot the wise who is not blind within," one answered up. "And seated with me here are my kin."

"Evil is rising up," the withered man started in a melodious tone.

"The mighty demons will not rest.

"They desire freedom from the abyss

"to destroy and to sever

"on this earth from which they had been expelled forever."

"What are you saying?" Navarro demanded.

Hanulot continued:
"Once the mightiest demons of hell ran rampant across the lands
"and nothing could resist their evil plans.
"The vile fiends coerced any living thing,
"defiling every facet of good this earth could bring.
"From animals to mankind, all fell short
"of what God had designed for each of their sorts.
"After Adam's fall, we all were corrupted by sin, you see.
"And that's why Jesus had to die to make us free.
"But to see man's rebellion these demons did not applaud,
"because humans are made in the image of God.
"With the evil power they possessed, they wanted to destroy mankind
"and every and all remnant of holiness God left behind.
"Satan assigned his most wicked demon, Diabolicus, to the lead
"for that hellspawn longed of God's vestige to be freed.
"But the Lord God, enraged by the demonic endeavors,
"snatched up the mighty demons and chained them to the lowest pit
forever."

Another of the scarred men piped in:
"Then God judged the earth,
"destroying with a flood all whom breath he was giving
"except on a massive ark, the prophet Noah and his family
"and the animals the Lord had led that would remain living."

The third spoke up:
"Mankind has survived and prospered under God's merciful hand,
"And the mightiest demons remain confined for their evil plan.
"But recently, through dark magic, with communication uncommon
"those who seek evil have communed with their sovereign,
"and the lesser demons have spoken of a powerful key
"that will unleash Diabolicus and unshackle his demonic army.
"With their anger having boiled for thousands of years,
"mankind will be hopeless if on earth they appear.
"The fiends hunger for human blood to spill
"And if this key can be found, all mankind they will kill.
"The forces of evil in this world long for it to be found,
"seeking feverishly this power to make those demons unbound.
"Beware warrior, the wicked will burst from cave and from den,
"in earnest to free the demons and bring mankind to an end."
"What a chimerical but impossible tale these men wove," he decided later
that night after departing from the men, choosing to dismiss the whole conversation
as a freakish bad dream come to life. So easily had they intertwined fantasy with the
truths of the Bible that he regarded their words as little more than idle rhymes. He

8

pressed onward to what he thought to be a more important use of his time, namely traveling to Avundar and finding reprieve from the past months' warfare.

Those thoughts quickly transported him back to the present crisis.

"How foolish of me not to investigate further," he lambasted. "Before me stalks three goblins, three others are cut down along the trail. Hanulot's words no longer seem so trivial. How I wish I would've lingered with the men and discovered who they really were and how they received their information. No time for regrets now. The goblins are on the move."

The trio came upon a clearing, scanning it carefully before proceeding. Navarro kept his footsteps quiet. The goblins were wary. One wrong move and they'd be alerted. From the tree where he hid, he noticed the next oak he could duck behind was a long, ten feet away. With three nervous goblins looking about, surely he'd be easily spotted if he tried to run it. He backed then stopped and measured the distance again. With three bounding steps, he dove, rolling on one shoulder, and with but a whisper of noise, his momentum carried him to that oak on the other side of the clearing's mouth.

The brutes turned, scanning the darkness behind them.

Peeking around the tree, Navarro gained a visual fix on them again, this time taking opportunity to note the goblins more carefully. He observed something unusual about them he'd not considered in the heat of battle against the others. They were heavily armed and armored.

Goblins are normally rank beasts, Navarro decided, their armor tattered and their weapons rusted or perpetually tarnished, making the vicious brutes less of a threat than they could've been. But these brutes look especially menacing. By their nature, goblins are wicked, heartless killers who hate every other race, rarely residing peacefully with their own kind unless under the fear of a dominant leader. They are willing to murder friend or foe for the most meager of rewards. Natural-born killers. These evil brutes equipped with immaculate armor and keen weapons means they'll be that much more dangerous.

Navarro had confronted goblins before on countless battlefields whenever they emerged to threaten peaceful communities. His responsibility was to protect the people of the lands from this kind of evil. But his life hadn't always been that way. Before he trusted Jesus Christ as his Savior, he used his abilities and acumen for his own selfish purposes, often to wrest goods from another or to steal a lady from someone else's side; however, God had different plans for him. After the Lord used a series of events to bring him to repentance and salvation, Navarro recalled how he prayed daily for wisdom and guidance. How and where could he be used by God? He sensed strongly the Lord wanted him to channel the same fighting caliber he used for shameful endeavors into battling the forces of evil.

He was a warrior, the paladin Navarro Silvinton. What a description, he considered, laughing quietly at a sudden thought. "What was a paladin?" most people asked him, for few knew about his calling. There were, after all, not many like him. With a dry wit, in his usual humble tone, he answered them, admitting that a "paladin" was just a fancy title for a warrior set apart for the service of the Lord. His next thought broadened his smile. The question following was always "You're a paladin?" He understood their doubt. His bronzed, corded muscles and long, sun-bleached mane made him look more like an island wave-rider than a champion of good.

Drained by continuous battles over the last several months, Navarro sought Avundar. During those months, without respite, he journeyed from one region to another, leading warriors to defeat throngs of bloodthirsty monsters only to receive pleas for help from an adjacent kingdom. And so it had gone continually, days quickly turning into weeks, and weeks rapidly becoming months. Never before had he seen such frequent and concentrated attacks from the wicked brutes. They seemed driven with unusual focus. Finally, after leading the Telitarian islanders in triumph over the monsters, and with no further pleas for his capabilities, Navarro longed for repose in Avundar's paradise. But now, with goblins stalking through these woods before him, he realized peace was not at hand.

Observing the foul monsters with disgust, Navarro turned his sword over and over again in his palm, his blade shimmering brilliantly whenever a sliver of moonlight splashed down through the tree branches. A crimson glow grabbed his attention. He looked down to its source. His sword's smooth richly colored ruby heart blazed with an inner fire.

"I know," he whispered, comprehending it sensed the evil of the monsters he was following. The weapon was a gift from God. Its keen, three-foot blade rose from a golden hilt, and the ruby rested within the crosspiece just inches below the blade, smooth and oval in shape. His sword was a beautiful weapon, Navarro admitted, but moreover a powerful one. Having wrested it from the lair of an evil Crimson dragon, the blade forged victory after victory in countless battles, its regal appearance unscathed by even the smallest scratch. The sword had seen action, he acknowledged, plunging into fiery skirmishes, blasting into hardened walls and even penetrating the mighty armor of a dragon's scales, but never had a blemish marred the tough blade. Invinitor, he affectionately called the sword, a name in his native island dialect which meant "the indestructible one."

"Relent," he instructed his weapon and immediately the fire in the ruby subsided, the stone taking on its deep-red opaque tone again. "Ever on guard," he praised it. It had saved him several times in the heat of battle. Invinitor's heart would glow when the presence of evil was near. How many times had that glow warned him of an enemy approaching at his back? How often had it given away the location of a hidden monster?

With sword in hand, he evaluated his foes. There were only three. Although evil and vicious beasts, he knew he could slay the trio in a matter of moments. Equipped with skills far above what these brutish monsters could hurl at him, he decided they'd be no match; however, he'd battled in enough campaigns to realize destroying these goblins would eradicate only a short-term problem.

"Goblins are cowardly," he said. "They would never venture out in such a small group to simply prey on unsuspecting victims, especially not in a land which was foreign to them. Those monsters, though warlike by nature, only fight in large armies, never as individuals or small groups; they gain their courage from overwhelming numbers. No, these goblins can't be a rogue hunting party, stalking human prey; they must be scouts, spying out the land and evaluating weaknesses. A greater threat lurks in the darkness for the people of Avundar. When a few goblins are spotted it usually means a gigantic nest of them hide somewhere in the shadows. For that reason, I cannot just leap into the group and snuff out their evil lives. I must trail them and discover their hidden lair."

Unexpectedly, the goblins veered off to the north, and Navarro raced to keep the brutes in his sight, surprised by their uncharacteristic resolve. Apart from fits of wreaking destruction, goblins were usually lethargic in everything they did. It was so unusual to see them move with such purpose.

Tailing only dozens of feet behind, he kept his footsteps hushed. He spied them turning down a treeless path and into a wide meadow which backed up to more dark woods, several hundred yards behind.

When the goblins stalked onto the open meadow, Navarro stopped short behind the final oak before the clearing, quickly weighing his options, watching the monsters march on, oblivious to his presence. The goblins, although resolved in their course, appeared distracted and not much time passed before he realized why. He could hear the Boss-Goblin and one of the others bicker. A few shoves were exchanged and one punch which didn't connect. Shaking his head, Navarro wasn't surprised at the creatures' demeanor. "So is the nature of goblins, brutish and warlike, even to each other," he said.

Pressing across the field twenty, forty, and eighty feet, the goblins put more and more open ground between them and The Paladin. Navarro felt frustration gnaw at the edge of his thoughts. He could do nothing about the escaping monsters. Scanning the field from one end to the other, he saw not a bush or a boulder he could hide behind. The only thing that even remotely presented itself was the tall grasses which the wind rippled up and down like the sea waves. The goblins moved fast, and with darkness crouching over the land for yet a few more hours, it would be nearly impossible to track them once they slipped in the woods at the back of the meadow.

"If I cannot follow them to their lair," he said, "I'll have to exterminate them now before they can extend any information to a waiting and malicious tribe."

Gripping his sword tightly, he sprang away from the tree and started to dash across the field. As he exited the trees something suddenly didn't feel right, and he stopped, the hair on the back of his neck standing up and a chill rolling over him despite the warmth of the waning night. The air took on a thick, electrical feeling, as if a lightning storm was about to strafe the field. When he looked up, not a cloud appeared in the starry sky. Glancing back toward the goblins, The Paladin noticed they looked even more troubled by the sensation than he did. They stiffened with fear, their bickers and fights brought to an abrupt halt.

"What's happening now?" Navarro questioned, disturbed that this peaceful land had suddenly become so dangerous during the months he'd been away.

Invinitor's ruby heart blazed again.

"Relent," Navarro ordered, but he sensed the strong presence of evil also. He glanced around the meadow, trying to discover the anomaly. Turning toward the goblins, he spotted it, not sure what to make of it at first. A fiery fist pierced reality and there it burned, suspended in the air right before the brutes' faces, forcing them back, their eyes bulging with terror. The flaming fist expanded, taking on a circular form and rapidly widening in circumference like a gigantic, disembodied, fiery mouth.

"A powerful wickedness emanates from that fire ring. A thick, overwhelming
dread, a hellish evil." When Navarro looked through the flaming circle he didn't see
Avundar's moonlit surroundings behind; instead there was only darkness, a black and
swirling mist, thick and impenetrable to the eyes.

The ring continued to grow, towering several feet taller than the goblins.
Navarro watched two of them topple, fear stealing the strength from their legs. The
third stood paralyzed, his frightful gaze frozen on the abysmal circle. Navarro
followed the goblin's stare and spotted something within the swirling mist. A hulking
shadow lurked in the churning darkness but melted back before he could get a sure
look. He suddenly understood this fiery ring for what it really was, a necromantic
ingress into reality. But from where?

"Help me, Lord Jesus," The Paladin prayed. "Prepare my heart to oppose
this evil. I feel I'm literally about to walk into the valley of death."

A monstrous fist thrust out of the fire ring, almost quicker than Navarro
could register, and snatched up the lone standing goblin by his vest and yanked him
into the mists. The creature's terrified scream trailed away into eternity.

Navarro withdrew behind an oak and watched the eerie scene before him,
unsure how he should react to this strange drama.

A different shadow approached the threshold of the swirling mists, this one
tall and ominous. It grew closer and closer to the fire ring and finally stepped
through! Navarro stared intently as the burly invader, crowned with a horned helmet,
closed on the two, downed goblins. He sensed the great evil this one emanated, the
wicked smell of death.

Strangely, the air grew chilly, The Paladin noticed, and he hugged closer to
the tree, not so much to get warmer but to be sure the invader didn't see him. He was
frightened. Suddenly, uncharacteristically, he wanted nothing more to do with this
situation. Taking a deep breath, he tried to shake the fear from his soul; he felt like a
trembling child in the first waking moments after a horrible nightmare. Never in any
battle, against any foe, had he experienced such overwhelming dread. He pushed his
thoughts through the cloud of intimidation and found clarity of mind. The invader
issued the fear, he concluded, its aura of daunting wickedness diffusing into the air
like an invisible, venomous mist.

"I'm being assaulted by demonically inspired fear," he said, guessing the
emotion to be a magical attack.

"Lord, you didn't give me the spirit of fear," Navarro prayed, gaining
strength from God's Word. "In the authority of the powerful name of Christ Jesus, I
command the aura of fear attacking me to dissolve and be no more." Like a dry leaf
caught in the wind, the fearful sensation blew away and was quickly gone.

As Navarro turned back to the muscular intruder and saw he too had noticed
the power of God shatter his evil emanation.

The invader's fiery eyes roved the tree line to locate the godly presence that
opposed his dark powers. His corded muscles rippled as he clenched and unclenched
huge fists. Navarro stood unmoving behind the tree, formulating a plan of attack
against this formidable monster, but after a brief moment passed without incident, the
invader slowly turned away. The Paladin was at first surprised it gave up on the

search so easily, guessing the powerful creature must be arrogant enough to think any opposition to his dark powers unworthy to be considered a threat. The monster went back for the goblins.

Reaching down with one huge fist, the invader snatched up one goblin by his armored breast plate, hoisted him to his feet, then even higher, lifting him from the ground.

Navarro stared closer, taking in the invader's stature. At first, from that distance, he couldn't discern monster's height, but it stood upright and straight like a man. But now, contrasted against the height of a five-foot-tall goblin, Navarro could see just how huge this apparition was. The sinewy invader pulled the goblin's face close to his helmet. The only part of his countenance visible was his flaming eyes. There they were, eye to eye, the goblin's feet dangling nearly two feet above the ground!

The intruder spoke, his words a dialect foreign to Navarro's ears, his voice reverberating like thunder across the clearing, and the goblin just stared, horrified. Again, the booming voice roared, and Navarro observed the goblin's response. Obviously understanding the giant, the goblin struggled to respond but fear had seized his tongue. With a growl, the giant flung the brute away, spinning him into the mist-filled portal, where eager claws latched onto him and dragged him screaming from sight.

He turned to the last goblin.

The giant is looking for some kind of information, Navarro comprehended. He seeks an answer these creatures don't seem to have.

"Don'ts destroy me," Navarro heard the goblin cry in his crude language. "I will find fer you, master. I will find fer you."

"What will it find?" Navarro questioned quietly, as the invader jerked up the goblin. The brute's next words stole that consideration and his breath away.

"Mercy, Master Zeraktalis. I will find the source o' power for you. Spare me, Dark Sorcerer!"

There was no mercy as Zeraktalis pitched the screaming goblin into the mists, but

Navarro hardly registered the monster's cry, his own thoughts dismayed. "Zeraktalis, the Dark Sorcerer! Here in this land! And seeking some mysterious source of power?" His heart felt numb. "Hanulot's words are culminating into a heinous reality right before my eyes. Monsters are boldly on the move in every land, the forces of darkness are furiously pursuing this source of power, but worst of all, this Zeraktalis is leading the quest!"

The name of the Dark Sorcerer carried his thoughts back a few years to the Kingdom of Sheliavon, the region adjacent to Avundar, where Navarro first heard of the feared Zeraktalis. The Paladin had charged in to assist that kingdom against a surge of invading monster hordes, who, as the circulating rumors stated, were being driven by the sorcerer's dark leadership. Consisting of only giants and goblins, the hordes should've been relatively easy to dispatch, regardless of size. When battling goblinoid hordes, it was well known that if confusion could be caused among their ranks, the brutes would turn on each other, break into skirmishes, and thus destroy themselves from within. Not so with these hordes. They struck, not like a hodgepodge of uncooperative tribes, but instead they melded together with a singleness of mind, becoming one huge, destructive entity. The combined horde rolled through human populations, overpowering army after army, demolishing town militias, and leaving hundreds, even thousands, dead in their wake. Because of the supernatural tenacity and boldness of the goblin and giant hordes, more than one of the generals fighting them suspected they were compelled, possessed, by some more powerful being.

Indeed, the rumors spread the longer war raged. Tales of some Dark Sorcerer controlling the dreadful monsters filled every camp that had come to aid in Sheliavon's rescue. Several even attested to seeing The Dark Sorcerer, but none who fought against him lived to tell about it. Many of Sheliavon's best fighters disappeared mysteriously in battle and their deaths were blamed on this Zeraktalis. The war produced tremendous casualties on the side of good, depleting nearly all the fighting men of Sheliavon before the warriors of Avundar and the Silver Elves could shore up the ravaged kingdom.

Even with the help of the fresh warriors, the battle remained tough. Newer forces were barely able to hold back the horde's momentum, with the reinforcements fighting courageously and stubbornly but to no avail. The horde vastly outnumbered the warriors. Navarro and several generals realized they'd soon be overwhelmed if they continued to fight power for power, so they planned and carried out strike-and-scatter tactics where the armies would sweep down on the horde, hit hard, and flee before the monsters could organize against them. Undaunted, the warriors pressed the same strategy over the ensuing weeks until over half the horde had been slain. Then one day, suddenly and without reason, the well-disciplined and organized goblin war machine splintered, the brutes reverting back to their usual chaotic demeanors, fighting in confused clusters and imploding in self-destructive skirmishes. It seemed the strings were cut on this puppet and it was left to flounder around on its own. In the following weeks the momentum swung completely in the favor of the rescuing armies and the monsters were herded and pressed back until they were finally pushed over the cliffs.

"I know you're here, Paladin of Christ!" Zeraktalis roared, jolting Navarro back to reality. "Why is it your kind is never far away? I grow weary of delaying my plans because of the interference of you God-fearing pests! Show yourself and fight. Let us see how great your faith is in your God, and we'll discover who will prove triumphant, the Christ-follower or the power of darkness."

Navarro nearly charged from behind the tree and engaged the sorcerer. He wanted to take his challenge and shove his words down his throat, but wisdom prevailed. Behind Zeraktalis, movement in the mist alerted The Paladin to more danger. Inside the portal, just beyond the realm of reality, stalked a growing number of hulking silhouettes. The shadows tore and charged at the smoking gateway. A huge clawed hand occasionally ripped through the mist and swiped at the air.

"The imposing sorcerer has mighty allies at his back," Navarro said. "Evil Ones never appear openly unless the odds are stacked heavily in their favor. At any moment those monsters could be unleashed, but something becomes acutely obvious. Although Zeraktalis knows I'm somewhere in the vicinity, he doesn't know exactly where. His fiery eyes still scan the tree line around the open meadow looking for me.

"I have to make a stand now," Navarro decided. "The power of Zeraktalis the Dark Sorcerer is legendary. If loosed upon the nations again, with swarms of eager, bloodthirsty brutes at his disposal, could any survive against his wrath? I have him here and now. Even at the cost of my own life, I must vanquish this evil one before it's too late.

"Lord, only you can lead me to victory in this impossible situation," he prayed, evaluating the odds. Looking to the ingress, he guessed no creatures could pass through the opening unless Zeraktalis summoned them. The claws swiping from the mists supported his supposition and reminded Navarro of a caged animal's restricted reach. The daunting task became apparent: he had to destroy the fire ring and defeat Zeraktalis. No small feat indeed.

I can't just charge out blindly against a creature with such incredible power, he decided. I must discover his potency to know what I'm up against.

Reaching down, he grabbed a stone, heaved back his arm, and launched the rock through an opening in the tree branches, and it thumped down several hundred feet to his right.

The sorcerer's head snapped in the noise's direction, his arm whipped out, and with a mighty shout, a branch of lightning soared from his fingertips. The bolt shredded the majestic oak it hit, spraying a shower of flaming splinters into the air. Although impressed and unnerved, Navarro fought through his fear and sprang away from the tree which concealed him. He raced behind the tree line to the left, angling himself for a charge. A second and a third enchanted shout echoed throughout the meadow before lightning ripped apart a young oak. The other bolt shattered a pine at its trunk where he'd just stood, collapsing the tree into the forest.

"Lord, help me!" he prayed as he separated from the trees and dashed onto the field toward the sorcerer.

Zeraktalis spotted him and turned. "I knew you'd show yourself, Paladin of Christ!" he roared, pointing flaming fingers Navarro's direction. "For your lack of wisdom, you Christ-fearers compensate with courage. But the days of the godly are nearing their end. Darkness will march against goodness and thrust it into the grave. Then wickedness will reign forever!"

"We all know the end of darkness," Navarro rebutted. "Jesus Christ wins in the end, and He alone reigns for eternity!"

"I'm about to set into motion a chain of events which will disallow that," Zeraktalis boasted.

The Paladin ignored the empty statement.

"As for you though," the sorcerer threatened, "your days are finished now!"

Navarro heard the ominous chanting as the sorcerer compelled magical energies for the next enchantment, but the paladin was still too far away to attack and knew he was an easy target on an open field. Thinking quickly, he snatched the goblin's dagger from his belt, spun it in his hands, grabbed hold of the blade, and launched it at the sorcerer.

Zeraktalis swatted away the spinning blade that winged for his head. The Paladin wasn't surprised by the sorcerer's deftness. But Navarro had achieved his goal. The incantation disrupted. Navarro's raced toward the sorcerer. His sword Invinitor dove toward the sorcerer's exposed gut. A quick chant created a radiant energy shield which refused the sword and sent it glancing aside. The Paladin reversed angles, sending the blade in low. Another quick chant elongated the shield and repelled Invinitor again. Tall Zeraktalis drove into the paladin, shield leading, as it again started up a chant.

Navarro tried to hold his ground but Zeraktalis' strength was Herculean. With a single shove of the shield, Navarro stumbled several steps back. The shield dissolved and the sorcerer's fiery hand raised, palm aimed in Navarro's direction.

"Tu-usima!" Zeraktalis roared in an arcane language, and one fireball then another rocketed toward The Paladin, the leading one thrusting straight for his chest.

With barely a second to think, Navarro instinctively leaped off to the side. He escaped the first attack, but the following fireball grazed his leg as he was airborne. He spun viciously, before he collided hard with the ground. Shaking off the pain, The Paladin leaped to his feet, snuffing out the flames biting at his boot.

Zeraktalis chanted again.

"You'll find trying to destroy me isn't as easy as picking off a trio of sniveling goblins," Navarro promised as he rushed in. "With the Lord as my strength, I fear neither you nor your dark powers!"

"Your faith in God is misplaced!" Zeraktalis roared. "Ek-esima!"

"I'm too late," Navarro roared in frustration. A bolt of lightning burst from the sorcerer's palm. Navarro saw it coming but his charge had him racing straight at it. "There is nothing I can do but..."

Using the momentum of his churning legs, he leaped into the air, turned a somersault, and the bolt zipping underneath his airborne frame. Without missing a beat, he touched down feet first and continued his charge, hearing the explosion of the lightning bolt as it collided against one of the forest trees.

"Ek-esima!" the sorcerer shouted again, unleashing another bolt.

Turning and spinning, Navarro barely escaped the path of this second, fast-moving lightning bolt. The deadly energies tore into his left arm, shredded his leather armor and ripped a deep gash which was cauterized immediately. The blast nearly knocked The Paladin from his feet. He winced in agony but knew if he had been hit straight-on, instead of glanced by that bolt, he'd be dead now. Again he heard the boom of the bolt slamming into a tree somewhere far behind him. Fixing his concentration back on Zeraktalis, he noticed the sorcerer had already made his way to the ingress.

"No!" he heard the sorcerer yell to the shadows in the mist. "I will finish him!"

Zeraktalis raised an electrified hand and turned in Navarro's direction. "You are quite the resilient one, Paladin of Christ."

"You haven't seen the best part yet!" Navarro shouted, sprinting at the fleeing sorcerer, ignoring the pain in his arm. "That's when I thrust my sword into your wicked heart!"

"Inescapable death is your only destiny, Christian! Seekominos Ek-esima!" A third lightning bolt rocketed toward The Paladin as the sorcerer stepped into the swirling mists.

In a desperate move, Navarro planted his heel, stopped his momentum, and purposefully let his feet slip out from under him. He fell onto his back just as the bolt zipped over him. Hearing Zeraktalis laugh wickedly, The Paladin leapt to his feet and turned to the gateway in time to see the sorcerer submerge into the mists. The flaming circle shrunk behind it until the final fires folded into the fabric of the air. "Inescapable death? What was he talking about?" Navarro asked. He'd fought in enough battles to know not to take evil threats lightly. Suddenly, he realized he'd not heard the last lightning bolt explode and he understood! He shifted to his left, and in his peripheral vision saw the bolt swiftly arcing back at him. He turned and swung Invinitor like a club, batting away the lightning before it slammed into him. The impact sent Navarro stumbling back several feet, but the energy careened away and looped back into the sky.

The Paladin looked to the bolt incredulously. "I can't get rid of this thing! It's designed not to stop until it's destroyed me!"

The bolt gained altitude, swept above Navarro, and plunged down at him.

"Lord, give me wisdom to prevail over this sorcery before it can finish me?"

His eyes followed the bolt as it dropped. His heart pounded out a rapid drumbeat in his chest as he stood his ground. He had no time to flee. If he ran for the cover of the trees, he'd be struck down long before he could reach them.

"Come to me," he coaxed, Invinitor grasped tightly in one hand. How would he thwart the plummeting lightning bolt this time?

Sixty feet.

Thirty feet.

Navarro heard the deadly cracking. He felt the prickling of the closing electricity.

At the last moment, he dove!

BOOM! The explosion tossed him awkwardly onto his seared arm, sending a flood of agony washing over him. No time to think about pain, he thrust his arms over his head to cover his face as a shower of flaming dirt clods pelted him.

A few seconds later it was over, leaving Navarro lying face down in the silence of the still night. Tentatively, he lifted his head, surveying the landscape for any foes, but it appeared Zeraktalis, confident his sorcery would destroy him, had not remained. He glanced over to the crater just feet away. Zeraktalis' lightning bolt had been defeated!

Leaping to his feet, Navarro pumped his fist victoriously before raising his hands toward heaven. "Lord, Your Word still remains unshakable. As you promised, 'No weapon formed against me can prosper!'"

The Paladin turned and looked to the spot where the sorcerer had disappeared, his thoughts filling with concern. *What does Zeraktalis want with the peaceful land of Avundar? Now that I know the Dark Sorcerer is leading the thrust, Hanulot's prognostic is terrorizing. But what evil relic or power could it extract from Avundar which would unshackle the mightiest demons of hell from their prison? And what kind of creature had such authority in the spiritual realm? It'll be hard enough to stop this powerful sorcerer, if it's indeed merely a mortal necromancer, and watch for demons at my back.*

Navarro surveyed the meadow once more, trying to digest the threat that

Zeraktalis and his plans posed.

"We'll meet again," Navarro uttered to the darkness.

"Christ Jesus, your power is beyond comparison. You are without equal," he prayed as he marched out of the meadow. "Now that the darkness is rising up, I know only Your strength can forge a victory against such a powerful, demonically inspired host. You alone can propel the forces of good to victory."

* 2 *

DARKER WORLDS

"Come on, Father!" Candace called as Kelt hesitated to wipe the sweat from his brow and catch his breath. Candace waved her cutlass playfully, daring him with a series of mock slashes and thrusts.

He watched her bounce easily from one foot to the other as she raced to the open field, her golden hair dancing elegantly in the early morning breeze. He set off after her again, still struggling for breath.

"I've never seen a deer run with such ease and freedom as you do, my girl. Where do you get such energy?" He laughed as he compared their endurance. For all her effort, Candace's tanned skin only glistened with perspiration. As he shook his head, drops of sweat spattered all about. "Your skills are definitely improving," he admitted.

"Improving?" she scoffed, amused. "You just won't admit your 20-year-old daughter exhausts her father in a sparring match."

He laughed lightheartedly at her words. "Exhaust me? I'm not so sure of that. But you certainly are out-racing me. Candace, you're quite a fighter but far from victorious in this match."

"You're practically defeated, Baron Kelt Veldercrantz," she giggled, using his monarch's title. She kept bouncing around, daring him, now with her padded sword leaping from one hand to the other. "Do you yield?"

"I've taught you better than that these past years," he warned, grave. Candace's countenance drooped. He doubted her eagerness had crossed the line into arrogance.

"Never count an opponent out until the final blow," he said and his face broadened into a sudden smile, easing her concern. "Now, let me see what you're made of."

She advanced cautiously. Early on her father taught her to react to an assault, not initiate it. Those who chose to drive in first exposed much about their fighting style, eliminating any element of surprise.

"Come on, girl!" he pressed. "The sun's almost above the mountain tops, and it's getting warm. I want to defeat you, and swiftly, before I drown in my own sweat."

"Defeat me?" she stammered, her eyes narrowing dangerously at the insult. She rushed him, quickly closing the distance. Kelt lost a step, not expecting the aggressive charge. The flat of her padded cutlass darted in high. Then dove low. Kelt deftly deflected the thrusts with his sword. She feigned a plunge for his chest, pulling his defenses up. Instead her cutlass arced down at his vulnerable thigh. *Easily enough finished*, she thought smugly.

But to her surprise, her father's padded sword darted down to parry the strike. She recovered in time to see the flat of his sword speed for her cheek. Thrusting her blade up to block, she fell into a backward tumble. Rolling with her momentum, she came back up to her feet a safe distance from her father.

"Impressive escape," Kelt complimented. "Let the chase begin anew!"

He charged, but she stood calmly, patiently surveying his potential attack pattern. His sword arced in at her side, and she almost committed her parry in the direction of the sideswiping attack. She quickly realized the strike would leave no room for a follow-up attack, and she knew he always left an open door for a combination. She waited half a second longer. Kelt whipped out a short sword from a scabbard strapped to his back, abandoned the leading assault. The second blade swept in low. Candace was alert. She leaped over the low sweep of the sword that nearly took her in the ankle.

"Excellent!" Kelt applauded. "That's the way to measure your opponent's maneuvers. Trust your instincts and not merely your sight. An experienced adversary tries to distract you with one attack thus opening you up for a completely different, lethal strike."

She slashed across at his head, forcing him to duck the sword, then slammed the bowing warrior in the chest with a quick knee thrust. "You mean like that?" she asked.

"That's exactly what I am talking about," he agreed from his crouched-over position. He sprang at her suddenly, wrapping both arms around her knees and pulling her legs out from underneath. She dropped flat on her back, her head bouncing viciously off the ground.

All went black.

"That hurt!" she grumbled, trying to shake the dizziness from her mind. "Sometimes our lessons do get rough, don't they?" She expected her father to respond. He didn't. She forced herself to one knee, rubbed the back of her skull, and tried to adjust her blurry eyes. But she could see nothing but darkness all around her. Rising unsteadily to her feet, she glanced around, seeing no one. She didn't even appear to be in the meadow any longer. Surrounding her in every direction were the twisted silhouettes of warped trees. With wide eyes, she slowly took in the scene. Her hands trembled with fright. "Where am I?" she whispered. "What's happening?"

Standing motionless in the dark, she felt vulnerable, helpless, and suddenly found herself hyperventilating. Her heart pounded like a rapid drumbeat. Feeling herself overwhelmed with fear and unwilling to let it paralyze her, Candace took slow measured breaths to calm her nerves. Quickly removing her cutlass's padding, she took one step forward, then another, and another. Slow and reluctant, she pushed forward into the unknown, apprehensive about what she might discover and trying not to imagine what could find her. Alarmed and frightened, she suppressed her fear. It could cripple her should she have to fight for her life.

Her mind spun into a blur as she tried vainly to rationalize the sudden change in scenery. Just a moment ago, she was on the plush meadow with her father, sparring and racing, and now here she was in a dark and eerie forest. *In this unreal forest*, she questioned, *where was her reality?*

At the crunching of a close footstep, she slipped behind a dark tree. Sword arm tensed to strike, she wiped the perspiration from her brow.

Another footstep sounded in the darkness and she drew closer to the cover of the tree. In an environment so dark, she guessed, any lurking creature likely had some form of heat-seeking perception. That thought did not put her any more at ease.

Confrontation seemed inevitable. She pulled her sword arm back and gripped the tree for leverage. "Ugh!" she squeaked, pulling her hand away quickly from the slimy tree, her lip curling in disgust as she wiped the sticky resin on her pant leg.

Again the heavy footstep crunched. She felt every muscle tense. Her breathing grew heavier. Her hands shook. Eyes darting frantically, she could see no movement anywhere in the darkness. "Remember your training," she whispered, bringing her breathing under control and relaxing her muscles. She knew if she was stiff and short of breath, she would surely succumb to an attack.

Still a new wave of oppressive fear washed over her, smacking her like an unexpected breaker and plunging her into the depths of fright. She needed help beyond her own skills.

"The Lord is my Shepherd, I shall not suffer need..." she found herself whispering. Those words from the psalm of David gave her courage, even began to erode the assault of fear. "Yea, though I walk through the valley of the shadow of death, I will fear no evil: for thou art with me: thy rod and thy staff, they comfort me..."

"You will receive no solace!" a booming voice roared out of the darkness, sending Candace's heart beating wildly. "Your God cannot help you here!"

With trepidation, she peeked around the tree, hands shaking badly. Glancing to the left, everything seemed quiet and still. *Where did that voice come from?* Her eyes roved slowly to the right, her vision slightly accustomed to the darkness. A towering shadow stood not more than twenty feet away from her. She immediately froze in terror. Blacker than the night sky, the shadow's fiery eyes penetrated the ungodly darkness. He stared straight at her!

She started to scream but found herself without strength. Louder than thunder, her heartbeat pounded in her ears. Her legs felt weak. The oppressive fear surged back in on her, almost suffocating her. To her ultimate terror, the ominous, blazing-eyed shadow stalked slowly toward her.

"There is no escape for you now!" his booming voice declared, hurting her eardrums. "You're in my realm now, in the land of darkness. No one can help you here! No one!"

Her mind pled for her to run, to flee with all the energy she had, but her muscles wouldn't respond. Her eyes were hopelessly locked in his fiery gaze, paralyzing her in his iron grip of terror.

"Look away!" she warned herself but any effort to resist fled away. No, it was stolen away as those flaming eyes, radiating an aura of the basest evil. They bored right into her. Piercing into her soul, they seemed to drain the very life from her. Slowly, the shadow advanced toward her like a cobra who had ensnared his victim with a mesmerizing gaze. All her years of training, all the self-control, and all her courage crumbled away into nothing, crushed by paralyzing dread. She felt powerless and utterly without hope. The jaws of death itself were about to close on her.

"Be strong and courageous!" She heard the words loud and clear in her mind. They were words she read often from the Holy Scriptures. The Lord gave this command over and over again in the Bible, and she knew they were words that could save her life! Finding renewed strength well up within, she tore her eyes from the shadow's gaze and pushed aside her fright. She was still afraid, she admitted, but she wouldn't let it doom her.

"You say no one can help me here?" she intrepidly cried, rebutting The Shadow's words. "Someone just has!" she said, turning her eyes heavenward. "Thank you, Lord Jesus!"

The Shadow roared as if pained by that Name and swiped at her with his huge gauntleted fist. She ducked low, just barely avoiding the hit. Thinking quickly, she thrust her blade at his gut, hoping to run him through. The shadow's arm whipped across with lightning speed, backfisting the blade away with force so great he knocked the cutlass from her grasp and sent it flying into the darkness.

"What else can go wrong?" she groaned, now weaponless and still without any bearings on her location. "When nothing else works in a fray, the best defense is to flee."

The Shadow swiped at her again, but she sprang aside, turned, and darted deeper into the woods, desperate to distance herself from her attacker. Once she was safe, she'd contemplate a plan to remove herself from this nightmarish land. But for now, her instincts told her above all else to escape!

Mocking laughter echoed behind her. "You cannot flee from me! I am the Dark Sorcerer, and this is my domain!"

The Dark Sorcerer? The name sounded so familiar, so ominous. *Where had she heard it before*? she wondered as she fled. She felt somehow that name was the key to her escape from this hellish place. But how? And why did it ring so dreadfully in her mind? "My father!" she remembered as she raced. When she was a young teen, her father had been troubled by that name. In those days, her father led his barony's warriors into a neighboring kingdom to war against this sorcerer and his minions. The monster throng, led by the Sorcerer, was eradicated, and the Dark Sorcerer had not been heard from again. All that seemed a moot point now. His heavy footsteps were pounding not far behind her!

The fear of being caught in his clutches increased her feverish pace, the silhouettes of the trees sped by on either side. Several minutes passed and the footsteps sounded as if they had fallen farther behind. She nearly shouted in elation. She was outracing him!

Dashing wildly, she prayed she would not accidentally run into another denizen of the darkness, and she begged God for the endurance to outrun this wicked monster. With no stars or moon in the sky, she had nothing to light her path as she raced through the forest. Her next step sunk her boot deep in mud, holding her foot and nearly throwing her on her face. The Sorcerer's footsteps closed in behind her.

With her other foot finding solid ground, she planted her heel and grabbed onto a nearby root, trying to pull herself up. "Let go," she growled, pulling up with all her might and nearly lost her boot as the quagmire relinquished with a defiant, sucking noise.

Finally her foot pulled free of the clinging mud, she darted forward again, her heart racing. Valuable distance had been lost by the delay. She didn't dare look back to see how much ground the sorcerer had gained on her, and she feared the sight of its fiery eyes would again steal the strength from her legs.

A dark tree appeared before her face, and she wove to the right just in time to avoid smashing into it. She didn't slow her stride as she dodged another tree and sprinted headlong into the eternal darkness. The Sorcerer's hideous laughter mocked her efforts, echoing dangerously close at her back. She wouldn't give in to hopelessness, though. Her father made sure throughout the years that above all, she must remember to never give up.

"This Sorcerer might be the master of this domain," she said to herself, beginning to gain a little confidence, "and he might be able to trail me in a straight sprint, but can he keep up with my dodging quickness? My only chance is to lose him among the twisted trees of his own forest." She veered to the right, rounding a wide, gnarled tree and wove again to the right before continuing her wild dash. She zipped to the left and dashed ahead a good dozen yards and cut right again, rounding half the girth of a wide tree, then bearing off to the left.

The hideous, mocking laughter echoed through the trees again not far behind, chilling her bones and making her heart feel heavy with helplessness. "I can do all things through Christ who strengthens me," she encouraged herself aloud through labored breaths, "even outrun this wicked creature in his own land!"

She slipped around one more tree and dashed headlong as fast as she could. Her ears, so sensitive to every sound in this desperate situation, still heard the Sorcerer's footsteps chasing her. For all her trouble, he didn't seem much farther behind her! How foolish she was to think she could outsmart this sorcerer in his own dark forest.

"Lord, help me!"

She ran upon a copse of crowded trees. Without slowing, she wove through and slipped sideways between the dense trees. The trees painfully slowed her pace. She banged elbows and knees to push her way through the murky forest. Her breath came heavy now, her legs feeling like lead, but terror kept her feet moving, and soon she squeezed through the copse and raced away at full speed again. Several long minutes passed, and her exhausting pace began to play itself out. Huffing now, she gulped for air. Her speed began to dwindle.

Hopelessness flooded in again. How could she escape? Even if she did somehow outmaneuver the sorcerer and elude it, what then? Would she have to hide forever? How did she get in this land? And more importantly, how could she ever get free of it? She wondered.

Unable to go any farther, lungs burning and muscles screaming for a reprieve, she ducked behind a tree, held her breath and wished she could quiet the drumming of her heart. The Sorcerer's heavy footsteps pounded in her direction. Her eyes went wide. She felt utterly helpless without her weapon. The pursuing footsteps grew closer. She could feel her heart booming in her chest. The footsteps stopped next to her tree and then silence eclipsed the surroundings for what seemed an eternity. Sweat poured down her forehead. Her stomach cramped, lungs burned for oxygen, but she didn't dare breathe and give away her location. She cautiously glanced around the side of the tree and saw those flaming eyes search the darkness. Throwing her back to the tree, she hugged as close to it as she could, trying to evade the Sorcerer's penetrating gaze.

She sucked in a desperate breath, but in the silent darkness, it sounded like a loud gasp. She heard the crunch of the undergrowth as a footstep fell, sounding like it was coming in her direction. Another footstep. Then another. *Should she run?* she wondered desperately. Her energy was drained. She didn't stand a chance of outrunning this untiring fiend. But she had to do something. If she didn't and just stood there, she'd be torn apart. One more footstep sounded toward her. She'd have to run.

The footsteps began pounding again, running. Her heart froze. Then the steps faded away as the Sorcerer dashed out into the wooded darkness. For a long time she stood paralyzed, afraid to move, afraid to breathe. When she could hear the footsteps no longer, she fell to her knees and gasped for breath, chest heaving, muscles shaking. "It's gone," she gulped. "It's finally gone."

Her hands went to her knees as she tried to support herself, breathing in precious air, inhaling, exhaling, every gulp of air renewing her strength. Several long minutes later, she pushed herself to her feet, still breathing hard.

"Now where do I go?" she wondered. She had no idea where she was, so she decided any direction would be a good place to start, except, of course, where she heard the footsteps disappear. She found a large stick lying on the thick roots of a tree and picked it up. Without her sword, she needed some kind of weapon, and a primitive club would have to work.

If she could find where she'd first arrived, maybe she could find clues to get her back to her reality. This all seemed so bizarre, but she had no other choice but to press onward. Carefully choosing the direction she thought she had come, she proceeded cautiously. Not a few steps into her journey, she noticed a shadow she didn't recall passing.

His flaming eyes opened!

She screamed and swung her club at him. The Shadow's thick arm swept across and shattered the weapon. *Run! Run! Run!* her mind urged, and she turned and dashed away.

She never saw the thick root, and the toe of her boot snagged it. She sprawled to the earth, banged her elbow painfully, and landed chin first onto the hard ground.

The Shadow dove on her. His strong hand latched onto her shoulder.

He tossed her over onto her back.

She bolted awake, heard herself screaming, her face wet with perspiration. It was daylight again. She was back on the open field once more. Looking up, she didn't see the flaming eyes of an evil sorcerer. The handsome, gray-bearded face of her father loomed, his strong arm supporting her head. Surrounding her were several younger warriors, members of her father's Elite Guard force.

"That was a bad fall, Candace. I truly didn't mean to hurt you," Kelt said. "How do you feel?"

"I've felt better, but I can take a beating," she joked, forcing a weak smile, feeling still badly shaken by her nightmare. Recalling now what had caused her fall and thrown her into that incubus, she threw her arms around her father's neck and held on tight, glad to be free of that terror. "I know you'd never mean to harm me."

Behind her, she heard several hushed sighs from the guards. Her father began to snicker.

"By the reactions of my men, they, no doubt, wish to be the ones receiving your embrace," he whispered teasingly to her, petting her long, golden hair. "My daughter, sometimes I have to remind myself that you're not my little girl any longer. You've blossomed into a woman of stunning beauty." He held her close. "I'm so sorry. Everything'll be well now."

"No, father!" she urged suddenly, pulling herself out to arm's distance. "I had one of those accursed nightmares! This one was as real as the ones I've had before. Something bad is about to happen. I can feel it. And I think I'll play some part in its fulfillment."

She watched her father's head drop, for he knew well her unusual gift. Or is it a curse? Several of her other nightmares had become realities.

She recalled with a shudder the most poignant and horrible evidence of her strange ability, a nightmare and an event that changed her life forever. She was just a little girl then and had come to her father that evening, tears streaming down her terrified face. She could barely speak through her weeping, but somehow managed to convey to him a dream that her mother would be murdered. That night he cradled her and sang to her, trying to comfort and tell her it was only a nightmare.

The next evening, his guards had discovered her mother slain outside the fortress walls.

Later, he gently asked her to explain as many details about the nightmare as she could remember. After many tears, she described it as well as a 5-year-old could, and Kelt discovered her description matched exactly the evidence of the brutal killing. He'd never discovered who the murderer was or why his wife had been killed. Her death had nearly destroyed him. Many in the fortress thought he'd never recover from his depression and sorrow, but his sad, lonely little girl pierced through his melancholy, and he realized he needed to be strong for her.

He knew his dear wife wouldn't wish him to stop living but would want him to raise a godly little girl who could have a positive impact on the world. He took those thoughts to heart and poured almost all his energies into training her. He'd decided he wasn't going to take any chances losing her, his only child, to some horrible misfortune as he had his wife. From an early age she learned the disciplines of sword-fighting and self-defense from her father and a myriad of other instructors. As a result of that tutelage, she progressed rather swiftly. Now as a mature woman, she was able to fight as well, if not better, than many of his soldiers. At least that's what Father told her. She'd started her training because of his concerns, but she developed a passion for it, surpassing even his expectations for her as a warrior. Although slender, she was deceptively strong. Every now and again he liked to embarrass her, telling her that her muscles were as taut as woven cords and toned to a perfection which put many of the male warriors to shame. Usually he said it when there were visitors to the castle, loud enough of course, for all to hear. How often she'd pinched him hard during those humiliating moments, but it meant the world to her he was so proud.

He used all other moments during those years to strengthen both the numbers and the skills of his army as well as overseeing the building of a tremendous outer wall to surround the fortress.

Consequently, and sadly, he'd neglected his faith. He no longer talked to

God. He no longer read the Bible. He didn't even take the time to teach her about the Word of God, instead entrusting the Captain of his Elite Guard Battalion, Simeon, to encourage her in godly ideals and to raise her up with a knowledge of the Bible. She tried to lead him back into fellowship with God several times, but each time he rejected her attempts, putting up a wall of resistance against her words.

It had been years since her last prophetic dream. Inwardly, she groaned of the implications of this new one.

"What did you see in your nightmare?" he asked.

She began to explain, but the horrible images forced her to hesitate. Kelt's hand gripped her shoulder, lending her courage. "Father, I'm unsure what this dream meant. It was horrible. More dark and hopeless than any I've had before."

Candace watched her father force away a troubled scowl, knowing he dreaded the fulfillment of another bad omen. The loss of his wife had nearly ruined his spirit. But she had to explain what this nightmare entailed, the whole frightening event. She'd seen too many of these visions come to pass. Hopefully, they'd have enough time to do something before this one became a reality.

"What did you see?"

"I saw evil personified. I was transported to a land of darkness and was pursued by a creature radiating the most hideous evil," she said. "He was a towering shadow, unrelenting and deadly, and his presence alone nearly drowned me in fear, Father. Other than his appearance, I don't know much about him. I have no insights into his motives or why he wanted to destroy me. I just know he hated me and my Lord Christ.

"Oh father, he emanated such demonic power. His appearance alone was hellish. He was tall and powerful and blacker than the darkness itself. Crowning his head was a scarred, horned helmet, and in the dark recesses of it burned the most terrifying flaming eyes. The loathsome wickedness he exuded melted away my courage. His gaze seemed to pierce into my very soul.

"He called himself the Dark Sorcerer..."

Kelt's gasp stopped her mid-sentence. Her words had drained the blood from his face. She heard the sharp clicks of metal as the men behind her father instinctively reached for their weapons at the mere mention of this evil.

"Many of the warriors spoke of him years ago," she responded, anxiety edging her words. "Who is he, Father?"

"He's the most horrid of fiends," Kelt answered. "But I thought he'd been chased away forever. All the world hoped he was gone. Oh Candace, what would that evil monster want with you?"

"I wish I knew. He chased me through a dark and twisted jungle like a fierce lion after his prey. No matter where I turned, he was there. Regardless of how fast I ran or how many obstacles I left in my wake, I couldn't evade him. Father, even with all my training, I have to admit I was scared."

Kelt firmed his jaw and flexed his shoulders as if shrugging off a deadly chill. "Of my current army, only my most seasoned fighters and I fought against the sorcerer's foul minions when they invaded Sheliavon."

Candace nodded. She was only a teenager then. Around the fireplace, she'd heard many horrifying tales of war. From these stories, she'd learned of hordes of brutes, an unusual collection of goblins and giants, who pillaged and savagely murdered humans in whatever town or settlement was in their path. The beasts had fought with no fear, unafraid of death and unshaken by any effort to stop them. Instead, with one mind, they ravaged the countryside, shredding Sheliavon's armies. Several warriors hinted in their tales that the dark souls of the monsters were possessed by evil, manipulated into a destructive extension of the infamous sorcerer, Zeraktalis. They told how the throng's strength seemed unbeatable, how nothing could slow this horde's momentum. Ultimately, it required the combined forces of Avundar and the remaining fighters from Sheliavon to bring the monstrous reign of terror to an end. Since that time, the sorcerer hadn't been heard from again. Kelt had hoped Zeraktalis had somehow been killed during the war. Now with the prophetic dream about the evil one, it appeared that wasn't so.

"Know well that as long as you're within my fortress walls, the Sorcerer won't reach you," Kelt boldly promised. But what she saw reflected in his eyes was concern and dread, and she easily discerned that he was recalling the destruction and massacre inflicted in Sheliavon years ago. But she didn't doubt his word. Knowing the stubbornness and tenacity of her father, she knew any promise he made, he'd keep.

Looking up to the morning sky, she watched brilliant rays of orange light pierce the peaks of the distant Lomonis mountain ranges, signaling the early morning sun was about to climb over the peaks. Candace smiled thankfully. A new day was beginning. The sunlight chased away the shadows, dissolved the dread of her nightmare, and gave her a renewed courage. She turned to her father, her azure eyes shining radiantly in the new day's sunlight.

"I know you wouldn't let anything happen to me," she said, smiling and playfully tugging at her father's beard. "You instructed me for situations just like this. You trained me to defend myself, so fret not, father. I can take care of myself just fine."

* * * * *

Sebultis Killion reluctantly stepped into the dark corridor and sealed the door behind him. His heart beat hard in his chest. He waited as his eyes slowly adjusted to the darkness. He'd been in this same blackened hall many times over the past long seasons. Yet the anxiety was always present. Straightening his shoulders, he steeled himself, lifting his chin majestically. Here he received his power, here he was endowed with his unearthly abilities, here he communed with The Master.

Master? The word stuck in his throat. He'd always been a self-made man with skills far outweighing others. A warrior without equal, he was the master over all he surveyed. So why was he gripped with intimidating fear whenever he isolated himself within this dark space?

He scowled away the question, knowing it was hopeless even to ponder. The Master owned him. Ever since that fateful day on the battlefield of Sheliavon when he'd first come face to face with that mighty creature and agreed to a pact with him, he was no longer his own man. He'd been a younger man then, a foolish man hungry for power and willing to get it no matter what the cost. But he had no idea that aligning himself with such an ungodly monster would cost him so much.

Was he foolish to accept The Sorcerer's offer? He could've gained great power on his own over time, but without the powers and resources given him by The Master it would've been nothing like the great and secret dynasty he'd woven throughout all the regions.

As he gazed down the dark hallway, he began to discern the outlines of the walls. It was time for him to move. With a confident gait, he started forward, ignoring the nervous pounding of his heart. The passageway was short and uncluttered, having nothing he could trip over or run into. Killion could walk this stretch with his eyes closed, but regardless, he scanned the corridor anxiously. Instinctively, his hands reached for the hilts of his twin dirks, the two-foot long knives hanging from the scabbards at his hips. Although he was aware the passageway was clear, he proceeded cautiously, never knowing if some demon had slipped from the realm of his master to haunt this corridor. If that was the case, he was ready. Preparation and an alert mind had always been his keys to survival in this dangerous lifestyle.

The corridor ended abruptly, not at a door to an adjoining room, but at a huge, blanketed wall. Through the darkness, he saw the waving shadows of the bulkhead. He reached out and grabbed onto one of the folds, jerked the thick curtain to the side, and uncovered the wall behind. Striding to the other side of the hall, he pulled away the remaining folds to reveal the rest of the wall and the huge framed device which looked like a mirror. As he gazed into its center, he did not see his reflection, but the abysmal scene of dark swirling mists.

Killion shrugged off his anxiety, gaining a renewed level of courage in the new, yet dim lighting. Just as his confidence began to gel, the huge swirling face of the mirror went black, again surrounding him in darkness. Knowing what was about to begin, he steeled himself. Once and again he'd been through this ordeal, yet it never seemed to lose its otherworldly, fear-inspiring aura.

A high-pitched wail pierced the blackness and sent chills down his spine. He glanced around cautiously, though in the dark he could see nothing. It always began this way, and every time he wondered if he'd live through the danger to see another day. From the side he sensed movement and turned. A shape flitted away into the deeper darkness. "Something else is in here with me," he growled.

Another movement to the right snared his attention. His dirks leapt into his hands as he spun. He spotted only the backside of some squat, leathery creature as it scurried out of sight.

Overhead, fiery stirrings caught his eye. Glancing up, he spotted one of the intruders, the ghostly image of a tattered, flying wraith, its face nothing more than a fanged skull with fire in sockets where eyes should've been. The fiend circled close to the ceiling, darting and weaving in the darkness.

"Demons," he groaned. "Demons are always the prelude."

Slowly and one by one demons oozed out of the brick wall and began pacing the open corridor. He easily spotted them, but they no longer attempted to stay concealed. "Ugly creatures they are," he said, looking at the squat imps, beasts not taller than four feet but savage-looking. Their gaping jaws were lined with razor teeth and stubby arms ended in wide hands with long, curved nails.

He was not overly concerned. Demons emerged whenever he prepared to commune with his master in this dismal hall. Still he didn't trust them. They were evil and murderous to their core. If Killion let down his guard against them for even a second, he'd invite their long, filthy claws into his back. But they wouldn't dare touch him, he thought. He was aligned with their Master, and they knew better than to disobey him.

Dozens upon dozens of the fiendish imps seeped into the corridor, crowding into a swarming mob behind him.

Looking at the intimidating scenario, Killion grew a bit nervous. Demons had always appeared during his summons in front of the mirror, but not this many. The fiends slowly closed in and began to gather behind him in a semi-circle, though staying a respectful distance away. His eyes narrowed angrily. Had The Master decided his usefulness had come to an end? Had The Master summoned all these demons to feast upon him, destroying his soul forever? Turning and spinning on the demons, he cut a dangerous circuit in the air with his dirks. It wouldn't be so easy to destroy him. If they wanted to execute him, it was not going to be without a fight. The dirks sliced across again, this time low, scattering the closest demons.

"Do you dare oppose me?" he challenged the fiends, pointing out the closest with the points of his blades. Most of the demons looked unimpressed, some looked at him dumbly, others shrugged their shoulders, chattering noisily with fellow demons in their hellish language.

"You're not afraid?" he roared, bringing his weapons back up threateningly. "I'll make you vile fiends fear! These blades are the 'Fangs of Hell,' gifts from your master and empowered to send your spirits back to the stinking abyss!" He approached, a wicked smile on his face, and this time they did edge back, their ugly faces staring dreadfully. With his confidence growing, he drove the fiends back farther and farther. The demons, however, seemed to look through him, past him, and it was not until he noticed the reddish tint diluting the darkness that he realized the demons' trepidation was not inspired by him after all. His heart pounded rapidly as slowly he turned back to the wall and fell on his knees.

In the midst of the blackened mirror, he watched two fiery eyes open slowly, dramatically. His master always had a flare for the spectacular. But today, was it the overture to destruction? How helpless he suddenly felt. Potential death was at his back in the form of scores of demons. Or if The Master chose, Killion could be destroyed by sorcery tossed through the magical mirror device. Times like this made him regret selling his soul for the prowess and power he'd been given.

"Your servant begs your bidding, my master," he humbly addressed the flaming eyes, fighting against his own steeped pride with every word.

"Have you found it?" a booming voice thundered from the mirror.

"Not yet, my master," he apologized, staring into those enraged eyes from his humbled kneeling position. "But we continue to search for it. We do have a premonition of where it may lie, but we won't know for sure until we infiltrate the area and seize the source."

"There is no doubt the emanation of power is within your land of Avundar. I've exhausted much communication with the major demons of the abyss, and although, from their smoking pits, they couldn't pinpoint the source, all evidences point to its existence there.

"I will send you fighters, monster warriors, to insure your victory. Your role is to find it! Don't disappoint me Sebultis Killion. You know what'll happen if you do."

Killion's hand went defensively for the scar on his bare, corded biceps, a blast burn torn into his arm during an unforgettable summoning of his master immediately after the disaster in Sheliavon. Killion and his army hadn't stayed around to see the end of the battle those five years ago. When the goblin horde marched against Sheliavon, he and his assassins infiltrated the homes of monarchs, deceiving them into thinking they were a visiting army from Avundar sent to assist against the monsters. By the time the horde besieged that particular monarch's stronghold, Killion and his men had already worn away the defenses through key assassinations. The brutes could easily ransack the fortress and destroy any opposition swiftly. But when the horde began to self-destruct shortly after being challenged by a coalition of Avundar's baronies and the Silver Elves, Killion pulled his assassins out of Sheliavon before they could be linked with the monster horde.

Tales trumpeted how the keen-witted Avundarians, although a smaller force than the horde, continually eroded the monsters' numbers, the armies attacking as one then retreating before the brutes could form any kind of solid defense and counterattack. Those adroit warriors came at them for weeks, repeatedly slicing into the throng's numbers before slipping away to safety. Then when another opportunity presented itself, they'd return, keeping the horde wary and back on the defensive instead of surging forward to lay waste to the kingdom. Under the Avundarian warriors' incessant attacks, The Master's once impressive war machine was cut down to only half-strength. At that time, The Master decided the size of the horde would be useless for his plans and removed his control from them, leaving them to battle with their brutish wits. Predictably, without The Master controlling them, the goblins and giants who had been an unstoppable fighting unit, fell apart into squabbling, disorganized bands which the Avundarians, united with the surviving Sheliavonians, easily picked off.

It was on that day The Master had summoned him before the mirror. To his surprise no demons entered the corridor. He was by himself before his Master, and his Master was not pleased. Fuming, cursing and roaring filled the corridor that day, but Killion could barely remember what was said; however, the emotion which permeated that room was something he would never forget--hatred, burning, fiery wrath! In the midst of the tirade, he felt a measure of the Master's ire. What he could only describe as a splinter of his wrath, a streak of fiery energy pulsed through the mirror and blasted him, searing his arm.

Killion shook off the painful memory and glanced back up to the mirror in time to see the fiery eyes fade to nothing, the whole room falling back into darkness. The demons around him melted into the walls and floors, withdrawing from the corridor. But Killion, lost in his thoughts, never noticed, being bogged down with confusion and doubt. He was recalling again that fateful day years ago when The Master's horde first began to overrun the people of Sheliavon. Instead of assisting that kingdom against the invasion, he'd decided to align himself with what he thought the most dominant personality he'd ever known. The Master promised him power and prestige beyond his wildest dreams, and now with his army of assassins and the backing of the Master himself, he had all that. So why, he wondered, was he questioning if that decision was the most profitable endeavor he'd ever made or the worst mistake of his life?

* 3 *
THE VERDANT WOOD

Hearing the unusual noise far below, Zakili the elf turned, curious, and dove for the nearby tree limb, easily catching hold and using his momentum to propel himself to the next distant handhold. He discovered the source of disturbance as he latched onto the bough. From his perch among the trees, he crouched on the limb and looked down on the procession with narrowed eyes, spotting hated Methlon at the head of his troublesome band. This wasn't the first time Zakili had seen that man in his kingdom, and he'd heard enough about him to utterly despise him. Methlon and his troupe called themselves merchants, and wealthy were they. But the majority of their riches was bloody money. The merchant Methlon was a schemer and often supplanted the belongings of others by initiating their murders and seizing what they owned. Zakili smiled mischievously. It was time the two finally met.

* * * * *

"Keep your weapons close," Methlon advised his two lieutenants.

From somewhere nearby a loon screamed, its shrill cry echoing through the towering cypress trees, causing Methlon, who was at the head of the merchant caravan, to turn nervously. They were following a familiar path through the forest known as Verdant Wood. It led to a natural fountain called Lifespring. The hooves of the horses pulling the wagons clopped quietly against the soft earth. Methlon wished they made no sound at all. He and his men were trespassing; it was not the first time.

The loud caw of another loon startled Methlon, and this time he yanked his sword from its scabbard and glanced around nervously. He turned and whispered to his lieutenants who, with finely polished rapiers in hand, pulled their horses beside him. Methlon tried to shrug off his uneasiness. This was the domain of the Silver Elves, and he was unsure how the elves would react to them this time.

"These elves is a strangely forbearin' bunch," Danatin, the man on Methlon's left, said hopefully. "They wouldn't dare attack us."

"We must take precautions regardless," Methlon instructed. "We don't know this people well enough to guess how they might respond to our intrusion."

"Why then are we carrying all this treasure into their domain?" the other man, Bozar, asked, sweeping his arm behind him and indicating the many wagons loaded with riches.

"The gold in those carts is our key to unending life and unequaled power!"

The men looked at Methlon dumbly.

"Fools, what race of people could refuse what we're offering?"

Danatin scratched his head, a confused look on his face. "They rejected all the other proposals we made. Why will this be any diff'rent?"

"We have never promised an award the extent of this one. When they see it, they won't turn it away. The glitter of so much gold easily bends the mind to compromise. This day our prize shall be won!"

The narrow road Methlon's caravan traveled turned in beside a grassy shore, and beyond those tall grasses the merchant leader could see the sparkling of a liquid surface, water belonging to the most pristine of springs. He immediately thrust up his hand, signaling the wagons behind him to stop. Dismounting, he gazed straight ahead, pushing through the tall reeds to get an unobstructed view of the spring's halcyon surroundings.

He lost his breath. This was like no place he'd ever seen. It was paradise! Tightly packed along the spring's far shores were lofty, ageless cypress trees whose thick branches seemed to reach to the high heavens, their vast canopies shielding the direct sunlight, allowing only slivers of light from the awakening sun to seep down. The swelling waters below caught the rays and surrealistically broke them into a thousand tiny sparkles. Colors exploded everywhere before Methlon's eyes as colorful flowers rose up among the lily pads and bright mushrooms populated near the cypress trunks. Many-hued butterflies floated on the gentle breeze.

"Lifespring," Methlon breathed in awe. A pair of loons flew from the trees and skidded to a stop near the middle of the spring, the water being so clear they seemed to be floating on nothing. The merchant leader stared for a long moment before shrugging off the enchanting trance. This wasn't the first time he'd viewed it; he'd been here several times before, but every visit seemed just as mesmerizing as the first.

"Where do we meet these elves?" Methlon heard one of the wagon drivers call from behind him.

"Be patient. They'll show," he called back before moving for the spring. He bent down, his knees sinking into the wet sand, and scooped up a double handful of water, gulping it down ravenously. "Life," he said with complete satisfaction before scooping in another handful of the sweet water. "The waters of eternal life."

"What are you doing here?" an echoing voice asked, the question resonating through the trees. It didn't wait for an answer. "Be gone!"

Methlon bolted to his feet and raced back to his caravan, his heart pounding viciously in his chest. Fear of retribution mingled with the eagerness to purchase this prized region, and Methlon didn't know whether to hide or cheer. But this was the opportunity he'd long planned. Many a sleepless night passed by over the past few weeks. The merchant-leader unable to quell the excitement caused when he thought on the incredible wealth he could attain by having ownership of this one spring. He hoped he'd finally acquired enough treasure to buy these elves' interest. If the offer wasn't accepted, he'd turn to more devious methods, but either way, he didn't plan on leaving until the spring was his.

Behind him, his merchants glanced around nervously. None could see a soul on the shore or on the road, the voice seemed to come from everywhere at once.

Hesitantly, Methlon cleared his throat and looked up to the tree branches, searching for the right words to say. "We've come to make a deal."

"No deals," the unseen person said. "Leave now."

33

Lifespring

"But this offer is unlike any we've ever proposed to purchase the Lifespring and its shores," Methlon promised bravely. "We..."

"No deals!" the voice interrupted.

"Listen, you stubborn elves! My caravan carries a load of treasure three times the worth of this small stretch of land. With that much gold you could buy the whole town of Senadon and the people who live there if you wished."

"We see your riches," the voice assured. "Now take it back where it came from."

"What!"

"We don't want your treasure, and we won't forfeit our spring no matter what reward you offer."

"Fools, I could buy a kingdom with this amount of gold!"

"Then that's what you should do," the voice suggested calmly. "For we will not accept your gold nor sell our spring."

Methlon slammed his blade into the soft ground in a fit of rage, splattering mud on his clothes and face. He turned to his two lieutenants, angry etched on his face. "These elves don't know the value of gold and they won't sell us the land!" he growled although they'd heard the entire dialogue clearly enough. "Take the fighters and spread out," he ordered. "Find the elf who speaks. He must be the leader. Once we have him in our clutches, he'll learn the value of compromise.

"I was actually hoping it would come down to this. We'll take the spring from these elves and still keep our gold. If any elves get in your way, cut them down without mercy! We must have Lifespring!"

Bozar turned and whistled back to the wagons in a broken rhythm. The wagon drivers knew what that meant. A call to arms. One reached behind his seat and pulled out a double-headed axe, another thrust his arm into the cart trailing him and retrieved a glistening broad sword, while yet another slid a huge war hammer, strapped to his back, up and over head and gripped it in his big fists. All along the caravan, the merchant-fighters drew their weapons, their faces turning grim as they dismounted and began to spread out.

"The men are ready to claim their prize," Bozar assured his leader.

"Since they won't accept payment for this spring, we must take it from them by force!"

"Not a wise idea," a different voice rebutted, causing the fighters to glance around, unnerved. This voice didn't echo from the tree branches as did the first. This one sounded close and ominous.

After a few anxious moments, one of the fighters cried, "Look!" and pointed to a tree limb stretching out above the narrow road before them. Methlon turned in that direction and froze in terror, staring at the unexpected sight of an ebony-clad figure who crouched easily on the overhanging bough. Trim and sculpted, with pointed ears and slender eyebrows, the man-sized individual was easily recognizable to Methlon. He understood his heritage. This was a Silver Elf, and his furrowed brow and the ivory-colored bow in his hands spoke volumes.

"You know you're not welcome. Get out of here now!" the elf commanded.

"But the treasure," Methlon urged, finally having someone visible with whom to plead his case. "We have ten wagons filled with the most fabulous goods in this land, all gold, a dragon's hoard."

"Which dragon?" the elf asked facetiously.

"It... it is a figure of speech," Methlon continued nervously as the elf handled his bow. "And we're willing to give all this treasure for this small stretch of land."

"You don't hear very well, do you?" the elf asked. "Get out now!" He fingered the silvery bowstring of his ivory bow, broken streams of sunlight playing off the weapon and accentuating the golden veins running up and down the bow's stock. He took a mark on the merchant below and without an arrow even stationed on his bow he pulled back on the string. The air sizzled and popped and impossibly a radiant arrow glowing like lightning materialized on his bowstring. Methlon could hear the crackling of its deadly energy all the way from where he stood.

"Do not, Zakili!" the echoing voice demanded.

"Zakili!" Methlon gulped, his face blanching when he heard the infamous name of the belligerent elf, recalling many a rumor about that one and having heard that no challengers who faced off against this elf fared well.

"I'm glad you know of me. It will save me the trouble of explaining what kind of demise you will meet at my hands. Besides, I sure hate talking to people I can't tolerate." A mischievous grin crossed Zakili's lips. "Say good-bye to the land of the living!"

"No, Zakili!" the hidden voice screamed.

The energy arrow streaked from the bow like a bolt of lightning, and Methlon dove to the side, eyes wide with fear as he sprawled face first onto the ground. The missile exploded into the nearest wagon, blowing apart one of its wheels, but never really getting close to hitting Methlon even if he hadn't moved. Methlon glanced back and was suddenly startled by the crashing din of the wagon collapsing onto its wheelless corner. Methlon covered up as a crest of gold items surged over the wagon walls, spilling noisily on the ground and half burying him.

Bozar and Danatin leaped on their horses, whirled them about and dashed away full stride down the road, leaving Methlon and the caravan far behind.

"Get the wagons back!" Methlon screamed, digging himself out of the mound of gold items. "Get those things moving and get them out of here!"

"What about this one?" whined the fighter whose horses had been hauling the wagon which now had the blasted wheel.

"Unhook the animals and take as much treasure as you can carry!" Methlon cried, his eyes narrowing in wrath as he spun back to Zakili. "You'll pay for this, elf! You and your kind will pay! We came peacefully to buy your land. Now this gold will be used to seal your doom!"

Zakili shook his head in disbelief. "Can I believe my ears? Are you actually threatening me?" He slid an arrow from the quill hanging on his shoulder and set his mark on Methlon. The merchant's eyes widened fearfully, and he froze. "Have you ever seen a man die when his throat is pierced by a shaft?" the elf asked morbidly. "His air is cut off, the victim painfully aware of his own fate. Death is certain but slow. There he fades with nothing he can do to reverse his demise, his eyes wide with the horror of knowing it is the end." He threw in a sinister laugh to add to the effect.

Methlon sluggishly backed away, careful to make no sudden movements which might cost him an arrow in his throat. Turning cautiously, he marched back to his wagon with as much pride as he could muster.

"Ahhh, enough of this," Zakili decided, quickly bored with the game. "This facade is over." He threw his wooden shaft aside and pulled back on his silvery bowstring, a lightning arrow electrified from the empty air. Taking quick aim, he fired. The radiant missile rocketed down and exploded the ground at Methlon's heels, sending him away in a wild sprint. Zakili laughed.

"We'll get our revenge!" Methlon's voice called back as he took lead of his retreating band.

"We'll be waiting!" the elf called back, still laughing. He nearly fell out of the tree, guffawing hysterically, as he watched the invading caravan awkwardly about-face and flee. In minutes, the only evidence the merchants had even been there at all was the broken wagon with its spilled remnants of gold and the din of them banging along the narrow pathway at full speed. "You came peacefully," he scoffed, mocking the merchant leader's words. "If you came peacefully, I'm as gentle as a dove!"

Zakili heard rustling in the canopy overhead and turned. From a nearby branch in the next tree, a figure swung down and landed on the thick limb beside him. He wasn't surprised to see the elf, nor was he taken aback at the angry scowl on his face. The elf glared at him with silvery eyes which sparkled more brilliantly than a pair of coins in the midday sun.

"King Gallatar," Zakili said in an overly polite voice, sweeping into a low bow.

Gallatar, an elf considerably older than Zakili, gazed menacingly, his expression not softening in the least at the exaggerated display of manners. "Insolent scion," he growled. Gallatar was slender and sculpted like Zakili, and bore a close, handsome resemblance. Gallatar's hair was peppered with gray, a sharp contrast to Zakili's stark black mane.

Zakili stared into Gallatar's silvery eyes, which were common among his race and gave the Silver Elves their name. Zakili was the only one of all his people who didn't bear the same metallic-colored eyes. His dark, gold-flecked irises contrasted as sharply with those of the rest of his race as did his wild and reckless character when matched against their conservative nature. But although an adventurous anomaly compared to the rest of his reclusive people, he'd always been well-received by his kin and had even found great favor in the eyes of the king. But over the past several months, his relationship with the king mysteriously began to disintegrate and Gallatar's undeserved intolerance toward Zakili drove the younger elf to the point of indifference.

"I commanded you not to fire on the merchants," Gallatar said slowly and indignantly.

"Please forgive me," Zakili pled in mock shame. "I'm so disappointed in myself. But I feel there's some good that came out of the conflict. You see, those were some real bad men, and I made them go away," Zakili finished, his tone dripping with sarcasm.

Gallatar spat off to the side, an elf's gesture of disdain.

Zakili looked into the king's eyes again, trying to discern where it had all gone wrong. It seemed the two of them had not shared a civil word with each other in seasons. Gallatar's angry attitude had swelled past the breaking point, and it seemed the few times the King would speak to him, venomous words streamed out. According to the King, there was nothing he did which was right.

Of course, Zakili knew his facetious comments only added fuel to the fire, but how else could he react to some of the accusatory and inane statements spewed from Gallatar's lips? Lately he'd not conversed with the King, aside from passing salutations, and it wasn't because he hadn't tried. He was spurned often and openly.

Only a year ago, Gallatar had looked upon Zakili's carefree nature with amusement, not wrath. King Gallatar enjoyed and was even intrigued by his daring courage and unconquerable personality during countless adventures beyond the borders of Avundar. And despite how the King playfully labeled his behavior "passionately insane," he'd always considered Zakili just another of his close-knit, elven family. So how had their relationship gone awry? Why such friction? Zakili felt so thoroughly alienated from the King. His father, Gallatar.

"You never listen, do you, son?" Gallatar said.

"Better than you think. I may have disregarded you, but I heard every threat those arrogant fighter-merchants said. They weren't going to be slow about shedding blood over obtaining this land--"

"No!" Gallatar interrupted. "This isn't the first time I have conferred with you about this. You're always on the edge of violence! It's bad enough we have to suffer those merchants coming into our land, trying to purchase Lifespring. Because of what you've done, next time they'll come with enmity toward the elves. You humiliated them, and even worse, you forced them to leave some of their goods behind. Those greedy merchants will want retribution and will likely return for it in the heat of anger. That lot will continue disturbing us with their offers for our spring, but additionally, they'll desire to be recompensed for the gold they lost."

"Did you hear a thing I was saying, father? Don't you understand? These merchants aren't merely bid makers, hoping to gain a stretch of the spring's shore. They're trained fighters who'll stop at nothing. They sought to shed elf blood until I intervened."

"Unlikely."

"I was right here, my king, overhearing the whole conversation. Methlon wanted to force you into forfeiting the spring, and he was going to kill any elf who got in his way."

"Impossible! They'd not dare challenge the Silver Elves in our own land. No one's been foolish enough to oppose us in our forest home in centuries. If we

37

Lifespring

leave them be, they'll grow tired of the fruitless game. If provoked, they'll continue
to be a nuisance to us."

Zakili looked to his mulish father incredulously. Never had the King so
thoroughly disregarded his words, especially about something as crucial as the
defense of the Verdant Wood. Zakili knew his father regarded him as the best fighter
and most apt general of all his elves.

"If we leave them be, they'll overrun us using an army that will outnumber
our small community of elves with odds even I shudder to think about," he argued,
drawing an angry huff from Gallatar. "And you know how much I love to fight!"

Below them, a quiet rustling sounded, and Zakili grew still. Entangled in
their argument, they hadn't realized somebody had inched up close underneath them.
The Elf Prince placed his finger to pursed lips, signaled his father to become silent,
and abruptly ended the dispute. Bending his ear low, he could hear someone talk
quietly. He determined the voice was heading toward Lifespring. With a short series
of bird whistles, he directed the many elven scouts concealed along the trees'
canopies to investigate and quickly bring back a report. Could those fighter-
merchants be bold enough to return and attack? He didn't doubt it. He'd seen
Methlon's type before, greedy and possessed, and didn't dare imagine how far this
man would go to get what he wanted.

"What is it?" Gallatar asked in a sing-songy voice which sounded like bird
whistles, a voice the elves had fashioned for use in covert missions.

Zakili only shrugged his shoulders as he tried to glance through the leafy
boughs to
the invader below. He spotted the glimmer of gold below the leaves and far off to the
side of the path. Gripping his bow tightly in one hand, the fingers of his other hand
played eagerly on the silvery bowstring. If these were the merchants, what folly they
must have in their hearts. They knew what would be waiting for them!

Leaves rustled overhead before an elf scout lit on the bough next to Gallatar
and Zakili. He bowed immediately in deference to the King and his son. "A fighter
in full armor," he reported of the stranger.

Below them to the right, the bushes were pushed away and a knight in
golden plate mail led his magnificent charger onward, making his way toward
Lifespring. Zakili observed the tall warrior, understanding how formidable this
single man must be.

The elf scout slid his sword from its scabbard, understanding the threat the
warrior posed also. "He must be a knight hired by the merchants," the elf guessed.
"I'll dispatch him."

"Overly aggressive today, are you, Maengh?" Zakili asked. "It'll take more
than one warrior to halt this fellow."

Zakili dropped down silently and crept up behind the knight, but the warrior
spun about, and with a metallic ringing, his sword leaped into his hand. Zakili
jumped back. "Hey, be careful where you go swinging that thing, wild man! Have
you been gone so long you forgot who I am? Is that any way to greet your friend in
his own home?"

"Hawk!" the knight acknowledged, smiling.

"Zakili," he corrected.

"Zakili?" the knight questioned, smiling wide and extending a hand the elf clasped. The visitor quickly reeled him in, crunching him in a quick bear hug. "I prefer to call you by your birth name rather than your battle name. But no matter what you call yourself now, it's always good to see you!"

"Likewise, my friend," Zakili wheezed through labored breaths until released from the hold. He noticed the knight squint curiously. It was a look he'd seen before; it seemed he'd detected something beyond the reach of his natural senses. He turned and looked upward toward Gallatar and the scout. There was no way he could've known they were up there, Zakili knew. Elves are masters at blending in with their environment and stay practically invisible unless they want to be seen.

"Well met, King Gallatar, Maengh," he addressed the two elves.

"Salutations, Navarro Silvinton," Gallatar greeted, now recognizing the man in the golden plate mail. "It's been seasons since we've seen you in our land."

"Yes, it has been a long time. Too long. Sometimes though, the demands on a Paladin can keep him from the people he loves most."

"So why the sword? Are you suspicious of the elves now? You know you're among allies here." Zakili questioned.

"I know," he admitted. "But I fear potential disaster in this region."

"What seems to be the trouble in our paradise?" Gallatar asked, his tone sarcastic.

"Trouble is the correct word, King Gallatar," Navarro agreed. "I know an ominous threat prepares to invade this land and all the regions of Avundar are in great peril." The Paladin looked to the elf standing beside the king on the bough and grew silent. One of the things Zakili had come to understand about his Paladin friend was his commitment to etiquette. Navarro wouldn't want one outside of leadership privy to events concerning the authority above him. "Can we talk in your private chambers, King Gallatar?"

"No need," Gallatar said. "I know what concerns you."

"I really don't think you do."

"You think those merchants you passed on the way through our woods are some kind of menace. Put your mind at ease. They're no threat to us."

"The merchants?" Navarro questioned before reflecting for a moment. "Oh, the merchants. I did see a group of traders, an unruly bunch really. In fact, I heard them long before I saw them, spitting curses against the Silver Elves, so I led my charger off the side of the road behind the cover of some bushes and watched and waited for their caravan to pass. The men were so embroiled in their own anger they didn't notice me among the bushes as they stormed by. I remember them now, and the sight did disturb me, but I've news much more--"

"Their anger will be short lived," Gallatar interrupted. "I know well of your covenant with your God, of protecting the lands from evil and defending them against all adversaries, but the merchants are more a nuisance than a threat. As you well know, there hasn't been an enemy in the borders of Avundar in your lifetime, and no adversaries have dared challenge us in the Verdant Wood for over a thousand years. The merchants' wrath is due to my son's disobedience to my commands."

Zakili looked up to his father, eyebrow raised, but he wasn't so surprised by the King's accusation as he was by Navarro's seeming absentmindedness. Navarro was as sharp-minded a man as he'd ever seen. Nothing escaped his keen senses it seemed, and he never knew him to forget anything. So how could the merchants who passed him only moments ago have been so dim in his memory? Something pressing disturbed The Paladin. Zakili filed that consideration away for another time and turned to Navarro. "They just didn't like the way I asked them to leave."

The Paladin looked to the scorched wagon and another wide burn mark on the road and laughed. "You asked them to leave with your usual manners, I see."

"Guilty," Zakili admitted, all teeth showing in an exaggerated smile.

Gallatar dropped to the ground beside Navarro, his face twisted in anger. "You're a Paladin, a champion of righteousness with special principles and powers given from your holy God," he accused. "How can you condone Zakili's reckless actions?"

The Paladin backed a step and bowed in apology. "I'm his friend," he explained, his tone serious. "I don't always agree with Hawk's maxims, but I'm not responsible for changing his characteristics."

"Zakili," the Elf Prince playfully argued.

"Hawk! Zakili! It doesn't matter!" Gallatar fumed, turning fully on his son. "It *is* important that you follow my commands. I am the King of the Silver Elves, and I will be for quite a long time. Although you are my son and the future king, you're still my subject! When I give an order, you will listen and obey!"

In response to Gallatar's explosive tirade, Zakili noticed Navarro back a step. Confusion etched his face. The Elf King was always calm and tolerant. Zakili knew The Paladin had only seen he and his father as best friends. This exchange was one he'd never seen between elves and especially never between the two of them.

The King stared into his son's dark, gold-flecked eyes, and Zakili could almost read his thoughts. Increasingly throughout the year, the King warned him about his hot-blooded temper and impulsiveness. Warned him? Zakili scoffed. He was doing nothing new; he'd always acted that wild. Until recently, his character had never bothered the King. It had actually entertained him. Zakili glanced over to his friend, seeing Navarro's dismayed expression. Much had changed in his relationship with his father in so short a time. He knew Navarro sensed the trouble.

* * * * *

"We must have Lifespring," Methlon roared over the noise of the banging wagons as they hurried out of the Verdant Wood, frantically putting distance between them and the elf Zakili.

"They is not goin' to let us have it," replied Danatin.

"Silence coward! You ran after the first arrow! Whether they're willing to relinquish the spring to us or not no longer matters."

"The spring is a wondrous sight to behold," Bozar added. "But why were we willing to pay such a great price for it? There are other springs in Avundar."

Methlon growled and shook his head. "Don't you fools understand? This *is* The Lifespring," he said, as if the name of the spring explained everything.

Bozar and Danatin just stared back, their expressions clueless.

"Consider the elves. They live for hundreds and hundreds of years. The elves drink from the spring's waters daily. There must be some connection."

"The waters extend life!" Bozar blurted out excitedly.

"Yes, finally you dimwits are catching on. But I believe it may do more than extend life. It may provide life indefinitely. The spring has some magical power about it. I'm sure of it! Why else would it be shrouded in such mystery? And how about Silver Elves dying of old age? I've never heard of one."

"But the elves won't sell it to us. How can we be gettin' at it?"

"The elves must die. Zakili in particular must be slain!" Methlon took a deep breath after saying that name. Just mentioning the elf made his back teeth grind. The Elf Prince had embarrassed him. Badly. One elf! One elf routed his entire caravan. Nobody did that to Methlon with impunity. "I vow Zakili will pay for his arrogance!"

"He coulda killed us if he wanted ta," Danatin said with a hint of fearful admiration.

"Silence! I know what he could've done. He could've killed us, and maybe he should have. But now his race will have to deal with the consequences."

"But how can we get t' them? They live in the trees. They're hard to locate."

"There is a way to get at these elves, and I have already prepared in case it did come down to this."

"How?" Danatin asked excitedly.

"I have contacts that will give me audience with a secret army of assassins. The Lurking Shadows."

The faces of his lieutenants went grim. The reputations of the Lurking Shadows preceded them. Methlon could tell by the reaction of his simple-minded warriors even they were as overcome with dread at the mention of the Shadows, as was most everyone who had heard of them.

A wicked smile crossed Methlon's face at the thought of enlisting assassins against the elves. The Silver Elves were formidable opponents whom nobody dared to challenge, not that there was any reason to war against the reclusive race. They were peacefully tucked away in their forest home, far from the baronies of Avundar, and rarely seen venturing out of their kingdom.

Now things were different. They had something he wanted. And he was willing to get it no matter what the cost. The Lurking Shadows were his answer. Li

They were the most mysterious and ruthless group in the land. No one targeted by the Shadows ever survived; thus, nobody knew much about them, and that made them especially dangerous. One wouldn't know if a Lurking Shadow dwelt in their midst, prepared to pull down their whole kingdom around them, until it was too late. The assassins had an extensive web of contacts throughout the lands, which kept the rumors flowing, fear instilled, and availability open. Methlon had even heard they had access to the spirit realm and could be aligned with demons. He waved off that thought, knowing assassins with the Shadows' degree of success would have some outlandish claims made about them. He discounted most of the rumors.

All that mattered to him was their accessibility. He heard they could be hired by anybody to do anything, but the price was high. Often more than most could pay. The cost was worth the task though, Methlon evaluated. The Lurking Shadows were always successful. They'd never been defeated in any conflict. Ever.

"The assassins will eliminate those elves," Methlon said. "They'll rid us of Zakili!"

* 4 *
NEVER A PLACE LIKE THIS

"I can hardly believe what I'm seeing," Navarro said, awe-struck and staring unblinking at the scene before him. Zakili had led Navarro from the Lifespring and invited him here to this graceful avenue of elven homes called the Elfstay. The Paladin had tried to reason with Gallatar, but the old king wouldn't listen, wouldn't even allow Navarro to expound on the potential problem. This concerned the Elf Prince. As long as he'd known Navarro, no challenge seemed to disturb him: not monsters, not dragons, not even demons.

What could unnerve The Paladin so? Whatever it was his father didn't want to hear it. His father's normally carefree, adventuresome nature had given way to this nightfall of distrust and, at times, paranoia. So Zakili ushered his friend away, discerning Navarro had some great burden on his heart. He took him here to the Elfstay, thinking it might provide him peace. Then they would tackle his concern.

Sunlight streamed through the breaks in the forest's high canopies, accentuating leaves with surrealistic sparkles. As Navarro glanced around, he saw vibrant and varied greens among the trees and on the grasses, and the richest dotting of reds among the wild strawberry patches and indigos upon the abundant blueberry bushes. Here and again, golden butterflies wafted across Navarro's path through the impressive avenue. He felt himself relaxing, the place drawing him into its promising peace, his ears being delighted by light-hearted melodious singing among the tree boughs.

"Welcome to my home," Zakili said, turning to face Navarro. He wasn't there. He looked behind. Far behind. Lagging way back, The Paladin glanced around, transfixed by the splendor of the elf homes. Zakili smiled, seeing wonder in his friend's curious expression. "The homes of the Silver Elves are unlike any in all the realms," Zakili explained. "The houses of the Avenue grow within the living trees themselves, the holes for the doorways and windows open in the trees naturally. Aside from the shutters and the doors, you'll find no clue of an architect's workmanship. These trees have been homes for my race for generations."

Navarro's expression went from wide-eyed wonder to gape-mouthed marvel. This was the first time Zakili had invited his friend this deep into the elves' territory before. Usually, time didn't permit such a luxury for him. Christian Paladins like Navarro always seemed to be busy with the work of God, never acting like he had time for simple pleasures like sparing and taleswapping, dancing, and singing. The kind of things Zakili loved to do.

"In all my adventures I've never seen a phenomenon to match this," Navarro said, still staring at the elves' housetrees. "I love the majesty of The Lifespring and the beauty of Verdant Wood, but by far the abodes of the Avenue outdo all their natural splendor."

"Ah, this," the elf stated. "This is just home."

The paladin shot a glance his way, shaking his head incredulously, grinning at his friend's nonchalant answer. "The elves' village is beautiful!"

"Follow me," Zakili encouraged. "I've got more to show you."

Navarro jogged up to the elf's side and they walked on, marching through the long avenue of Elfstay, housetrees lining either side. The farther they traveled, the more Zakili sensed The Paladin's demeanor gradually changing. He could tell Navarro was no longer awed by the beauty of Elfstay but grew more watchful, his eyes roving the shadows and any other place offering concealment. Zakili knew what was transpiring. Warriors have a sixth sense, an ability to 'feel' danger about them. The Paladin's senses were beyond anything the elf had ever seen though. Perhaps it was due to the endless adventures and battles, or maybe because he faced constant danger. But Navarro's senses developed to a point where it was natural for him to locate watchers no matter how well hidden. He knew Navarro sensed the weight of many eyes upon him. He knew he was being observed.

"You're the only non-elf ever to set foot into Elfstay, and there are probably many curious gazes investigating," Zakili said, hoping to put The Paladin more at ease. The Elf Prince knew his friend wished he could turn those senses off for this peaceful reprieve, but he was a warrior and they came automatically.

"Well met, Zakili," a female voice called from behind, causing both him and Navarro to turn. A slender woman parted from between a pair of tall bushes, her long mane of raven-black hair flowing down her supple, yet confident shoulders. Two others followed, both with the same dark tresses framing their thin faces, and all three clad in light summer gowns which fluttered about their ankles in the cool breeze.

Navarro bowed in deference to the elven ladies.

"As effortless and beautiful as the spring. As flourishing as the nature they live in," Zakili stated poetically. Navarro raised an eyebrow in admiration of their superior beauty, causing the elf to laugh. "That's more emotion than I'd seen any female evoke from you."

The Elf Prince quickly swept into a bow and continued on his way.

"Wait, Zakili," one of the women called out. "Who's your friend? I never remember meeting him before."

"I know we haven't," another confirmed. "He's the first human I've ever seen in the Elfstay."

Navarro stopped and bowed again in a courtly manner. "My name is Navarro Silvinton, close friend of Hawk Terishot."

"Hawk," one lady echoed, giggling. The others chimed in.

"Laugh not, Senetta," Zakili warned, slapping his hand to his forehead in exaggerated frustration. "I'm still teaching him to stop calling me that." He spun to Navarro. "Don't call me Hawk, especially in front of my own people."

"What's wrong with your birth name?" The Paladin asked.

"I have a fierce reputation to uphold," he whispered, giving his friend a furtive wink. "And my birth name's too tame for my image."

Navarro shrugged, and the women laughed in amusement.

"Well, are you refusing to introduce us to him?" Senetta asked, her foot tapping impatiently.

Zakili rolled his eyes and pretended embarrassment. "How thoughtless of me! Of course, ladies. This is Navarro Silvinton as he afore stated. Navarro, these ladies are Senetta and Monolique and Saranisen. Well met, one and all."

When they drew near, Navarro extended his hand to grip slender fingers in the usual courtly manner, but each maiden in turn grasped his hand with a solid grip and gave a strong shake. The Paladin cocked an eyebrow, and Zakili almost laughed at the surprised look on his friend's face.

"Their slender hands have deceptive strength," the elf said before turning to the ladies. "We must be on our way now. I'm sure we will have time to talk later."

"My sisters," the Elf Prince said when they'd left the three maidens far behind. "Very beautiful females."

Navarro nodded.

"They liked you."

"That's well, I liked them, too. They were nice young ladies. They'll make some elf happy one day."

"No. I mean they found you attractive. It's not often, in fact, probably never by my memory, that an elf maiden finds a human appealing, although the reverse is constant." A sudden memory made him laugh. "Once when I visited a human town, I stumbled upon a piece of literature from some love-struck author who happened upon an elf maiden. He was so enthralled with her beauty, he fantasized she'd seduced him and left him forever wandering, looking, bereft of love. What a joke! Elf maidens are very picky and very slow in romance. But today is a first, my friend. They were drawn to you."

"They were just courteous," Navarro explained.

"Believe me. I'm an elf, and I'm their older brother. I know."

Navarro simply smiled, waved off the comment, and kept on walking.

Zakili stopped, his mouth falling open in astonishment. "You're passing up an opportunity with an elven female?"

"What're you trying to do?" The Paladin demanded, raising his hands in surrender and smiling incredulously. "Are you trying to set up a courtship between one of your sisters and me?"

Zakili went speechless.

"Listen friend. Your sisters are beautiful and any man or elf in this land would be delighted to wed any one of them. Don't suggest that I marry one."

"No, no, I wasn't attempting such a thing," he promised, stumbling for words. "I've never seen a human, or an elf for that matter, act indifferently to them before, ever."

"Like I said, I thought they were beautiful young ladies."

"Yes, young," Zakili laughed. "The youngest of the three is nearly three score years old."

45

Navarro's eyes went wide in admiration. "I'm impressed at how well they have preserved themselves over the years," he said, then blushed suddenly and smirked in embarrassment. He remembered, in time past, his friend had clued him in on the difference between elf years and human aging. Being fifty years to an elf was akin to being a teen in the human timetable.

"You don't often involve yourself with women, do you?" the Elf Prince probed. He knew his friend purely as a warrior and one of the finest he'd ever seen in battle, but The Paladin's personal life seemed always a mystery.

"Never seem to have enough spare time, I guess," Navarro quipped.

"What kind of answer is that?"

"Earthly love may last a while, my friend, but my Heavenly Father's love is eternal. That's what I focus on. He cared about me even when I was a selfish, evil, God-hater and, He loved me enough to forgive me all my sins when I cried out for Jesus to become my Savior.

"God's love is forever satisfying and infinitely more complete than anything this world can offer. I know. I've tried everything this world has to offer."

"But your God could not forbid you the pleasure of a beautiful female, could He?"

"This is my life, and for me it is adequate."

"Adequate? That's all?" Zakili asked though he knew Navarro's simplistic answer cued no interest in the conversation. He couldn't let it go so easily though. This was the deepest he had been able to drag The Paladin into sharing about this area. And females were one of Zakili's favorite subjects. "You seem like a man who desires more than simple adequacy in his life."

Navarro nodded in agreement, and Zakili pulled closer, eager to hear the innermost desires of his paladin friend. "I used to seek fulfillment in many different pursuits. I used to think adventure would make my life worth living, only to find the quest for thrills mostly leads through seasons of boredom. For a long time, I strove to be the best fighter in all the realms, merely to discover no matter how many triumphs I forged, it was never enough. I used to think the meaning of life was to conquer as many women as I could..."

Zakili moved in closer.

"...but I came to the realization that that pursuit was hollow of any real meaning and left me feeling empty. But in the midst of being engulfed in all that sin, the Lord still had mercy on me, sending my grandfather my way to share the Word of God, the Bible, with me, teaching me God's plan of eternal salvation. There's no greater love than what God showed to me. He sacrificed His Son, the Lord Jesus, to redeem all races even though inwardly all our hearts harbor vile wickedness. Jesus died on the cross for our sin, suffering eternal torment for mankind's sin. He also proved His power, defeating death, hell and the grave and rising again from the dead on the third day of His own power so we don't have to go to hell, but instead have the chance to receive eternal life. What's a lustful rendezvous in comparison to the love of God?"

Zakili fell silent. He knew little about this religious stuff, but he knew

Navarro was deep into it. The curious thing was if someone were to ask him, The Paladin would say he despised religion, saying religion hasn't gotten anyone to heaven yet. Unashamedly though, he'd proclaim to know this Jesus who said He was the only way to heaven.

Heaven? Zakili wasn't even sure he believed there was such a place. But he knew Navarro did. He believed it with all his heart. He also believed in one almighty, universal God, and he even talked about Him as if a personal friend.

Zakili recognized their destination as they turned down a bend in the road. "We're here," he announced, seeing an opening to escape this line of conversation. "The Circle."

"Where are we?" Navarro asked as he walked into a copse of seemingly unremarkable trees. After several steps, he realized the uniqueness of the place. "Did these trees grow like this naturally?"

"Every one."

Navarro glanced into what he thought to be the center of the copse. He looked to a massive oak, its girth wider than the height of several men. His eyes traced the rows of trees which grew in concentric circles around the center oak. Each group of trees was equally spaced from the others and positioned in perfect ring pattern. In each consecutive circle, the trees became younger and younger, the oldest, of course, being the oak in the center.

"The Circle," Zakili began. "Each circle springs up during the generation of the specific elf king who rules. The great oak in the center represents the first elf king of our race. His name has been lost, but legends say the oaks of the forest, the toughest of the trees, were allies of the ancient elves. The center oak began growing when the first elf king took power. Each circle of trees afterward sprang to life under the rule of the next successive sovereign." He pointed to the outer circle, the youngest ones. "Those are the oaks which represent my father's reign. Out of nothing they sprang up and grew after he assumed leadership from his father before him."

"This is incredible," Navarro said in an awed whisper. He looked to his friend. "But why have you taken me here?"

"This place is unique. It's almost like there's a magic that abides here. Only you and I can hear this conversation."

Navarro laughed. "We're the only two here."

"I know that, you funny paladin, but even if this grove were crowded with people no one could hear our dialogue unless we willed it to be so, even if they were standing only a step away. That's the power of this grove."

"I know why you have brought me back here. But why the secrecy? The information I have is dire and needs to be spread throughout the countryside."

"I want to hear you out before anyone else does, and especially before my father convinces the elves to disregard your warning. Father has changed, and if he doesn't agree with what you have to say, he'll forbid it from the ears of his people. He's trapped in his own confused fantasy world where he now trusts nearly none of his own people and believes no enemies would dare assault his kingdom. You know,

47

Lifespring

just as I do, there's destructive evil out there."

"Indeed," Navarro agreed, then turned fully to his friend. "Do you remember the war in Sheliavon?"

"I do. I lost a number of good friends to the clutches of that possessed monster horde. Except for the united front of the Avundarian warriors, the brutes would've crushed all resistance in Sheliavon. And who knows, they might've turned toward our land next."

"Do you think the elves are prepared to fight in a battle of similar proportion?"

"Well, I'm always ready for a fight," the elf said energetically, yet his expression was edged with confusion. "But never have I heard you initiate a conversation about fighting, although it seems you always battle somewhere. War is my favorite subject, not yours."

Navarro raised an eyebrow, and Zakili ceased his inquisition and answered the question. "For the most part, the Silver Elves have become passive over the years since
the battle in Sheliavon. If war were to erupt in Avundar or even here in Verdant Wood I doubt we'd be ready. Now, if the Elfstay were full of fighters like me, I'd not worry, but they're all loyal to the king, as they should be, and assume his attitude."

"And he feels that never in a million years would an enemy dare attack the kingdom of the Silver elves," Navarro guessed.

"You've seen his attitude toward the merchant-fighters. They're trouble. Methlon is more dangerous and more persistent than my father'll give him credit. He grows bolder each time he enters Verdant Wood. Father understands not that stern words won't suffice when dealing with this man. Unfortunately, the other elves have adopted this attitude and will not take him seriously either.

"But you chased those rude merchants right out of your forest single-handedly."

"Action had to be taken. Methlon threatened violence. He couldn't carry it out today. I was there to stop him. But there'll be other days. That merchant has extensive resources and knows how to get what he wants."

"Lifespring?"

"Exactly. Methlon and his merchant-warriors think drinking the waters of the spring will give them eternal life."

"That's crazy."

"I agree. But they think the water has some magical property. They hear of the ages the Silver Elves, centuries-old ages, and equate that with the spring. Those fools! Silver Elves naturally grow to that age, spring or no spring. Lifespring has no potential to extend life. Its power is illustrated in the paradise-like surroundings which abound in Avundar through every season. Regardless, Methlon, driven by his false notion, desires to seize the spring for himself, and a man possessed won't quit until he gets what he wants. Or until someone stops him."

"It appears I've arrived at a dark time, my friend. And I wish I didn't have the foul news I've come here with. The darkness is about to thicken."

"What is it, Navarro?"

"I've battled The Dark Sorcerer in our land."

Zakili lost a step. He couldn't have been more stunned if Navarro had slammed his face with a war hammer.

* * * * *

Across the plains they rolled, a noisy and pompous caravan singing praises and blowing trumpets, heading straight for the castle grounds. Candace saw them from her bedroom window which overlooked the vast Ormantict Plains, having heard them from a mile away it seemed. She rolled her eyes at the gaudy train of banners flapping in the late afternoon breeze, each one displaying the same royal seal. This was definitely the arrival of a prince. She'd seen it too many times during the past couple of years, and she knew what it meant.

With the sun still a couple hours above the mountains, there was plenty of day left, but she glanced over to her plush bed and forced out a yawn, bored by the eyesore parade coming her way. Quickly, she slipped off her boots, pulled her dress over her head, then wiggled into her soft night gown. With a forlorn look toward the door, a door only she and her father had keys to, she sprinted the three steps to bed and dove into the silky sheets, throwing the layers over her.

"Good night," she told herself, hardly tired.

A few minutes passed before the expected knock on the door startled her. She'd not thought she'd be summoned this early. She closed her eyes, tried to remain relaxed, controlled her breathing, and attempted to simulate the rhythmic murmur of sleep. Again came the knock, this time even louder. She knew who it was; the thunderous pounding was unmistakable. Father. She knew the reason for the visitation: the arrival of the caravan meant she was soon to be courted by another prince. A quiet groan pushed from her lips.

How tiresome these royal arrivals had become. How agonizing to put on the same interested pretense in the over-inflated, self-absorbed tales the princes expounded, ever exalting themselves. Today, she had neither the endurance nor the patience to put up with the fronts of yet another vainglorious man. Maybe she could sleep the whole nightmare away.

Sleep? Nightmare? Those were dreadful thoughts to her after experiencing the horrible incubus earlier that morning. The flaming eyes of the sorcerer intruded into her thoughts. She immediately pushed that image away, reciting Scripture to ease her mind. "Whatsoever things are true, whatsoever things are honest, whatsoever things are just, whatsoever things are pure, whatsoever things are lovely, whatsoever things are admirable, if they be excellent and praiseworthy, think on these things." The wicked vision was gone.

She heard the rapping at her door one more time, and still refused to answer. She knew what her father was trying to do, and she loved him for the concerned effort. He had raised her from a child, instructing her and guiding her diligently every step, all the way up to adulthood. He wanted the best for her, she knew. But trying to find a husband for her, with the only prerequisite being he was of royal blood, was simply unacceptable.

A metallic click and she heard the doorknob turn and, with only a whisper of air, the door slowly swung open. She concentrated on her breathing. Quiet footsteps sounded in the room. Her father had entered.

"Oh, my little girl must've been exhausted," she heard him whisper to himself.

Her ruse was working. She forced down a smile before it could turn up the corners of her mouth.

"I'll just give her a little good night peck on the cheek and let her sleep."

She heard him step quietly over to the bed then felt the bristle of his beard on the side of her face. She did well to maintain her composure. The kiss was short, only a second or two, but to her it seemed like an eternity with his whiskers tickling her cheek. Finally he rose and she heard his footsteps fade away. This time she did allow a victorious smile. She'd pulled it off! She'd fooled her father. Maybe now he'd direct this prince back to where he came from.

The covers were peeled away at the foot of her bed! Her eyes nearly went wide open. What was father doing?

"I've tucked my little girl into bed almost every night of her life," she heard him saying in a baby voice. "And I've not missed an opportunity since she was 15. She looks so peaceful when she's asleep. So sweet. So innocent."

She felt him stroke lightly once then twice on the bottom of her exposed foot, nearly making her jump out of bed. Gritting her teeth, she tightened her toes and held her breath, trying to hold back the giggles from the tickling brushes.

"Yes, so innocent. I'd never have to worry about deception from my little girl," she heard him say before she felt him tease her toes and tickle her feet again.

"All right, all right," Candace relented, jumped to a sitting position, and pulled her legs defensively underneath her. "I'm up! Are you happy?" She was unable to finish her retort, watching her father laughing so heartily at her. She smiled, too. It was rare to see her tough, warrior father laugh.

"I've been your father all your life, as profound as that may seem. I know when you're asleep, and I can tell when you're pretending. When you are sad and refuse to admit it, I can sense that too. And most of the time I can read what you're thinking just by your expression. I would dare say I know you almost as well as you know yourself, my girl. I even know one of your few weaknesses," he admitted and reached for her foot.

Candace jerked away playfully, then changed her mind. She threw the covers aside and leaped at him, throwing her arms around his neck.

"I love you father."

"Mutual," he replied. "And I'm extremely proud of you. Now get dressed, please. The Prince of Normanway has traveled here to meet you. Put on your best manners and have an open mind. Trust me, being introduced to a prince is virtually painless, so don't run this one off. Although I've never met him, I've heard good things about him."

Probably a message about himself from himself, she thought.

"So up, up. He'll be in my chambers shortly. Be ready when I send a messenger down to get you." He kissed her on the forehead and exited.

"Here we go again," she mumbled once the door closed behind him. "If I didn't love father so much I would be insane to allow myself to go through this torture."

* * * * *

Candace took a deep breath as the messenger, one of her father's elite guards, opened the door to Kelt's chambers. She'd hurried and gotten ready, not because of any desire to see another prince, another suitor for her hand in marriage, but because she didn't want to embarrass her father. She knew it looked good for him and his barony if everything went as planned when royalty called. This was a game she'd grown quite used to over the past two years. She thought she'd seen every monarch or son of a monarch the world had to offer, but still they came. Today though, she wasn't in the mood for play-acting to inflate a prince's ego.

How did they all hear about her in the first place? she wondered. Somehow the word kept getting out about her, she was told, about the Baron's beautiful daughter. She was so tired of hearing herself defined like that. "I am more than some pretty trophy," she said. "Why am I never described as the Baron's intelligent daughter or the Baron's warrior daughter?" She huffed before dismissing the entire thought.

From the corner of her eye she spotted a second and a third guard emerge from the shadows of the corridor behind her, just as she was about to walk into her father's throne room. She considered that for a moment. The guards had been shadowing her, lingering on the fringes to protect her. She thought about her father and smiled. Her nightmare about The Dark Sorcerer in the early morning had him concerned about her, and he was holding back no precautions.

In she walked. She threw aside her casual gait and moved across the floor in a rigid, yet elegant prance. She tossed her head, sending her long golden tresses bouncing across her shoulders. If Father wanted her to put on a show, that's what he was going to get. Her long dress flowed out gracefully behind her as she strode through the faceless crowd of people, stopping only when she stood next to Father's throne.

"You look radiant as usual," Kelt complimented. He leaned toward her and gave an approving wink. She smiled.

"So this is the Baron's beautiful daughter," she heard someone say from the gathering of people. She used every ounce of willpower not to scream. The crowd parted, allowing a tall, burly man to step forward, his violet cloak flowing out wide behind him. "A woman more lovely than even the dreams inspired by the legend of her beauty," he said, stroking his goatee as he stared at her, sizing her up.

Candace replied with a forced smile.

"Oh yes. She will make a wonderful prize for my kingdom of Normanway," the prince appraised as he circled her, eyeing her closely. "I really do like this one. For someone not of royal blood, she's almost worthy of a man of my position. How did you keep this one such a well-guarded secret for so long, Baron Veldercrantz?"

What? Was she a live animal at the market? she wondered. He wasn't talking to her. He was simply talking about her like she was a good grade of livestock. She wouldn't have been surprised if the arrogant prince had come over and pulled up her lip to inspect her teeth.

"Excuse me," Candace spoke up, drawing the prince's and everyone else's attention. "I don't even know who you are. Would you mind introducing yourself, please?"

The whole room went silent.

The tall prince stared hard at her for a moment then turned back to the baron. "Does your whelp not know how to behave before a prince?"

"I, well..."

"Oh," Candace said. "You are the prince who has come to seek my hand in marriage." She turned to her father. "He's a better specimen than the others who have paraded into this castle." From the corner of her eye she saw the prince stick out his considerable chest at hearing her left-handed compliment, and she nearly laughed out loud. The one thing she learned about these princely types was they liked their egos petted. She turned to the prince. "Well, do you have a name, sire?"

Without even realizing his action, Kelt slapped his palm to his forehead, embarrassed at how the meeting had gotten out of control so quickly, and how Candace was adding momentum to its downward slide.

The prince strode up to her. "I am Perizar, Prince of the proud Kingdom of Normanway, slayer of many goblins and giants not a few, a warrior mighty in deed, and of the sword, a master. You're not familiar with my prowess?"

"Your accomplishments sound impressive," she admitted. "But no, I've never heard of you."

"You must lead a sheltered life, daughter of the Baron."

"Prince Perizar of Normanway, do you know who it is you've come to see? Do you even know my name? Let me instruct you: a lady's name is always a handy thing to know when you come calling for her hand and demanding her vows."

Perizar glanced helplessly to the baron.

"Candace," he mouthed silently to the Prince, trying to aid this faltering meeting as much as possible, though it troubled him this Prince couldn't even remember his daughter's name.

"You did say you're a master of the sword, didn't you?" she asked before he could even answer her previous question.

"A warrior whose skills are envied by most," he said.

"Do you think you could defeat me in a fray?"

"Candace," Kelt warned.

"I'm just curious," she explained. "When a person introduces himself with a long stream of titles following, I like to see if he's for real or just a bunch of hot air."

"I'm as real as they get, woman," Perizar answered coldly.

"Would you dare to draw on me?"

Perizar stepped back, staring venomously at her. "What is this, Baron? I come to your home seeking your daughter's hand in marriage, and she wants to fight me."

Kelt rose from his seat and swept into a low bow before the Prince. "I seek your forgiveness, your majesty. This hasn't been a good day for my Candace. She's a little
sullen tonight, not a normal thing for my sweet girl. Please accept my apologies."

Perizar looked at him, turned to Candace, then simply marched away, waving them both off. "Let's be gone from here," he ordered. "This whole meeting was nothing but a big mistake."

Two of Kelt's guards opened the chamber door and began to lead the Prince out, but he pushed them aside and stormed out of the room, his attendants streaming out behind him.

"No prince in any land is going to want anything to do with this barony before too long," Kelt huffed in exasperation once the room was cleared.

"Come on, Father," Candace replied. "Would you have really wanted me to marry that arrogant, over-inflated boaster? He didn't look at me as a person but like a piece of property. And that first statement of his--the Baron's beautiful daughter--that closed the book before he could even begin to read it. I know you want the best for me, Father. Believe me. That Perizar was far from it."

Kelt could only nod his head in agreement. "I know."

* * * * *

Late that night, Methlon pulled his charger up to an unfamiliar wooded region. Slipping from his horse and quickly tethering it, he darted into the dark copse. With the moon being new, looking like a black globe against the star-dotted sky, the night was dark, and he could barely see his own hand in front of his face as he pushed through the thorny bushes. He was running late for an appointed meeting and knew he had to hurry or miss his opportunity forever. With arms out in front to block any low-hanging branches from hitting his face, he pressed forward. That technique helped him push through the trail faster, until one branch he'd knocked aside, and consequently let loose too soon, snapped back and slapped him in the eye. He cursed the trail and the reason he had to be on it in the first place. He cursed the moon over Avundar for not illuminating the night with its soft glow. He cursed the branch which hit him.

His anger fled when he recalled the rewards promised as a result of this short journey. In an initial visit early during that day, the person he was to meet had instructed him to come alone, threatening to cancel the whole deal if even one other person was spotted. He accepted the terms willingly, evaluating that rewards would far outweigh inconvenience. They were supposed to rendezvous just before midnight, but now he wondered if he'd even find the destination in time in the pitch darkness. He reached for a tinderbox lying in a deep pocket of his coat, but reconsidered. If he lit a torch he'd expose his location to any watching eyes, or worse, his informant might shy away from contact. A few stumbles and many scratches later, he finally happened upon the copse of trees which were packed so tightly they looked like they huddled together for some secret meeting. He quickly rushed in. The night's darkness grew more menacing as the canopies blocked out even the dim light of the starry night. With hands cautiously out in front to feel his way, he hurried along, not wanting to be late and miss his opportunity.

"Methlon," he heard a voice whisper close to his ear. In the deathly quiet of the night it seemed as loud as a shout and almost made him scream. He stopped and turned in that direction. "Come quickly, Methlon," the voice directed. "You're behind schedule."

He rushed over in the darkness, banging his head on a low bough he could not possibly have seen in the intense blackness. He cursed the entire way.

"What do you have for us?" the voice asked.

"Let me see your face," Methlon demanded.

"You don't trust me, old friend?" the voice asked and Methlon scoffed. He hadn't held this contact with The Lurking Shadows for very long, and he certainly didn't trust any of those assassins enough to even remotely call one a friend. In answer to his request, several small sparks sizzled in the darkness and then a tiny lantern blazed to life, spreading a small circle of light around a dark-haired man with beady eyes and a perpetually mischievous grin. "Are you satisfied, my distrusting associate?"

"It's you Stoman."

"What do you have for us?" Stoman asked again.

"Nine wagon loads of the finest gold items."

"Our deal was ten," he argued.

"The elves blasted one of the wagons while we were using a road in Verdant Wood. That wagon was lost, but we were able to recover a fair amount of the treasure before we were forced to flee. What we don't have, the elves possess."

Stoman pulled away from the lantern, fading into the darkness.

"Well, do we have a deal?"

Stoman, hidden in the night, answered nothing.

"We have nine wagon loads!"

"The deal was for ten," Stoman's voice said calmly.

Enraged, Methlon pounded his fist against a nearby sapling, cutting a knuckle on a jagged branch stub. He ignored the pain and huffed in frustration. He needed the assassins, but it was becoming painfully clear to him they didn't need his gold. Thinking quickly, he decided he would have to throw in the only card he had to bargain with. It was the one he hoped he wouldn't have to forfeit. "Once the elves are destroyed the assassins have the rights to all the treasure spoils as compensation for the missing wagon load. But Lifespring is mine!"

Stoman's face came back into the lantern light, his perpetual grin nearly splitting his face.

"Your deal is satisfactory. I'll be in contact with our warlord tomorrow and inform him of your generous offer. He's committed to another project currently, but I'm sure he'll abandon that undertaking when he hears the news of such a tremendous payment in gold.

We must have your gold before we enter into the elves' kingdom. Meet us in the town of Senadon in two days. Somebody'll be waiting for you there. The appointed time will be midday. Don't be late this time."

"Are you sure The Lurking Shadows will be able to meet the task?" Methlon asked snidely.

"The elves will be destroyed."

* 5 *
MORE THAN MEETS THE EYE

The sound was unmistakable. The clanging of weapons ringing out through the Elfstay could only mean one thing. Fighting!

"Battle! Here in my elven kingdom?" Gallatar, King of the Silver elves, cried, the din shaking him from his sleep. He anxiously threw the covers off and leaped out of bed, pulling up his breeches and tugging on his boots.

"What's going on?" a groggy voice asked from the other side of the bed.

"Tarina, stay here," Gallatar commanded as he snatched up his sword. "There's fighting in the midst of the Avenue."

"What do you mean saying stay here, my King?" his queen asked, slipping out of her covers and grabbing her own sword. "Remember, when you married me you didn't just get a pretty face. I'm a warrior also." She set her sword into a series of graceful strokes and mock slices.

Gallatar didn't argue with her. Tarina had a strong spirit, a courageous spirit. It wasn't in her nature to question his commands, but she'd never allow him into any situation she wasn't willing to go up against herself. When he'd first met her a hundred years ago, she was the same way, loyal yet persistent. The years had put a few more wrinkles around her eyes and slowed her warrior reflexes some, but her personality had never changed.

Pushing his graying mane of hair from his eyes, Gallatar simply nodded to her and stormed out his chamber door. As King, he would lead the charge to dispatch whatever enemy had dared infiltrate the Elfstay!

As soon as he rushed through the doorway, his momentum came to a near halt. He ran face-first into the backs of a gathered crowd of elves, all cheering wildly as if watching some fabulous sporting spectacle. Beyond the throng, he heard the clashing of weapons.

"Get out of my way!" he roared, and the force of his yell caused the closest elves to scatter like a school of fish trying to dodge a predator. He shoved his way forward, commanding elves to make room for the king whenever he ran into a crowd too thick to push through. With every step, his face contorted into an angry, impatient mask. It took him longer to get through the press than he thought. Nearly every elf in the forest appeared to be there watching whatever was going on. Pushing the last few elves aside, he finally reached the front.

When he did, his eyes narrowed in anger.

In the middle of the Avenue, the paladin Navarro Silvinton parried away the two lightning-quick jabs of twin daggers. No longer donning his plate mail suit, but instead bare-chested and wearing only his breeches and boots, Navarro spun and thrust his double-edged sword straight out at his enemy. His opponent swiftly spun to the side and his sword came up empty. Again the daggers dove in, but without the armor on, Navarro had the fierce freedom to make precise moves and intricate cuts, blocking one dagger and ducking the other.

Navarro's sword slashed out, driving the adversary back. He pressed forward, slicing and thrusting. The Paladin's muscles churned with every precise movement, and Zakili's sisters who were watching the match from the front of the crowd didn't miss one move of the human warrior's technique.

Gallatar's lip curled up in anger as his hot gaze remained on The Paladin's sparing partner. His unruly son.

Zakili's daggers, twin knives with hilts fashioned in the likeness of winged tigers, spun in his palms as Navarro came back at him. Navarro's sword lashed out to cut across the elf's midsection, but Zakili dropped to the ground, allowing the sword to swoosh over harmlessly. He rolled to the side and sprang back to his feet. The sword easily reversed angles and came back in, this time low at the elf's knees. Zakili leaped, somersaulting over that attack and receiving a roar of approval from the elf audience. As soon as he touched down he came in behind the arcing sword, his daggers, which he affectionately called the Flying Tigers, diving in straight at Navarro's exposed ribs. The Paladin turned his torso suddenly. He flipped his sword in his palm so that he clutched it in a backfisted angle. The sword sliced across with impossible speed--his blade deflecting the double attack.

Monolique and Saranisen, Stiletto's youngest sisters, applauded loudly for The Paladin's swift counter.

Zakili leaped away, tossing one dagger then another at Navarro's broad chest. Too fast to be taken down by such a simple attack, the paladin batted the first dagger down and turned just enough to let the other fly past.

"Not the wisest attack," Navarro judged. "You're weaponless against an armed opponent." He waded in, his sword slashing across suddenly. Backed against a tree, the Elf Prince had no room to dodge the sudden attack so he ducked, the blade slicing overhead and tearing through the front of the oak as effortlessly as if it were butter.

"Playing for keeps, I see," Zakili said, one eyebrow raised questioningly when he glanced back and saw the great gash in the tree. He looked back to Navarro's unblemished weapon.

"No blade could be forced through solid oak like that without being broken! It's no wonder you say that thing is indestructible."

"It is a gift from God," Navarro stated matter-of-factly.

Zakili darted to the left in the direction of one of his lost daggers, and Navarro sped in that direction to intercept. The elf cut sharply and leaped feet first into unsuspecting Navarro's chest. The elf hit him solidly, stopping him in his tracks, but his light frame bounced off The Paladin as if he hit an unyielding wall. At least that was what he first thought, but Navarro, teetering back on his heels, waved his hands frantically, vainly trying to remain upright. The elf's second jump-kick sent Navarro reeling, and he finally toppled.

Zakili roared victoriously.

The crowd cheered wildly. Even Gallatar whooped loudly, unwittingly getting caught up in the excitement of the spectacle. Tarina, who had finally caught up to him, wrapped an arm around his waist, receiving a smile in return.

"Sly move," Navarro complimented, springing to his feet.

"I have more where that came from," Zakili boasted, his recovered daggers in his hands. "Give me a shovel, I'll dig my own grave!" he roared out his battle cry and charged full speed, daggers bared. Navarro's blade cut across sidelong, more out of self-defense than a counter attack, but the lithe elf's momentum brought him in fast and he somersaulted over the blade and Navarro, coming down at The Paladin's back. His daggers dove in. Navarro spun suddenly, his sword tucked closely, knocking the daggers aside.

"Incredible," Gallatar gasped, amazed at the agility and speed of both combatants.

He was so wrapped up in watching the fray he'd totally forgotten he was angry just moments before.

Navarro and Zakili slammed into each other, their weapons crashing together and grinding in close. With all muscles tensed, they stood stalemated, sword hilt locked up against daggers, piercing gazes not letting go of the other's eyes, beads of hard-earned perspiration rolling down their faces.

"Do you give up?" Zakili challenged.

"I must say you are a worthy opponent," Navarro complimented then started to laugh. "But why would I forfeit? You haven't come close to defeating me."

Zakili's blades shifted suddenly, and Navarro knew the elf was going to attempt his assault anew. He pressed in, keeping him locked up. A wide smile crossed The Paladin's face at a sudden idea. "Truce?" he suggested.

Zakili thought about it for a second, shaking rolling sweat from his face. "Sounds good," the elf agreed. "But who breaks first?"

The Paladin smiled suspiciously. "I will," he offered, immediately leaping out of Zakili's striking range and sliding his sword into its scabbard. He turned to retrieve his shirt hanging on a nearby limb, thinking the match to be over.

"Never ease up on your opponent! Especially if he is Zakili Terishot!" the elf roared before bellowing out his war cry. "Give me a shovel, I'll dig my own grave!"

The elf lunged at him, daggers leading. Navarro spun, evaluating the attack quickly and his foot snapped out in a vicious sidekick which slammed against the elf's chest, knocking him out of the air, the elf crashing flat on his back.

"If you plan to use surprise as your ally," Navarro jokingly advised, "never announce to your opponent you're coming."

"Brilliant suggestion," Zakili granted from his position on his back. The Paladin stepped to him, offering a hand, but the elf waved the gesture away, springing to his feet. "We must definitely try this again. I can't accept you having the last word in a battle."

Navarro laughed, then suggested, "What do you say about a dip in Lifespring to cool off?"

"That's drinking water. I have a better idea. Follow me." Zakili bolted through an opening in the crowd and sprinted off behind the housetrees. Navarro took up the chase.

"Where are they going?" Zakili's youngest sister, Saranisen, asked.

"I know exactly where they're headed," Monolique answered, a lascivious gleam in her eye. "Where all hot and sweaty warriors go to cool themselves."

"The Waterfall!" Saranisen realized excitedly, thinking she might know what her older sister had in mind.

"Shall we follow?"

* * * * *

"Excellent plan, Navarro," the elf yelled over the roaring water. Zakili stepped back under the pouring, water wall which streamed down from a twenty-foot precipice. Around him the shadows of surrounding trees began to recede as the morning sun rose higher in Avundar's cloudless sky, allowing the day's warmth to take hold.

"It was probably our only chance," Navarro replied, leaping onto a large, wet boulder close to the falling water. He was about to jump to one of the bigger rocks which was almost directly beneath the waterfall when he balked and stared in amazement. When the two had first charged into this section of woods, Navarro had only taken a glance at the waterfall, not noticing a bit of its detail as he rushed to strip off his sweat-soaked clothing and plunge under the alluring wall of water. But now, with a closer inspection of the falls, his mouth dropped open. Awed by the majesty of Lifespring and impressed by the elves' aptitude to create living architecture within the trunks of the lofty trees of the Avenue, he found complete wonderment as he stared at the sculpted design of the falls. The lip of the twenty-foot precipice protruded out impossibly far--so far he felt he could stable a dozen horses behind the falling water--but the stone should'ave collapsed under its own weight, not to mention the power of the roaring water. And it probably would've collapsed, Navarro perceived, if not for the two thick pillars of stone supporting it. He lost his breath in his amazement. Those natural pillars had been chiseled and decorated so intricately by the hands of elven craftsmen that they looked more like ornate columns than natural rock structures.

"After seeing the beauty of Lifespring, the allurement of the Elfstay and now this amazing waterfall, I may need an entire day to explore the rest of the rich wonders of your kingdom." Shaking away his awe, he leapt to the next rock and dunked himself under the clear, chilly cascade. The pounding liquid washed away his perspiration while beating away at his months of battle and travel fatigue. Bending his head back, he let the waters soak his gold-streaked hair.

"Hopefully, our sparring match has sparked the competitive nature of the elves," Navarro said. "If we can get them involved in competitive skirmishes among themselves, we might be able to incite them into action against the very real threat posed by Methlon and..." He let that thought trail off, but Zakili knew he referred to The Dark Sorcerer.

"Indeed. May it work," the elf declared, bending his head back and gulping in a mouthful of water.

Navarro laughed unexpectedly.

"What's so funny?"

"Did you see your father? He was caught up in the sparring match more than most of the other elves there."

Zakili snickered. "When he first broke through the crowd I thought he was going to burst into the match and throttle both of us for waking him so early."

"It was a shaky scheme, but I think it's going to pay off."

"I agree."

"But the potential threat of The Dark Sorcerer concerns me more than that of a band of warrior-merchants. I was told a premonition by a trio of mysterious men. They warned of the destruction of the world as we know it. They spoke of demons emerging and monsters running rampant. At first I doubted their veracity, but with the sudden resurgence of monsters in all lands and now the appearance of Zeraktalis, I believe The Dark Sorcerer has designs on more than conquering the baronies of Avundar; I feel he will stop at nothing short of Armageddon, the annihilation of all races."

"Well, what would make him think he could exterminate the populations of the world when his army wasn't even able to overcome the forces of Avundar's warriors so many years back?" the elf argued.

"He must've been searching for something then," Navarro guessed. "From the brief allusions I picked up from the conversation between the sorcerer and his minion, the goblins dispatched into our countryside hadn't yet located what they sought. Whatever it is must be something of great power, a force Zeraktalis presumes he can harness to destroy all the godly people of all lands."

"Well then, I'm safe!" the elf guffawed.

Navarro glanced to him with a sly grin. "You'll be next on the list. As many times as I've shared the saving gospel of Jesus Christ with you, you should know what to do."

"I do," he said weakly. "But..."

Navarro's eyes zipped away from Zakili and glanced toward the forest ahead, scanning the woods all about the waterfall. He noticed a slight rustling among the bushes where his sword lay! His fist tightened in frustration. If the invader were to spot his weapon and use it against him, all he'd have to call upon would be his fists and feet. That kind of match didn't thrill him. He was painfully aware how naked he felt without his sword at his side.

"What is it?" the elf asked, crouching like a jungle cat ready to spring. He'd noticed his friend's intense gaze and understood they had unwanted visitors hiding in the foliage.

Navarro signaled for silence as he tried to discern who or what the intruder was. A delicate-looking hand reached from behind a tree for The Paladin's breeches which he had washed moments earlier and was drying from a low-hanging branch.

60

Lifespring

Zakili stood up straight. "Don't do it!" he warned, hearing girlish tittering as the hand drew back. The elf suspected who the invaders might be. "Be gone, ladies."

Popping up over the bushes came the faces of Zakili's two youngest sisters, and Navarro retreated, face blushing, behind the wall of water. As powerful of a warrior as he was in battle, he was equally as modest about being undressed in front of women. The elf maidens stared at The Paladin's physique, regardless of the fact he was now only a blur behind the falling water, and despite their maturity, the elven ladies snickered and shoved each other playfully.

"I told you my sisters were attracted to you," Zakili called to his friend. "They even come to watch you bathe." Navarro made no response, and the elf understood how embarrassing and uncomfortable this must be for The Paladin.

"Please go," he bade his sisters, nodding back to Navarro.

The two swept into exaggerated bows and backed away. Giggling, they disappeared into the foliage. "Father enjoyed your battle this morning," Zakili heard Monolique call back. "I think you got his stale warrior blood moving again."

"Did you hear that, Navarro?" Zakili asked, his smile wide.

The Paladin stuck his head through the sheet of falling water to make certain the elf maidens were gone, the redness beginning to fade from his face. He pushed through to stand next to Zakili, the water shattering on his broad shoulders.

"Gallatar's warrior spirit appears to be revived after our match," Zakili cheered. "And it's likely, too, the other elves will energize."

"Excellent," Navarro responded. "Because the threats which have suddenly raised their ugly heads will wreak tragic results unless the elves become ready and unite."

* * * * *

This time she was sweating. Kelt came in again and again with a series of short jabs, finally ending the attack with a snap kick. Candace almost got out of the way, but his kick grazed her shoulder. He immediately waded in at her, having learned his lesson from the last sparring session. His girl had a lot of stamina, and he was unwilling to let her get out in the open and wear him out with all that running.

Candace's cutlass sliced across at his head, but he dropped to the ground, sweeping his leg, trying to take her off her feet. She sensed the attack and leapt, Kelt's sweep coming up empty. "Good move, father," she condescended. "You knocked me out the first time. I won't let that happen again."

"Then the training is working effectively," he said, springing back to his feet. "If you don't learn from a previous failure, you wasted the lesson."

Candace leapt at him with a flying sidekick that pounded into his gut and sent him stumbling back. Aware of her ever-alert father, she tried to sprint away when her feet touched down, but Kelt dove forward and grabbed her ankle. She fell face first to the turf.

A double trumpet blast echoed through the trees. His brow crunched in confusion, Kelt looked to the mountains and saw the sun hadn't yet climbed over the peaks. Why would he hear a double trumpet blast so early in the morning? He hadn't expected visitors today.

Candace looked to her father and groaned. She too knew what those double trumpet blasts meant. They sounded again.

"Our sparring's not yet finished for today," she said. "We can't let our lives be dictated by the arrivals of our 'guests.' We're at a draw right now. Let's determine a victor."

"I understand your apprehension," Kelt said. "But graciousness is part of your training. I want to make you a whole person, not just a good warrior."

"Father, you know your tutelage has sculpted me, and by no means am I beyond teaching, but you know how I feel toward these princes constantly disrupting our lives."

"You never know, Candace. One may be the man the Lord has directed here as your perfect match..." Suddenly Kelt let his sentence trail away. How foreign it sounded for him to mention anything about God. Years had passed since he'd last acknowledged Jesus.

Before Candace was ever born, he and his wife worshipped God fervently. He remembered both of them received Christ as Savior on the night when a traveling evangelist stopped by their fortress. In that time, it was customary to provide room and food for any sojourner without shelter for the night. They'd invited the preacher to eat with them, and later that evening, beyond the castle walls, he preached the gospel to whomever would listen. And whoever would listen happened to be almost everybody dwelling in the fortress, including his wife and himself. They never saw the preacher again, but they took responsibility for their Christianity and lived according to the precepts of the gospel, even being compelled to locate and purchase a copy of the Bible to share with the warriors and families living in the fortress.

Then one dreadful day, his dear wife, several years after Candace's birth, was murdered outside the fortress walls in almost the same location they had knelt together and cried out for Jesus to save them from their sins. Overcome with grief and bitterness over her loss, he slowly drew within himself, blaming God for her death. With his desire to serve the Lord quelled, the other warriors' faith began to wane, for they had looked up to the baron as their shepherd in the absence of a pastor. Now nobody would share the Word with them, and help them study, save one.

Only faithful Simeon, captain of the Elite Guard Battalion, remained steadfast. It was Simeon who took on the responsibility of teaching the Scripture to Candace. He often quizzed her on what she had studied, prayed with her, and was a constant comfort since her mother's death. Even now as a grown woman, she and Simeon had a close relationship, and Kelt was glad for it. Although Kelt failed to mature her in the fear and nurture of the Lord, God still found grace to assure she was raised up as a strong Christian.

"And you'll never know if you find the right man," Kelt continued, "if you continue to challenge every prince who comes here to a fight and drive them away."

"They ask for it, Father. After all, how much can one person brag on himself? I don't see how they can stand themselves, and to think this is the person I'd have to live with the rest of my life. Just to hear them crow for a few minutes is almost unbearable, to listen to it my whole life would be torture. I just like to put some of their self-glorying claims to the test."

"Well, it appears you get to challenge another one today," he said, throwing his arms high in surrender. "Maybe this time you can get the match you wanted. And I hope you do whip him. I don't want to think all this sparring was for nothing."

Candace rolled her eyes at her father's sarcasm, but Kelt only laughed, put his arm around her shoulder, and lead her back to the fortress.

* * * * *

Candace slipped her feet into a pair of elegant, indigo sandals and stepped over the open shutters to hang her towel. The sunlight streaming through the windows glistened on her tanned arms, warming her after her cool bath. This day promised to be comfortable, as was usual here in Avundar, the land of perpetual springtime. So why was she overcome with an icy sensation that ran down her spine like someone just poured glacier water across her back? She forced away the chill, swept across the room in her flowing dress, grabbed the door handle, and swung it open.

Reflexively, her fist shot out when she found herself standing face to face with a man just on the other side of her door. He threw a hand up in defense, but Candace recognized him in time to pull back her strike. The bearded man smiled warmly at her. "Simeon," she apologized.

"I was coming to summon you," he explained. "You can put your weapons away."

She looked down to see that her hands were tightened up, ready for action, and she shrugged, embarrassed.

"Your father's ready to see you. He seems quite thrilled with this young prince. He thinks you'll be in for a real surprise."

"I'm sure I have a treat waiting for me," she said. "Does he think he's the perfect man for me this time?"

"I don't know," he answered honestly. "But try to hold your sarcasm. I know you grow weary of this entire courtship thing, but a little tact and courtesy goes a long way. Remember our Bible studies? Your Bible knowledge is meaningless unless you apply it to the way you live."

"I know what I ought to do, but it's so hard. Do you know how disgusted I get listening to all these braggarts glorifying themselves? Not one of them looks at me as a person. To them, I am the would-be, crowning jewel to their kingdom, nothing more. Sometimes it's so difficult, my old friend."

"I haven't met this one yet," Simeon explained, "but if your father says he's a surprise, he must be somebody worth your while. Give this one a chance. Your father is a good judge of character." He winked and departed, quickly turned a sharp corner, and was out of sight before she could even begin her next question.

She huffed helplessly. Father had always been protective. When it came to her future, suffocatingly so. He had initiated this whole suitor thing a couple years ago in an attempt to find her a prince. She was entertained by it at first, but now it was getting out of control. Father was admitting anyone who made claim to royal blood. How obsessed was he that she be a princess?

Today she had to put a stop to this whole tiresome cycle.

"Don't be late," Simeon called back from the far corridor. "You know how he hates to wait."

Breathing in deeply, she tried to quell her frustrations, straightened her flowing blue dress, and walked through the open door, her steps anything but determined. She knew exactly where to meet Father, in the same place he held counsel with anybody of importance, in his so-called "throne room." Her father was but a baron in the land of Avundar, a land with no king, just a loose republic of baronies. But despite the lack of royalty in the land, her father had a penchant for using fancy royal names for the rooms and ceremonies in his impressive fortress. Why he was so enamored with royalty she did not know. From her brief experiences with their kind over the past couple of years, she could think of nothing she would less want to be. She didn't understand why he wanted to emulate them, other than for their riches. By far he was much nobler than any she'd met.

From the shadows, she sensed two individuals step in line far behind her, and she knew right away they were a pair of her father's elite guards guaranteeing her safety. She turned and smiled to the young men and continued on her way.

The few minutes it took to traverse the lighted hallways seemed like an eternity to her as visit after previous visit replayed in her memory. She dreaded this next meeting more and more with every step. A couple of hours had passed since she'd heard the trumpet blasts from the field. By now, she was sure the prince had made himself feel right at home. She took a deep breath and steeled herself for the ordeal, but it took several minutes until she thought she was ready. When she finally stood in front of Kelt's closed chamber door, she paused, anxiety setting in once again.

"Your best behavior," she reminded herself, and hesitantly reached for the handle. Listening carefully to the noise on the other side, she heard a cacophony of male voices discussing a confusion of topics. She listened more intently, trying to discern information about this visitor who had so impressed her father. After a long moment, she heard
nothing which gave her any clue, so with a resigned sigh she turned the doorknob and walked in.

"Candace!" she heard her father announce too cheerfully. "We haveth been waitin' for you! We haveth been waitin' for thisth very moment!"

64

ple"Have we?" she mumbled under her breath, scrutinizing the pronoun. And why was he slurring his words? She looked around the gathered crowd, trying to appear as elegant as possible as she walked forward, but she felt especially nervous today. Carefully, she glanced around but saw only the familiar faces of her father's guards and soldiers and some of the fortress' ladies. She exhaled a sigh of relief.

Just as she began to feel more comfortable, one unfamiliar face, then another emerged from the crowd and stalked to the front, until finally the number of alien visages equaled those she recognized. Something about this meeting felt terribly wrong.

From behind a crowd of seasoned warriors around the baron's throne emerged a tall man, gait confident, his presence demanding respect. His vestment, a tight, sleeveless shirt, clung to his sculpted torso. A flowing garment woven into the vest rolled over his shoulders and flowed behind him like a cape. The stranger bowed low, sweeping an arm out wide in front as she approached. When he rose, his black eyes gazed into hers. She shivered as a chill again coursed down her spine.

"Salutations," he addressed her. "You're even more beautiful than your father or the rumors of the land have informed me."

She wanted to rebut the tiresome description with a sarcastic comment, but nothing came. She knew it wasn't because she was trying to be on her best behavior. Something about this man truly frightened her. The vision of fiery eyes burning in the depths of a scarred helmet flashed through her mind suddenly. Then was gone. The Dark Sorcerer? What does he have to do with this prince?

"Candace," she heard her father call from across the room, shaking her out of her thoughts. She turned and saw him raise a goblet in the air. "Meet Prince Sebultis Killion!"

"Some just call me Kil," he said with a smooth inflection, causing those closest to burst into laughter.

"Kil?" she echoed, not joining in the mirth, not at all liking the phonetics of the name.

"Don't worry about how it sounds," he grinned, showing his teeth and reminding Candace of a hungry wolf. "Just how you say it."

Candace backed away a step.

"He hasth come from afar," Kelt explained, his voice sounding unusually lazy. "Thomehow the secret about my fair daughder hasth gotten out and is bringing in heirs from even the most distant kingdoms."

"What secret?" she protested under her breath.

"Killion," Kelt continued. "My apologies, Prince Killion has come to seek your hand in marriage, my daughter. And he's willing to have the ceremony performed tonight."

Candace's mouth dropped open in shock. She stared unbelieving at her father who swayed in his throne.

"This is a time to celebrate!" Kelt announced, setting off a chorus of cheers, mostly from the visitors, Candace noticed. "My precious daughder will soon be a princess, something she deserves!"

Standing to his feet, he climbed up on his throne and stood on the seat, raising his goblet into the air. "Bring more wine! Let the festivities begin!"

Candace stared unbelievingly at her normally reserved father who now held his cup under a huge wineskin. In horror, she watched him gulp down the pale-colored liquid then reach out to refill his container again. She strode up to her father's throne, avoiding eye contact with the stranger named Kil and motioned Kelt closer with one finger. Eager to hear her, he knelt, but before she said her first word, she eased the goblet from his hand.

"Father, I don't wish to be married to this man," she whispered, feigning a smile so those watching wouldn't discern a problem.

"Well why not, girl? You've not challenged him to a duel yet. With that omission, I'd think you would find this prince a man of character above the rest."

She backed away, embarrassed by the total disregard for keeping the conversation private. It was the drink that was affecting him, she knew, trying not to be offended. Apparently, he'd been celebrating long before she arrived. That worried her. She never saw him drink anything that would alter his thinking. She never saw him drink any intoxicating substance ever. And where did he get the wine? They kept no such things in their home. One glance over to Kil answered her questions. He pointed to one of his wineskin-totting men and directed him toward Kelt.

"He's had enough," Candace declared sternly before the man even got close. Her eyes narrowed when she looked back to Kil. Had he laced her father's drink with some kind of mind-bending drug? She turned back to Kelt. "Father, he scares me!" she whispered forcefully.

"Do you not trust my judgment?" he asked overly loud. "It's my love for you Candace that has helped me in making this decision. I only want the best for my precious daughter."

She smiled bitter-sweetly, discerning his words were true but surmising it was more than his love for her which forced him into this rash decision. Something evil was taking place in this throne room. Killion was deceiving her father, she knew. Killion inebriated him to twist his goodly intentions toward whatever end this prince hoped to achieve by marrying her.

"Your father is a wise man," she heard Kil's voice say over her shoulder, nearly making her jump. "We spent a good hour discussing. Together we decided this is a good thing. Albeit, you might not think so now, in the future this union will prove profitable for both houses, and it'll change the course of history in the land of Avundar forever."

Candace succeeded in not casting a condemning stare at the man and instead turned back to her father. "Reconsider, Father. I feel something evil about this man who so coolly calls himself 'Kill.'"

"I have. Many times in my own privacy I've mulled it over these past years. I never wanted to give you up. I've always wanted to hold you close under my protective arms, but I've slowly come to realize you're not my little girl anymore. You're a grown woman, and as your father, I wish to make just one last parental decision for you, one that will make you comfortable for the rest of your days and give you a better future than I can give. I want you to dwell in the lifestyle of a royal monarch."

Candace's face dropped. She knew her father spoke from the deepest concerns of his heart. And as long as he remained drunk--and most likely drugged-- there would be no way to reason with him.

A heavy knock on the door broke Candace from her miserable thoughts. Slowly, the door opened, allowing a messenger to stick his head into the room. "Prince Killion," he summoned, "an emissary from your court has an urgent message for you, sire."

Kil's brow furrowed angrily. Candace didn't miss the expression. The man put on a courtly smile immediately, though, when he turned to Kelt. "With my most humble apologies, I ask you to excuse me," he bade, receiving a nod from Kelt. "I'll return shortly, Baron Veldercrantz, once I've discovered what information my servant has carried from my kingdom." After a deep bow, he exited out the doorway.

"Father, there's something sinister about him. I don't trust him."

* * * * *

"There had better be a good reason why you drew me away at such a crucial moment," Kil threatened, once he and his emissary got out of earshot in the courtyard.

"I'd never disrupt your work for foolishness," the other man promised, his voice quivering as he looked into Kil's dangerous stare. "Did the herbs work as well as hoped?"

"The baron's mind became clay in my hands," Kil said matter-of-factly. "Now tell me why you interrupted me, Stoman!"

"A task."

"A task? You come to me with information about some fool who has offered us gold to assassinate someone? I work to achieve a prize many times more valuable than all the riches we could ever earn! I'd kill you right now if I wasn't engaged in this whole charade."

"But he promised nine wagon loads of golden items and the rights to the spoils after victory."

Kil came close to Stoman's face, his dark eyes bored right into his servant. "Do you understand what I'm about to gain here? Within this woman is the key which will unleash our opportunity for power like we've never known. This woman Candace has an untapped force about her that I think she doesn't even know about yet. I believe she embodies the mysterious essence of power The Master has confirmed is within this land. And you break me away from my deception to inform me about a task. No amount of gold is worth what we're about to wrest from here!"

Stoman inched back, imagining any number of ways crafty Kil could strike him down. Although his leader appeared unarmed, he carried any number of hidden weapons, and if he didn't use those, his hands and feet were deadly by themselves. If

Kil didn't kill Stoman for interfering with his plans, Stoman knew The Warlord would surely destroy him for not conveying what he thought to be essential information, so he steeled himself and spoke up.

"The merchant leader was reluctant but eventually relented any claims to the elves' treasure after he lost one wagon when traveling through their forest kingdom. He was willing to yield all the treasure, but more importantly and definitely more interestingly, he desires only a small area in Verdant Wood known as Lifespring."

Kil's snarl faded. "Lifespring," he said with a calming interest. He grew silent for several long minutes, causing Stoman to shift uncomfortably. "Tell me more about Lifespring."

"Possessed by the Silver elves since history unwritten, it's a natural well fiercely guarded by that race. The exact location remains a mystery to most since it's never been mapped; however, the merchant Methlon somehow knows its exact bearings. The trees surrounding the spring have eyes, I've heard. The elves will know if anyone has infiltrated their forest from the very first step."

"You've done well in discovering this information. Go on."

"Lifespring is legendary to all the storytellers and historians of Avundar. Rumors abound of its supernatural powers. Some even think drinking the waters of Lifespring will stop the body from aging, and that's an attribute even the most gifted wizard's magic can't boast. I also understand the spring is the heart of Avundar's spring-like climate, the spring's waters being the lifeblood that makes the land so fertile--"

"Why hadn't I thought of it before?" Kil blurted. "The power of Lifespring must be what we're truly looking for!" He thought for a moment. "But what about the woman? She still may play a significant role. I can sense her untapped abilities, and she isn't a prospect I wish to slip through our fingers. However, the Lifespring of the Silver elves would seem to be the more logical essence of power. Instruct your merchant we'll complete the task for him. Then once victorious, we shall slay him and take his precious spring."

Killion spun on his heels and marched toward the fortress, leaving Stoman to his task.

* * * * *

"That's terrible!" Kelt cried after hearing Kil's story. "But with your leadership restored to your kingdom, I'm sure the coup d'etat will be swiftly put down. And all of my forces are at your disposal to eradicate this problem."

"I thank you, Baron Veldercrantz," Kil said, sweeping into a low bow, "but that won't be necessary. Once I've returned, all the kingdom will rally back under my control. Baron, meeting you was an honor. I've never been received by someone so noble who was not of royal blood. If only there were more men like you, the kingdoms of every land would be utopia, now wouldn't they?"

Kelt accepted the compliment gratefully, delighted to receive such an honor from a prince. He was never so mistaken.

"Where's your lovely daughter? I'd like so much to bid her farewell before I depart."

"Summon her to the throne room," Kelt ordered, snapping his fingers to one of his guards. He turned to Kil apologetically. "She's departed to her bedroom. She said she wanted to be properly prepared for your return."

After several long moments the guard finally returned, perplexed. "Sir, I could find Candace nowhere in the fortress."

"What?"

"Her dress lies crumpled on the floor in her room, and her armor and sword are missing. I searched everywhere, but she's disappeared."

Another man rushed into the room, this one adorned in leather chaps and smelling of dirt. Kelt recognized him as one of his horse ostlers. The man bowed quickly in apology for his appearance. "I heard you look for your daughter, sir. She departed moments ago. With her pack stuffed and flung over her shoulder, and adorned in her armor, she took her mare Eliom and rode out."

Stunned, Kelt stared at the man. "Candace has run away?"

* 6 *
GREATER THAN LIFE

"What're you doing out here this early?" Navarro heard a sleepy voice ask.
He looked up and pushed his hair from his eyes. He was careful to place a finger in his book to retain his page. With the morning shadows long and the birds singing their first melodies, he was surprised to see anyone up so soon. He especially didn't expect to see this individual--one of the last to finally settle and go to bed last night. Rising from his seated position against the tree, he bowed courteously to the King's daughter Saranisen.

"Well, good morning to you, too," he teased.

A grin lit her face at seeing Navarro's contagious smile, then she yawned profoundly and placed a hand over her mouth. She started to apologize, but The Paladin laughed and waved off the gesture.

"I hope I haven't disturbed your sleep, especially after a long night of dancing under the stars."

"You saw that?" she asked, smiling.

"Yes, I saw you and your sisters and about half of the kingdom out there on the plains sing and dance yourselves to exhaustion. Travelers' tales about the dance of the elves do no justice to its beauty. It looked so exhilarating, I joined in as well. Predictably, my dancing was awkward compared to the elegance of the elf style. Still, it was fun."

Saranisen giggled, and Navarro was uncertain if it was because of his statement or because she was trying to imagine a human dancing with the elves. He smiled that consideration away.

"Well, I apologize if my reclining here was too loud and woke you so early this morning," he joked.

"No, actually it was Monolique who shook me and pointed you out. I was going to leave you to your solitude, but she asked me to find out what you were doing."

He smiled at her lie. "This just seemed to be a quiet and comfortable spot to rest."

"You've been out here with your book since sunrise. I saw you studying that same book last evening before sunset. I'm curious. What enthralls you about that literature that it keeps drawing your attention to it again and again, and why would you be out here this early in the day with it?"

He pointed upward. "Right above me is a break in the canopy, allowing some sunlight to warm me and to read by, so I sat down by the tree to fellowship with God for a while."

"Fellowship with God?" she asked skeptically, her face twisting in confusion. "How do you communicate with God by reading a book?"

"There's much more to communing with God than reading a religious book. I gain strength, encouragement, and joy from this book. I can get alone in a quiet and peaceful place to converse with God in prayer. I listen to Him talk to me through His Word," Navarro explained, nodding to the book in his hand. "How about you? Do you take time to communicate with the Lord God?"

"The Silver Elves worship Sistal, the nature goddess of Verdant Wood. We don't really talk to our goddess and neither does she talk to us. We guard and protect these woods which she entrusted to us, and we offer sacrifices of the fruits of the forest during the full moon. A moral life, stewardship of these woods, and worthy sacrifices are all Sistal demands of us. That's the elves' way to commune with our goddess. But since you are a human, I'm sure she's not your god."

"You are correct. She's not. But I am intrigued by your belief. I discern you assume there are a variety of different gods which any individual can choose to follow."

Saranisen nodded her affirmation.

"Now I am curious. In your opinion, how many gods do you think there are?" he asked.

Saranisen shrugged her shoulders, scratching her temple as she thought. "That's hard to say. I've never been asked before. I guess it all depends upon how many different communities of people there are. From what I understand, each race worships a different god, and there are even different gods for various cities. I guess there has to be about five or six score gods out in the world somewhere," she answered confidently, thinking she had given The Paladin an accurate answer.

Navarro deferred to her answer with a nod and a smile.

"Which one of those gods do you think created the heavens and the earth?" he asked.

Saranisen looked to him sheepishly. This time she had no answer. Guessing a roundabout figure for the amount of gods was one thing, but pinpointing one exact god for such a task was an entirely different challenge. "I really don't know," she finally answered after a long silence.

"Can I tell you which it was?"

Saranisen shook her head eagerly. All of this was new information to her, ideas she'd never considered. She'd always been cognizant of the physical realm, never delving into the depths of her religion which centered around an impersonal goddess. Intrigued, she sat down across from Navarro and leaned in. What God could create an entire world and the sky above?

"What I'm holding in my hands is the most powerful tool in all of history," he said, opening the book to the place he had marked with his finger. "This is the Word of God, the Holy Bible, a book the Lord has kept incorruptible and indestructible no matter how many different hands of the different generations it's passed through.

"I worship the God of this Bible, not because He's my favorite of all the hundreds of other gods, but because He said He is the only God. He is the God who spoke the world into existence, the people, the animals, everything. Have you ever looked up into the night sky and seen the countless stars?"

"Yes."

Johnny Earl Jones

"He created every one of them. He created the infinite heavens just by speaking it into existence! And He's so mighty, so awesome, so huge, that the Bible says even the heavens can't contain Him. But yet a God of such magnitude knows each individual personally. He knows you, Saranisen."

"He does? He would spend his time knowing about the fourth child of an elf?"

"He would. He knows how many hairs you have on your head. He knows all your needs. He knows your desires. He knows what's important to you, and the things important to you become important to him."

Her mouth fell open. "Your Deity actually cares about me and is interested in me?"

"He is."

From the corner of her eye she noticed others gravitating toward the conversation. Elves began to file into the once-empty avenue, their curiosity piqued. She feared the distraction might end their discourse, but she noticed Navarro's concentration was solely on her, not on the growing crowd.

"Now there is one problem, and it's the problem of every race of every land," he emphasized, turning the pages in the Bible. "See, read here."

"It is appointed unto men once to die," Saranisen read, "but after this the judgment."

She looked to him. "Why will we be judged?"

"Good question. God tells us here," Navarro said, turning several pages back. "The Bible says all have sinned and fall short of the glory of God, but it additionally says the wages of sin is death."

"I.. I'm not sure if I like God," Monolique decided as she walked over. "It sounds like there is no hope when we die."

"God knew that. So He loved us enough to send His only perfect Son to save us from His just wrath, and *gift* us with eternal life through Christ. He requires only that we believe on Him."

Saranisen and Monolique drew forward, hands on knees in anticipation.

"God's Son, the Lord Jesus Christ, willingly gave up His position, His glory, His laud to become a man and to die a cruel death on the cross for us. But the Bible says He didn't just get nailed there and die. On that cross, Jesus took upon Himself the sins and wickedness of mankind, and there, God the Father had to turn His back on His only Son, laden with our sins, and pour out His fury on Jesus Christ!

"Jesus died on that cross for our sins. But the best news is that three days later, of His own power, He rose from the dead, having defeated death, hell and the grave for us. Jesus has granted us forgiveness and eternal life! Everybody's sins must be punished. But the person who has *not* trusted Christ for forgiveness must pay the penalty for his own sins. The person who cries out for Jesus to save him already has the penalty paid for his sins by Jesus on the cross. There's no other way to heaven but through Christ Jesus."

"What must I do to be saved from God's wrath?" one of the elves behind the sisters asked.

"Yes, please tell me," Saranisen pleaded.

Navarro flipped his Bible a few pages forward. "Here, God's Word says: if you shall confess with your mouth the Lord Jesus and shall believe in your heart God has raised Him from the dead, you shall be saved. For with the heart man believes unto righteousness, and with the mouth confession is made unto salvation. For whosoever shall call upon the name of the Lord shall be saved."

"That's all?" another elf asked skeptically. "I would think a gift as spectacular as eternal life would demand some great feat to be accomplished to prove your worthiness."

"That's precisely the point. None of us deserve eternal life, and there is nothing we can do to earn it. We can't make ourselves worthy. The Bible says 'by grace we are saved through faith. It is the gift of God, not of our own efforts.' It's all about what Jesus already did for us!"

Saranisen waved the other elf's doubts away and looked into The Paladin's eyes. "What must I do?"

Navarro rose from his seated position and knelt before them. "Fall on your knees and tell Jesus you need help. You're a sinner who needs a Savior. Cry out for His mercy and He will hear you. Believe and you'll be saved. Salvation and forgiveness are not found through religion, but by a relationship with Christ."

He took Saranisen and Monolique by the hand when they knelt by him, but they quickly had to make room as several of the elves nearby joined them, dropping to their knees.

"Why are you elves standing around?" Navarro heard a voice demand tersely from behind the crowd. He recognized it as Maengh's. "Everything this human speaks is nonsense. Why listen to him any longer? Move on!"

The curious crowd began to ooze away, and Navarro wasn't surprised to see the vast majority of them turn away after Maengh's comment. Some snickered about sin, others sneered about a need for a Savior. Navarro was saddened that so many spurned the words of life. The Paladin had met many elves during his adventures, and without exception, they all had deep moral character and were reputed citizens among and outside their own people. Most considered themselves good, not sinners in need of a Savior. But The Paladin knew it was impossible for anyone to get to heaven by just being moral. They needed Jesus. He's the only Way to heaven.

The handful who remained bowed their heads.

"Lord God Almighty, we humble ourselves before You, broken and convicted by the power of Your Holy Word..." Navarro began.

A short distance away, Zakili watched. Not so long ago, Navarro had shared his testimony about Christ. The elf had listened intently and felt the power behind the words. He had almost given in that day. He had almost become a Christian. He was fond of the idea of a loving, heavenly Father. He was mesmerized by this Jesus who cared so much for Zakili that He would actually die so that Zakili could live. Zakili even enjoyed the thoughts of a place called heaven, where there'd be no more sorrow, no more tears and no more pain. But certain things he wasn't ready to give up yet. He didn't think he could live up to the expectation. Forsake all his own schemes to live in obedience to God? *No*, he thought. He was not quite ready for this Jesus Christ yet.

He turned, truly admiring his friend's dedication and faith. Maybe some day, he speculated. Maybe some day he would take this Jesus up on His offer of eternal life and peace. But not now.

* * * * *

They swirled about Kil and crawled around behind him, all of them ugly and vile. Would he have to stomach these wicked, otherworldly fiends every time he talked to his Master?

Slowly, he walked through the dark corridor. Although the demons filling the hallway were aflame, they burned a black fire so the lightless walk was even darker. He could barely see them, but what he could make out made his lip curl in disgust.

Sensing evil diving in close, he stopped. A demon plunged down just inches from him. The sharp teeth of its fleshless jaws would have ripped his face off if he hadn't halted. The fiends were getting too wild and too close. Whatever the Master had schemed up, whatever evil he'd concocted, drove these wicked beasts into an uncontrolled bacchanal and pushed them past the limits he could stand.

"The Fangs of Hell," he growled and his twin dirks leapt into his hands, both flaming hungrily. "An award from your Master. These hellish blades have the power to end even your existence on this world, to send you to the stinking abyss. Don't try me, vile fiends. I'll extinguish any of you in a second." He slashed the flaming blades through the air. Any demons too close fled. He knew they understood the power of his blades; not long ago he'd sent a handful of arrogant spirits back to the pit.

With a light source to guide him now-- the flames of his blades--he marched on confidently, shifting his eyes back and forth, watching for any surprise attacks. He didn't trust a demon's motives for a second, knowing they'd lie or turn on him with every chance they had.

Several tense moments later, he finally stood before the huge, curtained wall, the gateway to his communication with his Master. Shoving his blades into their hilts, he let the room fall back into blackness and waited a moment for his eyes to adjust to the darkness, then he stepped to the wall and pulled back the curtains. He stepped back a respectful distance, knelt and looked to the wall. Soon the mirror-like gateway radiated a dismal glow. Hellish mists swirled and plumed in its frame. Instinctively, Kil raised an arm to protect his eyes. He'd knelt before this mirror countless times and although it hadn't happened yet, the mists always seemed on the verge of shattering the mirror surface and sending shards flying everywhere. The mist dissipated suddenly, blanketing the corridor in darkness once again. He'd seen this enough times to know what was next. A pair of fiery eyes opened in the midst of the dark mirror.

"Master," he said respectfully.

74

Lifespring

"Stand, my servant Kil."

He obeyed, blowing out a quiet, perturbed huff. He hated the term servant when applied to him, but he wasn't foolish enough to reveal this to his Master. Nor was he foolish enough to challenge his authory.

"I have news for you, my Master."

"Speak."

"I think I've discovered the mysterious essence of power we seek."

"You think?" the voice asked mockingly.

"I *have* discovered it, my Master. And we will possess it before the moon sets three times."

"How can you be so sure?" the eyes asked, and Kil heard the tinge of doubt. Was The Dark Sorcerer testing him or deriding his confidence? Really, he had no guarantee that Lifespring held the key of power to release demons, but that was his gut feeling. He trusted his instincts. Besides, he knew to withhold potential information from the sorcerer was akin to Stoman withholding essential discoveries from him and would reap the similar punishment--sadistic torture and slow death.

"My men and I go to wrest this key from the hands of a people who have no clue of their closing destruction. They'll be slaughtered like unsuspecting sheep and before they even realize doom has fallen upon them, the dead will be piled high. This kingdom will be brutally ravaged and the capture of the key assured." All was silent for a moment as the fiery eyes blazed more intently. Kil understood the malicious nature of this sorcerer. The description of the coming massacre only whetted the sorcerer's evil appetite for bloodshed and carnage.

For Killion, life and death were flip sides of the same coin. He was an assassin and an extremely effective one. Killing was a way of life for him. He did it well, and he was paid handsomely. He had gained a reputation among his Lurking Shadow assassins as bloodthirsty, but that wasn't true. Unlike the sorcerer, whose appetite desired death continually, for him murder was his business.

"Prepare the way, my servant. Capture the source of power. I will gather my army and send them against Avundar. Your assassins will join them to secure the land for my arrival. My lieutenant, long-time stationed in Avundar, will seek you out. He has information you'll find vital to your conquest. The forces of good will soon be crushed, and God Himself will flee from this world. All lands on this world will be suffocated in my iron grasp!"

* * * * *

"This is where the goblins disappeared," Navarro said to Celemonte as they pierced the veil of trees surrounding the grassy meadow. He looked around. The surroundings appeared peaceful. His sword Invinitor was unaffected by the return to the scene, its ruby heart remaining deep red and opaque. By all evidences, the evil had departed. And that was what troubled him. Without any solid evidence, he couldn't persuade the Council of Rulers, the respective leaders of baronies and townships, along with the Elf King, who oversaw the diplomacy of Avundar. After all, the inhabitants of Avundar hadn't suffered invasion since any of them could remember. Why would they think it possible now?

Zeraktalis had covered his tracks well. Although The Paladin's word held quite a bit of pull, without one shred of evidence that Avundar was targeted by the Dark Sorcerer for invasion, he wouldn't be able to convince the rulers.

Navarro glanced about the lea which was full of quiet shadows. The woods encompassing the meadow no longer seemed peaceful to him. Every shadow concealed potential wickedness. Every dark space hid a bloodthirsty monster. The Paladin shook the disturbing thoughts from his mind. But if the monsters did come to Avundar--and after seeing Zeraktalis standing in the midst of their land, he was sure they would come--the dark images invading his thoughts wouldn't be far from the truth. He'd fought in enough battles to understand the surreptitious movements of monsters, and the destruction they could wreak at a moment's notice. And if the Council of Rulers were as complacent as King Gallatar, especially without solid evidence to jar it, they would be completely unprepared for the imminent onslaught.

"Lord, help us."

* * * * *

"The proud elf king won't offer much resistance against our invasion," Kil, Warlord of the Lurking Shadows, told his gathered assassins, his voice echoing throughout their dim, capricious lair. "Those complacent elves think no one would dare to attack their kingdom. So confident are they that they refuse to prepare for possible attack. We'll use that to our advantage and slaughter the entire race like dumb lambs."

"But how do you know so much about them?" Stoman asked, in total awe as Kil finished unfolding his plan of attack. He was usually Kil's point man to receive news about the land, but here he was hearing fresh revelation from his warlord about the reclusive elves of Verdant Wood.

"Frequent spies. I have many in every region," Kil explained. He tapped his finger to his forehead, and a wicked smile lifted the corners of his mouth. "Information is my forte."

"But spies among the Silver Elves?" Stoman asked respectfully. "Surely they'd know if one of our assassins impersonated one of their kind by physical differences alone. And we have no reprobate elves among our guild of assassins. How did you infiltrate their society, my Warlord?"

"It requires special sorcery to pierce the lair of the goodly elves," Kil explained with uncharacteristic patience as he looked over a sea of quizzical faces. He always his assassins guessing and perpetually remained several steps ahead, never foolish enough to forget these were murderers who were as heartless as he. He feared no one. If any of his assassins challenged him, he summarily destroyed them and hung their carcasses from the rafters as a warning to all the others. He knew they feared him but he wasn't so naïve to think they wouldn't supplant him if given the slightest chance. "It takes a unique spy," he continued cryptically. "The Master gave me the power to make an elf."

"What?" rang throughout the room.

"The Master handed me a fearful extent of authority to command his resources. Some things are grotesquely curious, such as our goblin guards, while others are altogether deadly. Such is the case with the spy among the elves, a spy who can masquerade as anyone he wishes."

Kil spread his arms out wide, gazing toward the center of the room. "Make room for Ironfist, the elven spy of the Lurking Shadows!"

The assassins turned and looked about the dim lair, trying to catch the first glimpse of this mysterious spy. For several suspenseful minutes nobody stepped forward, filling the lair with impatient questioning. Kil observed the addled men with interest, a mischievous smile splitting his face. Then from the midst of the throng a burly viking rose and pressed his way forward. The assassins stared, knowing he hadn't been among them a brief minute ago. A lane cleared before him, none willing to hinder the great man's strides.

"Well met, Ironfist," Kil said, clasping wrists with the huge man while holding back chuckles at the confused expressions of his men. "Greet your fellow assassins, the Lurking Shadows."

The burly viking turned to the men, his long, braided beard swinging as his wide torso came about. "To kill 'n destroy in the name of the Master," he saluted gruffly.

Saying nothing, the assassins stared curiously at the huge man.

"This is the spy who dwells among the elves?" one finally asked.

"The very one," Kil said.

"Wouldn't it be obvious to the elves this fellow wasn't one of their race?" another Lurking Shadow dared to challenge.

"Not necessarily," the 7-foot-tall viking answered.

A chorus of laughter sprang up from the crowd.

"The last time I checked, elves grew no taller than six feet and have never had a beard!" one voice cried sarcastically, feeding the venomous mirth.

"My horse looks more like an elf than he does!"

The laughter exploded into a deafening roar. Ironfist kept his resolute stance and gave no indication he was affected by the throng's chides. Kil calmly marched up beside the viking and stared at his men, his dark eyes unblinking. The assassins saw the deadly seriousness on his visage, and they fell so silent they could hear the quiet groan of the catwalks goblin guards stood upon overhead. "Now that you have their undivided attention, Ironfist, make my assassins believers."

"With pleasure."

Without warning, the huge viking's countenance blurred and slowly melted away. His burly chest and thick arms convulsed and contorted, issuing sickening snaps and squishing noises. Grotesquely, his torso caved in and his limbs thrust deep into their sockets, becoming shorter. His whole body looked as if it consumed itself.

A number of curious whispers and a few profane expletives filled the air as the normally unshakable assassins watched this unusual display. Kil stood calmly to the side, his gaze shifting from Ironfist to his entranced warriors.

Ironfist jerked, his frame compressed and writhed. His height diminished. His beard dissolved completely into the still melting flesh of his face. Slowly, his blood-shot eyes rolled back into his head. His body ever shrinking, he turned away from the men captivated by this strange metamorphosis. To their amazement, even the clothing Ironfist wore began to melt away and change.

When Ironfist finally turned back, he had a completely different visage. Instead of veined eyes, they now shone in silvery brilliance. His burly physique was no more. He had the tight frame of a lithe fighter.

He was an elf.

"He's a shape-shifter!" one assassin cried, daggers drawn.

"A lycanthrope?" another questioned, and the air filled with the ringing of metal as weapons appeared in hands everywhere.

"Calm yourselves," Kil ordered. "Ironfist is much more valuable to us than a werewolf. Comrades, this is a jothenac, an ally sent from The Master himself, and he has the ability to transform into whomever he desires. Beware of course. He destroys any he chooses to emulate. Hope none of you see your own face begin to stare back at you. It'll be the last thing you see."

Ironfist bowed deeply, sweeping his arm across in the usual elven manner. "In this form don't address me as Ironfist," the jothenac warned. "I'm the elf king's guard and messenger, Maengh."

"This is how you received so much knowledge about the elves," Stoman said, his tone one of awe at his resourceful leader.

Kil accepted the praise as if it was expected, then turned to the jothenac and indicated the throng of assassins with a wave of his arm. "Maengh, inform my Lurking Shadows of all they need to be alerted to before the attack. I go to finish preparations."

"Together we'll win Lifespring for the lofty purposes of The Master," Maengh began, stepping to the forefront as Kil melted back into the shadows. "With the capture of the spring a new order will dawn, a new authority designed by The Master to crush all godly resistance and give us free reign over the entire world.

"Our blitz against Verdant Wood will produce tremendous carnage," he said, inspiring a cacophony of cheers and yells. "The elves won't be prepared. The king refuses to believe any would dare attack his domain. After slaying one of his most trusted guards and assuming his identity, I began to poison his thinking, to convince him no army would foolishly risk battle with the elves in their own forest. They're invincible, I continually tell him, giving him a false sense of security. He thinks it's a reasonable assumption. No army in memory has ever challenged those elves in their own forest where they seem invisible among the trees. The elf king will absolutely not prepare for the attack. He sees no need. His pride and overconfidence has blinded him. These elves trust their sovereign's judgment, so they too think they'll meet no conflict. Their apathy will play right into our hands, for I know their secret places. I have discovered their defensible areas and planted seeds of contention among the elves themselves. Lack of knowledge on the enemy's part has been a strength to the elves. I've stripped that from them. The borders of the Silver Elf community are wide open for attack."

A triumphant roar tore the air in the shadowy den. Assassins clapped each other on the back, salivating at the thought of easily conquering the legendary Silver Elves and attaining their mysterious spring.

"Only one problem may stand in our way," Ironfist added gravely. "There is one anomaly among these elves. But only one." The men quieted and turned back to the jothenac. "The Silver Elves number less than our army. Typically, the elves agree uniformly with the views of their arrogant king.

"But beware of one elf who is not like the others, one who may cause more trouble than we expect. When any of you confront him, concentrate your attacks solely on him until he's destroyed. He'll prove to be our greatest obstacle, for he has the charisma to ignite his people's will to fight. Watch for him! Destroy him swiftly! His name is Zakili!"

* 7 *

LIFE AND DEATH DECISIONS

"Put your weapons away!" Methlon growled to his anxious lieutenant Bozar. "Have you any idea of the place we're about to enter? This town is lawless, and the last thing we want is to bring any undue attention to ourselves or our goods." Methlon thumbed behind him, alluding to the caravan of wagons following his lead.

They were closing in on Senadon, a town governed by gang rule where the tough bullied the weak into subjection. Methlon knew the possibility of confrontation was extremely high here and prepared thoroughly for this visit. In each of the nine, horse-drawn wagons were two heavily-armed merchants, trained to fight with tenacity. Skirting the fringes of the troupe were numerous, mounted, merchant-fighters who acted as escorts. The wagon's contents were covered so not to tempt any crafty highwayman to go after their riches. The gold items clanged noisily under the tarps pulled tight over each wagon. The merchant leader smirked. Even if the gold was uncovered, he knew his battle-hardened merchants were more than enough insurance against any band of thieves. Robbers were never a problem for Methlon's troupe.

Senadon was offered by Stoman as a rendezvous point to meet with a representative of the Lurking Shadows. But as they neared the town gates, Methlon realized he had no clue where to find his contact. Stoman told him he'd know when he found his contact, but the merchant feared having to wander aimlessly in this dangerous town. Although he was accompanied by a skilled band of fighters, he still didn't relish the thought of parading his treasures around before a population of outlaws.

A group of three rugged characters marched out from the city, traveling on the dusty road in the opposite direction of the caravan. Methlon eyed the men for an uncomfortable moment hoping they might've been the contacts Stoman hinted at. They kept their path, looking over the caravan briefly, then never looking back. Methlon growled in frustration. He wanted to conclude this meeting with the mysterious assassins quickly. "They're murderers," he grumbled to himself. "I don't trust them. The sooner this foul business is completed, the sooner I can remove myself from this forsaken town, and the sooner Lifespring will be in my hands."

A lone individual, looking equally as hardy as the previous three, slipped around the tall columns that marked the town's entrance, and headed toward the caravan. Methlon, eager to be through with the assassins, addressed the man quietly. The Senadonian made a profane gesture and kept walking.

"That's not him either," Methlon growled under his breath, hating the cryptic game the assassins played with him. "If they're willing to accept my riches, they should at least make it easier for me to find them." Considering for a moment, he realized he'd no other choice but to tolerate their secretive ways, and he ceased his complaints. The Lurking Shadows were only a temporary necessary evil. There was no other way to wrest Lifespring from the elves. He'd tried bribes. He'd tried an assault, which, of course, became a disaster when Zakili opposed them. But what his gold and his schemes could not accomplish, these assassins could.

The caravan passed through the town gates unceremoniously, drawing many stares. Methlon nervously ran his fingers through his stringy hair as he glanced around the streets of Senadon. His horse plodded along the baked road, kicking up choking clouds of dust with every step. Compared to the green fields and lush forests rich in Avundar, desolate Senadon didn't look like it belonged. The town was filthy, the buildings coated in grime and ages of dust. Even the indolent folks, who spent their lives lurking in the shadows of the beaten edifices, and those begging for coins, appeared dusty.

With every second which passed, Methlon's decision to arrive in this forsaken town to enlist the services of the Lurking Shadows seemed a growing mistake. The weight of hidden eyes was upon him. He sensed his band was watched from every shadow. Although at least two dozen warriors protected him, he hardly felt safe. His defenses would stand against a band of highwaymen, not an entire town of outlaws. He dismissed his trepidation. He had a lot more to lose than wagons filled with gold. Eternal life was at stake. If he abandoned the rendezvous with the Lurking Shadows for fear of the townspeople, he'd forfeit any chance to possess Lifespring. *Only if he owned that spring could he have eternal life,* he thought, *and once he owned it, eternal life would be his to merchandise to the highest bidder.*

"What do ya got in those there wagons?" a surly voice demanded from the shadows, shaking Methlon out of his thoughts.

"Tis gold," another voice answered from across the wide street. "Lots o' gold, I reckon!"

Methlon's hand went for his sword as he scanned the sides of the streets, hearing voices emanating from the shadows of saloons on either side. He couldn't pinpoint where for many saloons lined the street. Taking a deep breath, he steadied himself, and eased off the hilt of his weapon. The last thing he wanted was trouble here in the streets of Senadon. If he retaliated, the whole town might storm him and his men. Was that what the assassins wanted? If so, they'd have their treasure with no labor having been done.

Waving his lieutenants closer, he dropped his hand on his blade's hilt. With Danatin and Bozar trotting up beside him, Methlon felt his confidence grow. He began to feel in control again and that was what he needed. With his men on either side, he felt at ease to look more objectively at the unsavory town. On both sides of the wide street, he noticed a fair number of saloons with various rough-looking characters loitering in the shadows with mugs and wineskins. Squeezed next to every other drinking spot were brothels, bustling with young, yet used-up-looking women motioning seductively to passersby, as well as inns and dining halls, which no doubt doubled as sleeping quarters. He could hardly believe such a forsaken town was alive with so many people, but he easily understood why he'd not heard much about this community. Few traders would dare venture into this place.

"All of this is nice scenery," Methlon mumbled facetiously. "But where's the messenger Stoman promised?"

The press of staring eyes grew heavier.

Ahead of the caravan, a fighter staggered out the saloon door into the sun, squinted his eyes, and wielded a stained sword in his hand. He stumbled down the battered steps into the dusty street, a chorus of protests at his back. "He got what he deserved," the fighter called back into the saloon. He turned when he heard Methlon's caravan and stood defiantly in the middle of the road.

"Regroup men!" he called up to the tavern. The force of his own outburst sent him staggering back a few steps.

"A hostile drunk," Methlon groaned. "This could be a problem." The challenger was brawny and probably an imposing fighter if not so inebriated. But to Methlon, he looked like nothing but a drunken fool. He watched as six more fighters pushed their way through the protesting crowd at the saloon's door. They knocked several people to the floor as they made their way down the stairs and gathered behind the burly drunk--apparently their leader.

"Looks like we gots some mersants visitin' our town, men," their leader slurred. "We isthn goin' ta become risch today! Just look at dose wagonsth full o' stuff. Let'sth welcome them to our home."

With a metallic ring, Methlon's sword was in his hand. No one could openly threaten his gold. He stared at the drunk men. All around him, the distinct metal hum of swords being drawn could be heard from every shadow, and Methlon realized painfully the wrath of the entire town might fall on him and his men. There was no way to win. If he didn't fight, his gold would be lost. If he did, he might forfeit his life. Methlon cursed Stoman and the Lurking Shadows for requiring him to come to this lawless town. The six drunken men and their equally drunk leader advanced. The fighters on the wagons grew anxious.

"Ruskin! What are you doing?" a commanding voice demanded from farther down the street.

The leader of the mob, Ruskin, turned, seeing a tall, sculpted individual easily saunter out of a dark alley and into the wide road. "How do you know my name?" he asked curiously, his blurry eyes not recognizing the man.

The newcomer gave no reply, only continued to march forward.

"Stay out of this stranger," burly Ruskin commanded, steeling his nerves.

"What are you doing?" the newcomer asked again, this time more forcefully.

Curious, Methlon observed the man as he approached the gang, his swagger confident, his expression fearless. The man was slender, but Methlon could see his sculpted muscles work under his clinging shirt. A long cape flowed over his shoulders, sweeping out wide under the gentle push of a passing breeze and made him look more ominous.

"You're drunk, Ruskin. Leave now or die."

Ruskin glanced around the street, an arrogant glimmer in his eye. He didn't recognize anybody who stepped forward to side with this man. In this lawless town, gang rule controlled the street, and no one was willing to jump on the side of a cause unless it was going to profit them. A crooked smile crossed Ruskin's face as he stared at the lone advancing man. It would be the newcomer against him and his six fighters. "An easy kill," he spoke back to his men, laughing. "Who are you, fool? I demand to know the name of the one who would so unwisely threaten Ruskin the Great."

"Kil," was all he said.

"Destroy him," Ruskin ordered, and his six men raced toward the newcomer, encircling him.

Methlon didn't like the chances for this lone man. He was surrounded on all sides by fighters who drew their weapons and clapped them noisily against their scabbards, obviously attempting to disturb his confidence. The lone warrior stood in a relaxed pose, no weapon in his hand. The battle would soon begin, Methlon knew, and with six swords against bare hands, he knew it would end just as quickly.

"This is your last chance, Ruskin," Kil warned. "Leave or die."

"Do it now!" was Ruskin's answer to his men.

A sword plunged at Kil from behind. He side-stepped the clumsy attack and punched the man in the back of the skull as he stumbled past. That drunk tumbled against a swordsman on the other side of the circle. Another attacked from the side, hacking across with his blade. Kil dove and rolled, the sword only nicking his flowing cape. He came to his feet right in front of two of the drunks, who both sliced high at his head. Kil ducked and the blades crossed. When he sprang back up, he stared into the eyes of a man whose face was locked in a silent scream. Kil kicked the dying man away. His twin dirks were suddenly in his hand. He heard someone stomp up from behind, ducked, and mule-kicked backward. His foot slammed into the fighter's midsection, stealing his breath. He never got it back. Kil spun, driving one dirk then the other into the inebriated warrior's exposed back.

Kil yanked his blades free as two more drunken fighters came at him. Defensively he pulled back, right in range for the warrior behind him. With a roar, the drunk's sword slashed down. Kil sprang to the side and launched one dirk with the flick of his wrist. He didn't see the results of the attack as the other two drunks closed in, but the sudden scream and the way the two pursuers balked at the sight of their friend's anguish told him his toss was deadly accurate. The brief delay of the two drunks was costly. Kil flipped his dirk in the air, caught it by the blade, then snapped his wrist forward. One fighter fell away, clutching his throat.

The other balked momentarily, fearful from the carnage Kil had already caused, but the drunk's fear didn't last long. He had a blade; the stranger had lost both of his. The victor seemed obvious. He charged in, his sword slicing viciously. Kil ducked the drunk's attack too easily. From the corner of his eye, he spotted another blade plunging at his back. With the agility of a cat, he spun to the side and heard an earsplitting scream behind him. Looking back, he saw the light go out of the man's eyes; his companion, who had missed Kil, had inadvertently driven his blade into his companion's sternum.

And then there was one.

"Kill him!" Ruskin commanded.

The final fighter looked around nervously at his fallen friends. Reluctantly, he looked back to Kil who stood cross-armed, staring back at him with cold eyes.

Although drunk and angry, he had enough sense to understand he was overmatched. Quickly jamming his sword into the scabbard, he stepped back, took a deep breath, and walked away with as much dignity as he could muster.

"Kill him," Ruskin demanded again. "Or I'll kill you."

Kil casually strode over to one of his victims, tore a dirk free, and took aim. "It's not wise to turn your back on an enemy, especially when he's a cold-blooded killer!" The dirk whistled from his hand, piercing the retreating fighter in the spine and forcing out a scream that echoed through the street like a siren's wail. Methlon, who was some distance away, clamped his hands over his ears. Ruskin froze in fear. In horror, Methlon watched as Kil, apparently hearing enough of the fallen man's agonized bellows, plucked his second knife from the other victim and walked to the crawling, gnashing man, grabbed a handful of hair, lifted up his head, and unceremoniously he finished the foul job.

Kil stood up straight, pushed his cape back over his shoulder, and rubbed a stain on the knee of his breeches. Methlon didn't know what to think. This one man had destroyed six lives and had only a few wrinkles in his clothing and a dirt smudge to show for his trouble. Turning, Kil's gaze fell on Ruskin.

"What did I tell you, Ruskin," Kil asked coolly. "Didn't I give you the choice to leave or die?"

The burly drunk went for his sword, his hands shaking visibly.

"You chose one over the other," he went on. "You see dear Ruskin, there are consequences for every action. In your case, you and your men could've departed with your lives. Instead, you decided to challenge me! The consequence of that is death!"

Drunk Ruskin's sword came out defensively in front of him as he retreated slowly, his eyes never leaving the dangerous man.

"Do you know these?" Kil asked, holding up his bloody dirks. "Do you know what these are?"

Too terrified to speak, Ruskin stared wide-eyed at the man, seeing the blood of his slaughtered men dripping from the blades.

"These are the Fangs of Hell."

Ruskin gawked at the knives, imagining he saw the blades ignite into flames for a second as Kil spoke the weapons' names. He blinked his drunken eyes and looked again
but noticed only the metallic glimmer of the blades. "What kind of man are you?"

"Farewell Ruskin," was his only answer before he flicked both his recovered blades with blurring speed. Methlon on his steed could barely keep up with the movements, but a muffled scream led his eyes to Ruskin, who had caught both blades in the face. The merchant leader turned away from the grisly scene as Ruskin fell dead to the ground.

"What's wrong with the mercenaries in this town?" Methlon heard Kil ask rhetorically. "You give them a chance to live and what do they do? They choose death anyway." Kneeling down, Kil stripped a leather bag from dead Ruskin's belt. Opening it up, he fingered around in it a moment before throwing its disdainfully back at the body. "Not even enough money to bother with.

"Looks like you have quite a number of wagon loads there," he addressed the caravan, turning squarely to Methlon. "Might they carry gold?"

Methlon instinctively went for his sword.

"Ease your concerns, Methlon," Kil exhorted, making the merchant leader infinitely uncomfortable. Methlon had no clue who his man was, yet the warrior knew his name. He glanced over to dead Ruskin. The mysterious man knew his name too.

"You seek a certain guild of assassins," Methlon heard him presuming. "This gold must be for them."

"Yes," Methlon answered eagerly. "You're the messenger sent to meet us?"

"The messenger?" he echoed skeptically, a knowing smirk raising his lips. "The messenger. That is correct. I'm the messenger for the Lurking Shadows."

"Excellent. Take me to your warlord then. We have important business to conduct.

* * * * *

"I cannot believe I decided to come here," Candace grumbled, turning down a shadowy alley and tugging her cloak tighter. After seeing a brief glimpse of the bloody battle raging right in the middle of the street, she felt safer tucked away between the buildings and away from everybody. At first glance, she thought the face of one of the combatants looked familiar, but she didn't want to stay around long enough to determine who it was.

A large rat darted out from a pile of rubbish, gnashing its yellow teeth at her, its jaws frothing saliva. The animal was diseased, she recognized, and if it bit her she'd be overcome with the same contagion with no hope of a physician in this desolate town. The rat scurried at her threateningly. Her reactions were sharp though and just as the rabid creature lunged at her, her cutlass snapped out, intercepting the rat and cutting it down.

After getting over the initial shock of the huge rodent's charge and her reaction against it, she breathed easier and considered her ability with her blade. Exhibiting poise in a controlled fighting atmosphere against her own father was one thing, but to wield a cutlass against a hostile adversary with such quickness and confidence, even if it was only a rat, was something entirely different. Her father's tutelage had prepared her well.

"My father," she groaned. "How foolish was I to leave home to only end up here in Senadon, the town of the mercenaries. This isn't the life he intended for me, standing in a stinking alley in a stinking town with a bunch of smelly people." She sighed. "He wanted much more for me than this. But that was where the problem came in didn't it? He agreed to marry me to some man I didn't trust. Father's so enamored with the royal lifestyle, he was willing to freely hand me to a prince he knows nothing about!"

She shook those thoughts from her mind, wiping her blade clean on the rat's backside. *Something wasn't right about that whole meeting,* she thought, looking back to Prince Killion's arrival. *The whole thing was unannounced, not even my*

85

Johnny Earl Jones

father received word he was coming. It all felt so evil. Oh, and then when I arrived in his chambers, I couldn't believe what I saw. Father was drunk! Even in his depression following Mother's death, he never tried to quell his pain with wine. I don't know what Kil did, but somehow he deceived father into drinking those spirits. If that wasn't bad enough, I suspect he must've laced it with some mind-twisting drug. Father isn't weak-minded; he'd never so easily given into anyone without investigating his background to assure my own good.

She looked to her cutlass, her sturdy and trusted companion. *This might prove to be my only way to gain a livelihood now. There's no way I can go back, not with that wolf of a man Kil waiting for me. So here I am, in Senadon. And to survive, one has to be skilled with the blade. Father told me my skills are exemplary, but how did it all come down to this?*

She had only a saddleful of possessions she'd strapped to Eliom who she'd hidden in the forest outside of Senadon. *How empty my life feels right now. All my hard-earned skills are going to be only as valuable as the person who puts a price on it. Lord, give me wisdom.*

A noise from behind turned her about. Her cutlass swept across defensively as she scanned the alley, looking for the foe. She saw nothing. Probably just another rat, she surmised. To ease the sudden tension, she zipped her blade through a series of quick thrusts and slices, pretending she was battling some imaginary adversary. Having defeated that one, she took a deep breath, pulled her cloak about her, and tugged the cowl down to put more shadow on her face. She wanted her gender to be hidden as long as possible, knowing it would cause her many problems. With her blood still rushing, she played out another cut and jab sequence against a different fictional opponent, landing strike after effective strike in swift, accurate combinations. As she considered the challenge and the danger, her blood rushed even faster, and she went into a deadly dance in the middle of the alley.

She would survive, she decided. She knew she was just as good as any of the vast number of hirelings populating the town.

She would be a mercenary, she realized. The reviling thought struck her hard. She felt filthy just considering the level she'd be lowering herself to. She was a good fighter, able to hold her own against any brawler in this town, she guessed, but her valiant nature convicted her as she considered leading her life as a warrior-for-hire who'd do anything to make enough coins to live off of. This way of life opposed everything she ever learned about being a Christian, about being obedient to God. She couldn't be a mercenary!

But what else was there for her? Life for a lone woman was dangerous indeed, but being a woman of principles in an unscrupulous town only compounded her problems. Unfortunately, returning to her father's fortress wasn't an option. She had to survive somehow, but could she sear her conscience and make this lifestyle work? Candace stopped and leaned up against the alley wall, a forlorn sigh escaping her lips. Dejected, she stared down the narrow, littered lane, the putrid odor of decomposing refuse assaulting her nostrils.

"This isn't my way," she said, wagging her head. "Why? Why did Father try to force that evil man upon me? What was it that so tainted his reasoning?"

Frustrated, she kicked at a broken mug, sending it skipping down the alley. "He was only doing what he thought would be best. He's always wanted a better life me, and I love him for that. But why did he fall to Kil's charisma and wine? Inebriated, there was no reasoning with my father. But now, if he's sober I can convince him. I can warn him. Kil was evil. I could see it in his eyes. Being drunk, father couldn't. I'm sure he'll listen to me now."

She turned. "I love Father dearly and wish to go back to him, if for no other reason than to tell him for the final time how much I care about him. He deserves that. He's painstakingly raised me since my mother's death, pouring all his time and knowledge into me. I must go back."

She took a step back toward the wide street, her mind on home.

The noise sounded again behind her. Candace whirled about, glancing around the alley. Again she saw nothing. She turned back to continue.

"Well met."

Candace leapt back, her cutlass swiping across defensively. The man easily lurched out of the way.

"You're a quick one with that blade."

"Who are you?" she asked, deepening her voice to hide her femininity. Her cowl was still low and she was thankful for that, its shadows masked her smooth chin and full lips.

"You're the stranger here," the man said with a mocking laugh. "You tell me who you are, young fighter."

Candace balked, not knowing what to say. She pointed her cutlass menacingly, thinking this confrontation might come to arms. The man waited patiently however, making no threatening gestures toward her.

"You're a stubborn one," he said. "My patience is great, friend, but don't put it to the test. My time is valuable, and I do so hate to be ignored. Now, what are you called?"

"Simeon," she blurted, the name of her mentor being the first male name to come to mind.

"Well Simeon, what're you doing walking the forbidding alleys of Senadon?"

She only shrugged.

"How foolish of me," he said, chuckling. "You're an alien to this town and its dangers. My guess is that you were trying to avoid the massacre in the middle of the street."

Candace nodded.

"Just as a word of advice: as dangerous as the streets are, they're the safest place for you. There you can blend in with the crowd and be almost invisible. To isolate yourself in the back alleys or anywhere else invites trouble."

"I can handle myself," she said, menace in her deep voice.

"I'm sure you can," he laughed. "Let me introduce myself. I'm Stoman, point man for the most extensive and powerful guild in all of Avundar. I noticed your inexperience with this place, but I also observed your deftness with the blade. You might prove to be quite a formidable opponent, and for that reason I'm persuaded to pay you a special visit. We don't ask many warriors to join us, only those we sense have the prowess to fight well, those whose fealty and skills will be devoted to our organization."

Candace listened warily.

"Perhaps you have heard of the feared guild I represent, the deadliest assassins in any land, the Lurking Shadows."

"I've heard of them," she said calmly, although panic gripped her soul. She steeled her nerves and swallowed hard. "Why would I be met by a representative from that renowned association?"

"We're not above seeking fresh warriors for our group," Stoman explained. "Very few are singled out, but when we find a warrior with the potential to be a skilled assassin, we're more than willing to extend an offer. None have refused our proposal.

"Let me correct myself. There are none who still live who have rejected the offer."

Candace understood her options: join them or die. "The prospects are definitely interesting," she lied, fighting back the trembling in her voice. "I've heard of these assassins since my younger years. All rumors say they are indeed a powerful guild, one to be feared. How could I refuse such an honorable position?"

"Not so honorable," Stoman smirked. "You're going to be a murderer."

He spoke aloud her exact thoughts. "Lord, how do I get out of this?" she mumbled under her breath. Her mind began formulating schemes of escape, turning them over in her mind and eliminating those that wouldn't work. She couldn't live a life as a paid murderer, and she couldn't dwell in the midst of ruthless killers. But by the rumors she'd heard, the arm of the Lurking Shadows was long and able to track its victims anywhere. If she did escape, where would she go? The last thing she wanted to do was run home and bring the wrath of the Lurking Shadows crashing down on Castle Veldercrantz.

"This life is quite rewarding," she heard him say, breaking her away from her thoughts. "There isn't a king in any land who wields as much power as we do, not only in this land but also in the surrounding kingdoms. This is my only offer, Simeon. I think you know the consequences of the wrong decision. Do you join us?"

A long moment passed before she could say anything, her mind a jumble of confusing thoughts. She refused to be part of their bloody lifestyle. The only question was whether she wanted to die now or later. No, she decided, she wouldn't die. She would play the part for now and find a way to elude these assassins. Despite her mistake, she prayed that somehow the Lord would open up a way of escape.

"Could there be any answer but yes?" she replied.

"This is good," Stoman cheered. "We have never had a female warrior in our guild before."

Candace's face blanched under the cowl. He knew!

* * * * *

Candace squinted her eyes against the bright sun, her cowl removed, her gender revealed. Despite the weight of dozens of eyes peering at her, she marched onward, not showing her fear. Although uncomfortable walking to the lair of the Lurking Shadows, she felt confident she wouldn't be bothered, not when walking side-by-side with one of the assassins. She kept her face straight ahead, refusing to make eye contact with the many, many warriors piling out of taverns to get a look at her; however, she stayed alert, using her peripheral vision to locate any avenues of escape.

"All things work out for the good of those who love the Lord," she remembered from Simeon's teachings when she was a teenager. She wanted to cling to that promise, but what good could come of her getting mixed up with the Lurking Shadow assassins?

As she walked, she noticed from tavern after lazy tavern on either side of the street, drunken and indolent warriors lounging under the shadows of the eaves. When they caught a glimpse of her, the sluggish men suddenly came alive, rushing to the bannisters and shouting out suggestive comments and lewd whistles. That set off a chain reaction, drawing more onlookers from every bar, the once quiet street erupting everywhere with excitement. She spun about and stopped, staring into the bustling shadows on one side of the street as disgusting and lascivious comments assaulted her ears. Under her unyielding gaze, the men quieted.

"It doesn't matter if they are dirty mercenaries or royal suitors," she said under her breath, "they all have the same juvenile mindset."

She turned again, facing the other side of the street, and with both sides stared down the whistles lessened, the comments came to a halt. Stoman watched curiously at her method of silencing the rowdy men. But now that she had their attention, her playful spirit kicked in. She pranced forward in a long showy gait, tossing her hair back teasingly, refusing to look to either side. Stoman shook his head at the impossible woman as both sides of the came alive with cheers again.

Several minutes later, their short journey finally brought them to a huge prominent edifice which looked relatively free of the age-old grime covering the other structures in the town and appeared several times larger than even the biggest inns. Stoman stopped and stared up at the small dark windows situated above long, ornate eaves some two stories from the ground. He looked like he was trying to discern something. A moment later, he was on the move again, marching to a dark alley adjacent to the magnificent building.

"Follow," he ordered, his voice stern.

Candace stared at the man hard, trying to weigh her options, knowing they were few. This was the guild house of the assassins, she guessed, looking to it and comparing it to the closest buildings of the town, seeing how this one stood out like a jewel among coals. And being this close to it, she knew escape was impossible. If she ran away now, could she get away? There'd be no telling how many assassins would stream out of their lair and hunt her down. And even if she could get away from any pursuers, could she get out of town. A guild as rich and powerful as the Lurking Shadows had probably bought the allegiance of the whole town and word would spread quickly to capture her before she reached the town gates. So, what options did she have left?

"Approach," Stoman demanded forcefully.

She stood her ground, her arms akimbo.

"Simeon, this is the way to--"

"Candace," she corrected.

"All right," he agreed, exasperated with the stubborn woman. "Are you having apprehensions? You know you have nowhere to hide. You've seen my face thus you must follow me, Candace. If you turn away from us now, the assassins won't rest until you're slain. You can choose life and power or you can face the coldness of death. The choice is yours."

She mused over his words momentarily, unable to escape his line of reasoning. Her limited knowledge of the assassins was enough to remind her of how extensive the group was. Even from her teenage years she remembered hearing the assassins had tentacles which stretched out over all of Avundar, and therefore providing no place she could hide. She felt a headache coming on. With a resigned huff, she started into the alley, her hand inconspicuously dropping to the hilt of her cutlass.

Before they traveled too deeply into the alley, Stoman stopped abruptly just inside the shadows. His hand skimmed over the side of the wall for a few seconds, then stopped. He placed both palms on a specific plank and pushing with all his body weight, a section of the wall swung to the side. Candace's stared in marvel at the secret door. He waved her in. Having no other option, she obeyed, mouthing a silent prayer as she stepped into the darkened room. A dull boom behind her signaled Stoman had sealed the door.

She was in near complete darkness, only the thin beams of sunlight seeping through the shuttered windows provided scarce light. "How can this be your den if you can't even see in it?" she joked despite the dread filling her heart.

"You can'ts, but we cans," came a gruff, inhuman voice from high above her. She looked up, seeing a burly shadow walk through the cords of sunlight.

"But for those who cannot," Stoman's voice called from farther away than she thought him to be, "we have these."

A flint sparked in the blackness, kindling something which swiftly became a hungry flame. Light filled the corner of the room from that single torch, igniting a narrow circle with dancing and dazzling shimmers. Candace lost a step. Gold! Mounds of gold items and treasures littered the cavernous room from one side to the other, piled high against every wall. On the far end of the building she noticed several doors and imagined they led to more rooms with even more treasure. She strode in closer to inspect the riches as the room increased in brightness and she noticed the floor feeling soft beneath her only to find under her feet was the plushest fur rug she'd ever walked on. Her fear of the Lurking Shadows increased. What power they must command to demand such wealth from those who desire their services.

An otherworldly grunt from above drew her attention away, her eyes shifting to the elevated windows. She noticed a long catwalk about ten feet from the ground, the exact height for a Lurking Shadow to peer through the shuttered windows. *So that was why Stoman was looking to the windows,* she realized. He was looking for some kind of signal from the sentry, but when she saw who the signal giver was, she recoiled. The sentry wasn't even human. The burly creature stared at her with beady, bloodshot eyes, smacking its large jaws and gesturing with his hands. Several more gravitated toward the brute from farther down the catwalk. She put her hand to her mouth in horror and shock, but a ground-level snarl snatched her attention back down. She turned and saw a handful more of the brutes separate from behind the treasure piles. Suddenly the room seemed infested with them.

"Goblins," she heard Stoman say matter-of-factly, as he finished lighting the last torch in the wide room before placing the one he was carrying into an empty sconce. "They make good lookouts. They need no light to see by which makes them particularly valuable, not only against intruders but also against any assassin who becomes ambitious and tries to dip into the Warlord's hoard."

"But goblins," she said in disgust. Not in her wildest nightmares could she imagine those monsters dwelling anywhere in Avundar. Since her childhood, she'd been taught goblins were evil creatures, the antithesis of the purity Avundar symbolized.

"No need to worry, my apprentice assassin. Our Warlord only stations them here in the treasury. They're not allowed entrance into any of the other rooms of our guild. Goblins are savage villains, but totally harmless to any Lurking Shadow," Stoman said. "Watch now. Come meet our newest acquaintance." He called to the slobbering goblins.

The goblins sprung over the catwalk railing to the treasure-littered floor. With snorts and grunts they neared the woman, sniffing at her eagerly. The goblin sentries on the floor closed in. Candace tried to back away, but they came from all sides, enclosing her. She drew her cutlass.

"She does smell tasty," Stoman said, a lascivious smile on his lips. "But respect her for what she is, my monsters. She's a warrior, and if our Warlord allows it, she'll soon be a Lurking Shadow as well."

"Get away," she growled, her cutlass arm cocked back, her eyes furtively scanning the room for possible exits. She could no longer act out this facade. Somehow she had to escape.

"Do be a sociable guest," Stoman bade, laughing. "Meet your new allies."

"Where are the rest of the assassins?" she asked, hoping to slow the goblins' advance. She wondered why the lair of the most prominent assassins in Avundar looked so empty.

"The majority of them are occupied unloading the payment of a wealthy merchant who hired our services."

"It must be quite a haul," she said to keep the conversation moving, to keep the goblins away.

"A tremendous hoard for the task they are..." his words trailed off, eyes suddenly reflective. The goblins, too, were attentive no longer. They sniffed the air nervously. And Candace, spooked by their weird behavior, slipped away into the tight shadows under the far catwalk.

"Back to your posts!" Stoman screamed, but it was too late. A loud boom against the side wall echoed through the room. Stoman and the goblins winced. Candace stood stock-still in the shadows. A secret door flew open and a dozen stern-faced men rushed into the room. Arrows sprayed throughout the room and knocked out a number of torches, and felled several goblins. Another entered--a grim man the others gave a wide girth--obviously their leader.

"Prince Killion," she hissed. What was a prince doing in this den of assassins?

"Where were the lookouts?" Kil asked too calmly. His eyes locked with the wary gazes of Stoman and the surviving goblins. The majority of the men who preceded him faded backward and spread out behind him. "Where was my signal to enter? Any bunch of rogues could've crashed in here and overrun the place!"

"Not all are Lurking Shadows," Stoman said nervously. He noticed several unusual faces among the assassins and tried to deflect his Warlord's wrath. "Methlon and some of his merchants."

"You've embarrassed me in front of them!" Kil said, ignoring Stoman's question. "Someone must suffer for this very serious error! No Lurking Shadow leaves his post or abandons his duty without the reward of death.

"Close the door," Kil commanded. One of his assassins broke away and slammed the door shut.

Candace eyed the secret door, her nerves edged on panic. Of all the doors in the wide chamber, that was the only one she knew was an exit. But even though the room was considerably darker now with several torches extinguished, she'd still be easily spotted if she dashed for the secret door. What could she do? It wouldn't take long before the assassins discovered her hunching in the shadows. She threw her head back in disgust. Her eyes locked onto the catwalks overhead. Perhaps there still was hope.

"You'll be the example!" Kil roar as he pointed out one goblin. Stoman and the remaining goblins scattered. The doomed goblin tried to follow, but the throng of assassins cornered him, formed a semi-circle, and closed him into a far corner of the building. Kil stepped through them, removed his cape, and handed it to an assassin. His fingers spread wide, signaling his men to spread out and give him a wider arena. "Draw your sword," Kil said. "I will use no weapon." He tossed his dirks to Methlon then turned to the goblin. "If you defeat me in battle, you may go away with your life. You know the consequences if you don't."

Nervously, the goblin yanked his broad sword from the scabbard on his back. Kil approached with an easy gait, barehanded. The goblin grinned evilly, his brutish instincts providing courage. The man was truly unarmed. Candace noticed the apparent mismatch with little concern; a sharpened sword against bare hands.

The victor was obvious.

The goblin charged, hacking across at his leader. Kil ran forward, ducked under the cut, and as soon as the blade passed, he slammed his shoulder into the goblin's gut. The brute stumbled back against the wall. He got his feet under him and looked questionably to his sword. His upper lip curled into a snarl, and he charged again.

Candace couldn't have called for a better diversion. With the Lurking Shadows facing the battle in the far opposite corner, she leapt for the catwalk. As her fingers snagged the high walk, a splinter drove under her fingernail. Without a good hold, she couldn't pull herself up. She dropped softly to the floor. Glancing at the secret door, she longed to dash for it and flee from this nightmare but understood that was impossible. The keen assassins would kill her before she got halfway there.

With the din of battle still raging, she leapt again. Her fingers barely caught hold. Her left hand slipped and ripped a fingernail, but her other hand grasped long enough for her left to grab hold again. Denying her pain, she hoisted herself up, and laid very still on the catwalk. *Now what?* she wondered.

The sounds of battle decreased and she knew it was almost over.

Kil hammered the goblin's face with a series of quick punches and leapt out of sword range. Predictably, the goblin's blade sliced across weakly and too late. Kil was there a second later, pounding again, one, two, three punches into the goblin's bruised and bleeding face. The goblin swung again, the blade coming around in a sluggish arc, an apparent sign it was worn down and had little energy left.

"Enough," Kil said with finality. He came in behind the blade, punched the goblin hard against the side of its jaw and set it off balance. Kil jumped on the brute, wrapping
an arm securely around its neck. With the other hand, he reached over and grasped its chin, twisting sharply. A resounding crack filled the room, and the brute crumbled dead to the floor. "I feel much better now." He spun to Stoman and the remaining goblins. "Why were the goblins not at their posts?" he demanded.

"I... we..." Stoman stuttered, sincerely terrified.

"We can't have any mistakes at this crucial point," Kil interjected. He walked over to Methlon and retrieved his blades. "The guards must be at their posts at all times! There are no variations from that directive, do you understand?"

Stoman shook his head and the goblins darted for the ladder leading back up to the catwalk. Candace panicked. They would find her easily. She looked around for any hiding place. There was none. A beam of sunshine sparkled in her eyes and she turned, seeing the small shuttered windows.

"We've received our gold and now our task to take Lifespring is before us. And this, my assassins, will be our most important venture ever."

Methlon's brow furrowed curiously. "The assassins are only conquering the elves so I can exploit Lifespring for my own purposes. How could slaying the Silver Elves be of such great importance that it overshadows their past endeavors?" he mumbled quietly.

"The Silver Elves will fall to us!" Kil declared, sending up a raucous cheer from his assassins. "Lifespring will be ours!"

"Ours?" Methlon questioned, and his lieutenants drew defensively tighter.

Kil laughed. "A slip of the tongue," he apologized. "What I meant, sir Methlon, was we would secure the spring for you after we have slaughtered the elves. And so easy it will be." He put an arm around Methlon's shoulders. "We'll be upon them before they comprehend death is at their door. By the time they do realize, it'll be too late."

Candace took in the information, horrified. She wasn't too familiar with the Silver Elves, but she'd heard enough to understand they were a beneficial race, a people who guarded the source of Avundar's largest river. A reclusive race, they rarely ventured into human towns and never bothered a soul. Whatever ill fate Prince Killion planned for them, they certainly didn't deserve.

"My liege," Stoman said with the highest respect. "I have brought in a new recruit for the Lurking Shadows. A beautiful woman fighter, one who'd add a new dimension to our future missions."

"Liege?" Methlon questioned. "I thought you said you were a messenger. You are the Warlord of the Lurking Shadows?"

"The very one," Kil said and waved the man away, fully turning to Stoman.

Above on the catwalk, Candace lost her breath. Prince Killion was no prince at all! He'd masqueraded as royalty to get to her. Someone hired him to take her from her father's castle. Her fear increased tenfold. Her eyes darted to the goblin's ladder. The brutes were halfway up, but bottlenecked by one goblin who stared curiously at the conversation.

"Where is this female?"

"Right there," Stoman said, swinging around to introduce her but seeing she was not there. "But she was--"

"Men, spread out and find her," Kil ordered. "She must be a spy."

The assassins scattered, inspecting shadows, opening doors, and speeding through to other rooms. Others overturned sizable items which might provide a hiding place.

Candace felt her heart pound hard. It wouldn't be long before they found her on the catwalk. She looked again to the secret door. Oh, how she longed to be at that door! It looked like a redeeming icon, a way to escape her decision to come to this accursed town in the first place. "Lord, I wish I could fling that door open and run free, leaving this nightmare behind me."

The goblins were starting up the ladder again.

The secret door swung open suddenly, unexpectedly. A moment later, it slammed shut again, a resounding bang echoing through the room. Candace gawked at the sight. There was nobody near to open it. It was as if the door opened at her very wish! The goblin at the top of the ladder halted, gazing to the secret door.

"The door!" Kil yelled, spinning in that direction. "The female has escaped out the door! Follow and slay her!"

She heard the stampede, and the violent voices as they stormed out into the alley. The first goblin clambered onto the catwalk. Candace jumped to her feet and shoved the shutters open, slipping tightly through the small windows and onto the eaves. Maintaining her balance, she shuffled to the end of the building, seeing the disturbance on the street as townsfolk scattered from the rampaging assassins.

A trumpet blast sounded from the window then, the goblins alerting them of her escape.

She thanked God that the nearest building roof was in jumping range and leapt, noticing ahead a pathway of adjoining roofs. With light footsteps, she dashed atop the roofs, making her way for the town gate. She thought of the secret door, still puzzled how it opened and closed seemingly of its own volition, but it opened to her the way of escape she so desperately needed. God had spared her. But now, she couldn't just go home and hide in the castle. Danger was about to fall on the elves of Verdant Wood. She had to warn them.

* 8 *
THE DARKEST MINIONS

Lightning ripped across the gloomy afternoon sky, outlining Krylothon's hulking silhouette at the tower's turret. Standing nine-foot-tall, with six muscular arms, a skull which looked like a gigantic spider's, and powerful wings folded onto his back, Krylothon was a nightmare come to life. The three goblin messengers reared back at the sight, looking to each other with fearful stares and shoving for one to press forward. This day was especially stormy and dark, and the winds whipped across the high reaches of the Black Fortress with violent force, tossing the goblins in the strong gusts. There they stood, frightened, as they stared at the mighty Krylothon. His back was turned to them as he looked down upon the jungles of the island Genna Fiendomon far below. Morbidly, they understood some or all of them might not return from this assignment. The Dark Sorcerer commanded them to relay an order to dangerous Krylothon.

"You go," Gorik, the burliest goblin, grunted and pushed away the smallest goblin with the butt of his spear. Gorik was not one of the smartest goblins, but he did have experience communicating a message to this deadly monster. He'd been unfortunate enough many years ago to bear news to wicked Krylothon. That first time he didn't understand why it took three goblins to relay one message. After the initial encounter, he understood perfectly. And now he found himself compelled again to bring an order from Zeraktalis himself.

He had come so close to death the first time, he still trembled whenever he thought about it. On that initial trip many years ago, his previous troupe had walked intrepidly before the wicked one, carrying a message from the Dark Sorcerer, thinking Zeraktalis' word alone guaranteed them unwarranted power. They were never so wrong.

"Krylothon!" the leader of the group called out boldly that day, feigning no respect, pitting his bravado against the creature's prowess, thinking the word from the sorcerer would grant him impunity from the giant usurper's fiery wrath. His folly spelled his doom. Gorik's eyes could barely keep up in the following seconds. With swiftness impossible for a creature of such great size, Krylothon spun on the goblin. All six of his massive arms converged on him, his huge fists quickly crunching the goblin, allowing only a breathless, silent scream. But Krylothon wasn't through. With one snap of his vicelike mandibles, the usurper clipped off the goblin's head and stole his life.

With disastrous speed, he destroyed the second goblin with the swipe of three claws, but Gorik was able to blurt out The Dark Sorcerer's order before he fled. He knew if he hadn't, Zeraktalis' punishment would be long and excruciating-- inevitably death. The monster lashed out at him, raking deep furrows in his back, but Gorik didn't slow. Racing for the exit, he barely escaped with his life.

Krylothon was a demon spawn, Gorik remembered from fireside tales. Krylothon was the greatest of the demon spawns unleashed on the world. Usurpers they were called, powerful and evil, and as far as his dim mind could comprehend, invincible. Krylothon, like all of his usurper kin, was sinewy and strong; one of his arms was the girth of Gorik's blubbery waist. To him, usurpers looked like some weird mix between a small dragon and a giant spider. Although standing only nine foot tall, Krylothon bore the physical traits of the towering dragon race: a long tail, considerable wings and a scaly hide. Its skull, however, looked like the stuff of nightmares. Powerful insectoid mandibles clamped menacingly like a deadly vice. Eight, multifaceted eyes focused on the dark, looming clouds while his carnivorous mouth, bearing hundreds of serrated teeth, gnashed impatiently behind those wicked mandibles.

Krylothon's imposing appearance was nothing compared to his nasty temper.

Gorik shoved the youngest of the three in the back with his spear again, prodding him reluctantly forward. He knew this goblin would die. He knew Krylothon would surely destroy him, but Gorik wasn't concerned. Like all his wicked ilk, he had no compassion, only the desire for self-preservation, and if it took this young goblin to die so he would remain alive, so be it.

"M..Mi..Mighty Krylothon," he heard the young goblin stutter, his voice cracking in terror. Gorik wondered if the goblin would simply fall over dead from fear. Gorik had felt that horror before, but fortunately for him he'd never been the *first* messenger sent the usurper's way. "Da master demands ta see ye in his chambers."

Krylothon just stood there and continued to stare at the boiling storm. Gorik couldn't believe it! The goblin got the whole message out and still remained alive. Gorik turned to dash for the doorway leading into the fortress, but before he could take his first step, a form streaked by him and disappeared into the darkness of the corridor. It was the first goblin running for his life. Gorik jolted forward, raced for the doorway, and pushed back the other goblin who was also beating a path to escape.

Neither turned to see the hatred seething in Krylothon's spiderlike eyes.

* * * * *

Darkness. It permeated the Dark Sorcerer's chamber like an impenetrable veil and here Krylothon waited, enraged, his huge fists clinching frequently. Impatiently. Zeraktalis had ordered him to these chambers--had ordered--and he wasn't even in his sorcery chamber upon Krylothon's arrival. The giant usurper stalked across the room, his nocturnal vision allowing him to see as well in the darkness as he did in the daylight. He slammed his huge fist against the marble wall, venting his rage and crunching a gaping crater. The usurper was enraged enough that Zeraktalis would command him to do anything, but the sorcerer's absence only threw salt on his wounded ego.

Krylothon punched the wall again, shattered the marble, and sprayed chunks of rock into the air as he bellowed out a cavernous roar. "Eventsss aren't taking placcce the way they ssshould," he hissed, "and it'sss all the fault of the sssorcccerer'sss. If I were in charge, there would be no delay, no incorrect decccisssionsss. Only dessstruction and victory!"

"I was there the day Zzzeraktalisss ripped a portal into reality and ssstepped onto the land of Avundar. I sssaw the peaccceful rolling hillsss and the lusssh treesss sssspreading out asss far asss the eye could sssee. How I long to razzze that land, ssstrafing the treesss with unquenchable firesss and bending the inhabitantsss to their kneesss before I unmercccifully torture and kill them. But no, I am playing a waiting game behind the leaderssship of the Dark Sssorcccerer," the usurper continued.

He was tired of waiting. He wanted to destroy--the common, driving force behind the actions of all demons--but Zeraktalis was delaying. "The Dark Sssorcccerer mussst be dessstroyed, then I will lead the wicked hordesss against all the landsss of the world!"

Footsteps echoed in the corridor, drawing the usurper out of his thoughts. Krylothon crouched low and growled a mystical sentence, flames suddenly licking his huge palms. "You will feel the power of my flamesss!" he hissed menacingly to the sounding footsteps. The echo pressed right up to the door and the usurper grew anxiously, waiting for the door to swing open. "You will die!" he promised under his breath.

The footsteps continued marching onward. Krylothon's muscles relaxed as the echoes trailed away down the corridor. With a word the flames in his fists extinguished. "Probably a goblin guard," he guessed.

"Krylothon!" a booming voice echoed from behind and the usurper spun, seeing Zeraktalis standing cross-armed at his back. He didn't try to guess how the sorcerer got in the room, but shouted an enchanted phrase and whipped his suddenly flaming hands in the direction of the sorcerer, launching six fiery spheres at Zeraktalis.

Responding with an arcane roar of his own, the Sorcerer waved his arm in a circular pattern, creating a sizzling energy shield. The fire balls collided against the shield and exploded into a kaleidoscope of brilliant colors. Behind it, the Sorcerer remained unscathed.

Krylothon cursed in defiance of Zeraktalis' spell-wielding prowess. Roaring another arcane chant ignited the usurper's top two hands with white fire and he hurled the lightning-bolt spells hard at the sorcerer. With impossible poise, Zeraktalis roared out similar archaic syllables, two lightning bolts exploding from his gauntleted hands and colliding with Krylothon's, the sorceries shattering each other with a colossal boom, throwing splinters of energy throughout the room, and the usurper covered his eyes from the fallout. He heard another dark phrase uttered, and looked up in time to see Zeraktalis cast a fireball at him. Before he could react, the flames slammed into his chest, blasting the air from his lungs, searing his hardened scales, and throwing him head over heels against the wall, crunching his impression into the marble.

"I am the Dark Sorcerer! Do you defy me?"

Forcing himself to one knee, Krylothon gingerly clutched his smoking chest, pulverized marble cascading off his broad shoulders, his spiderlike eyes glaring at the sorcerer with hatred as deep as the pits of hell.

"I won't only defy you, I will dessstroy you!" Krylothon threatened, roaring successive chants which sent a barrage of lightning and fire the sorcerer's direction.

But with a quick phrase and the wave of a hand, the fiery attacks shattered against a suddenly materialized and impenetrable energy shield. But before the usurper's defeated spells had completely dissipated, Zeraktalis chanted and heaved a fireball, which Krylothon barely escaped. A lightning bolt followed and cut the behemoth's legs out from underneath him. The usurper crashed hard on his side. Indomitable, Krylothon quickly pushed himself to his feet, dreadfully hearing more chanting. He looked up in time to see a tidal wave of fire crash down, forcing out an anguished roar from the depths of his dark soul.

Burned and scarred, unyielding Krylothon grunted away the pain of the attack, rising to his full nine-foot tall height, his upper lip curling in unrestrained hatred. Quickly and stubbornly, he pointed his hands toward the sorcerer, ignoring the burning pain, and began a hissing chant of his own.

"Stop this foolishness, Krylothon!" Zeraktalis ordered, holding out a fiery hand to emphasize his point. "I know your desire, mighty usurper, but I know also your great impatience..."

Krylothon stopped his chanting and listened, eager saliva still dripping from between his teeth, and his massive chest heaving with each breath.

"Don't make me destroy you, Krylothon. I have grander plans for you, General of my dark hordes, plans to destroy and terrorize mankind like never before! Unite under me and evil will reign supreme over all lands. I've located the energy source and soon it will be in my hands. With this key, we'll unleash the most vile demon lords from the bottomless pit, but to prelude them all will be the mightiest of all demons, the most destructive fiend ever to curse the world's existence--the arch demon Diabolicus!"

A wicked smile raised the corners of the usurper's carnivorous mouth. Plans suddenly seemed headed the way it had dreamed. The demon spawn's disastrous lusts boiled hot.

"When released, death and destruction will raze every land! Once Diabolicus is freed, mankind in all lands will have no hope of escape!"

* * * * *

A scream pierced the dark night and Zeraktalis knew the monsters were on the hunt again. For days, he'd heard their struggles from the lofty heights of his fortress and was delighted by it. Rarely over the past several years had Zeraktalis spent much time on the island of Genna Fiendomon, leaving the rulership of the various monster tribes to his general, Krylothon. During his departure to the hellish underrealm, his dark horde had grown hungry for blood. By the sound of the many growls and cries that came to his ears, he could tell they were carrying out their murderous bloodlusts upon one another. Wanting to see his wicked brutes in action, his desire had driven him to the jungle floor.

After the disaster in Sheliavon, after his horde had practically beaten down all resistance from that kingdom, they were still defeated by the influx of warriors from neighboring Avundar. How ironic, he thought, that the heat of his vengeance would first crush the republic which thwarted his conquest so many years ago. Following the loss in Sheliavon, the sorcerer actively sought the powers of the demonic. He spent years with the cryptic and deceptive fiends as he delved into whatever knowledge they had about weapons that would defeat the godly and rid the world of this self-proclaimed Almighty God, Jesus Christ. Demons were liars. That was their nature even among themselves, so it took him years to cut through the deception to get the information he desired. Once he did, he discovered the existence of a key which would unlock even the mightiest fiends which God had chained during the flood of Noah. And now all the verbal frays and twisting lies proved worth his time. The end of the godly was near.

As silent as death, he stalked through the twisted trees of the jungle, searching for the vicious play of life and death being acted out by his minion. He didn't have to wait long. A group of three goblins stalked through the misty darkness, wielding spears and trailing something the sorcerer couldn't see. The brutes drew up close to a tree, surveyed the environment, but not five feet away, in the darkness, stood the sovereign of Genna Fiendomon. Zeraktalis watched the occupied brutes with amusement, sensing death was near. The sorcerer knew these goblins, like all the other nocturnal predators, were endowed with the ability to see another creature's body heat in the dark. He chuckled quietly, thinking as close as he was they were unable to see him. He was of the blackest evil, and the most powerful heat-seekers wouldn't find him in the dark of the night if he didn't wish to be found.

Zeraktalis followed the goblins' stares to a low branch where he found their prey, spotting the dim glow of a thin shape twisting its way across a branch. He glared angrily at the salivating goblins. "Just a snake?" he grumbled in an archaic language. In the deathly silence of the dark jungle his words sounded like a snap of thunder. Startled, the goblins' eyes darted around nervously, trying to discover if they'd been trailed, hoping that, as the merciless rule of the jungles of Genna Fiendomon often dictated, the hunter hadn't become the hunted. After a long moment of careful surveying, they concluded the noise to have been a phantom sound of the mysterious swamps. When they turned to stalk their prey, they discovered it had disappeared. The goblin who initially spotted the snake dashed to the tree and poked around with his spear, hoping to dislodge the animal from its concealment. The other goblins rushed over, their spears stabbing into the branches as well.

Hoping for better killing elsewhere, Zeraktalis turned away from the pathetic hunt.

And that's when the trap fell.

From behind his back, the sorcerer heard a sudden chorus of growls and snarls. Branches broke and the ground thumped with the heavy footsteps of predators. Zeraktalis turned, hearing the terrified hoots of the goblins. Ambushing the goblins were a half-dozen hairy, lupine brutes, swinging clubs and war hammers. The smell of sweaty, wet dogs permeated the air. The Dark Sorcerer recognized the burly, wolfish brutes to be monsters known as masnevires. The 6-foot-tall creatures bludgeoned the goblins savagely and drove them to the ground. One goblin desperately got his spear up and thrust it at the belly of a charging masnevire. The tip pierced through the brute's leather armor. The wound wouldn't have been mortal of itself, but the momentum of the charging masnevire drove the spearhead deep, thrusting through armor then into his gut.

Zeraktalis watched the struggle intently, his fiery eyes blazing in delight; his monsters were both fierce and savage. The time had come to unite his monsters, to assemble the ferocious tribes into a single, cohesive fighting machine. These brutes who had tasted nothing but the black-blooded corpses of other dark monsters would soon dine on the flesh of the creatures Krylothon called warmbloods--humans.

The vicious lupine masnevires slew the goblins in moments. Throwing their prey's beaten and lifeless bodies over their huge shoulders, the masnevires trudged away. The sorcerer began to turn away, encouraged by what he saw, but he sensed he should linger just a moment longer.

As the pack headed off, one curious masnevire looked back, spotting a small sack which had fallen off one of the goblin corpses. Since he wasn't weighed down with a dead goblin, he rushed over, a greedy smile on his canine face. His impaled and dying companion grasped onto his ankle as he passed by. The downed masnevire pleaded for him to remain and help, his voice coming out in a weak gurgle. The cry fell on deaf ears. The covetous masnevire growled in disdain, kicked the dying monster in the face, and continued to his prize.

Zeraktalis looked on, interested. The monsters were without compassion, merciless, bearing the fruit of their dark souls. So much the better.

The masnevire knelt down and scooped up the sack, a sneaky smile splitting his face as though he found some special trinkets the others overlooked. He tore the sack open from the top and peaked inside, but before he could view the contents, the marshy ground erupted under his feet. Two thick hands clasped onto his legs and pulled him downward. Yanked down torso deep, the unfortunate masnevire yelped and screamed to his companions. They looked in his direction, but they never took a single step to assist. One masnevire mouthed that he was doomed, causing the trapped brute to thrash and wail wildly. Desperately, he beat on the thick arms pulling him down, then he screamed, his countenance panic-stricken as agonizing pain racked his submerged legs. The masnevire pounded furiously at the arms. Over and over again he pounded and kept on pounding. Surprisingly, the grip loosened and the masnevire immediately grabbed onto a loose root with one hand, intent on pulling himself out while pounding the thick arms with his other fist. Suddenly, the massive beetle-like head and thick shoulders of the subterranean attacker erupted through the dirt, the mass of the creature nearly bowing the wolf-monster in half at the back. Its huge serrated mandibles opened wide and clamped down on the skull of the terrified masnevire, ending its struggles.

Death! The Dark Sorcerer breathed in the sensation. His monsters were ravenous. When united, they'd be unconquerable. Behind the savagery of his dark horde, Zeraktalis knew he'd soon capture the key to unleash the limitless wrath of the

Johnny Earl Jones

archdemon Diabolicus on the world.

* * * * *

Midnight had fallen. Except for the sporadic lightning flashes from the rolling thunderheads, oppressive darkness reigned.

Resounding booms pealed through the night, drowning out the rumble of thunder as a dragon swept across the sky, propelled at impossible speeds by its mighty wings. The wyrm's eyes were ablaze in the intense glow of its nocturnal vision. Miles whisked by in moments as the dragon skimmed the treetops. Its head jerked back slightly, and the beast slowed, its flight now taking on a wide circular pattern over one section of the jungle.

"Down!" came a booming command from the base of its neck. There sat the Dark Sorcerer, his eyes flaming brilliantly, overshadowing the dragon's larger eyes. The huge wyrm spotted a clearing and flapped to the jungle floor. Touching down gracefully, its clawed feet sunk into the marshy ground under its immense weight.

Zeraktalis leapt from the dragon, and surveyed the mist-shrouded jungle with his piercing gaze. He stood on dangerous ground. In this section of the island ran the most wicked and deadly packs of all monsters.

He waved the dragon away. The great, majestic beast leapt into the night air with a flap of its massive wings and disappeared in the darkness, leaving the sorcerer alone.

Inhaling the gloomy atmosphere, Zeraktalis turned toward the jungle trees. Creatures undoubtedly were already converging on him from the shadows. His observations earlier that night confirmed the chaotic and merciless behavior of his monsters. He would harness this.

A challenge awaited him. His years of absence had grown weeds of rebellion and independence in these brutes, especially in his powerful general Krylothon. His conversation with the giant usurper revealed much of his mutinous attitude. Zeraktalis needed to subject his army again. Then he could conquer the world.

He recalled the dialogue:

"I sssussspect you will employ a different ssstrategy than the one usssed in attacking Sssheliavon," Krylothon had hissed in response, his voice dripping with sarcasm. In that war, neither Krylothon nor the usurpers were included in the onslaught, and the giant usurper still harbored bitterness. Krylothon often boasted the victory would've been theirs if the demon spawns had been involved.

"My overconfidence was the cause of defeat there," the Dark Sorcerer admitted. "The warmbloods, the humans, were more courageous and resourceful than I anticipated. But now, fate requires our first victims be the warmbloods responsible for my horde's defeat.

"Evil will be recompensed on the Avundarians, the ones who aided the men of Sheliavion and triumphed over the goblin army. Releasing Diabolicus from the chains of the bottomless pit requires us to first pierce the land of Avundar and rip away the supernatural power key to freeing the demon lord. Then we exterminate the goodly from all lands!"

Krylothon's spiderlike eyes gleamed evilly. "Sssinccce the unleassshing of my kind onto the world from the abyssss, mankind has been a bane to our desssire for absssolute power. Thossse humansss, although physssically weaker, are sssurprisssingly troublesssome creaturesss. Their God keepsss a hand of protection over them. But onccce they're eradicated, God will have nothing more to do with thisss world, and it shall become the domain of demons and evil! Onccce and for all, we will overthrow Jessssussss Chrissst'sss promise to cassst all of usss into a lake of fire!"

"The chained arch demons were able to give us only a general location," the sorcerer said. "Without access to the surface world, they were unable to disclose the exact vessel of supernatural power. I've provided for this setback. Planted in Avundar are several spies and one thinks he's found the origin of the energy source and as soon as we unite the dark horde once again, we'll attack!"

"There will be sssome difficulty in that," Krylothon said.

"What!"

"You haven't lead them for yearsss. In their chaotic mindsss, you're asss good asss dead," Krylothon said, the sorcerer picking up a wishful hint in the usurper's tone. "Thossse monsssstersss have created a world of their own on thisss isssle. They won't allow a ssstranger to disssrupt their livessss and mold them into what he wantsss them to be."

"If that is so, they've forgotten their terror of the Dark Sorcerer," Zeraktalis growled. "And you've done a poor job as the commander of my horde, Krylothon. These monsters will dread me again. They will know who their master is once more!"

That conversation had driven him here, to the most dangerous terrain in Genna Fiendomon, probably the most dangerous area in the world.

"Krylothon," he roared, his booming voice resounding off the surrounding jungle. Being hungry for power and having commanded the usurper to meet him there, he didn't wish to be delayed any longer. He'd been detained in the stinking pits of the underrealm for too long while communicating with demonic forces. He was ready to march against all civilizations now, eager to destroy all semblance of good so God would abandon this world. Then evil could reign forever.

Hearing a quiet rustling among the trees, Zeraktalis turned. The noise, faint at first, approached rapidly, relentlessly. Scanning the mist-shrouded environment, he searched for a potential assailant and began to chant a destructive spell. From the darkness erupted an echoing boom then cracking, and splintering, shattering the silence of the jungle. A huge cypress splashed down onto the marshy clearing only ten feet away from Zeraktalis. Blurred by the steam rising from the swampy jungle stood an awe-inspiring, six-armed silhouette, his muscular arms and his wings stretched wide.

"Krylothon," the sorcerer acknowledged. "You're late."

The giant usurper bowed deeply, careful to keep his facial expression hidden as his mandibles and needlelike teeth ground together in deep hatred for the fiery-eyed fiend. With tremendous self-control, he swallowed his swelling pride, taking on the facade of obedience. Zeraktalis chuckled to himself, understanding the emotional struggles going on in the usurper's mind. The demonspawn was powerful and chaotic to the core, not used to taking commands from anyone. But ever since he was beaten into submission, and because he didn't have the vital information Zeraktalis wielded, he had to take on a subservient role, which was completely foreign to his nature.

"This is our first and biggest challenge in uniting the dark horde," the sorcerer said. "The key to uniting the monsters again is to bring the creatures of this domain, the slilitroks, into subjection. By causing this tribe to submit to me once more, the other tribes will fall in behind with little trouble."

Krylothon grunted in agreement. The slilitroks were mysterious and fearless creatures. And as mighty as he was, the giant usurper was wary about ever treading this land without several other usurpers at his side. One slilitrok was a formidable foe by itself; however, these monsters always ran in packs, making them even deadlier. And they were among the most difficult to destroy.

During Zeraktalis' absence and acting as ruler over Genna Fiendomon, Krylothon would often invite underlings to the mountain fortress to wrestle a slilitrok for the entertainment of the usurpers. At first glance, a slilitrok didn't look menacing, but Krylothon understood its abilities.

On one particular season, the chieftain of the ferocious canine monsters called masnevires had grown extremely arrogant and overbearing, so much so his fame spread all the way to the Black Fortress. In the guise of an event to pay homage to the "great" masnevire, Krylothon set up a feast for the chieftain and a number of his captains, asking for a display of the chieftain's fighting prowess. He readily agreed and the usurper provided as an opponent a slilitrok, a cadaverous monster looking like a thin and sickly troll. The masnevire approached, wielding a mighty battle axe; the slilitrok had only the vicious nails of its bare hands.

The battle didn't last long. With the cheers of his captains behind him, the masnevire chieftain pounded his opponent to the ground and decapitated the fallen monster. Thinking victory won, he turned to face the gathering of usurpers, arrogantly pushing out his considerable chest.

The masnevire never understood his doom. Ignoring the cries of warning from his captains, the chieftain, being caught up in the moment, lifted his axe triumphantly to the strangely grinning usurpers. Krylothon remembered incredibly how the slilitrok had placed its skull back on its neck. Through its incredible ability of accelerated regeneration, all sinews had rejoined, allowing it to stand as a whole creature again. It was then the masnevire felt the long, dirty nails reach from behind and grab his exposed throat. The slilitrok ended the poor creature's life.

Despite his concealed hatred for the Dark Sorcerer who had overpowered him earlier that day, the usurper felt a sense of fearful respect for Zeraktalis and his bold plan to recruit these most dangerous monsters first.

"Let's move," the sorcerer snapped, plunging into the steamy jungle. "The slilitroks abide among the fens. I will march into their swampy stronghold and make them understand the power of the Dark Sorcerer."

"The ssslilitroksss abound around the outer perimetersss of the isssle thusss making it an awesssome tasssk to put these creatures under subjection. There are many a fen within thisss jungle and packsss of ssslilitroksss in each one."

"Then we convince them one at a time!" Zeraktalis asserted, turning to his burly general. "And they will be convinced, even at the cost of losing many of them to a display of my power."

Drawing close to a bog, the sorcerer sensed the presence of many shapes skirting in close among the shadows. Undaunted, he marched forward. From behind, he heard Krylothon's great mandibles gnash anxiously. A quiet chuckle escaped. Krylothon was the most powerful warrior he knew beside himself but here in the swamps the usurper appeared a little unnerved. Rightly so, he mused. Slilitroks never surrendered and never grew tired. Worst of all for their opponents, they didn't seem to die.

Several concealed figures dashed away from behind the trees in the Dark Sorcerer's path. Several other fleeting shapes shifted back and forth behind the trees as the pair pushed forward. Step after step, the sorcerer drove deeper into the jungle, and the glimpses of the shapes became more and more frequent, giving him prospect of a soon confrontation. Three steps later, the dark jungle suddenly came alive with wiry shapes and beady, red-glowing eyes. The slilitroks flooded out from everywhere, it seemed, standing as a grotesque wall before Zeraktalis and Krylothon. The monsters were fantastically gruesome, more hideous than even Zeraktalis remembered them to be.

"This is perfect!" Zeraktalis roared, laughing sinisterly. "The mere sight of these monsters will paralyze their victims with fear! With their numbers at our command, there will be no army who can withstand the dark horde!"

Krylothon concurred, staring at one of the tall, gaunt monsters. Perpetually skinny, its mottled skin clinging to its ribs, a slilitrok looked like a ridiculous caricature. Each had bony legs and long thin arms that ended in wicked claws that hung down past its kneecaps. Each dangerous hand sported fingernails so sharp, they could strip the hide off a goblin in mere moments.

Moving slowly and threateningly closer, the slilitroks growled at the two intruders, chomping their gaping jaws lined with sharp crooked teeth and flailing their long arms.

"My pets," Zeraktalis cooed as the slilitroks gathered in greater and greater numbers. "The time for victory is upon you. The moment to destroy has come!"

The monsters stared curiously at the sorcerer, obviously unsure what to think of the power of his words. These brutes were more animal than humanoid, Zeraktalis remembered. None had intelligence greater than a dim-minded goblin, so the creatures lived primarily by instincts. Though unintelligent brutes, they were capable of picking through sentences to understand what was said. For that reason Zeraktalis' words to them were short and direct. "Join me, my slilitroks."

The monsters howled questionably to each other while Zeraktalis stood resolutely and patiently, unable to comprehend the animal growls and truly unconcerned about the topic of their primitive conversation. On the outskirts, he noticed more of the brutes trickling in to join the slilitrok pack.

These creatures understood danger had stalked into their territory to challenge them in their own domain. Normally, they'd have surrounded and overpowered any invader who foolishly dared to pierce their swamp, but the sorcerer knew in the back of their mind they sensed an uncommon threat. One slilitrok roared over the din of the others, voicing something in its indecipherable tongue. The others grew quiet until the loud slilitrok was finished. Then they all barked and howled to each other again. A different slilitrok rose its rasping voice over the crowd, apparently addressing the loud one.

Zeraktalis watched the exchange curiously, recalling slilitrok packs had no real leaders. They operated in one accord without a chieftain to guide them. They were obviously trying to select a speaker for the throng. Separating from the rest of the pack, the loud slilitrok howled at the sorcerer, its glowing eyes narrowing dangerously as it stomped forward, its deadly hands slicing the air viciously. The sorcerer couldn't understand the crude language the monster spoke, but the message the creature conveyed seemed clear enough. It was issuing a challenge.

The sorcerer grunted in disappointment. He'd already been challenged by Krylothon, beat the usurper into submission, discovered his horde wasn't ready for battle, and now was being defied by a creature who used to be part of a subservient fighting force. When left undirected for just a short period, monsters reverted back to their wild ways. Zeraktalis' extended absence had left the brutes without guidance for too long.

An arcane phrase later, the Dark Sorcerer's gauntleted fists blazed with ebony flames. The advancing slilitrok halted and examined the sudden sorcery. Behind it, the others hooted louder to encourage it to brave the fire and destroy the intruder.

After all, slilitroks couldn't be killed.

The slilitrok trudged ahead one fearless step after another, and seeing the sorcerer in a relaxed stance, not preparing for attack, only elevated its growing confidence. Closer it drew, its ridiculously long arm winding back for the first swipe. Still, the sorcerer remained unmoved.

Krylothon lurched in front of inactive Zeraktalis and intercepted the slilitrok. The usurper's deadly talons lashed across and sliced through the creature at the waist, spinning its torso some ten feet away from its legs.

The slilitrok throng went silent, and Krylothon turned on the mob, roaring victoriously, spreading his wings wide and displaying his deadly arsenal of talons, vicelike mandibles, and serrated teeth. Energetic rustling in the saw grass where the torso landed turned the usurper, his arrogant show suddenly losing his pomp. In his battle rage, he'd forgotten a key aspect about slilitroks.

The torso crawled back to its other half and quickly began to reform, tendrils and sinews reaching out and impossibly reforming, pulling the monster back together where it had been ripped apart. Several dead leaves and other refuse were caught among the sticky entrails and became part of the monster as well. The gangly slilitrok sprang back up as a whole creature again, standing boldly, not intimidated by the usurper's attack.

In the background, the mob whooped and howled loudly.

"Impressive," Zeraktalis said. Although he'd seen the slilitroks' accelerated regeneration process in the past, he never failed to be astonished by their curious ability.

The slilitrok's wide claw swiped across at the sorcerer's skull, bringing him back full alert. The sorcerer's flaming fist thrust up and batted the attack away. Backing a cautious step, the slilitrok howled in rage. Zeraktalis wasn't impressed. Even these ruthless killers grew overly haughty and careless, he decided. The clumsiest of fighters could parry away such a reckless strike. It swiped in again. Zeraktalis ducked the swing
and backhanded the creature to the side.

"It's time to make an example of this insolent creature," Zeraktalis said coolly to his general. "By so doing, the rest of these brutes will realize who their true master is."

Predictably, the slilitrok got to its feet and rushed in again, this time a hideous scream blasting from its wide mouth. Zeraktalis turned and faced the brute squarely, seeing the fearless look in the brute's eyes. The slilitrok obviously thought its continuous assaults would wear him down so it could kill him.

The din of the cheering slilitrok mob increased behind it.

With one enchanted word, flames erupted from both fists as Zeraktalis thrust his arms toward the charging brute. A double stream of fire exploded from his hands, slamming into the monster, stopping it in mid-step and setting it ablaze. The slilitrok let out a hideous wail. In ghoulish amusement, the sorcerer watched the brute's eyes go wide when it realized its burning flesh was not regenerating. Flailing and thrashing, the brute screamed and beat at the flames, trying to extinguish the hungry fire. Moments later, with a final hideous shriek, the monster collapsed to the ground, a stinking and charred lump.

The throng of once noisy slilitroks fell silent. Concerned eyes looked from Zeraktalis' flaming fists to their smoldering, unregenerating brother. Slilitroks feared nothing, the Dark Sorcerer knew. Nothing but his sorcerer's fires.

"Any more challengers?" Zeraktalis roared and for a long time the creatures stood motionless. "Join me again, my pets. With you in my ranks, our horde will march unstoppable!"

He watched the monsters scrutinize him, visibly more careful than before. Again they continued howling in their guttural, animalistic language. Before he could wonder what formulated in their dim minds, a tall slilitrok stepped away from the throng and stalked aggressively toward him.

"How many more of these will I have to destroy?" he said. With an utterance, the flames licked his fists twofold. Unflinching, the slilitrok pressed forward. The sorcerer raised one flaming hand threateningly, but the creature stopped ten feet away, its mouth twisting weirdly. Zeraktalis couldn't discern its intentions until a crude voice forced its way from the creature's throat.

"Master," it said.

* * * * *

The secret door flew open and a pair of rugged-looking warriors rushed in. "Did you locate her?" Kil roared, stopping the two men instantly in their tracks.

"She was nowhere to be found, my liege," one of the men dared inform him after a long uncomfortable silence. "The only females we could find were in the brothels."

"Did you inspect them?"

"Yes sire. We searched every room, even breaking up lecherous rendezvous to see if the women matched the description Stoman provided us. She wasn't among any of them. None of the other parties had any success in finding her either. Many still search the town."

"She couldn't have simply disappeared!" Kil said angrily. "And what was she doing in our lair? She couldn't be a scout aligned with any other guild. It makes no sense. All others fear the power of the Lurking Shadows too much to dare send a spy. They all know doom would fall on them."

"Could she possibly be a scout tracing the moves of the Lurking Shadows," Methlon offered. "Perhaps she is following your actions and putting up facades of her own to disguise her intentions. She might be a spy from a guild outside this town."

"A spy from another town's guild?" Kil pretended to consider. Kil's eyes shifted to the merchant leader. He held back his murderous stare. Arrogant Methlon had no privilege to expound his opinions in the Lurking Shadows' lair. With great effort, Kil let the moment pass. After all, Methlon would guide them to the essence of power the Master desired.

"She did seem unfamiliar with the town," Stoman agreed.

Kil turned on the man, piercing him with a dangerous stare. Stoman backed away nervously. The Warlord saw the fear in his eyes and approached with a hungry snarl. Although his second-in-command, Stoman knew his safety was hardly secure. The woman hadn't yet been found, and he was responsible for bringing her into their den.

"Who is she?" Kil demanded. "Stand here before me and tell me what you know!"

Stoman stepped up tentatively, his hand instinctively dropping to the hilt of his weapon. Suddenly conscious of that action, he quickly withdrew his hand. If Kil saw him approach threateningly, the Warlord would destroy him on the spot. Stopping a safe distance from his Warlord, Stoman took a deep breath and began his narrative. "The woman wandered the back alleys, away from the main street, the places which are strewn with garbage and infested with diseased animals. No sane person familiar with Senadon would willingly have gone back there.

"But when I spied her, I sensed an aura of confidence. I watched her, observing her swordsmanship, and as is our custom with worthy newcomers, I dropped down and offered her a proposal to join our guild of assassins.

"She acted ignorant enough about the entire lifestyle of Senadon, was even apprehensive about her choice. If she's a spy, she's a good one. I sensed no agenda. It seemed she wasn't even looking for us."

"That's strange," Kil said, stroking his goatee. "What was her name?"

"She told me it was Simeon," Stoman answered. "No! That was her ruse. Candace! Her name was Candace!"

"Candace?" the Warlord echoed. "The disgruntled daughter of the baron? What part could she play in all of this?"

Kil turned to Methlon. "I must ask you to leave now. My men and I must prepare for the siege. With maps exposing their every weakness, the elven defenses will be rendered useless against the power of my mighty assassins. The Silver elves will be exterminated before the sun sets on the morrow."

"How will we be informed when you have secured Lifespring for us?" Methlon asked suspiciously.

"My dear Methlon, we extend the privilege of you and your fighter-merchants accompanying us. You'll watch the destruction of the Silver elf race with your own eyes!"

"And participate in it?" Methlon asked vengefully. He received a nod of approval from the Warlord. "Kil, you're an evil man," he complimented, grinning wickedly.

"I will rendezvous with you and your troupe at the inn when midnight has fallen. By this time tomorrow you'll bath in the victory of your captured Lifespring."

Methlon and his merchants shuffled out of the den with springing steps. Their conversation resounded with hushed whispers of unending life and unfathomable riches.

"We kill the merchants tomorrow," Kil said once Methlon's troupe departed. "The legends of this spring are too numerable to be ignored. This must be the place the Master seeks. It's our responsibility to capture the spring before resistance can rise against the Dark Sorcerer's invasion force. The merchants presume we'll win Lifespring for them.

But after we begin our march in the Verdant Wood, fall on Methlon and his men. Slay them. Lifespring will be ours!"

* 9 *

UNHEEDED DANGER

"Unbelievable," Candace said and shook her head in disbelief. She snapped the reins sharply. Eliom galloped faster. Candace spied night shadows from an unusual cropping of bushes on the wide Ormantict Plain. Frightened, she steered Eliom clear and kept her eyes darting in the darkness as she raced from Senadon. Candace feared the possibility of the Lurking Shadows' long arm reaching around her in the night, ready to ensnare her.

"Goblins! Wicked assassins! Here in Avundar!" she cried, shaking her head in horror. "Not even legends of old testified of evil lurking within our republic. Yet I saw it! Monsters and murderers nest here in the midst of the baronies!"

Eliom began to slow again. Candace snapped the reins lightly. "Not much longer now, girl," she encouraged her horse. "The forest ahead is our destination. Once we've arrived safely, we can rest, find food, and a pool to drink from. Keep your strength up."

She patted the horse's muscular neck then gingerly snapped the reins again. As if understanding that reprieve lie ahead, the charger huffed determinedly and raced onward. Candace smiled at her valiant charger. She'd received Eliom as a gift from her father on her fifteenth birthday. The horse was a wild, young pony then, and it was Candace who broke her. She trained and fed her, disciplined and loved her. And their relationship grew so close, Eliom would let no one ride her but Candace. Over the past five years they were inseparable companions and had developed an unspoken language of their own.

Eliom was a loyal horse, and Candace hated to run her all night, but the animal sensed her urgency and fear, and sustained her thunderous pace. Eliom had run for hours with no break and no water. The charger's coat glistened with sweat. Her mouth frothed. Now their destination was in sight and soon Candace would reward her faithful charger with the rest she deserved.

Ahead loomed the vast Verdant Wood. This home of the Silver Elves was the unfortunate target for the wicked Assassin Warlord Kil. Philanthropic Candace was truly frightened for them, even though she knew none of the elves nor knew much about their culture. She understood the danger which would soon pounce on the unsuspecting lot. Her back teeth ground together as she envisioned the face of sinister Kil who controlled this extensive and infamous army of murderers.

Under Eliom's thundering hoofs, yardage disappeared behind them and the forest rose up quickly, just several hundred yards ahead. Doubts began to creep into Candace's mind. How would the elves receive her? Would she be shot down as an intruder? Would the reclusive elves even heed her warning? She had heard rumors the Silver Elves were not fond of other races. They rarely trafficked with humans or other heritages. Within Verdant Wood, they were self-sustained and self-sufficient and had no need to trade or merchandise. They had everything they needed, enabling them to cloak their race in a shroud of mystery to the outside baronies. She might not be welcome in the mysterious home of the Silver Elves, but what other choice did she have?

Kil's strategy was to execute the entire race.

Countless times during the night she pondered veering away to the north and gaining the assistance of her father's army, but to convince him would cost valuable time.

She feared the deception against her father would be so strong, she may never get him to move his hand against the Warlord of the Lurking Shadows, thinking he was some princely suitor.

The forest swept up quickly under Eliom's relentless pace, but Candace hardly noticed, her concentration turned inward. She felt she chose correctly to warn the ill-fated elves. Any trouble would be worth the effort, if she could even in some small way ruin the murderous plans of wicked Kil.

"Thank you, Lord!" she praised as she considered the events which brought her into the Lurking Shadow's lair and then into earshot of the assassins' schemes. Had the Lord orchestrated Kil's arrival, Stoman's invitation, and even the door of escape from the assassins' lair to bring her charging to the aid of the elves? She believed so. "Thank you for trusting me enough to help good prevail over evil."

The forest was upon her, massive boughs hung low like thick arms barricading the tree line. Blasting out a determined snort and having received no other instruction, Eliom lowered her head and thundered into the dense forest.

"Slow, Eliom!" Candace yelled, finally snapping out of her thoughts. Her charger's momentum was great, and even though she pulled back hard on the reins, they plunged into the thick of the trees. It all happened so quick. Eliom skid past a half-dozen trees and wisely ducked as she came upon a low-hanging tree bough. Candace spotted the bough they sped toward, knowing she wouldn't be able to move in time. She couldn't duck low enough.

"Oh Lord," she cried. "Move!" She prayed either her horse would make an impossibly abrupt turn or that the limb wasn't there. Neither option seemed realistic. She closed her eyes and winced, bracing for the painful impact. A second passed, then two. She was still on her horse and not groaning in agony. What happened?

She looked and saw no bough before her. Glancing back quickly, she witnessed the thick limb--which should have peeled her out of the saddle--no longer in its original position, but bowed back impossibly. Now that she was safely past, it creaked slowly back to its initial place. Candace's jaw dropped. The bough had moved to allow her by, unhindered.

"Elf magic?" she mused aloud, then quickly dismissed the supposition. "They don't even know I'm here yet. And besides, I've heard Silver Elves don't possess the dark powers of sorcery. So what caused that limb to move?" Her mind raced, trying to discern the impossible answer, but she came up empty. Then she remembered the events of the past day. *Senadon. When I was forced into the den of the assassins, hopelessly trapped on top of the catwalk, I longed for escape out the secret door. I wished for it to open so I could run free of that horrible nightmare. In response it swung open wide and provided a diversion allowing escape. Now here in this forest, a limb sweeps out of the way at my desperate urging. What's happening around me?*

Telekinesis? she wondered. *Could I actually be moving these objects by the power of my mind? I've heard of individuals who were empowered with that ability, had listened to rumors of people who proclaimed to possess this gift since birth. But in every case, the person was either dabbling or fully grounded in the dark arts of necromancy or witchcraft. Being a born-again child of God, I've never been ensnared by the allurement of wizardry, so I can't turn there for an answer to these strange occurrences. But I also can't deny the truth of these things happening. I've seen them with my own eyes!*

Could there be a possibility somebody could innately be born with the ability to move objects with the mind without magical assistance? If I'd always been gifted with telekinesis, why am I discovering it so late?

"My training," she audibly answered. "Maybe I've always had this gift but it was buried under my unwavering dedication to my disciplines."

Feeling compelled to put her speculation to the test, she slipped from the saddle. She spotted a stone in the grass two trees ahead. She stopped, bent on one knee, fixed her eyes on the stone and concentrated.

"Move," she commanded, holding out her hand to catch it.

The stone didn't budge.

Candace grunted in disappointment. "Maybe it takes a little more preparation," she guessed, shaking away the defeat and staring hard at the stone again, focusing her mind on its shape, its grooves, guessing at its weight.

"Come to me," she said. It still didn't move. She tried once again. It lay unmoving. Aggravated, she marched over to the stone and tossed it deep into the woods. "You'll move now!" she cried to the disobedient stone.

Climbing back on Eliom, she spurred her charger forward. Her failure with the rock was quickly out of mind. The threat to the elves resumed paramount importance.

* * * * *

A soft breeze wafted through the foliage, stirred the warm morning air and quietly rustled the shimmering leaves of the forest. Suddenly the bushes burst aside, and two racing shapes sped by.

"Keep up if you can," Zakili challenged his friend.

Navarro matched the elf's pace, his legs churning feverishly. It was everything he could do just to keep stride with the elf. Their race began in the avenue called Elfstay, now several miles behind them, and Zakili's pace hadn't ebbed one bit. The elf was a full foot shorter than Navarro, his legs shorter, as well as his stride. Where did he get all the endurance and speed? Zakili often dubbed himself as the fastest thing on two legs. The Paladin began to believe him. During adventures and battles, Navarro often ran for multiplied miles or even days to relay a warning to an endangered town. He pushed forward with endurance and strength he received from the Lord in prayers offered as he dashed to his destination. But now his legs screamed for a reprieve. His lungs ached for air. He'd kept up this wild sprint for what seemed forever.

"We're almost to the finish," Zakili said, his voice not winded at all. "Lifespring. Last one there..." he stated, smiling, all teeth showing. With a sudden burst, Zakili jolted ahead, moving at impossible speed. He left Navarro behind, stunned as The Paladin tried futilely to catch up. Thirty seconds later, The Paladin pushed to the spring's shore, stopping next to his elf friend who stood against a tree, arms crossed and not even breathing hard.

"Fastest thing on two legs, huh?" Navarro asked, forcing his words out between heavy breaths.

"You're a witness," Zakili said. "And a victim of it."

Navarro smirked at the confident elf, but hearing the chatter of water fowl behind him, he turned. They flapped down and skidded onto the spring's halcyon surface. Amazed, he took in the sight. The water was so pure, so transparent, the birds appeared to bob in air. A few distinctive quacks later, they paddled into tight formation, like a miniature, peaceful armada.

"What a scene," he decided. "What a contrast to the scarred battlefields I've seen, littered with the carnage created in wars of man against monster, and more often, man against man."

Sun rays pierced through the high canopies of the cypresses, illuminating the swelling spring below with a dancing show of radiant sparkles. Surrounding the shore of Lifespring were ageless trees and bushes swelling with berries which only magnified the place's beauty, and Navarro imagined this is how the Garden of Eden must've looked.

"Thank you, Lord," Navarro praised, awestruck by God's creative handiwork. Constantly, he roved wherever trouble raised its ugly head. With monsters rising up against communities so frequently within the past months, he'd not had the pleasure of visiting this forest, his adopted place of repose. The peace and beauty of the Silver Elf Kingdom, Lifespring and the Verdant Wood was beyond his ability to express. Whenever he thought about it, his heart was strangely warmed. For him, this was home.

A dreadful consideration pushed to the forefront of his thoughts, shattering his peace of mind and furrowing his brow.

"I know that look," Zakili said. "You're always confident. Always joyful. Why the dark cloud over your countenance?"

Navarro rubbed a hand over his face, trying to negate his expression, not cognizant his alert companion could read his concerns.

"There are many a wonderful memory at this spring," The Paladin started, trying to redirect the conversation. "I remember the first time I set eyes on Lifespring. I must've sat back against a tree for half the day just listening to the peaceful gurgling of the water, well, until some stranger named Hawk disturbed me."

"No! No!" the elf corrected. "Zakili. The name is Zakili. And beside, you're not going to sidetrack me like you so often try to do in our conversations. We are warriors of kindred spirits. I can tell something concerns you."

Taking a deep breath and squaring his shoulders, Navarro looked Zakili in the eyes. "I fear for your kingdom's future. I fear for the fate of mankind. I traveled back to the meadow yesterday hoping to uncover any clues to The Dark Sorcerer's schemes of conquest. I found none, not even a sign he or his brutes had been there. It's almost as if he turned away from Avundar. I know better. He's coming. I can feel it."

"And the problem is?" Zakili questioned. "I'm ready for a good fight."

"The sorcerer's looking for something," Navarro explained. "That much I could discern from his demands directed at the goblins. I'm not sure he knows what he's looking for yet, but if it's found, the end will come. I don't believe The Dark Sorcerer was probing Avundar just so he can conquer this republic. From the implications of what he said on the meadow that day, he's trying to uncover a source of power he thinks will somehow unleash the demons in the bottomless pit to raze this world and slaughter all who live."

"The Silver Elves will be ready, no matter what this sorcerer or his minions can throw our way," Zakili said confidently. "Our battle in the avenue has stirred the warrior spirits inherent in my race. This morning I was awakened by the clashing of weapons just outside the Elfstay. The elves are excited about their skirmishes. Energized. They're becoming the fighters the Silver Elves have always been throughout the ages. That makes my heart feel good. It was aggravating knowing I was the only one who liked to fight of my whole generation. They hone their skills again. Just think, all it took was for me to beat you up in the midst of the avenue."

"You beat me up?" Navarro asked, chuckling. "Interesting. I thought we ended in a truce.

"But, indeed, I'm encouraged by the resurrection of the elves' battle tenacity, and their renewed passion for engagement. In retrospect, Sheliavon suffered carnage all across the kingdom due to their lack of readiness against such a fierce horde. I saw too much death and destruction in those days. But I've seen just as much these latest seasons in other lands. The nations' battlegrounds begin to resemble Sheliavon's. Thus far I've led kingdoms and islanders to victory over the swarming monsters. But if the sorcerer grips the brutes' dark souls and possesses them as he did in Sheliavon, the threat will grow much worse.

"My friend, I no longer enjoy fighting, but when evil arises I'll dive into that danger and eliminate it in Jesus' name. In the Bible, God promised if I was obedient to Him and trusted Him, I'd be invincible until I complete the pathway He laid out before me. I'm going to fight for His honor to the end. And I won't let the Silver Elves suffer defeat."

"I know you won't, my friend. And I comprehend the demands which come with being a holy fighter and have never opposed your decision to choose such a lifestyle. But while we're on the subject, questions linger in my mind.

"You see, I use life to its fullest. Drain it for all it's worth. But my friend, your entire life is devoted to service for others." Zakili hesitated, then glanced curiously. "Does your God permit you to have.., well,.. fun?"

Navarro laughed. Zakili feared nothing, but when the conversation turned spiritual he always approached with reverence. Navarro knew the elf was serious, a rare moment indeed and understood he was offering a heartfelt question. Before Navarro could even extend an answer though, Zakili started up again.

"The Silver Elves enjoy their recreation," the elf continued. "For example, on any given night you may find my people rollicking carefree on the plains under the starry sky. Our spirits are light because our gamboling is what makes our lives so tolerable. And then we have our women...."

Navarro held out his hand, respectfully silencing him. He knew if he didn't his friend would predictably turn this conversation in a direction he really didn't care to go. "I see where you're leading, and I appreciate your concern, but contrary to what you may believe, my life's not just battles and danger. I never know what each day may hold and that's what makes it so exciting. Life's such an awesome adventure to me, and the Lord gives me the strength to be victorious in it every day."

"I love adventure," the elf admitted, "but even you must admit the monotony of life can sometimes drown that."

"Life can be monotonous, if I let it. But if I remain thankful for even the smallest things, not taking anything for granted, life remains worthwhile to me. Even in times of difficulty, I search for wisdom that increases my faith and strengthens my resolve which could've never been gained in times of ease. It's all about perspective. I can either view my life as a morbid, joyless duty, or I can see it as an exciting opportunity to serve mankind and glorify God. I choose the latter."

Zakili pulled in close. "But is there any fun your God allows?"

Navarro smiled, sensing his friend was pressing for an answer which was no longer characteristic of him. "Such as?" he asked.

"All right. Let's take my sisters as an example," Zakili said, leaping back and motioning histrionically with his hands. "Now, any three of them would be a delight to any elf. They'd be like a dream for any human to have as a mate. Then comes Navarro after a long absence and visits the elven wood. He has three of the most beautiful elven ladies panting and falling over themselves to get at him..."

Navarro smiled, and he crossed his arms, entertained by his friend's narrative.

"...And you know what Navarro says when his friend tells him his sisters find him intriguing? He says they'll make a few elves happy one day. I'm not alone in my belief that the greatest pleasure in this world is to share company with an attractive woman. It makes the game of life worth living. Even the greedy quest for riches seems foolish if there are no women to spend it on. Now I demand you tell me: do you not like females or does your God forbid you that pleasure?"

"I thought we addressed this already."

"We did, but you somehow evaded giving an answer."

"Well, here it is. I don't *need* a relationship with a woman to make my life fulfilling. My faith relationship with the Lord makes me complete and full of joy."

Zakili stared, one eyebrow raised strangely. "Then that means your faith demands celibacy. I don't think I could live that type of lifestyle. You're never allowed the pleasure of being with a woman?"

"In the past I pursued women to satisfy me. But now as a Christian, I haven't met anyone I desire to extend a relationship or give wedding vows to. And I'll not dishonor the Lord by taking the fleeting pleasure of a lustful physical relationship," Navarro retorted.

"Why not? Life is full of fleeting moments, now isn't it?"

"This much is true, but that fact only reinforces what I believe. The things of this world all pass away to dust eventually. Only those things done by the power of God will last, and only those who believe in Christ will live forever."

"Are you sure about that?" Zakili asked. "You put a lot of trust in something you can't even see. Look around! The world's right at your very touch. Personally, I prefer the tangible. Don't you remember the sensation of another warm body close to yours?"

"Enough," Navarro said, laughing at Zakili's failed attempts to bait him. "You received your answer."

"Of course I did, but I refuse to believe your God would deny you the wonder of a mate."

"My God doesn't deny it."

"What?"

"I choose to abstain. One of my covenant commitments to God was not to entangle myself in relationships with the opposite sex. The lifestyle of a Paladin cannot afford the luxury of quality time with a mate, so the Lord gives me the strength to refrain from those desires."

"So you consciously and willingly picked that way to... you choose to..." Zakili balked, stumbling over his words. "That's self-punishment, man!"

"I knew you'd lead me here. As hard as I tried to avoid it, you still pulled. You don't give up easily. Understand this my friend, my past caused much hurt to many. I used women as objects of lustful pleasures, luring them away from their mates, destroying marriages, and damaging potential marriage relationships.

"Those are evils I can never reconcile.

"But since Christ saved my soul, He forgave those past sins and took away the condemnation which easily comes with their recollection. It's because of my prior lifestyle I've chosen to refrain from all relationships with women.

"I refuse to draw close to anyone again for fear of hurting them and bringing shame to the glory due Christ's name.

"But that doesn't mean I don't enjoy life or have fun."

"Name one thing you do that's fun." Zakili challenged.

"I could give you a list. But keep this in mind, things some consider fun may not be to others. I used to think fighting was the only thing worth living for. Now, I'd trade all that conflict for enjoying a peaceful sunset or reading a book. Here's an example you can relate to. You think singing and dancing in a moonlit glade a pleasurable moment, while hypothetically, I could think elven sport is senseless and a waste of time."

116

Zakili glared at him and his gold-flecked eyes narrowed into slits. "You think dancing in a moonlit glade is senseless and a waste of time?"

"I said *hypothetically*. I did enjoy dancing with..." Navarro paused, seeing his friend crouching like a cat about to pounce, a playfully dangerous look in his eye.

"Nobody says that about frolicking under the stars!" Zakili roared, ignoring his friend's statement. He plowed into the unprepared paladin, driving him backward. Navarro latched on. He quickly shifted his weight to turn the elf's momentum to his favor. Dragging one foot behind, he tripped Zakili's churning legs. The two went into a jumble of limbs, bouncing and tumbling until they splashed down into the cool waters of the spring.

Zakili tossed his head back, his wet ebony mane swinging behind him as he roared in laughter. "Now that, my friend, is what I call fun!"

Navarro swept the hair from his eyes and nodded in agreement. "That was interesting. But it doesn't compare to this!" Grabbing hold of Zakili by his scale mail shirt and by one pants leg, he hoisted him overhead.

"Relinquish your hold, Paladin, or I'll be forced to react with a counter you'll never forget."

"Agreed," Navarro said. "Happy landing!" With a mighty thrust, he heaved Zakili behind his back and heard the elf splash hard in the waist-deep water. Zakili leapt up. He turned to the Paladin, his daggers spinning in his hands. Navarro sensed the attack. Quickly, he brought his sword about. One dagger then the next darted in. Invinitor whipped across and cut sharp angles, parrying away the blades. The elf stabbed in again. Navarro retreated back, and the daggers came up empty. The Paladin didn't see the root several inches above the sand as he stepped back. It caught his heel, forced him off balance and sent him backpedaling. Zakili tackled him around the shoulders and drove him into the shallow water.

Zakili was up first. His daggers, the Flying Tigers, dove in at opposing angles. Struggling to gain his footing, deft Navarro sliced his sword up and across, deflecting both blows. Across came another dagger. Invinitor darted up to parry the attack. The impact from the colliding weapons sent Navarro splashing onto his back. The elf sprang at him, daggers bared. Reacting quickly, Navarro tucked his legs in close. Zakili descended on him. The Paladin's feet launched out, slamming into the elf's gut and heaving him into deep water. The elf splashed down and disappeared under the surface.

"Excellent counter," Zakili complimented once he sprung up from the water.

"That's what staying focused and not chasing after women'll do for you," Navarro teased. Zakili chuckled and trudged back toward the shore. Navarro was already laid back in the shallows of the cool water, hands behind his head, he gazed up toward the cypress canopies.

"Oh, how I long for the peace these woods afford after each dangerous mission. It is the refreshing I need before I move on to the next evil uprising. I should enjoy this relaxation, but I can't. Belying the tranquility of this shady spring is the tumultuous brew of disaster the sorcerer plans.

"But I'm ready for battle and for death if need be. I pray Avundar will be

117

Johnny Earl Jones

prepared. I pray the Silver elves will be ready."

"Oh, we'll be ready," Zakili promised. "As sure as I'll knuckle you down every time we fight, the elves will beat apart whatever that sorcerer can throw at us."

Navarro smiled incredulously at his friend, his emerald eyes sparkling as the sunlight reflected off the water. "You have a penchant for tale-telling, my friend. No one but you can so effectively change and rearrange history until what never happened sounds as if it did. I'll allow you your tales. Because what I really like about you is you never grow tired of *trying* to beat me. No matter how many times I defeat you."

Zakili's Flying Tigers twirled in his hands. Navarro understood what that meant. He sprang to his feet. Invinitor leapt into his hand. With daggers spinning, Zakili pounced. Navarro's blade darted up and sideways, parrying away the dagger from the left. Then the right. Undaunted, the Elf Prince pressed in. Zakili struck with precise and measured blows, coming in fast and furious. Hard pressed, Navarro whipped Invinitor to and fro, repelling the Flying Tigers. This left The Paladin with no room for error in his defenses. Keeping the daggers at bay, sparks flying from the colliding blades, Navarro slowly turned the elf and worked him toward the deeper water. Several slashes and parries later they battled in waist-high depth. Zakili came in with a one-two combination to the right. Navarro easily deflected the daggers and shoved the elf back with his driving sword. Before the elf could stop and storm back at his friend, Navarro slammed his blade into its scabbard and dove into the water.

Zakili spotted his shape swimming fast under the clear surface, and he took up pursuit, trudging as fast as he could through the water. Then suddenly Navarro stopped and sprang above the surface, his sword in hand. The elf followed his intense gaze to shore. He understood the paladin's honed instincts had sensed somebody nearby. With the possibility of attack by greedy Methlon and now also a supernatural sorcerer, Zakili didn't take any chances. The Flying Tigers spun dangerously in his hands.

An elf swung down from the high branches, caught hold of a bough and dropped to the shore. He bowed to the two friends. Navarro put his sword away and Zakili's daggers stopped spinning. The newcomer's expression showed them he wondered why they were bruised and battling in the Lifespring.

"Reuben," Zakili saluted. "What news have you which would interrupt our morning exercise?"

Navarro rolled his eyes, drawing a smirk from the elf messenger. "Lookouts spotted a single human enter the Verdant Wood from the Ormantict Plains. At this moment they're tracking her every move. I didn't wish to alarm the King that a solitary invader had pierced our kingdom. I come to seek your counsel. We can engage this intruder and point her out of our domain."

Zakili mulled over the information for a moment. "A decoy?" he questioned, looking to Navarro.

"The possibility is high. When the merchants stormed out of the forest, vengeance laced Methlon's words. He wanted to destroy the Silver Elves, and in his bloodlust, he could've already amassed a strike force."

Zakili turned back to the messenger. "If this female is a decoy, the invasion force won't be far behind. Reuben, lead Navarro to the location of our uninvited guest. I'll personally put all the lookouts on alert for approaching armies."

"But Prince, King Gallatar wouldn't approve," Reuben pled. "Without solid evidence there are raiders on the move, he'll have nothing of it."

"Regardless," Zakili said. "I don't relish the thought of allowing my people to be slaughtered because they're not prepared. If need be, I will circumvent my father's authority."

* * * * *

Candace's sense of urgency quickly turned to frustration. She had wandered through the elves' forest for nearly half an hour and hadn't seen the first sign of them. "If they won't show themselves, let them find out about the peril on their own," she growled. She shook her head and dismissed her impatience immediately. "The threat to the elves is terribly real. What was I expecting? Silver Elf guards posted in the trees screening visitors?" she asked. "How am I going to find these people?"

She looked around. "Now if I were an elf, where would I hide?"

Pulling up on the reins, she stopped Eliom then slipped from her saddle. Elves had an affinity with nature, she remembered from childhood tales. They could be hidden all around her, and she'd never even know it. Kneeling, she slowly and deliberately inspected her surroundings. For the first time since bursting into the forest, she allowed herself to appreciate its majesty. Ancient, towering trees stood as an innumerable army of sentinels, their high canopies reaching to the sky. Swaying gently in the breeze, the canopies allowed slivers of sunlight to rain down on the forest floor below. Garnishing the foliage around tree trunks were colorful splotches from nature's palette: bright blues on blueberry bushes and the splashes of red from endless strawberry patches highlighting the vibrant, shimmering greens of the forest grass and leaves. Blooming flowers encompassed every spectrum in the rainbow. The forest floor spread out before Candace like a never-ending carpet, and she caressed the rich turf, noticing the texture was as inviting as some of the most expensive eastern rugs she had ever stepped on. She resisted the urge to take off her boots and run her toes through the soft grass.

A faint smacking sound to her side brought her back to reality. Looking over, she saw Eliom munch on the rich grassy carpet. She smiled bitter-sweet. Poor Eliom hadn't ate or drank since their long flight from Senadon. She petted her horse's thick neck, proud of the brave charger. In response, the steed let out a contented snort.

Running her fingers through her hair, Candace wondered what to do now. As her eyes roved the forest again, she noticed something peculiar behind them. Moving away from Eliom, she glanced at the hoofprints in the grass. In every direction the grass looked untrampled and untouched--everywhere except where they had trod, she noticed curiously. An eerie feeling washed over her, and she felt as if they must be the first to have ever walked on the living floor of the forest. She had the terrible feeling she trespassed on holy ground.

Eliom nibbled without falter.

Candace glanced back up to the boughs, noticing how the branches twisted and wove so completely they appeared to form a great blanket overhead. "Perhaps the elves travel along the canopy's branch system," she guessed. "This would explain why the grass seems untouched and possibly why I've seen no elves if they even know I'm here.

"But if they do, why have none come to meet me? Why are they playing this game of concealment?

"Here I am in their very kingdom, raced all the way from Senadon to warn of doom, and they'll not even show their faces! Is this what'll happen when the invaders come?" she cried to the treetops. "Will you just sit back and let them destroy you?"

"I doubt that'll be the case," a strong voice answered from behind her.

With her cutlass leaping into her hands, Candace spun and spotted a stately man leaning comfortably against a tree, one foot propped back against the trunk. She looked him over, noticing he seemed too sinewy to be an elf.

At that moment glad to see anybody, she found herself intrigued by his sudden appearance. His damp shirt clung to the muscles of his sculpted chest and abdomen. She stared.

"Good day, my lady," he said, dipping into a deep bow. When he swung back, he ran his fingers through his wet, sun-bleached hair and swept it from his face then locked his eyes with hers, a disarming smile brightening his face.

Not conscious of her action, she beamed in response, returning the stranger's contagious smile, staring into his emerald eyes. "Who are you?" she spoke too softly for him to hear.

"Are you lost?" he asked politely, his question awakening her from her musing.

"Uh, no," she stammered. "I'm born again."

He laughed lightheartedly. "No. I meant are you lost in these woods?"

Distracted by the man's looks, and drained from fatigue and anticipation, she realized she'd let her guard down. Taking a defensive step back, she raised her cutlass. "Who are you?" she demanded, her mind swirling with disjointed thoughts.

"That's not important. What's your business in the elves' land?"

"In the elves' land?" she balked, still struggling to disengage her curiosity. With much effort she silenced the confusion in her mind and regained her focus. "I've come to warn the elves of terrible danger, of an onslaught which will destroy their whole race. All the way from the town of Senadon have I raced here with this urgent message. But why am I telling you? You're no elf."

He looked to himself, feigning surprise. "I'm not?"

Candace's sneered, not appreciating his sarcasm, especially after searching so long to find somebody and then embarrassing herself with her reactions to this man.

He laughed, lighthearted and friendly again, pushing himself away from the tree. Advancing until he was a few steps away, he stopped and swept into a bow.

"My name is Navarro Silvinton, a paladin and close friend to the elves reigning over this forest kingdom. If you've come to warn the elves of danger, that is of highest concern to me. Tell me about this invasion of which you speak."

Candace didn't answer at first, suspicious of this unlikely encounter. Although she couldn't sense wickedness from this man as she had from deceitful Kil, she wasn't taking any chances. The Assassin Warlord had misled her father into thinking he was a prince when he was nothing more than a killer.

And now here was this man calling himself Navarro. Could this self-proclaimed friend of the elves be another potential assassin in the midst of unsuspecting victims? After all, what was the probability of a human dwelling among a people known reclusive and unreceptive of other races? "I refuse to disclose any information until I stand face to face with an indigenous resident of this forest. How do I know you can be trusted?"

"Very good question. I'll return it to you. How do I know I can trust your motives in this wood?"

"Not long from now you'll experience evidence of the dire words I bear," she warned. She watched Navarro intently study her--as if he were trying to detect a lie.

"Fair enough," he said, seeming satisfied with her veracity. Placing two fingers to his lips, he screeched out a loud whistle to the trees, then called, "Reuben!"

A quiet thud sounded behind her. Candace spun about, her blade leading the way. She spotted the slender individual, standing barely taller than her five-and-a-half foot height. His eyes glistened a metallic hue, his arms crossed comfortably. Although she'd never seen one, she knew exactly what stood before her, the long slender eyebrows and the pointed ears giving away his heritage. "A Silver Elf," she said awestruck. Allowing her guard to come down, she turned back to Navarro, staring into his emerald eyes. A smile brightened her face as she considered how much more appealing she found his eyes than the those of the newcomer elf. *Where did that thought come from?* she questioned, shaking away the distraction. Events were too dire for an infatuation.

"This is Reuben. One of the inhabitants of this forest and one among many sentinels who tracked your journey through the woods," Navarro explained. "Don't fret about the elves not knowing if someone enters their wood, young lady. You were monitored from the moment you set foot in their domain. Hidden in the great system of branches are no less than two score elves watching over the forest's borders."

Candace looked to him, frustrated. "Then why did no one address me upon my arrival? Why was I left to wander among these trees for so long?"

Navarro's face softened in true sympathy. "The elves have their own way," he said. "As you've already observed, I'm not one of them and can't pretend to fathom their reasoning."

The Paladin turned to the woods behind him, exhaling a short whistle. A moment later a muscular, snow-white stallion trotted to his side, his flowing mane cresting in the soft breeze.

"Celemonte," Navarro introduced, seeing Candace admiring the fantastic beast. "You too must be a lover of horses."

"Indeed, and your charger is absolutely majestic," she said. A brusk snort turned her, and she saw Eliom had taken notice as well. She giggled when the horses had sighted each other and drew near.

"Let's ride, Candace. I'll introduce you to the Prince of these woods, and you can tell him of your warning. That's if you trust enough to follow me."

"I don't know why, Navarro, but I do trust you. I'll let you lead me to this prince." Candace said, not letting her apprehension show, dreading conferring with another, possibly pompous, member of royalty.

* * * * *

"What information have you discovered of our invader?" Zakili asked as Navarro broke free from the tree-lined trail.

"By all appearances our intruder seems innocuous, but I discern she is formidable and potentially dangerous."

The Flying Tigers spun eagerly and a hungry smile raised Zakili's lips.

"The encouraging thing is she's on our side. And she bears news you'll find of great value."

The Paladin motioned back to the tree-lined trail. Zakili, his battle lust quelled, dropped his daggers to their sheaths and followed his friend's outstretched arm, his gold-flecked eyes falling upon a woman with radiant, flowing hair, stepping fluidly, confidently toward the pair. With one hand, she gently led her mare, with the other she had a relaxed grip on the pommel of her sheathed cutlass. The elf knew an easy touch could turn that weapon for a quick draw and jab. His warrior spirit grew suddenly excited. He sensed this woman was a great fighter.

"This is our invader," Navarro said. "Candace Veldercrantz, daughter of Baron Kelt. This young lady has raced here all the way from the mercenary town of Senadon with a warning of --"

The elf pushed right past him, cutting Navarro off in mid-sentence, and strode before the golden-haired woman. "Candace Veldercrantz, I am honored to meet such a distinguished daughter of the fine baron," he said, bowing. "I am the Prince of this forest kingdom, Zakili Terishot. I welcome you to the home of the Silver Elves, Verdant Wood." He bent low, took one of her hands, and gently kissed her wrist. But after feeling her calloused palm, he looked to her curiously. "Tough hands for a baron's daughter."

"Is a baron's daughter not allowed to have strong hands?"

"Of course," he fired back. "I just didn't expect such pleasantries on a woman of such beauty."

"Trust me, Prince Zakili, there's more to me than my looks. Many men have made the mistake of thinking I was nothing but a delicate flower. I can assure you I'm as tough as any adversary that can be thrown my way."

"And that's so exciting to me! I love a woman who knows how to grind out a good fight. But mistress Candace, your point is well taken."

Navarro grinned, shaking his head at the strong-willed clash. "Well, now that we've all met and become friends, there's plans to be made. Danger is aimed for Verdant Wood and we must prepare."

Zakili winked confidently. "I've already put the plan into motion against any imminent attack."

"King Gallatar is convinced no one would dare oppose his elves. How were you able to persuade your father to ready his forces?"

"My father's attitude hasn't changed. He may never budge from his stubborn demeanor. However, there are some things a King just doesn't need to know."

Navarro shook his head again, certainly not surprised. "You mean like when his unruly son's controlling the situation behind his back."

"Don't laugh yet. Not all's quite in place. I alerted my father's advisors to a possible attack, but with the appearance of only a lone female to use as bargaining leverage, they weren't alarmed.

"Although our invader does seem a formidable and worthy opponent," the elf added in deference to Candace.

"The word from the advisors is like a word from the King. If they speak it, the people will heed it. And if Candace's warning is as terrible as you hint, then I may have the determining factor to rouse these elves to arms."

"We've no time to waste," Candace said. "Let us find those advisors."

"Indeed imperative," Zakili agreed. "At this moment they confer with Father about added sentinel perimeters. But even offering this small request with the scant information they wield, they 'll face an uphill battle. This graver news should give us the edge needed against Gallatar's unyielding resolve. And I'll not be shy about making a commotion to get their attention."

"You never are," Navarro said. "Then it appears we'll have the opportunity to convince the advisors and Gallatar at the same time. From what Candace told me, the forthcoming army may be the greatest threat your kingdom's ever faced. We'll need the skills of *all* the Silver elves to win the day."

Outwardly, Navarro appeared confident all would turn out well, but inwardly his soul was heavy. His friends would suffer the death and heartache which always followed war's footsteps. And with the appearance of the Dark Sorcerer days before, he wondered how much darker times could become. Forcing a smile, he faced his partners. "Let's make our way back to the Elfstay, and pray the advisors will heed this urgent warning."

Zakili nodded and leapt for the closest bough, grabbing hold and launching himself, flipping, to the next handhold. Off into the forest he disappeared.

"Mount your charger, Candace. We go to the Elfstay," Navarro instructed.

Navarro lifted his eyes heavenward as he drew near his charger. "Heavenly Father, we need You in this dark time. Evil emerges from every side. In Jesus' name, give us wisdom as we prepare." His voice turned melodic as he sang, "I will lift up my eyes unto the hills from where my help comes. My help comes from the Lord, the Master of heaven and earth. You promised no weapon formed against us shall prosper. Lord, I cast my trust fully on you."

As Candace climbed into her saddle, she glanced over to the man, increasingly intrigued by him. She knew his prayer was private, between him and the Lord, when he walked to his war horse, but she couldn't help but eavesdrop. A smile lit up her face. Not only was he handsome, but he explicitly trusted God.

"Follow me," Navarro called out, winking playfully.

Candace grinned. Never had she trusted any man outside of her father and the Captain of his Elite guards, Simeon. Although she didn't quite understand why yet, she was quite comfortable in this Paladin's presence. She would follow him and without suspicion.

* * * * *

"We must attack now, Master," Kil said as he gazed up to the flaming eyes in the giant mirror.

Silence.

He edged backward, unsure how the Dark Sorcerer would react to his demand. When he'd prefaced this request by expounding the events prompting this summons, he felt his Master's ungodly anger radiate through the mirror device. He empathized, for he, too, was enraged. After Candace's escape upon overhearing the plans of genocide, he desired to slit Stoman's throat for bringing her to the lair. Witnesses were present though, Methlon and his merchant warriors. Though he planned on murdering them later anyway, he wanted no one to see him strike out in unbridled, uncontrolled rage.

He really had no proof Candace would, after hearing his schemes, dart to Verdant Wood and warn the elves. Anyone else would be frantic just to escape The Lurking Shadows' lair and flee for their lives, unconcerned with the fate of anybody else but themselves. But from the brief encounter with Candace at Castle Veldercrantz, he was certain the tenacious woman didn't run for home after escaping Senadon. More likely, she was alerting the elves to the imminent assault.

Given time to prepare, the elves could be formidable, but Kil's desire was to wipe them out quickly and with as few casualties to his own as possible.

With Candace being an outsider and the elves confined behind their walls of reclusiveness, the elves' distrust would buy The Lurking Shadows time to pierce the wooded veil and slay them all. To do that, his assassin army must attack with haste-- leaving no time to wait for the sorcerer's foul monsters. Kil forced back a wicked grin. He wanted nothing to do with the unspeakable creatures Zeraktalis would march into this land. He was a self-made warrior, his army an extension of his prowess. The Warlord wanted nothing more than to show the Dark Sorcerer the extent of power he wielded.

But he knew he'd never say those words for fear of being annihilated.

"Destroy the Silver Elves quickly and without mercy," was the only response from the dark face of the mirror. The flaming eyes went black, leaving Kil alone in the darkness.

124

Kil's upper lip rose in a twisted smile, he roared triumphantly, and his dirks, the *Fangs of Hell*, sprang into his hands. "Death to the elves!" he cried, his voice reverberating through the hallway.

* * * * *

"Salutations, good King Gallatar," a youthful elf addressed his liege, bowing deeply as he halted just inside the doorway to the king's capricious chamber.

"What do you want, messenger?" Gallatar asked gruffly, he and his advisors glaring collectively at the poor elf.

He balked, searching for courage to speak before his perturbed ruler. "My apologies, good King. My intentions weren't to disturb any important counsel you may be engaged in, sire. I've come only to announce that the Prince requests to--"

He never got a chance to finish his statement. Zakili bulled through the doorway, moving the ineffectual messenger to the side. Following closely behind were Navarro and Candace, both bowing respectfully to the King. When The Paladin glanced back up, he saw Zakili march to his father's throne, paying as much homage to the King as he would give an average horse. Navarro shook his head incredulously, understanding his friend's impetuous nature had started them off at a disadvantage already.

Simmering fires in King Gallatar's eyes reinforced his fear. Silently he prayed the news of approaching danger would outweigh the discourtesy of the King's son. Zakili turned quickly to Navarro and gave him a furtive wink. *What was he up to?* The Paladin wondered.

"We have grave tidings, father. Our forest kingdom will soon be engulfed in war. We must set positions now before it's too late!"

Gallatar stared hard at him, not uttering a response. Navarro didn't know how his friend could convince the king to prepare for battle with this meeting starting out in such a confrontational manner.

The only bright spot was when the advisors appeared concerned with Zakili's warning.

"Did you hear me, father?" the Elf Prince asked. In an effort to salvage some of this negotiation, Navarro reached for his friend's shoulder to reel him back, to shake Zakili back to his senses before their whole plea sunk in the depths of Gallatar's wrath. Zakili strode for the throne faster than The Paladin could react, leaving Navarro grasping empty air. "Invaders hurl themselves at us to cut down our people and steal the land from us! If we don't warn the elves and rouse them to arms, they'll be slaughtered, leaving only an extinct nation, a testimony to your self-deluded stubbornness!"

Gallatar thrust his palm out, his austere stare silencing Zakili. "Have you forgotten whom you're talking to? Who do you think you are? Barging in here like this was some common room and telling me--telling me!--what must be done! I am King! I will not remind you again! When you enter you'll pay the same deference as any other elf who would walk in here, do you understand?

125

125

Johnny Earl Jones

"As far as invaders go, impossible!" the Elf King kept on. "Even if those troublesome merchants hired an army to enact revenge against us that throng would be as ineffective as Methlon's men. Hidden among the trees, our home and sentries would be invisible to them. Any who challenge us here in our woods would only prove their ignorance. I think there are none so foolish to attack my people in our own land."

Maengh, the King's guard, standing to the side of Gallatar's throne, patted the king's shoulder in agreement.

"No? The merchants would've struck that day if I hadn't intervened!" Zakili retorted sharply. "They're possessed by their own greed," Zakili went on, "and won't let anything keep them from our Lifespring.

"In their mind, no obstacle is too big. They think Lifespring will give them eternal life, and that's the quest of every race of the short-lived humans. They'll not stop until they have what they want or until we stop them. We must act now, Father, before it's too late.

"We have information verifying the attackers think us unprepared and vulnerable; they think to destroy us swiftly. We must stop those dangerous men now..."

"This is foolishness!" Gallatar exploded, his brow furrowed in rage. "Those merchants couldn't even locate a single elf on their last visit until you made yourself visible to them. How can they defeat us if they can't even find us? This whole scenario is ridiculous and a waste of my time! Be gone!"

"But there is more," Zakili said, swinging his arm back to indicate the woman warrior next to Navarro. She bowed nervously and started slowly forward.

"More foolishness? Who's this?"

"This brave woman is Candace, daughter of Baron Kelt Veldercrantz, a monarch to our north. She's darted into our kingdom to warn us of a dire threat she overheard."

"What would a human, a female human no less, know about what may threaten the mighty Silver Elf nation? Your absurdity has gone on long enough, Zakili--"

"He speaks the truth!" Candace interrupted, immediately bowing in apology for the discourtesy.

Gallatar eyed her suspiciously, but noting her manners, remained silent so she could continue. Navarro saw a glimmer of hope.

"Yesterday, I heard the wicked plot against your people with my own ears. These merchants are the least of your concerns. They traveled to the mercenary town of Senadon and have hired an army of killers, The Lurking Shadows, a mysterious force of assassins with immeasurable power! With intentions to slaughter all the elves and conquer the Spring as their own, they pose a danger this nation has probably never--"

"Where did you learn this information?" Gallatar asked dryly, cutting her off mid-sentence.

"I was hiding in the shadows of their lair when they expounded their

126

Lifespring

schemes."

"Hiding in their lair," Gallatar echoed, eyebrows raised skeptically as he turned to his son. "Did you hear that Zakili? She was conveniently concealed in the quarters of potential enemies and just happened to overhear a plot against the Silver Elves. What nonsense is this? Does it not sound too coincidental? This entire delusion is impossible! I don't know what game this human is playing, but I tire of it already. Remove her from these woods and sternly advise her never to return!"

"Your judgments are incorrect," Navarro interjected, walking boldly before the king.

"You too, Navarro?" Gallatar questioned, shaking his head in disappointment. "I would never have imagined you caught up in such foolishness. You model wisdom and prudence, but it appears your friendship with my militant son has ensnared you in his pugnacity as well."

"I don't disagree with your assessment of the Prince. Zakili is quite aggressive and sometimes warlike, but in this case, his tenacity is beneficial to your people. With the wave of destruction preparing to wash over Verdant Wood, he's the breaker wall who can unite your race in opposition against the onslaught.

"It was God's providence Candace should be in the assassins' lair the same time their plans were announced. She's a messenger sent by the Lord to warn your kingdom. He put her in the right place at the right time, and Candace risked her life to alert you. Heed this exhortation before the danger is unleashed on your forest kingdom."

Gallatar rose from his seat, his face a mask of rage. "I don't believe in your God, Paladin, nor do I believe He's in control of these circumstances. All these tales the three of you bring sound like paranoid delusions, concoctions of battle-hungry and battle-warped minds. I've more important things to consider than an impossible threat from a race of people to whom we're invisible. Now leave and bother me no more, or I'll throw you out with my own hands!"

"What if?" Navarro argued, trying to insert some sort of rational into the quickly unraveling conversation. "What if this isn't a big game as you surmise it is? What if this strike force is as lethal as we suspect and is left to pierce Verdant Wood unopposed. Too many times have I seen devastating consequences resulting from leadership's indifference toward the warning of a closing threat. Many, being unaware of what was to come, never had a chance.

"I don't want to see this happen to my friends, the Silver Elves. I don't want to relive that horror here in Verdant Wood. Every moment we delay buys more opportunity for the enemy to shred what meager defenses we have and tear this nation apart. When they come, and if we're unprepared, there'll be no turning back. No rethinking of decisions. It'll be too late to act once they're upon us. Without organized resistance against their massive army, the end will surely come. Personally, I wouldn't be willing to accept responsibility for the loss of so many lives."

"Get out!" Gallatar screamed, drawing concerned stares from his advisors. Navarro noticed their unnerved expression. "Get out!"

"Good King," Navarro volleyed, "there would be no harm in testing your elves' battle-worthiness."

"Depart from me now!" the King exploded, leaping from his throne to the main floor.

Navarro, then Candace, swept into a respectful bow before leaving the King's chambers. Zakili turned unceremoniously and marched out.

* * * * *

"I knew the news of an encroaching army might not go over well," Candace admitted, hanging her head after the failed conversation with the Elf King. "But I had to warn the elves and give them a fighting chance."

"You were brave to venture out here with the threat of the Lurking Shadows at your back," Navarro said. "You did everything you could. But King Gallatar's decision has eliminated any chance of uniting the elves into an army."

"For us to survive this, the Lord must do something miraculous."

Candace lifted her countenance, looking into Navarro's emerald eyes. "You're impressive."

The Paladin stared back, pointing to himself and shrugging questionably.

"Yes, you. I meant to thank you for backing me in the King's chamber. You didn't have to; after all, you don't even really know me, and you had no proof what I said was the truth.

"If it means anything, I appreciate your efforts. You touched the King's sensibilities more effectively than having some stranger warning him of a yet-unseen invasion. Our admonition may not have fallen on deaf ears. Your words captured the attention of the advisors."

"We can just hope it wasn't an effort that'll prove too late." Navarro said.

The sound of hooves turned the two as Zakili, on his bay charger, broke free of the forest camouflage. The Paladin's piercing eyes locked with Zakili as he approached, trying to read the elf's emotions.

"I thought you said you made provisions against the invasion force," Candace said, expressing her concern.

"Remember, I said I didn't have things quite in place yet. Even if an elf army doesn't materialize, we still have a few resources to help. My sisters are skilled with almost any weapon, and they are deadly accurate. I know. I trained them myself. The three of them, plus myself, can provide a missile assault while you and Navarro can strike from the ground. Yet there's one other I can recruit; he's a fierce warrior with a great hunger for battle. The only problem is he's a guard who's close to my father. His name is Maengh, and despite his loyalty to the King, I think I can convince him to battle alongside us."

"Seven against several thousand," Candace measured up the odds grimly. "Doesn't sound like a fair fight."

"You're right," Zakili agreed. "Clearly, it would take several thousand more of them to make it much of a challenge for us! Let them come! Give me a shovel, I'll dig my own grave!"

Navarro laughed, entertained by his friend's unusual battle cry and unwillingness to be rattled by the hopeless situation.

"Help us, O God," Navarro lifted his voice, his words strong and confident and coming out in song. "God, You're our refuge and strength, a very present help in trouble. Therefore we will not fear, though the earth be moved, and though the mountains be cast into the sea; though the oceans roar and be troubled, though the mountains shake with the swelling flood thereof! Who's an army of assassins in your sight, O Lord? We will trust you; You'll provide the victory!"

Zakili turned, obviously awed by The Paladin's confidence.

Candace stared, her crystal-blue eyes wide, her mind a jumble of thoughts as she considered this man and his faith, admiring his composure. She'd never seen a man of God quite like him.

Any dread she had flew away.

* 10 *
NIGHTFALL

Lurking Shadows.

They were everywhere.

She couldn't see them in the darkness, but she sensed them drawing in closer from every side. *How'd she stray so far from the Elfstay? And what prompted her to wander in the woods in the dead of night knowing The Lurking Shadows would attack at any moment?*

The ringing of drawn swords pulled her out of her worrisome thoughts. *What would she do now?* She left her cutlass back at the housetree. Surrounded by killers, she felt utterly helpless without it. "My father has trained me well for battle," Candace said, "but what can I do barehanded against an army of sword-wielding assassins?"

She turned and from behind a tree spotted the glimmer of eyes, sending the chill of fear through her heart. She turned the opposite direction. Several dozen eyes stared from the blackness. She felt like the only prey in a forest full of hungry predators. Spinning in yet another direction, she grew desperate, her heart beating fast. More eyes stared at her. She was surrounded. From among the predators approached a grinning silhouette. In horror, she watched, paralyzed, as the shadow advanced. Slowly. Steadily. Promising death. She wanted to pull her eyes away and flee, but her legs didn't respond.

"You should have known you couldn't escape us," the grinning shadow said coolly. "You've only prolonged the inevitable."

Candace groaned as each ominous syllable forced chills down her spine. Prowling forward with the fluidity of a tiger, the shadow stalked closer. Closer. One step then another brought it out of the night shadows and into the open glade. The dim starlight revealed the lithe shadow with close-cropped hair for who he really was.

"Kil!" she screamed.

"At your service, daughter of the baron," he mocked, bowing deeply before his twin dirks sprung into his hands. "You weren't conversational when I visited you at your home. Maybe now you'll have more to say. A starting point would be pleading for your life. No, you'd never do that, would you? You are a proud one.

"Oh yes, I know much about you, Candace, more than you ever feared. For instance, I learned you desire to cross swords against would-be suitors. I didn't receive that challenge upon our initial meeting in your father's throne room. Would you like to fight me now?" he offered teasingly, his dirks crossing and slicing the air viciously.

"That's a brave proposition to make against someone with no weapons," she said. Her pride screamed for him to give her a weapon. Her pride wanted to shove his words down his throat. But she wondered who she was fooling. She couldn't match up against the Warlord of the legendary Lurking Shadows?

Kil glided slowly forward.

"A real man wouldn't fight a woman," she jeered.

"I'm not going to fight you. I'm going to kill you."

She felt her heart beat rapidly in her chest; Kil's chilly, death-promising threat made her realize the finality of this encounter. With Lurking Shadows everywhere and no weapon to defend herself, she fearfully understood she was going to die. She shook away the hopelessness. But with allies so near how could she give up? Somehow she had to find a hole in the surrounding wall of Lurking Shadows and run for the safety of the Elfstay, and dash to the side of Navarro Silvinton. Together they and the Silver elves would turn these assassins away. *It all sounds good,* she thought, *but I have to get through this pack of killers first.* Frantically, she scanned every direction. To the left, she saw eyes peer at her through the darkness.

She spun to the right.

More eyes.

"Lord, You promised there'd be a way of escape," she prayed under her breath. "I'm trusting You. There'll be no hope to get away unless You provide it." She spun back to Kil, stubbing her toe on a fist-sized rock. Gritting her teeth, she bit back the pain. The assassin drew closer, and her eyes went wide in dread. Although her situation seemed to cave in on her, she suddenly saw a ray of hope. A slim ray, but one nonetheless. Kil closed ground quickly. Candace bent, scooped up the rock, discovered a second one, and snatched it up as well. "I've got a weapon now," she threatened, heaving back her arm.

The assassin looked to the stones and laughed.

"There's nothing funny," she said. "I have excellent aim and a strong throwing arm. I'm dangerous with these things."

Candace grinned, seeing her threat had stopped his momentum. Silently, he circled her, cautious now, she noticed, in deference to the missiles she wielded. She pulled to the side in a curving pattern which took her farther away from dangerous Kil. The warlord quickly reacted and moved to cut her off, but when she heaved back her arm and balked a throw, the assassin stopped, crossing his blades before him. She started moving again and although she'd gotten him slightly to the side, she knew he was quick enough to intercept her before she could ever get into full stride. She glanced behind him briefly and miraculously saw no eyes in the darkness.

An opening!

If she could get past him, she could run free. She hoped the Elfstay was in that direction. Kil was her only obstacle.

Hurling one stone at him, she dashed headlong, her gaze focused on the exit. Kil never flinched. The flat of his blade batted the stone out of the air. This was an unexpected setback, but she wouldn't let that slow her. She had one more stone, and Kil was closer. The assassin smoothly stepped in front of her, his arms folded and a cocky smile on his face. Still running, she launched her other rock, the biggest of the two, just as she got within six feet of him. Although off-balanced, she got off an accurate throw, forcing Kil to duck. The action bought her only a second but that was enough. Candace raced past him into the dark cover of the trees.

"Destroy her!" he yelled from behind. The next sound to assault her ears was a chorus of sharp whistles followed by the thud! thud! thud! of several objects randomly slamming into the trees closest her.

"They're shooting arrows at me!" she screamed in a crescendo of anger and fear. A buzzing noise vibrated her left eardrum for a second, and she realized an arrow had come within inches of her skull. She was absolutely terrified. Her surroundings were pitch black, enemies hounded her, and worst of all, she was totally defenseless against the whistling arrows. Increasing her despair, she doubted she even ran in the direction of the Elfstay! "Lord, help me!"

A shadow stepped in front of her from behind an oak. "I'll help you," he promised sinisterly. "I'll help you to your grave!"

"Kil!" she screamed in terror, her mind whirling. *How'd he get in front of me?*

He latched onto her and seized her in a bear hug, pinning her arms. She felt more arms grab hold and pull her feet out from under her. She landed hard on her shoulder.

Her eyes snapped open as she rolled over on her back, her mouth agape in a silent scream. She laid very still for a moment, staring up at the unusual ceiling.

Silky, elven sheets twisted tightly around her all the way to her ankles. With her shoulder throbbing, Candace took a deep breath. She realized she'd fallen off the bed in the midst of an extreme nightmare. All was dark except for the pale, greenish glow shining through the curtains. Slowly, the hard beating of her heart and the anxiety caused by the incubus ebbed. She inhaled another deep breath before attempting to twist free of the bed sheets.

Her mind reflected back on the day. Shortly after the unsuccessful meeting with the King of Verdant Wood, the Elf Prince introduced her to several of the Silver Elves. Candace easily struck up a friendship with three in particular, Zakili's sisters: Senetta, Monolique and Saranisen, vigorous women having a charm she'd never seen in any king's daughters before. They led her to a private area along the river and there she bathed, washing away the dirt and perspiration of her flight from Senadon. Left hanging on some close tree limbs were beautiful elven garments she knew the sisters left for her. Feeling silky against her skin, the soft, blue material drew a contented sigh. When she slipped on the elegant sandals, she wanted to melt. She'd never felt anything so comfortable on her feet. Upon returning to the Elfstay, they offered her a bed to rest in. With the forthcoming danger, Candace was aware she needed to be her best to help them. The sun was still high when she lay down, but once her head hit the pillow, she was unconscious. She slept past sunset.

"Thank you, Lord," she prayed silently, understanding the Lurking Shadows must not have attacked. The only noise she heard outside was singing. Singing? Getting her arms free, she stripped away the rest of the sheets and got to her feet. She poked around with her toes and discovered her sandals' location, but once she found them and slipped them on, she felt like melting again. Using great will power, she forced herself not to get too relaxed. Stretching and yawning wide, she shook off her sleepiness.

The singing outside echoed softly through the avenue, wafting into the housetree. She started humming the tune the multiple voices harmonized. Recognizing those words, she suddenly felt encouraged by the melody. She swung the door wide and stepped outside only to stare in awe. The glow she'd seen through the window was no fire or lantern. Gawking, she watched as thousands of fireflies swarmed around two long poles driven into the ground. Combined, the insects shed more light than a dozen lanterns.

"They love the nectar we coat the sticks with," she heard a female voice say to her. She looked over and saw Monolique.

Gathered by the fluorescent glowing was a fair-sized crowd, some moved to the rhythm of the song, others clapped lightly, while yet others had their eyes and hands lifted to the heavens. In the midst of them, she spotted Navarro, a book in his hand as he led the elves in song.

"Sing unto the Lord a new song!
Sing unto the Lord all the earth!
Sing unto the Lord, bless His holy name;
Proclaim good tidings of His salvation from day to day.
Declare His glory among the nations,
His wonderful deeds among all the peoples!
For the Lord is great, and greatly to be praised!
He is to be feared above all gods!
For all the gods of the nations are only idols.
But the Lord made the heavens..."

She wiped away a sudden tear, feeling godly admiration and respect for this man Navarro. In the face of destruction, he was rejoicing before the Lord, sharing his confidence and joy with the Silver Elves despite impending doom. He had nothing to lose by just leaving to a place of safety. Having warned the elves, he could let them fare the assault as best they could. After all, this wasn't his home nor his people. Yet he chose to stay, chose to fight, chose to see this all the way to the end. She felt tremendously proud of him and was overjoyed there was a man who lived what it meant to be a Christian.

Suddenly overwhelmed with emotion, she wept. The heartbreaking whirlwind which drove her from her beloved father's fortress to the lawless town of Senadon then finally to Verdant Wood had finally caught up with her. She let all defenses down and sobbed uncontrollably, her tears washing away the anguish from the arduous trip, her blurred eyes continually being drawn back to the man Navarro Silvinton. Her sad countenance slowly became a smile of admiration.

She sensed several of the elves draw near, one placing a comforting arm around her shoulder while another gripped her hand, lending her strength. She looked to them, noticing one was Monolique, the other she'd not met yet. She was surprised and grateful for their compassion.

"Come with us, Candace," Monolique invited. "Navarro is leading us in worshipping the God of the universe, Christ Jesus. Come on. The Lord is our strength!"

Candace smiled at the elf's excitement. "How long have you been born again?"

"I received Jesus as my Savior two days ago. He's forgiven my sin and given me eternal life!"

"I could tell by your enthusiasm you've been saved!"

"What do you mean?" Monolique asked, smiling.

"With every sentence you radiate joy."

"Is that strange?"

"No! That's awesome! It's always great to see the joy and excitement of a new Christian."

"Do you mean I'm not always going to be this excited Jesus loves me and saved me from hell?"

"If you choose to be you can be excited about Jesus all your life," Candace said. "And I really can't think of anything better to be excited about."

Monolique gave her a grinning nod. "Good, let's go worship!" She latched onto Candace's hand, and they raced to the praising throng.

"Bless the Lord, O my soul!

And all that is within me,

Bless His holy name..." she could hear Navarro leading in song.

Following Monolique's lead, Candace circumvented the crowd, and to her ultimate delight the elf steered them right next to Navarro. The Paladin turned and smiled, nudged Reuben and handed him the Bible, pointing for him to take the lead.

Nearly overcome with emotion again, Candace stared into The Paladin's eyes. Imminent danger was near, but Navarro looked peaceful and confident, no hint of worry. Most impressive, though, was the way he gently looked at her, his smile amicable, welcoming. *How different was his glance than those lascivious stares of other men!*

"How are you feeling?" he asked, giving her a warm embrace around the shoulders. "A little rested and renewed I hope."

Candace seized him in a tight hug, staring into his emerald eyes. She wanted to speak. She wanted to express her deference, but clinging to him made her feel like a little girl caught up in a bout of infatuation. She was in the arms of a handsome man who actually loved the Lord with all his heart. Admittedly, when she first saw him in the forest, his wet shirt clinging tight to him, she was enamored. But now she realized her attraction to his spiritual fervor overshadowed even his good looks. Navarro pulled away. Candace reluctantly relinquished her grasp.

"You look absolutely elegant in that elven gown," he complimented, taking her by the hands and observing her soft, bluish, garment flowing down to her ankles. "Cute toes," he teased. She was adorned in strappy elven sandals instead of her boots.

She blushed and crossed her feet.

"There's excitement in the camp!" Navarro shouted over a crescendo of praise and clapping. "Several days ago, I baptized Reuben after he received Christ as his Savior. And within the past couple days, he's been busy baptizing. About twenty elves have come to trust Christ, His death, and His mighty resurrection."

"Twenty?" she asked, scanning the crowd. "It looks like you have three times that number here."

"The Lord's always at work. He's touching hearts as we speak."

"Come. Join us in lifting up the name of Jesus." They melted back into the wide circle of elves. Reuben looked Navarro's way when The Paladin rejoined. Navarro gave the elf a thumb's up and mouthed for him to finish. "You're doing a fantastic job!" Navarro encouraged.

Uplifted, Reuben's voice grew louder as he finished this last psalm. Lifting his arms in thanksgiving to the Lord, he nodded to Navarro who stepped forward, took the Bible, and began to pray. "Almighty Christ Jesus, Maker of heaven and earth, Lover of my soul, the Rock of my salvation, only at Your matchless name will every knee bow and every tongue confess You are Lord..."

A tear coursed down Candace's cheek, and she forced back the welling sobs. This time her emotions were inspired by the abundance of joy she could barely contain. The Lord was saving the souls of these elves, a race of people she guessed was hearing the gospel for the first time.

"Thank You, Lord!" she prayed silently. She knew the great number of elves gathered to hear Navarro preach this night came because of the joy of those elves already reborn.

She agreed with Navarro. The Lord was working in individual lives and preparing hearts. "Lord, You're not meeting these people for the first time. You've known about them all along. Now You prepare hearts. Your Holy Spirit will change many, many more people from being eternally hopeless into Christians living the victorious life You have promised. Thank You, Lord!"

* * * * *

With the vicious slilitroks again under his submission, Zeraktalis believed the other monsters would swiftly follow. He had forgotten about the giants. This race was least in number but most intelligent and the strongest of all the various tribes inhabiting the island--and with the exception of the slilitroks, the deadliest.

"I will crushes 'im" the Dark Sorcerer heard a shaggy-headed giant threaten. Zeraktalis squared off against three of the brutes on a treeless knoll which rose up above the thick forest. Days before he had sent out a party of goblins to announce his arrival on this particular knoll, demanding the giants bow their wills before him and unite with the rest of his monstrous horde. He never saw those poor brutes again. They probably ended up in a giant's stew pot. That meant little to Zeraktalis. All that was important was they passed his order to the giants before they became dinner.

"I will grinds 'im with me own back teeth," the largest giant argued, shoving the shaggy brute aside, glaring down at the flaming-eyed intruder. Brawny even beyond what was normal for a giant, the huge monster flexed threateningly. Veins the width of spear shafts coursed to the surface of his skin, gritted teeth showing large and yellow, and all along his bald, tattooed head bulged more huge veins.

"You don't know who you stand before?" Zeraktalis asked, his voice strong, voluminous.

The bald giant balked. He didn't know why. He'd never hesitated to destroy any foe before nor showed fear in the face of any adversary. So why was he awestruck by a creature he was three times the size of? Was it the confidence and power of his voice? Or maybe the aura of dread it radiated like a venomous cloud?

"Why does ye hesitate? Crush him!" came a cry from a giant behind.

"Baricon. If you take one more step against me, I will burn you to ashes on the spot!" Zeraktalis threatened, then uttered several arcane syllables. His gauntleted hands ignited in flame.

From under the shadows of his thick brow, the bald giant's eyes went wide.

"How do ye know me name," Baricon asked, still hunched as if to attack but unable, unwilling, to carry through.

"Has your memory grown so dim in so short a time? I am Zeraktalis, The Dark Sorcerer!"

The burly giant stepped back cautiously, eyeing the fires licking the sorcerer's fists. Zeraktalis tasted the fear, his dark soul consuming the sensation. Looking into the giant's eyes, he read the doubt and the trepidation of this mighty monster and understood Baricon was playing the consequences of attack over and over again in its mind.

"What are ye waiting fer?" the shaggy giant chimed in again.

"Shut up, Sheklok! We is dealin' with somethin' bigger than all o' us."

"Ye mean that single, small creature callin' himself the Dark Sorcerer?" Sheklok asked. "He's little bigger than a goblin. Check yer eyeballs, Baricon. Ye are the chieftain of the giant clan. Ye are three times his size. Why fear ye this little nuisance? One pound of me fist will rid us of this problem."

"This is The Dark Sorcerer," Baricon emphasized.

"The Dark Sorcerer is dead," Sheklok argued. "Krylothon has told us so."

"Krylothon was wrong."

"Was he? What has this puny invader done to make ye think otherwise?"

Baricon turned back to the sorcerer, the giant's eyes narrowed dangerously, his yellow teeth bared in an evil grin. Under the pressure of his tightening fists, great knuckles popped. "I will crush ye."

"How much do you doubt?" Zeraktalis asked, raising one flaming hand in the direction of the giant's face.

The bald giant stepped back again, reluctantly. A battle raged in his mind between bruising his inflated ego in front of its clan for not attacking, or risking possible, violent death.

Movement behind Baricon caught the sorcerer's attention. The giant Sheklok charged. Alerted by the heavy footsteps, Baricon heaved back his massive right arm and pounded the racing Sheklok in the midsection, forcing the air from his lungs and doubling him over. "Do ye want t' die that bad?" Baricon screamed.

"I is not goin' to submit to this impostor!" the shaggy giant protested. "And even if he was the sorcerer, I isn't willin' to become a slave to him either. Let me at him, Baricon. Dark Sorcerer or no, I is crushin' him."

"Let this one approach," Zeraktalis ordered.

Baricon hesitantly pulled his arm away, his eyes pleading with the shaggy giant not to continue with this folly. Sheklok hesitated after hearing the threatening power of the sorcerer's voice. Zeraktalis felt the fear radiate from Sheklok, multiplied many times over. He remembered this particular giant, one of Baricon's closest lieutenants, as always the wildest and most loyal fighter. Being constantly at the giant chieftain's side, Sheklok had heard Zeraktalis' commanding voice as often as Baricon had when they were part of this great monster throng. Deep in his dark soul, the shaggy-haired giant knew who he stood before.

"I am your master."

Shaking away his fear, Sheklok roared and beat his chest with one fist while raising his huge treetrunk club with the other. One other thing did Zeraktalis remember about this giant. He was the most arrogant and prideful of all. As Sheklok charged, Zeraktalis evaluated he was also the most foolish.

"Slilitroks!" Zeraktalis called as the shaggy giant's club plummeted at him. His arm bolted upward. A single arcane word roared from his helm releasing a flaming river from his open palm which tore through the weapon and left only a smoldering stub in the giant's blistered fist. Sheklok screamed in agony and rage.

The giant's eyes bulged when it saw a horde of slilitroks at Zeraktalis' back rushing up the knoll from the twisted jungle. The pounding of hundreds of feet filled his ears as wicked, death-promising howls chilled his black blood. To Sheklok's ultimate humiliation, Zeraktalis stood staring at him, fist still flaming, wicked laughter reverberating from his helmet.

"He commands the slilitroks!" Sheklok heard one of the giants behind him scream.

Up the knoll they rambled, wave after wave of the gangly, disproportional slilitroks, howling and gnashing their teeth, long arms dangling to the ground, knuckles scraping the turf.

"Destroy him!" Zeraktalis said, pointing to Sheklok.

The brutes charged fearlessly at the giant, the sharp nails of their long fingers slashing wildly. Sheklok swatted one away, then another as he tried to dance away from the creatures. The slilitroks were fast pack hunters, surrounding the giant completely, giving him no avenue of escape. From front and behind raking claws and sharp teeth tore into Sheklok's legs and abdomen. The giant screamed as pain racked his lower body. He pounded on the slilitroks with huge fists, crushing several, but for every one he crushed two more were there to take that one's place. Frustration caused him to panic as he realized for every blow he inflicted, he suffered dozens more. Sheklok was a true warrior, never giving up no matter how difficult the challenge, but fear siezed his heart at what he saw happening around him: the broken bodies of the smashed slilitroks were regenerating, the beasts re-engaging in battle.

Sheklok looked pleadingly to the other giants and one of them started forward but Baricon spread out its huge arms, barring the other giant from helping. The bald giant looked sadly into Sheklok's hopeless expression, then to The Dark Sorcerer whose fist still burned with flames. Baricon turned away from the scene, shaking his head.

Stubbornly, Sheklok fought on, fists pounding the monsters all about him, but his hope was fast fleeting, his legs being torn to ribbons, and back and gut raked terribly. He glanced back murderously at his leader Baricon, betrayed, but several well-placed slilitrok slashes later, and a scream ripped from the giant's throat, his gut ripped open. The pack converged on the doomed behemoth, toppling him. As the giant collapsed hard on his back, the slilitroks swarmed over him, jaws chomping, claws slashing.

"Do you have any doubts now, Baricon?" Zeraktalis called over the noise of the violent struggle.

Without a moment's hesitation, the bald giant fell on his face, paying homage and respect to The Dark Sorcerer, and answering, "Ye are the master, mighty Zeraktalis."

* 11 *
THE BLACK SIEGE

Methlon felt his hands growing cold and numb despite the warmth of the night. It was the charger, he realized. The beast felt like ice. The animals were unnatural; although giving the appearance of a horse, their thundering pace hadn't lessened in hours, and when he looked to its face and saw the beaming red dots where its pupils should be, he had the uncomfortable feeling he was riding something otherworldly. Methlon remembered Kil had told him these were gifts from the Master.

Methlon, staring nervously, hugged close to the neck of the ebony charger as it thundered across the vast Ormantict plains. Under the cover of Avundar's moonless night, the Lurking Shadows swept like a black swarm out of Senadon, rolling unerringly toward Verdant Wood. The merchant-warrior's mind spun with fear and horror as he wondered what he got himself into. When Kil invited him and his merchants to take part in the massacre, he'd been all too ready to join them, but that was more to insure against betrayal than to participate in a bloodbath.

But after what he saw during this journey his sensibilities were stunned.

Earlier that night, as a prelude to the assault, Kil and his assassin army veered in the direction of a traveling caravan of merchants. The horrible scene Methlon witnessed was forever seared in his mind. The army slammed into the caravan. The assassins sliced apart the unsuspecting men ignoring their pleas for mercy and destroying everything which breathed before racing off into the night.

Most chilling was, he knew they killed the men only for sport.

Hours later, here he was, with the wind blowing hard on his face. Methlon took a deep breath and steadied himself. With the destruction of the Silver Elves, Lifespring would be in his hands and the ungodly alliance with the assassins finished forever. He looked to the eastern horizon and could see a faint line of pink precede the awakening sun. The tree line of Verdant Wood was coming up fast.

From his lead position, Kil glanced back and flashed a murderous grin at the unsuspecting Methlon.

* * * * *

Under the weak light of early dawn, a lone charger carrying a hooded rider pulled up to the outskirts of the elven woods.

"Identify yourself!" a voice cried from the boughs of the trees. The words echoing all about the branches made it impossible to discern the speaker's position.

Yanking the cowl off, the rider stared up to the tree limbs, his pointed ears and slender face accentuating his elven heritage.

"It's you, Maengh!" the voice in the tree limbs called excitedly. "Thank God in heaven. Prince Zakili has looked for you throughout the night. He'll be glad to see you've returned."

"Not as glad as I to see him," the elf rider replied, a wicked grin splitting his face.

"Come quickly! Zakili wants an audience with you immediately."

"Can you tell me why?"

"Does it matter?" the lookout replied incredulously. "The Prince of these woods has summoned you, Maengh; that should be enough reason, I think."

"I'll tell you why he's summoning me," Maengh began.

"That's not important," the lookout interrupted. "I'm only to relay this urgent message to you. Your responsibility is to answer Zakili swiftly."

"There's a reason why all this seems so pressing. Look to the dim horizon. Do you see the throng thundering toward Verdant Wood?"

"Is that..?"

"That is the death of the Silver Elves!"

"What?"

"And I am the death of you!" With lightning speed, Maengh notched an arrow on his bow, fired, and sent it flying into the tree branches. A scream and a cacophony of broken branches shattered the still morning air as the hidden elf plummeted dead to the ground.

"I've dwelt among you for all this time," Maengh mocked evilly. "I know where all your hiding places are! I've exposed you, secretive elves. Your race is no longer invisible to outsiders!"

Maengh the jothenac turned to the western field, fangs protruding over thin elven lips as he laughed. Kil's forces were advancing quickly. "It appears the elves aren't prepared for the slaughter which will stain their forest crimson with their own blood. The Master will have Lifespring this very day!"

Moments later, The Lurking Shadows charged the elf kingdom under the powerful legs of their demon horses, tearing through the forest like a swarm of hungry locusts devouring a ripe crop. Ironfist, in the guise of the elf Maengh, was swept up in the fury of the battle-hungry assassins, his own blood lust raised to a murderous pitch, pushing him deep into the woods. He took the lead with Kil.

"The elves are caught completely off guard and will be utterly unable to regroup once we've fallen upon them!" the jothenac assured. "The elves' body count will be high before they realize the extent of what's hit them." Ironfist laughed, his confidence grew with every mile The Lurking Shadows infiltrated the forest with no sign of resistance. "Our assault is proceeding perfectly! Just as I planned!"

Under the power of the demon chargers' legs, the assassin army pierced deeper, splitting ranks a mile from Elfstay. Kil led his men to attack the elves from the west while Ironfist drove his contingent to the east. The assassins closed in to trap the elves in a pincer attack.

* * * * *

Methlon, caught up in the fervor of the moment, never saw the assassin pulling up just behind him with a dagger aimed at his back. Staring at the distant housetrees, he daydreamed of living in them soon, never suspecting betrayal. With no motion apparent in the elven avenue, the assassins would fall on the sleeping elves and wipe them out quickly. *Fitting revenge*, Methlon thought, a wicked smile on his face. Just then, the assassin closed on the merchant-warrior, and his dagger plunged down.

The weapon never hit its mark. An arrow slammed into the assassin's chest with a dull thud, flipping him backward off his horse.

Methlon and the majority of The Lurking Shadow attack force charged ahead, never seeing the attack on one of their own.

The rear guards who witnessed the unexpected assault pulled their horses to a stop, yanking bows off their backs and notching arrows. They glanced about the forest, scanning from trunk to canopy, but finding no opponent. Before leaving Senadon, Ironfist meticulously familiarized them with the locations of the lookout posts and the most readily used networks of tree boughs. As they peered around desperately for archers, that information became confusion in their minds. Woven tree boughs appeared as nothing more than a jumble of unremarkable canopies to their untrained eye, causing their eyes to dart to and fro to locate their hidden attackers. After a long moment passed, they still found no one. The small contingent of Lurking Shadows looked to each other. Was this all their imagination? The dead assassin with an arrow lodged in his chest belied that theory.

"The arrow of a scout who has fled from the scene," one rugged assassin suggested, pointing to his fallen comrade. "We will catch up with the main force and follow Kil! Together we will slaughter these elves!"

An arrow knocked him from his horse.

"Where are you?" another burly assassin roared to the unseen enemy. "I'll kill you all! And I'll ravage a lovely elf female for my trouble!"

"I don't think so," sang out a beautiful voice. "This elf female won't stand for such!"

Dropping from the branches overhead and springing out from behind the trees, the Silver Elves pierced the flanks of the surprised assassins with sword and bow. The forest exploded into a flurry of action. Senetta, the oldest of Zakili's sisters, led the attack, diving in with sword swinging.

The sudden attack dropped several assassins. But the strength of The Lurking Shadows' numbers drove the defenders backward. Assassin blades repelled the elves and quickly swung the momentum back in The Lurking Shadows' favor.

"For Master Zeraktalis' prize!" came a shout from several assassins, a battle cry stirring them to greater heights of fanatical zeal. Although they had never seen their mysterious and unseen commander, the knowledge that he had even mighty Kil in subjection wove a shroud of fear over the army.

The burly assassin hastily directed the Lurking Shadows into crude ranks and pressed back the sylvan warriors. The Shadows pressed in to consume the tiny group of defenders. With all in hand, the burly killer turned to Senetta, gawking lecherously at the beautiful elf woman. "Well met, elf," he hissed lewdly, licking the blade of his large sword. "I've never spoiled an elf female before."

Senetta's sword whipped across in response.

"Dead or alive, I'm sure you'll make great sport!"

"You barbarians are all alike," Senetta said. "Tall on brag, and short on brains."

"I killed a merchant last night with my bare hands. I'll not give you the same privilege." The assassin's sword hacked across in a backhand swing. Senetta reacted quickly to the swift attack. Ducking under the blade, she heard the *whoosh* of the weapon close to her ear. She retreated fast from his reach.

The assassin sneered and started back at her with a slow, confident swagger. "You don't have to perish," he promised. "The rest of the elves'll be slaughtered, but I can spare you as my little love pet."

"I'd rather die," she said as she stared into the eyes of the muscular, scar-faced man.

"As you wish," the assassin said and charged in. His blade slashed at her midsection. Senetta stumbled back fast, unharmed but was unable to launch a counterattack. The Shadow pursued. His sword lashed out wildly back and forth as she rapidly retreated. Senetta noticed a pattern in his thrust and slash attacks. Weighing just over a hundred pounds, Senetta knew she'd be run down by the huge man if she tried to stand and parry. His blade drove in. She spun to the outside, the sword tip only slicing the folds of her blouse's fluffy arm. His momentum pushed him past. Senetta turned and her blade whipped out and managed to slice a shallow gash in his arm.

"I'll rip you to pieces for that, wench!" he roared, turning and taking his sword in both hands, chopping down at her. "You can't be that lucky again!"

Senetta retreated out of his range.

"Not luck," she said, repeating what she often heard Navarro say. "God's in control, and He's on my side."

The assassin lunged. With a single fluid movement, she slid to the side. She barely escaped the assassin's thrusting sword. The assassin was swift, but she was no novice to battle. Her older brother Zakili had taught her well.

The assassin's sword ripped across at her again, this time diagonally. With no way to dodge this strike, she ducked, and charged right at him, her sword leading.

The assassin fought to stop the momentum of his sword and bring it back in time to parry. Before he could, his side exploded in pain as a thin elven blade pierced his leather armor and jabbed into his ribcage. Curses and profanity poured from his lips as he slipped to the ground, the light in his eyes dimming.

Around her, the din of battle raged powerfully and she raced to the aid of the nearest elf. With only a handful of elves by her side, she understood that, man to man, her group would be overwhelmed by the trained killers' greater numbers.

She was also quite aware the elves' fighting skills were unhoned. After all, they hadn't faced an adversary since the emergence of the giant and goblin horde in Sheliavon. Swords rang out and sang in the morning air in clash after clash after clash.

By all counts the smaller elf contingent should have been easily dispatched.

But the zeal of the Shadows couldn't compare to the dread the elves. If these killers rejoined the main force when they attacked the Elfstay, all was lost. Valiantly they fought on, resisting the assassin backlash, never giving up. The killers had no real leader to organize and rally them. The elves charged and quickly withdrew in measured surges, skillfully and efficiently picking them off. Several long moments later, Senetta and her hardy bunch overcame the enemy and forged a victory. Not a single Lurking Shadow was left standing.

* * * * *

Wind blew hard on Kil's face. The fragrance of blooming flowers filled his nostrils. The home of the unsuspecting elves was almost in range. Eager spittle wet the sides of his mouth. He patted the weapon still secured in its scabbard. Feeling one of his wicked dirks, called the Fangs of Hell, lent him greater confidence.

Kil's demon chargers broke free of the last stretch of woods, bursting onto the wide lane of the Elfstay. Lined on either side by rows of elven housetrees, Elfstay's streets were empty. The Lurking Shadows proceeded, silent as death.

"They will die in their beds," one assassin chuckled, drawing hungry grins from the closest murderers. "As you have said, my Warlord, the pride of the Elf nation has turned to their downfall!"

Positioned in the midst of the still avenue, Kil considered his strategy, stroking his goatee. "To just rush in and slay the elves as they slept would prove no contest. And with the rumors I've heard, these people are deft fighters, I desire to kill some myself. To take on a real challenger, one worthy of my caliber. One worthy to die on my blades."

The assassins turned to their savage warlord and looked at him quizzically. They expected to have crashed into the houses and stained their blades with the blood of the Silver elves by now.

Kil noticed their murderous stares and laughed insanely. "Awake you doomed elves! Your end has come!" He turned to his men. "Now, kill them all!"

Letting out a bloodthirsty cry, they leapt off their demon steeds and fanned out, storming through the doors of the housetrees with blades flashing. Kil sprang off his horse, his dirks leapt into his hands and blazed to life with hellish fire. Like a panther he waited, ready to pounce on any escaping elf. He drooled at the possibility some of the elves would rouse themselves to action before his men killed them all.

He thirsted for battle; however, only a moment passed before he discerned something was amiss. From one housetree after another the assassins emerged, their murderous glares muddled with confusion, their weapons free of blood.

"There are no elves," Methlon said. "The abodes are abandoned!"

Kil suddenly felt as if plunged into icy waters, numbed by the impossible news. In his shock he didn't even consider why Methlon was still alive.

"We've been exposed!" he growled angrily, casting his eyes toward the high branches, his mind consumed with rage as he remembered the one who escaped him in Senadon.

"Candace. I'll make your life a living hell for this!" He turned to his men and cried out, "Be on guard! The elves have prepared for us!"

"I couldn't have said it better myself!" a voice called out from the trees. "Let the rout begin!" Several sharp whistles cut the air, turning Kil in time for him to see several assassins fall in a shower of arrows. Elves dropped from the trees and stormed out of every shadow, piercing the amorphous cloud of invaders from all sides and throwing them into chaos. Sword rang against sword, and the battle was on full.

An elf sliced across with his short sword in one hand and a dagger in another, but the burly assassin he engaged stepped back quickly, lurching to the side and avoiding the hit. He came back in just as strong with a pair of long daggers, hacking at the elf in a blur of silvery blades. The sylvan matched his barrage, blades striking the assassin's with intensity, parrying away the attacks. Quickly and silently, Kil slipped behind the engaged elf and drove his fiery dirk into his ribcage, his life stolen so quickly, he didn't have breath for a dying cry.

"Our forces outnumber these fools, my assassins!" Kil roared. "Slay them! Slay them all!" He turned to battle again, the master of stealth, looking for a new victim. He was hungry to finish another legendary Silver Elf, longing to sink his blades into as many elves as possible. He pushed one of his assassins aside and took on that man's elf. "Your death has just arrived," he said, grinning wickedly.

The elf didn't respond verbally, his short sword slashed across, causing the Warlord to back slightly. The elf came at him, his sword reversing angles, but Kil's dirks were up in a second, batting away the blade with a double strike. This time the Warlord surged in, his blades a fiery blur as they blitzed the overmatched elf. Once and again, the elf batted the whirling blades, barely able to keep up with them, as he backpedalled in a hopeless retreat.

Kil pressed in mercilessly, sensing the kill, his twin dirks darting in from differing angles, forcing the elf to strike one blade and duck the other. His left dirk plunged down in an underhand strike and the elf reacted quickly, his sword darting across to parry the attack. The elf only had a moment to react when he saw the real strike, the right dirk slicing across low.

The elf tried to spring away, but before he could, the Fang sliced a deep gash in his thigh. The leap became a stumble then a fall, and Kil pounced, his boot stomping the elf's sword flat to the ground while the point of his dirk lowered toward the fallen elf's throat.

"How symbolic this seems," Kil sneered. "The elves fallen, my army with a knife to their throat ready to deal the finishing blow. Today, my poor elf, your doom is sure." The Warlord stopped for a moment, taking in the cacophony of ringing and clashing weapons mingled with his assassins' war cries. The dirk in Kil's right hand bore back for the finishing blow. "Your death calls!"

The dirk arced down quickly, fiercely, but met sudden resistance, his blade never getting close to the downed elf. His dirk was locked up between the crossed hilts of two ornate daggers. His deft warrior instincts alone had his left dirk in place. He pulled back in time to counter a lightning-quick barrage of dagger strikes from a fierce black-clad elf. The sheer ferocity of the attack drove Kil back.

"You have too much confidence for a man wagering with his own life," Kil's opponent mocked, his daggers spinning energetically in his hands. "Your assassins have chosen the wrong people to attack. *Your* demise has come! You have just encountered Zakili!"

"Zakili!" Kil hissed venomously.

"The one and only."

"I've yearned for an opponent worthy to sink my blades into and here you stand," the Warlord said. "I've heard much about you Zakili. It'll be an honor for you to die on my blades."

"That'll never happen! And it's no honor to have your stinkin' assassins in my kingdom. I'll throw every one of your carcasses out of here before lunch!"

With explosive quickness, the warriors surged at each other. Fiery dirk clashed against dagger. Once and again, sparks flying wildly. Zakili's left dagger jabbed in straight. The other hacked across high at the assassin's skull. Kil reacted quickly. His right dirk arcing up and parrying away the high dagger. He spun to the side, narrowly avoiding the other blade. Kil ducked behind the closest tree to regroup. Zakili didn't allow a reprieve. He made a sharp turn, a Flying Tiger slicing down at his foe. Kil spun away again, the dagger barely missing him.

"Your skill does justice to the accolades surrounding your name," Kil admitted coolly and condescendingly. "I'm impressed."

"I amaze myself sometimes," Zakili returned sarcastically, pursuing the invader.

"I've tested your temperament and your speed. Now I know what to expect from you. You've revealed much to me of your fighting style in these first few moments. Many have thought themselves a threat to me. You may prove better than they, but I know how to crush you."

"Don't get too confident," Zakili warned. "I have a whole repertoire still to unleash on you."

Kil blitzed in. His fiery dirks sliced across in a high-low combination. Zakili met the attack head on. His dagger sliced to the side to parry a sideswiping dirk. His other dagger hurdled to intercept the other plunging dirk. Onward Kil pressed. He drove the elf back with fast-moving combinations. His dirks lashed across in a dizzying blur of flames and steel. Hard pressed to keep up, Zakili parried the attacks feverishly. He managed to stay unscathed. But he couldn't get back on the offensive.

"I'll take great pleasure in killing you," Kil said. "The legend of Zakili will go down with these woods."

Kil jabbed in suddenly. His dirk darted for the elf's belly. Zakili slammed his dagger down hard. The elf's blade smacked the dirk to the ground. From the corner of his eye he saw the other dirk speeding for his throat. With impossible speed, his second dagger leaped up and knocked away the attack, careening the blade to the side.

Realizing his mistake immediately, Zakili tried to pull back. His odd angles

145

left him wide open. Kil's foot snapped out and plunged into the elf's gut, throwing him to the ground. The Warlord pounced, his dirks diving in to finish the foul deed. Landing on his back, Zakili's feet kicked out, slamming the airborne warlord in the midsection and thrusting him back.

"That's compliments of Navarro Silvinton," Zakili replied. He had experienced that same counter when sparring with The Paladin. This time he was on the punishing end. "Is that all you've got?" the Elf Prince challenged, springing to his feet.

With a groan, Kil leaped up and charged. Zakili matched the Warlord's rage. The weapon masters colliding with the power of two rival armies. Flaming dirks and tiger-hilted daggers slashed and countered. The two jabbed and parried in a deadly, macabre dance. Like two hungry predators they clashed again and again, blades diving and weaving. The combatants twisted and thrust, jabbed and collided. Neither were able to gain the upper hand. Both warriors came at each other in dizzying speed. Each tried to find an opening in the other's defenses but to no avail. The fury of their skirmish echoed throughout the Elfstay and drowned out the cacophony of battle around them.

Zakili's daggers plunged in from differing angles. Kil leaped back. His dirks sliced across to knock away the hungry blades. The left was a clean parry, the right was a glancing hit, and the elf's dagger slashed his arm.

The Warlord sprang away, quickly evaluating the injury. "Little more than a flesh wound," he spat. His eyes burned with anger as he considered the Fangs of Hell; five strokes were more than sufficient for his dirks to snuff out any opponent's life.

Yet the elf still stood.

"The second biggest mistake you made in your life was attacking my home and my people!" The Elf Prince said, and his daggers ripped across at his foe, forcing him back. "Your worst mistake was engaging me! Nobody violates this kingdom without feeling the sting of my blades!"

His left dagger came in low and jabbed up. His right cut across in a backhand swipe. Kil got his defenses up quickly. He parried the strikes, but got his arms crossed up in the process. Leaping, Zakili's leg snapped out in a jump spin kick, blasting Kil across the jaw and sending him stumbling.

Scrambling to gain his balance, the Warlord grasped onto a tree with one arm. Zakili was already charging when he turned.

In a desperate maneuver, The Warlord heaved one dirk, blade over hilt, toward the elf. The throw was precise but deft Zakili stopped, swung his daggers across and swatted away the flying blade. Kil had no doubt the elf would defeat the attack, but the attack slowed his momentum, buying the Warlord valuable time.

"This is Zakili! The one Ironfist warned us about, " Kil cried to his battling assassins. "He's the catalyst behind the elves' resistance. We must destroy him! When he falls, the rest of the elves will fall!"

Zakili glanced to the side and saw a number of assassins turn and break away from the larger battle and storm his direction. "Now it's time for a real fight!" the elf roared. "Give me a shovel, I'll dig my own grave!"

* * * * *

Rolling in like silent death, Ironfist's troupe roared past the curiosity of the Circle, the concentric rings of oaks, and surged in the direction of Elfstay. "Ahead is where we join Kil and begin the annihilation of the Silver Elves," Ironfist said.

"Stop where you are!" a strong voice commanded. Ironfist, at the head of the throng, wearing the guise of a great viking again, pulled up on the reins, bringing his black charger to a cautious trot as he glanced about for enemies who should have no knowledge of their arrival.

"Who are you?" he roared to the trees, not spotting a single soul. In the distance, he heard the unmistakable din of battle and grew anxious. "There should be no battle!" he growled to himself. "The elves should've been caught completely unaware." Behind him, the other assassins slowed, their weapons drawn, eyes searching murderously for adversaries. A hundred feet ahead of them, a lone warrior stepped out from behind a thick oak, holding out his outstretched palm, signaling them to stop.

"Who does this fool think he is?" Ironfist snarled. He studied the man a moment, recognizing he was no elf, his muscular build and blonde hair easily gave that away. Offhandedly, he thought he recognized the man, but laughed at the consideration. It didn't matter. As far as he was concerned, this man was just another enemy to be slaughtered.

"Turn back now, and you'll not suffer loss," the lone warrior instructed.

"Cut him down!" was the jothenac's only response, pointing to one of his archers. "He wears no armor, only cloth garments. Put an arrow through his heart!"

The archer took aim and fired.

"Be gone, fool," Ironfist spat as the arrow took flight. He turned to order his men forward when he heard a sudden *clang!* The incredulous expressions of his men caused him to spin about.

"He swatted the arrow away with his sword!" the archer interjected.

The lone warrior spun his sword once in his hand then pointed the blade at Ironfist. "Save yourself and your men! Leave now!"

"Again!" Ironfist roared, pointing to his archers.

A barrage of arrows launched at the sword wielder. His sword swept across once. Then again. He knocked several lead arrows out of the air before he dove behind the closest tree, narrowly escaping the storm of missiles. When the arrows passed, he stepped back out again. "Is that the best you can do?" he asked. "Remove yourself now!"

Ironfist yanked on the reins, stopping his horse in its tracks, trepidation edging his rough features as he stared at the impossibly adroit warrior. He realized suddenly where he'd seen this man. This was the Prince's Paladin friend, the one who'd been infecting the others with his sharing of the Bible. His guess had been that the man was just sojourning briefly in Verdant Wood. He thought he'd have been gone by now. Navarro Silvinton was his name, he remembered dreadfully, hoping he hadn't made a fatal oversight in his attack plans. "Charge!" he roared.

With each bearing a heavily armed assassin, the demon chargers bolted forward.

"Our enemies have arrived!" Navarro yelled back, and the woods came alive. Arrows rained down on the assassins and took down the lead attackers. Darting from behind trees and dropping from the boughs came a surge of elves led by Reuben, Candace, and Monolique.

Quickly reacting to the sudden opposition, Ironfist grunted out several orders and the assassin mob formed into tight ranks as they slammed into the forest defenders' battle lines.

Two horses thundered Navarro's direction, one rider wielding a spear, the other a spiked mace. Their ranks were tight, and they closed on him quickly with the proficiency of warriors who had fought together often. The spear thrust for his throat. The spiked mace dipped low then arced up, angled to club him under the chin. Navarro turned slightly. In a double-handed slice, Invintor batted the spear shaft into the swinging mace. Navarro slipped under the tangle as the riders streaked past.

The black steeds wheeled around and sped in his direction again. Navarro stood, his sword twirling. Just as he expected, the riders positioned themselves so he'd be caught between them. The demon chargers raced in. The mace swept in low again, leading the attack. The spear came in low for his gut.

"At least they aren't attempting to get me with that same failed attack," the Paladin said facetiously. Seeing both their weapons in motion, Navarro bent low, muscled legs taut. He leapt just as the spiked mace came across, somersaulting over the low-angled weapon. With unparalleled agility, his sword arm lashed out, slamming the spear point to the earth while his legs kicked out wide, knocking both assassins sideways off their horses.

Navarro leaped on the first man. The Paladin slugged him under the chin with a mighty right upper cut, rocketing him into unconsciousness.

The other started to rise, but Navarro lurched over. His left hand snapped out and blasted the assassin on the side of the head. Resilient, the assassin shook it off. He pulled a knife from his scabbard and slashed at The Paladin. Navarro's foot shot out and kicked the blade from his hand. Resetting his balance quickly, The Paladin's other foot snapped out and pounded the assassin in the gut, doubling him over. Navarro's elbow slammed down on the back of his head. The invader saw nothing but darkness as he dropped into the unconscious world.

Turning, Navarro spotted another adversary bearing down on him. This one obviously seeing how easily Navarro dispatched the last two, didn't try a weapon attack. He snapped the reins hard. The demon charger rampaged forward. "This one's attempting to trample me," Navarro said with a laugh. "How original!"

He started to dash out of the way, the simplest way to defeat the attack, but changed his mind and stood his ground as the demon charger quickly approached. Being a great admirer of horses, he looked to the beast forlornly at first, knowing he'd have to cut the animal down. Then he remembered this steed was not equestrian but an otherworldly monster wearing a horse's appearance. The demon horse rushed in.

His sword swept across, but at the last moment, he spotted a crossbowman taking aim at him. His trigger finger pulled. Navarro dove, the bolt just whizzing past his head. His angle threw him to the side, and the thundering steed passed by only inches away. Navarro landed on one tucked shoulder and rolled, his momentum carrying him next to a skirmish where three assassins overwhelmed one elf.

The closest assassin noticed him immediately and turned, his blade slicing in a roundhouse strike. Navarro was quicker. The Paladin ducked the strike then jabbed the pommel of his sword into his adversary's gut, doubling him over. He hammer-fisted the assassin on the back of the skull, dropping him to the ground. No sooner had the first fallen prostrate than a second attacked. A scimitar sped toward The Paladin's throat. His sword Invinitor leapt up and deflected the curved blade. The assassin came at him again, the scimitar hacking down low. Swift Navarro punched out straight with his sword in hand, the pommel slamming between his eyes, the scimitar bouncing harmlessly off downward-angled Invinitor. Navarro lurched, punching the disoriented man hard against the temple. The assassin did not rise.

"Now it's even!" he encouraged the elf, having only one adversary left to battle.

But with his senses screaming, he turned to the crossbowman who notched another bolt and saw the man's eyes following him. Although doubting he'd close ground before the crossbow was again armed, Navarro dashed the assassin's way. The assassin fumbled at the sight of the racing paladin, nearly dropping the bolt. Navarro thanked God silently. There was no way the assassin would have his weapon ready now.

In his peripheral vision he spotted a dark shape bearing down on him, the surprisingly swift demon horse had wheeled about to make a run at him again. Out of pure warrior instinct, Navarro lashed his blade across, taking the demon horse's front legs out from underneath it.

With incredible agility, the assassin rider leapt away from the crashing charger, landing in front of Navarro, his hand axes chopping wildly. The air came alive with metallic ringing as The Paladin brought his sword up to parry the quick, two-handed attacks. Relentless, the assassin assaulted, axe chop after axe chop falling.

Each time, Invinitor cut the attack short, the assassin getting close but not making a single hit. *Small consolation,* Navarro thought. *Valuable time was slipping away. By now the crossbowman had rearmed his weapon.* He sensed he was now in the cross hairs.

The axe-wielding assassin's short flurry started to play itself out, his chops coming in less frequently and with less power. Navarro, a veteran of countless battles and having seen this scenario many times, waited patiently for the right time to strike.

Noting the assassin's arms growing heavier with each swing, he surged in, his sword slicing across high and diagonally, drawing both of the attacker's axes up to block. The Paladin saw the opening he was waiting for. His foot snapped out, slamming the man in the midsection and blasting the breath out of him. He spun quickly, his elbow swinging across to smash into the man's cheekbone, snapping his head back. His left hand released the pommel and with fingers out straight and thumb tucked underneath to form a ridgehand strike, his arm thrust across and crashed into the bridge of the man's nose, slamming the man to the grass.

Somehow, through the cacophony of battle, Navarro heard a dull click, and he turned, his senses roaring danger. The crossbow! There was no more time. Trusting his God-enhanced senses and warrior instincts, his sword darted in a tight arch, his keen eyes spotting the bolt speeding his way. With a sharp *clink*, Invinitor smacked the missile, careening it harmlessly into the raging battle.

Navarro dashed at the crossbowman. Obviously knowing he wouldn't have time to reload, the assassin threw the crossbow to the ground, drawing his sword. Invinitor lashed across.

The assassin barely got his blade across to block the strike.

Invinitor came across again.

The assassin parried.

Navarro worked his sword feverishly, keeping the crossbowman on his heels, never giving him a chance to go on the offensive. The Paladin's sword play was just a distraction disguising the real attack. Occupied with staving off the blade, the assassin didn't notice Navarro's footwork. Slipping in close to the invader, Navarro's leg scooped low. He hooked the assassin behind the heel. Navarro yanked his foot awkwardly forward.

The assassin briefly lost his balance, waving his arms to right himself. Before he could, The Paladin's upper cut crashed squarely under his chin, jettisoning him into the dark world of unconsciousness.

A rider swept by, and his sword arced across at neck level, but Candace ducked suddenly, the attack coming so close she could feel the displacement of the air just above her head. She sprang back up, sword arm ready, but the assassin had already sped to another arena of the battle.

"Tis a shame to kill so lovely a catch. Just doesn't seem right not to toy with you before you die," she heard a surly voice lament from behind her. The hair on the back of her neck stood on end. She spun to the sound and found herself staring into the face of a monstrous, leering viking. His big hand reached for her, but Candace stepped back, her sword whipped across, and she smacked away his fist with the flat of her blade.

The viking jerked his stinging wrist back and eyed her evilly. "This isn't a game for the weak or the merciful, girlie," he growled and yanked his huge war axe off his back. He heaved it over his shoulder, and unleashed it in a diagonal cut.

Agile Candace sprang backward, barely escaping her legs being cut from underneath her. The viking drew his weapon back in and arced a mighty two-handed chop at her again. She fled. The axe chased. Candace quickly dashed the two steps it took to put a tree between her and the strike. The tree shook violently. Ironfist's massive axe, having missed her, slammed deeply into the trunk instead.

As the giant viking heaved to dislodge his deeply-embedded weapon, the reality of the situation suddenly hit her. This was no test. This was no sparing lesson where she could learn from her mistakes. She was no longer fighting for fun. She was fighting to stay alive!

"You're my kind of girlie," the viking said. "Full of spunk and fire. I'll enjoy getting my hands on you."

"Here's your chance!" she promised as she blitzed in and whaled on the huge man. Her blade slashed several short measured strikes before he could react to her suicidal bravery and bring his axe to bear. Retreating a step, he heaved back his axe and it sliced down, cutting through the air with a great *whoosh!* Candace danced quickly out of range. The axe head burying itself into the sod.

"Only small scores," he said as he yanked his weapon free from the earth and looked to the shallow cuts.

"Enough small scores add up to victory," she argued, not intimidated by the brawny man. She stormed him again. Candace knew his huge axe was too bulky to allow him a quick strike at her. She slipped in low, her blade slicing across his abdomen once, twice, three times, cutting his thick wool armor and drawing blood.

The axe cleaved across.

She dove for the ground. The battle axe clipped some of her trailing hair then bulled past harmlessly.

"You will die!" Ironfist promised, slowly. Deliberately. He tried to stomp her. Candace sprang to her feet and fled. The huge viking took up pursuit, his long gait easily catching her. Latching onto her shoulder, he forcefully spun her about.

Off-balanced, she stumbled. A backhand slap whipped across her cheekbone and stung the side of her face.

Knocked off her feet by the force of the strike, she landed hard against the roots of a tree. The back of her head slamming against the trunk. All she saw was darkness and explosions in her mind. Crumbling to the ground, her head throbbing from the impact, the world spun as she opened her eyes to get her bearing. She saw the viking approach, his axe raised overhead. In vain, she tried to rise. Her dizziness forced her back to the ground.

The viking closed on her, sauntering menacingly. Laughing evilly. "Well is this not a delicious sight? It's time to return blows now, girlie."

Navarro spotted Candace's attacker from across the battlefield. Fearing for Candace's life, he turned to help. An assassin engaged The Paladin before he could dart to her aid. The murderer never stood a chance. Navarro's blade rammed against the Shadow's sword and knocked it from his hand. A left hook sent the assassin reeling. Navarro had no time to finish him. The Paladin raced toward Candace. He watched the viking close quickly on her. He would never get there in time.

"Candace!" he cried, hoping to shake her from her confusion.

Miraculously, she heard his cry over the din of battle. She shook the dizziness away enough for her to look up and see the viking heave the heavy axe down at her. Her heart raced. There was nothing she could do to stop it!

"No weapon shall prosper, Lord!" she screamed in prayer. "Send it far from me!"

To her utter surprise, the viking's axe obeyed. Its momentum stopped in mid-air and reversed angles, flying backward and ripping free of her assailant's hands.

"Sorcerous are you?" he asked rhetorically, trying to hide his shock. "No problem. I'll kill you with me bare hands!" The viking reached for Candace's throat.

Candace fought back the groping hands, but the viking was quick. One massive hand slipped through her defenses and clamped on to her throat, squeezing off her air. She felt around frantically for her sword. Nothing. Desperately, she gripped his hand and dug in with her nails. His grasp didn't relent. She couldn't breath! Her mind started to dim from the absence of air. She felt consciousness slipping away, the sight of the huge viking's crooked smile engraved in her mind. Would his murderous face be the last thing she would ever see?

A dueling pair of fighters danced past Navarro to the right. The Paladin spotted a dagger sheathed on the passing assassin's hip and didn't miss his chance. Quickly reaching in, he snatched the small blade from the sheath and turned to Candace's opponent. He flipped the dagger once in the air, caught it by the blade and launched it the fifty feet separating him from the viking.

A pained scream shook Candace back to alertness as the large hand around her throat fell away. She gasped hard life-giving air. Surprised, she looked to see why the viking, moments from her death, had released her. His hulking form stumbled into the woods, a dagger lodged into his side.

Who rescued me? she wondered, stunned. She found it hard to believe someone could see her plight through all the chaos. Before long, she was staring across the violent field at Navarro.

"You?" she mouthed.

Her eyes locked with Navarro's just as he belted another assassin with his backfist, dropping that one off to the side. His playful wink and contagious smile confirmed to her he'd been the one.

Unable to resist his charm, she beamed, sensing an emotion warming her soul she had never experienced before.

But at the same time she felt ashamed and embarrassed. Even though heavily engaged in the throes of battle, Navarro had alerted then saved her from certain death. Despite her prowess in swordsmanship, and her deftness at one-on-one battles, she became painfully aware she'd never been instructed about the dizzying confusion and pace of actual battle. But before she could even begin to sort through her whirling emotions, she stared in horror.

A spearman charged Navarro from behind!

In a courtly manner, The Paladin bowed to her, and she thought he was insane. She started to call out, to point, but before she could even begin Navarro spun. Invinitor sliced a high-to-low angle and smacking the spearhead into the dirt, ripping the weapon from the assassin's grasp.

How did he know The Lurking Shadow was behind him? Candace wondered as she eyed the explosive Paladin. The assassin stumbled forward, but Navarro's elbow jabbed across, slamming the murderer's face and standing him upright, dazed. A mighty jab to the jaw sent that assassin stumbling to the ground. Another quick bow to Candace, and he rushed back into the heat of battle.

From across the field, someone else stared at Candace.

Stoman had ducked behind a tree when he saw her, his face pallid.

"Candace Veldercrantz," he groaned. "This is the woman I recruited. After feigning to unite with us days ago, here she fights against us. How colossal a mistake for me to lead her to our lair. She heard Kil's scheme, then warned the elves of our assault. They were waiting for us all along!"

Another elf raged past, but Stoman hugged tight against the tree, unseen. "We'll fall to these elves today," he said, dropping his head plaintively into his hands.

The Silver Elves bit into the confused ranks of the assassin contingent, chopping the once larger force into a dwindling remnant. The assassins didn't give in. They fought with a tenacity and fierceness which marked their reputation.

Several more elf fighters went down.

With Navarro leading the charge, the elves surged into the assassins' ranks. The elves broke the Shadows' forces into confused mobs and scattered them with swift and deadly attacks. The Lurking Shadows were unable to regroup and backlash on them. Navarro led the elves in tight, relentless formations. They smashed into the clusters of assassins and effectively split the enemy's forces further.

"Divide and conquer!" Navarro roared. He and the elves pierced the broken assassin ranks. Before the loons had wailed out their first screams of the day, the battle had been won.

Ironfist ducked unseen behind an oak's trunk, grabbed hold of the dagger in his side, and jerked it out. Somehow he muffled his pained scream. Looking to the bleeding wound, he knew he was hurt badly. He'd no time to let that slow him, knowing his viking form would be easily spotted and hunted down. His physique began to melt suddenly behind that tree. Moments later, when the metamorphosis was complete, Ironfist reemerged.

As Maengh the elf.

On the far end of the forest battle ground, Stoman slipped away from his hiding place and raced away as fast as his trembling legs could carry him, not daring to retrieve his demon charger. The thought of Candace haunted him with every step.

She had warned the elves.

And it was his fault.

* * * * *

In the Elfstay, the Lurking Shadows closed on Zakili like a pack of ravenous wolves. They'd been told that killing Zakili would break the back of any resistance. However, the only survivors they expected were a handful of elves. Instead, the elves had been waiting for their attack.

The assassins became a circular wall around the Elf Prince, surrounding and isolating him.

"Destroy him!" Kil screamed to his assassins, pointing to the Elf Prince. "Once he's dead, the elves will fall without contest!"

One drove in at the Elf Prince, his sword diving for Zakili's heart. Easily sidestepping the attack, the elf sent his daggers into motion, slamming once, twice, knocking the blade point toward the earth. He turned to retaliate. But from the corner of his eye he spotted something speeding toward his skull and ducked. A spiked club arced over his head.

From his crouched position he heard footsteps from behind.. He leapt and dove into a tumble, coming down on his shoulder. A spear narrowly missed pinning him to the ground. Zakili quickly sprang to his feet.

"Not bad for amateurs," Zakili quipped sarcastically. "Maybe next time you can manage to hit me."

"Oh, you'll be hit," promised a sword-wielding assassin. "Then we'll string your dead carcass high. You'll be the last thing your elves see before we close their eyes in death." He blitzed in, his sword arcing across swiftly.

Zakili leapt backward, thrusting the Flying Tigers diagonally at the arcing blade. With reactions much quicker than the killer could have realized, his dagger hilts crossed, forming a V-shape, parrying the blade and locking it in place. The assassin tried to pull his blade back. The man left his ribs exposed, and Zakili saw the opening. The Elf Prince's leg snapped out in a side kick that crashed into the assassin's side. Zakili's daggers leapt off the sword, uncrossed and drove forward and into the man before he could react. Two more assassins blitzed, and Zakili danced to the side, his previous opponent collapsing to the ground dead.

"Never make empty threats against the Prince of Verdant Wood, you parasites! Those threats'll die with you!"

The club wielder swatted across furiously, thinking to catch the elf off guard. The alert Elf Prince ducked. The weapon barreled over his head with a mighty whooshing sound. Zakili leapt back up ready to put the Flying Tigers to work, but the assassin reversed the momentum of the club, forcing the elf to spin away.

"Now!" the club wielder roared to his partner.

Glancing quickly behind, Zakili spotted the other assassin jabbing down with his spear. Too adroit to fall to such a rudimentary attack, he spun and dove toward him. The Elf Prince rolled to his feet right beside his adversary. One step brought him face to face with the man. The assassin tried to shove the elf away with his spear shaft, but the Flying Tigers exploded into action and finished off the spearman.

"This elf's only one warrior! Destroy him! Destroy him now!" Kil ordered. The circle slowly began to tighten.

Zakili knew there was no escape. He couldn't survive the assaults of such a throng single-handedly. "I guess I'll find out sooner than I wanted to if Navarro's

God is real." Looking into the snarling mob, he sent his daggers spinning in his palms. "Do you think I'm finished? I'm just getting warmed up!"

The assassins rushed into the midst of the circle.

The Prince kissed his tiger-hilted blades. "You want to challenge me? C'mon! I'll be the last thing you ever see!" With the flick of each wrist the daggers went flying. A pair of screams pierced the air. The press of The Lurking Shadow mob halted, their attention drawn to their suddenly fallen fellows, a dagger deep in the face of each. Never one to miss a moment, Zakili dove, rolling to his feet between the downed Shadows and snatching his daggers. "Who's next!"

"Kill him now!" The Warlord roared.

Driven by Kil's threatening taunts, the mob pressed back in.

All the commotion didn't go unnoticed on the battlefield around them. The elves saw their charismatic prince surrounded and under attack. A group of elves broke away from their foes, speeding to Zakili's aid. The remainder fought feverishly to stave off the murderers left behind.

Zakili spun, and his dagger whipped across and took one more Shadow out of the fight. In came another and the elf danced to the side, striking once, twice at the sword carving his way, turning the attack harmlessly downward. He had no time to finish this adversary. He sensed another storm from behind. He turned and dipped low, ducking an arcing sword blade just in time to keep his head. Darting up behind the sword swing, his twin daggers jabbed out, driving into the man's belly.

The mob circle continued to tighten until Zakili had only a few feet of maneuvering room. "Who's going down with me?" he threatened He knew to help his Silver Elves win the victory he had to vanquish as many opponents as possible before he was run through with a sword.

The din of yells and clashing blades erupted on the outer rim of the assassin mob, and Zakili quickly turned a curious eye.

Hoots and war cries filled the air. Zakili spotted his elves charging around trees and plowing his way, their efforts exciting the furious prince into a frenzy. The Flying Tigers slashed wildly, striking assassins on almost every turn.

"I love you guys!" he cried to his fellow elf warriors, as they, incited by Zakili's bravery, fought through the battle-hardened invaders with unrelenting zeal.

"No mercy!" Kil roared, sparking his assassins against the smaller elven force's surge. Battle lines blurred and elves and assassins scrambled into one amorphous brawling mass. Under Kil's leadership, the trained killers stormed back with deadly fury, forcing the elves back on the defensive.

Zakili roared in frustration. The elves were vastly outnumbered and many might be slain for daring to rescue him. To make things worse, the invaders weren't going down easily. He judged this army to be the best trained and deadliest he'd ever encountered. He knew his outnumbered elves had to be drained, not getting a second's reprieve from the onslaught.

"Battle on, my brave warriors!" Zakili exhorted them, yelling words of encouragement. "We'll win this day! Look not at their numbers. You're Silver Elves, a majestic, unbeatable people. Victory's ours! Fight with the dignity which

155

has characterized our race for centuries. Make me proud!" Zakili battled hard and furious, leading his weary elf warriors, most so exhausted only their adrenalin kept them going. *How much longer could his contingent of elves last against this vicious assassin army?*

An assassin swept up on the prince's blind side. His cruel blade arced across for the elf's ribs. Zakili sensed the attack, spun, roaring, and with a double barrage of his daggers he pounded the attack away. Lunging forward, skull leading in a head butt, his forehead splattered the assassin's nose.

Another lurched at him, delusions of grandeur filling his mind as he imagined cutting down this legendary elf. Just as the assassin's blade lashed out, Zakili turned fully on him. The killer found himself staring into the elf's gold-flecked eyes. Flashes of silver and crimson were the last things that assassin saw. His lifeless body dropped to the ground, a victim of Zakili's slashing blades.

Sensing an enemy at his back, Zakili spun again, locking stares with the blackest, most evil eyes he'd ever seen, his adversary's wicked grin mocking him.

"Kil!"

As swift as lightning, a pair of flaming blades drove across at Zakili's skull. Thrusting his daggers into the attack, he successfully careened the blades to the side. The force of the blow pushed him off-balance. Kil pursued. His dirk stabbed down. The elf quickly shifted his legs and only suffered a small nick. Zakili knew he wouldn't gain his footing quick enough to stave off another thrust, so he threw himself into a backward roll. Just in time. Kil's blade narrowly missed tearing out his throat. Zakili rolled back to his feet a second later, his blades crossing in front of him.

"Fight on, my worthy opponent!" Kil said. "But it'll be in vain. This kingdom is doomed. Your elves are exhausted and will soon be overrun by my throng. Your people are barely holding out against my warriors. My army is more vast than you could ever imagine. At this very moment, the rest of my assassins storm in to lay the final crushing blow to your Silver Elves!"

"Too bad you won't be here to see it!" Zakili roared. The Flying Tigers slashed like silvery blurs. With equal fury, The Warlord jabbed and parried, narrowly knocking each dagger blow away before it could get to his throat.

The elf's left dagger jabbed in but was parried. His right slashed across. Kil sucked his belly in and barely missed being gutted.

Relentless, Zakili blitzed in, left dagger diving in low. Kil pounded it down. The elf's right slashed across again, forcing Kil to lunge backward. The elf leapt forward, his foot snapped out and slammed into the Warlord's chest, sending him stumbling backward and colliding with one of his own men. The collision righted Kil, but shoved his man into the lethal blade of his elf adversary, and that man's scream joined the piercing cacophony of battle.

Kil lunged, and jabbed his dirk at the prince's face. Zakili spun to the side. His daggers arced wide, one blocked the dirk, the other angled for Kil's ribs. A fiery dirk smacked the attack down. The Fangs of Hell sliced plunged for the elf's chest. Zakili intercepted that strike with his two daggers. The Warlord's left blade leaped up from a low angle, forcing the elf back.

"Come to me," Kil hissed. "Death awaits."

"You're right about that much," the elf agreed. "Your death."

Zakili's daggers went into a vicious blur as Kil's exploded in a dangerous fury. Daggers and dirks clashed and ground and rung out, echoing under the forest canopy. Moments later, still no victor, breathing hard and with sweat rolling down their brows, they pushed away, eyed each other and stalked in a wide circle.

"I don't want a dance," Zakili said. "I want a fight."

"And I want your head on the tip of my blade," Kil replied.

"Come and get it!"

The mighty foes clashed again, blades jabbing, slicing, clanging, and crashing, again and again, seeking an opening but finding none. The barrage of weapon blows came quick and heavy. The ringing of dagger against dirk drowned out the chaotic noise of battle around them.

In the distance, Zakili heard the anguished roar of another elf taken in battle. He glared at The Warlord. This man brought death and war into his Verdant Wood. If his elves didn't survive, he was determined that the warlord of these assassins wouldn't either. He stormed in. His daggers ripped across in a double chop. Kil started to bring his dirks in from the sides to strike the elf's open ribs but the speed of Zakili's attack afforded no time.

In desperation, Kil's dirks whacked across one, two, knocking the daggers aside. Zakili spun with the momentum, coming back in again. His daggers slashed sidelong for the assassin's face. The fiery dirks leaped up, parrying the daggers away at the last moment. With impossible skill, the dirks twirled in Kil's palm, and he plunged them at the elf's head. Zakili, crossed his blades, catching one dirk and quickly shoving it into the the other falling Fang, narrowly escaping having his eyes gorged out. Undaunted, Kil retracted and his blades jabbed in at the elf's midsection. The Flying Tigers, like silvery lightning, zipped across, parrying the deadly strikes.

"Ironfist comes!" one assassin said, spotting a distant throng stampeding their direction. The distraction cost him his life. An elf blade pierced his wicked heart. The doomed assassin's cry rallied the others, pushing them to new heights of savagery. The Lurking Shadows pressed in on the smaller elf contingent, condensing the battleground, squeezing the elves into tighter, less effective battle groups.

Zatrus the elf found himself steadily losing ground as four assassins singled him out; blade after blade after blade slashed at him. He did well to effectively ward off the multiple attacks, his own skills heightened from years of tutelage spent under Zakili. The attacks were wearing him down though, his breath coming hard and his twin blades moving slower. He had no opportunity to turn the tide. His multiple attackers kept him completely on the defensive. As he battled on, his arms grew heavier. Dreadfully, he remembered Zakili's words: Only with an offensive will you prove victorious. You'll never defeat your enemy with defense.

Zatrus, unable to counterattack, knew he would surely die.

A blade came in from his left. Zatrus parried it. A jab from the front. His left sword swiped across in time to block it. Another from his right slashed at him,

157

but just as he moved to counter this attack, in his peripheral vision, he spotted a blade plunging for his ribs from the left. He knew he could defend against one, but not both.

An elf leaped to his side, knocking away the blade diving for his ribs. The new elf thrust his sword forward suddenly, taking down one Shadow. The assassins refocused their attacks now that this newcomer had arrived. The elf was already driving at them with blurring chops and slices.

"Baliesto!" Zatrus cried, as he too joined in. Both he and Baliesto had once shared instruction under Zakili.

"At your service," Baliesto said as he raged against a pair of Zatrus' opponents. "I finished my adversary and saw you needed assistance. I don't recall you being present when we gathered with Navarro Silvinton. So, I knew you needed me."

"What are you talking about?" Zatrus scowled as he fought back the assassin who nearly took him down several times in this fray, finally able to work in his adroit attack sequences in amid his parries.

"Last night I received Jesus Christ as my Savior. I asked the Lord to forgive me of my sins. Live in my heart. If I die, I know my eternal destiny. I'm going to heaven.

"You, on the other hand, are doomed if I were to let you die before the Lord saves you."

"What!" Zatrus roared incredulously, but the dying scream of Baliesto's foe stopped him in mid-thought. Now it was one-on-one for the pair, indeed something Zatrus was greatly thankful for, but the foreign words of Baliesto echoed uncomfortably in his mind.

The growing thunder of hooves turned heads. The throng was upon them. Cheering loudly, the assassins, who hadn't expected such a ferocious battle from the elves, welcomed the added arsenal of Lurking Shadows. The victory cry of the assassins turned to dread when from the forest emerged not Shadows riding demon horses, but white chargers ridden by Silver Elves.

And led by one majestic man.

Navarro's contingent smacked into the pressing assassins like a great wedge, breaking them apart and dissecting their ranks with victorious accuracy. The rout was on. With renewed hope, the elves cut into the Lurking Shadow throng.

Kil wasn't the first to recognize the futility of remaining in battle. .

The Lurking Shadows must flee, The Warlord realized, *or they would all surely perish. The element of surprise had been destroyed. These driving elves must have defeated the detachment led by the jothenac.*

Zakili jabbed suddenly. Kil zipped his dirks crossways, barely parrying away the attack inches from piercing his heart. Kil's blades bounced off the clash and reversed angles coming low at the Elf Prince. Zakili's daggers easily batted them down. The Warlord's strike was hardly an offensive attack. It slowed the elf just enough for Kil to yank one man over and push him in the wild elf's direction.

158

Johnny Earl Jones

"On more favorable ground we'll finish this!" Kil declared, looking Zakili in the eyes before turning and disappearing into the confusion of the battling throng.

Zakili tried to take up chase, but three wicked Shadows engaged him. Summarily, the Elf Prince had finished them all. He wanted Kil!

Hearing an unearthly screech, he turned. A red-eyed ebony charger reared up, Kil riding its back. "Abandon the fight, my Lurking Shadows!" The Warlord cried. "We've been betrayed into the hands of our enemy! Flee now, for the day'll come when, beside The Master, we'll crush this foe!"

The assassins, who no longer overwhelmed the elves, readily complied. They deserted the battle and raced for their demon chargers. Many a Lurking Shadow never made it, cut down by pursuing elves.

By the time the sun fully rose into the clear Avundarian sky, the plague was removed from the Verdant Wood. Zakili roared in victory. The Silver Elves accompanied him with a corporate mighty cheer.

* * * * *

"He was nearly dead," Zakili said, stunned as the elf The Paladin had knelt before jumped to his own feet.

"He's healed me!" the elf Simbolan exclaimed. "My wounds were mortal. Now I feel better than I ever have!" He turned and bowed at Navarro's feet.

"Arise!" The Paladin commanded. "My friend, you were healed by the the power of God, not by me. If you'll bow, bow before the Lord Jesus Christ. I'll seek you once the elves have recovered from this wicked assault, and I'll share with you the knowledge and hope of the God who's so wondrously regenerated you.

"Now go. Find any who're in need and report back to me."

The elf shook his head gratefully before racing off, a beaming smile on his face.

Navarro staggered, but quickly righted himself before taking a deep breath.

"Paladin, you've healed many this day," Zakili said. "But do you still suffer a wound from battle?"

"No. I become drained when the Lord's healing power flows through my mortal frame. I'll be fine shortly."

"So, how many notches can you add to your pommel?" Zakili asked eagerly.

"None," The Paladin said, and the answer nearly knocked the elf over.

"You didn't kill a one of those fools?" Zakili screamed indignantly.

"I won't take the life of another man," The Paladin explained. "The whole purpose of my being isn't to kill people but to save them."

Zakili's mouth fell open from shock. "You didn't..?"

Navarro drew his sword which hadn't a trace of crimson. "I can't stain my blade with human blood," he confessed. He replaced his sword and raised his fist. "But there are quite a few incapacitated assassins lying around."

Zakili guffawed, although to Navarro it sounded more like a sigh of relief. "For a moment, I thought you were telling me you just stood around and watched."

"Never my friend. I love these elves almost as much as you do. I would defend them to the end."

The Elf Prince smiled and turned to his fighters. "Finish off any Shadows who still draw breath."

"Wait!" Navarro said, halting the eager elves.

"Wait? Wait for what?" Zakili questioned.

"The Lurking Shadows are murderers. The Silver Elves are not. Show their injured mercy."

"They showed none of my fallen elves mercy."

"The Silver Elves have character," Navarro emphasized. "The victory is won. To repay their wounded evil for the wickedness they've shown would be a great sin and a dark blot on your people's benevolent reputation."

Zakili stared hard at him for several moments, grunting, "All right, Paladin. What is it that you want?"

"Bring those Shadows suffering wounds to me. I'll heal them. Then without weapon, we'll release them to return back to their lair. The long walk across Avundar will give them plenty of time to appreciate the mercy of the Silver Elves."

"Navarro!" The Paladin heard from behind, breaking off his conversation with the Elf Prince. "Maengh looks like he's hurt bad. He suffered a vicious stab in the back."

Navarro turned, seeing Simbolan at the tree line assisting the limping Maengh his direction. The Paladin rushed to him and helped Simbolan rest him gently on the ground. Gingerly, he placed his hands over Maengh's wound and began to call out for God to send His mighty healing through the elf. He stopped suddenly, his warrior senses tingling as if danger was very close. He looked around and saw only the elves rushing busily about on the open field. Seeing nothing threatening, The Paladin closed his eyes and prayed again, ignoring the warning signal from his senses.

* * * * *

It wasn't until the sun passed its zenith in the sky that the costs of the clash were summed up. Scores of Lurking Shadows had been slain in battle, not to mention dozens of the merchants who had incessantly trespassed in Verdant Wood. But strangely enough, most of them were found with an assassin's knife in their back.

Over 20 healed assassins had been escorted off the battlefield.

The losses to the elves were not as great. Less than thirty lost their lives, but the results were devastating. New bloodthirsty recruits could always be found to replace the lost assassins, but the elf fighters who gave their lives defending their home were gone forever.

"We're a family," Zakili told the assembly of elves that afternoon. "We'll take care of each other. Those who've lost loved ones won't go without. We'll all provide for one another. I'll assist in every way and as often as I can. As Prince of Verdant Wood, I give you my vow."

Candace listened to Zakili, admiring his fortitude. She compared her previous presuppositions of royalty with the actions of Prince Zakili. To her shame, she recognized she had stereotyped anyone who bore a noble's title. Zakili was not the selfish, stuffy person she always thought princes to be.

She turned and looked about until she spotted a lone figure leaning against a tree, one foot propped back against the trunk, his eyes closed and head down. Navarro was praying. She felt a strange twinge of emotion. So sedate as he leaned against the tree, The Paladin radiated strength. Other than her father, she never thought any man to possess such unspoken might.

But she felt something more than admiration for The Paladin. She felt... She shook her head vigorously to clear her thoughts, sending her golden hair tossing. She couldn't feel that way about a paladin.

Yet, she did.

* 12 *
REGROUPING

Zakili's face was stolid as he watched a torch ignite each funeral pyre. The evening sky was striped with billows of smoke. The tongues of flame consumed the piled wood and fallen warrior indiscriminately. Tiny embers took wing and fluttered away into eternity.

Navarro stood at his friend's side without words. What could be spoken to comfort the Prince of Verdant Wood after twenty-six of his people were murdered by the Lurking Shadows? What could he do to take away the pain?

There was nothing, he knew. The Paladin only hoped his presence would lend the elf strength. Looking to his friend, Navarro's heart weighed heavily. Zakili stood unblinking, speechless. There was no sign of rage on the elf's countenance but neither was there grief; however, The Paladin understood. Zakili was, after all, the commander of the elf defenders and the massive responsibility for the lost elves assuredly pressed down on the proud elf's shoulders.

Navarro turned his eyes back to the field and to the twenty-six flaming mounds. Yesterday, twenty-six elves were living, breathing, enjoying life, and an irreplaceable part of the Silver Elf community. Now they were no more, forever swept into eternity.

Further out on the plains another gigantic bonfire raged. This one, lit earlier, was constructed to destroy the bodies of the fallen invaders. No one gave that distant fire any notice.

As Navarro glanced around, he noticed the King was missing. When recovering the slain bodies of the elves, Gallatar hadn't been found. Could he have been captured? He doubted a disorganized, endangered mass of fleeing men would consider a captive a priority. Where was he?

Hearing the muffled sobbing of many elves behind him grabbed his attention, and thoughts of Gallatar left. Navarro's face grew grave. Sadness seemed so unnatural for the Silver Elves. Now grief overshadowed the disposition of the whole race. Death had slaughtered dozens in its savage jaws. *Death is a hideous thief,* The Paladin knew all too well, *stealing not only the lives of the wicked but those of the innocent.*

He'd seen the ruin and the wreckage left every time he departed from a scarred battlefield. Horribly, that same scene had replayed here, the last place he would've ever expected it.

The Paladin's heart broke when he thought that for some of the slain, death took far more than their lives.

As Navarro glanced back, he noticed several of the elves who had received Christ bravely put aside the sadness of their own slain family members to comfort those who lost loved ones. He knew they faced an uphill task when he caught the expressions on the majority of the elves' faces: grief and futility.

The burden of their loss nearly crushed Navarro's heart. The Christian elves tried their best to give words of consolation to families of the fallen, but their attempts seemed fruitless. They knew all the elves who were slain and were quite aware that the majority of them had shrugged off salvation days before. Those who rejected the gospel had dropped into a Christless eternity.

What could be said? They were in a better place? A lie. Outside Jesus they knew there was no hope in the afterlife.

Having faced the same scenario many times before, Navarro guessed the elves probably said nothing about eternity at all instead of the negative truth.

If he could find good in this sadness it was this: a handful of the slain were born again days prior to the attack. He knew they were in the Lord's presence at this moment.

Candace brushed up beside Navarro, gripping his shoulder firmly, comfortingly. The Paladin looked to her, and she began to offer encouragement but was speechless. Navarro understood. The despair was just too deep. Navarro offered a smile. She reciprocated, but tears welled up, and she hung her head, overwhelmed. Tenderly, Navarro placed his arm around her shoulder, and she fell into his chest, sobbing.

"Do you hear the cries of this people, Candace?" Zakili said, breaking his stony stare over the pyres. He walked up to her and gently grasping her arm. "Do you sense the grief which has swallowed the whole Silver Elf nation?"

Candace nodded sadly.

"It's only because of you that we have this," the elf said.

Candace looked to him in confusion.

"He's right," Navarro said. "There is sorrow here, and there is pain, but the Silver Elf nation still lives. Without your warning we would burn in an enormous pyre to an extinct people."

"We owe you a great debt of gratitude, my friend," Zakili said, bowing deeply.

She smiled modestly, closed her eyes, and lay her weary head back against Navarro's broad chest, gripping his strong arms for support. The past two days emotionally and physically drained her. She left home in disappointment only to happen upon Kil's fearsome band and overhear their wicked scheme which led to this terrible time.

Her eyes sprang open as she realized her actions. What was she doing? She shouldn't be holding on to this man. He was a Paladin. Drawing on her memory of conversations with the Elf Prince, she recalled that Navarro made a vow to abstain from women. Though her actions were innocuous, she understood they could easily be misconstrued. She sneaked a glance up at him, but he didn't protest. He stared out over the blazing pyres.

"The loss of the fallen will grieve us for a long time," Navarro said. "They should never have died. They had centuries of life ahead of them." His face grew stern. "Human greed. All this evil perpetrated because of the merchant's contemptible greed. They wanted Lifespring, and their wicked schemes cost the lives of twenty-six elves undeserving such a fate."

Zakili's daggers leapt into his hands, his eyes wild. "I didn't see the body of Methlon among the pile of corpses," the elf growled. "He's responsible for this! He and that assassin Kil!" With arms spread wide to the multiple pyres, he roared into the night. "More than a score of brave fighters' lives ended, victims because they defended their own home. Yet craven Methlon and Kil still live! This should not be so!"

The Elf Prince turned to Navarro, daggers spinning. "They must die! If there be a God out there, I swear to him I'll not rest until I've destroyed them both!"

Navarro took a step forward to calm his friend, but Zakili's sisters fell in around him. The Paladin nodded, proud of the elf maidens for stepping up to the challenge of comforting their fiery brother.

"Be at peace for now," Senetta demanded gently. "We all want justice. But even if you could slay the whole remnant of the invading army it wouldn't bring back those who we've lost--"

"I don't want the rest of those fools," Zakili growled. "I want only Methlon and Kil!"

"Your paths will cross again soon, of that I'm confident," she assured, kissing her brother on the cheek. "But remember, the fight was not yours alone and neither is the burden of the grim consequences.

"Every fallen elf died valiantly for the survival of the Silver Elf nation. They willingly paid the price for our victory."

"My courageous brother," Monolique said, "We all backed you concerning the forest's defenses, trusted you, and you didn't let us down. You led us victoriously through this terrible assault. We've emerged scarred yet triumphant!"

Zakili's expression softened.

"And as we backed you in battle, we'll back you now in the aftermath," Saranisen added. "Our thoughts no longer linger about those evil men, my strong brother. Let's remember those who gave their lives for our freedom and our survival this last time. Bid our final farewells."

Zakili smiled gratefully to his sisters. "Rage and pain has reddened my eyes so that I saw only our adversaries. Forgive me for my irreverence to our courageous warriors.

"This is the time to honor them for their brave sacrifice. Vengeance will come. But as you, my sisters, have so eloquently pointed out, this isn't the time nor the place."

He turned and cast a quick glance to Navarro who started forward. With the pyres in the background, Navarro started the memorial for the fallen by asking all to bow their heads and kneel in prayer.

Navarro prayed and preached at many gravesides and pyre sites, but never was any so hard as this one. These twenty-six funeral pyres belonged to friends and Christian brothers. He knew those who received Christ now rejoiced at seeing their mighty Savior, but losing them grieved him sorely. Sobs of sadness from the surviving loved ones squeezed his heart.

With every word of prayer, every syllable of consolation and even into the

Bible recitation tears threatened, but The Paladin did well in holding back his emotions. The memorial service only lasted a few moments, the crackling of the burning wood filling the silence between Navarro's words. Then with a final prayer and final amen, it was all over. Navarro turned away from the throng and walked away into the darkness, his grief overcoming him, and tears raced hot down his cheeks.

His Christian brothers were at peace, he reminded himself again, and shrugged off his tears. It was the survivors who'd have to bear the scars. The attack, although an utter failure for the assassins, would haunt the minds of the elves forever. When was the last time their realm was invaded? Probably more than a century before the birth of his father's father. No elf could even remember the last time a foe trod into their domain. Navarro wagged his head sadly. Centuries of peace under the rule of the Elf Kings had suddenly been shattered.

"Elf Kings?" he considered. "Where is King Gallatar?"

Since Zakili's father hadn't been among the casualties, Navarro glanced back to the elves and panned the throng, looking for the salt-and-pepper head of hair or a stately gait, anything to give away the King's presence. Nothing.

Navarro approached his friend. "Where's your father?"

"Elsewhere?" Zakili answered, his tone uncertain.

"Elsewhere?" Navarro echoed, his brow furrowed. Zakili's lack of concern troubled him. Several days before, when he'd arrived in Verdant Wood, he witnessed Gallatar explode at his son. When the crisis rose against the elves, he watched father and son war against each other concerning the forest kingdom's defenses. He knew something ill brewed between the two. As long as he'd known Gallatar and Zakili, the two had shared a lively, respectful, and sometimes competitive relationship. Had their kinship been tainted with bitterness so quickly and so completely they'd lost all regard for each other?

"Look to the east!" an elf cried from among the throng, pointing toward the wide plains. "A company of riders is headed this way!"

The song of drawn weapons rang through the night.

With darkness fallen, Navarro couldn't see the figures the elf pointed out. Silver Elves had keen eyesight and could see shapes easier on the darkening field than he. Fearing the advancing figures assassins possessed to dare another campaign, Navarro ripped his sword from his scabbard. Behind him the elves formed defensively, willing to fight again Navarro knew, and die, if necessary, for their home.

Candace walked grimly to The Paladin's side.

With one arm, Navarro scooted her protectively behind him.

"What're you doing?" she protested. "If there's to be battle, I'm willing to fight!"

Glancing back, he smiled, immediately soothing her flustered expression into a gentle grin. "You're correct. You proved yourself on the battlefield."

"Yes I did," she said, accepting The Paladin's approval gladly and walking to his side once more, her cutlass drawn.

"Zakili, who is it?"

"Whoever it is, I see only five riders." He studied the shapes a moment longer. "Put your weapons away," he instructed the elves, receiving several unbelieving stares.

A few moments later the figures ambled up to the pyres; embers flew all about them. The tallest rider pressed his charger into a gallop and headed straight for the friends. An undercurrent of hushed awe rode the elven throng as the rider pulled short of them.

"It's King Gallatar!" several shouted.

Candace, Navarro, and Zakili stepped back and bowed respectfully. The King trotted his horse to them. Without even a word, the scowl on his face spoke volumes.

"What has happened here?" Gallatar finally demanded.

Zakili looked around as if the scene spoke for itself. "The army you said would never dare attack attacked!"

Gallatar sat speechless.

"We have defeated our foes, father. We emerged triumphant over our attackers."

"What of the pyres?"

"Our victory was not without cost. Twenty-six valiant warriors lost their lives defending our home. But if we hadn't been ready, if we hadn't acted on my instincts nor heeded the warning of the baron's daughter," he said, swinging his arm Candace's direction, "then you would now find the rotted remains of an extinct Silver Elf nation! But no, father. We live! Verdant Wood's still our home. The Silver Elves have emerged victorious. We paid a terrible, high price for our victory, but in the end we won!

"With the help of Navarro, Candace, and all the elves, I've preserved our people from annihilation!" Zakili turned to the silent crowd, raising his fist to the sky. "May the Silver Elf nation live forever!"

A great cheer exploded from the once-torpid crowd.

Gallatar turned to the other four riders as they drew near. They were his advisors.

"You were in on my son's schemes to remove me from Verdant Wood today," he accused, and by the expressions on their faces there was no denying it. "You coaxed me to travel to a phantom meeting at the Council of Rulers to give my son reign of my kingdom?"

"His plan was sound," one dared say. "The battle plan he showed us was phenomenal but needed the unhindered skills of every elf to be successful."

The others nodded in agreement.

Gallatar's angry stare fell heavy over them.

"And with you, Father remaining in the wood, there was no possibility to prepare our defenses," Zakili interjected. "You would never have permitted the elves to organize into a united front, because you stubbornly choose to believe no adversaries would dare attack the Silver Elves.

"That's why the advisors led you away. It was I who convinced them to deceive you, to lead you away from the forest. Once you were out of the way, I, as your son, used your authority, saying it was by your word that the elves should ready for battle. If your wrath is to fall anywhere, it should fall on no others but me."

In the illumination from the raging pyres, Zakili watched the anger escalate in his father's countenance. The Elf King turned from his son to his advisors, his face twisted in anger. They shrank back from the king's dangerous glare. Gallatar turned back to Zakili, snarling, but the prince stood unimpressed, one hand resting on his sheathed dagger.

"What's the problem with you, Father? Are you enraged because you weren't controlling all the affairs? Was it because I misappropriated your royal authority to mobilize our people? If that's the case, then it's rightly so, but look Father! The Silver Elf race is preserved!"

Gallatar's heated gaze dropped when he realized there was no retort against Zakili's argument. He felt the weight of stares from the entire assembly of elves as they watched the interaction. He urged his horse off to the side. "Follow me, son."

Dismounting from his steed when the two were a considerable distance from the crowd, Gallatar locked stares with Zakili. The Elf Prince observed his father suspiciously, noticing the gentle smile on his face appeared forced.

"That was a brave thing you did, Zakili. You saved our people and our home, albeit at the cost of more than a score of our fighters. You were quite ingenious in the way you removed me from the scene to masquerade as my purported mouthpiece..."

Zakili saw where this monologue was leading.

"...You're a crafty and manipulative individual, let me grant you that. And this will be the last time you use your trickery on my elves! Henceforth, your voice will never have weight to establish a directive of mine! Do you understand? My elves will be commanded to heed no words unless they come from the lips of my advisors or myself. And they'll be expressly forbidden to follow any of your schemes!"

"My schemes led the elves in a resounding victory over an enemy bent on annihilating us!"

"Enough! I have spoken."

"The elves live to see another day," Zakili said, wagging his head in shock. "Do you not find joy in that? What's happened to you, Father?"

* * * * *

Kil stormed through the huge chamber, shoving over a marble statue in his way. His fiery dirks slashed into the nearest pile of coins, scattering gold across the floor. His face contorted in rage. None of his fearless men dared approach, lingering cautiously in the shadows and shrinking back whenever their leader drew near. They knew Kil was enraged enough to slice open the throat of the first who got in striking range.

For good reason. The Lurking Shadows had been defeated, their assault on Verdant Wood an utter failure. The flawless plan to take the elves unexpectedly and slay them in their own beds had turned completely against them. Instead, the Shadows became victims of a surprise attack.

"How could we have been defeated!" Kil roared.

None of the men dared answer. They saw the insane look in his dark eyes and understood it wouldn't take much for him to snap into a bloodthirsty killing frenzy.

A guttural roar tore from his innermost being, rage and fury resonating like the howl of a ferocious beast. His fist shot out and slammed the wall. "The Lurking Shadows have never been defeated!"

He stomp another lap around the room. His fiery blade lashed out and took the head off a golden statue which was part of payment for the assassins' services. Ironfist thought Kil would burst if he didn't release his anger soon.

Then suddenly Kil stopped, his visage surprisingly serene. That troubled the jothenac more than his rage. Now he questioned whether he should've rode out of Verdant Wood to the Shadows' lair. Sometimes he didn't know what to expect from this mysterious human. The Dark Sorcerer Zeraktalis had sent him to *serve* this man to establish an outpost for the sorcerer in this land. Ironfist didn't understand why; and he considered the word "serve" hardly applicable concerning obedience to any human. But in the short year he'd known Killion, he gained great respect, even fear, of him. This assassin was as dangerous as any monstrosity he'd ever known.

"Candace," Kil said, slicing the arm off the decapitated statue, blowing apart his peaceful facade. "Candace warned the elves of our coming."

All became deathly silent.

"I saw the woman riding among the elves who conquered Ironfist's contingent," he spat, firing a heated gaze the jothenac's way. Ironfist faded farther back into the shadows. "She was the woman, the baron's daughter, who was led into our lair and then escaped bearing news of our invasion.

"She was the one Stoman led into the den."

Kil scanned the throng and, with not a directive given, the crowd separated as a reluctant figure was pushed to the forefront. Stoman. Gracefully, Kil strode over. Stoman winced as those closest faded back. With a wide smile, The Warlord casually laid his arm about Stoman's shoulders.

"You've been my right-hand man for several years, one of my most efficient spies, one of my most flawless assassins. Always have you paid attention to detail, conducting our affairs effectively and secretively.

"Like a brother."

Stoman smiled weakly.

Kil's arm whipped around Stoman's neck suddenly and squeezed. Stoman gasped as his air was suddenly cut off.

"I lost half my army this morning, fool! And all because of your one blunder! It was you, Stoman, who led Candace to our lair. Because of you, she heard our invasion plans against the Silver Elves! And it was because of you we were slaughtered by the elves this morning, by elves who should've never known anything about our attack!"

Kil tossed him to the side. Stoman clutched his throat and gulped for breath.

"This is a shameful loss," Kil stated calmly, his voice echoing throughout the lair. "This is the first time The Lurking Shadows have ever failed. It's something I can't let go unpunished."

He glared down at wheezing Stoman. "Draw your sword."

Stoman, in a humbled position on his knees, stared up fearfully to his warlord.

"You have served me faithfully for many seasons. Arise now and draw your weapon. I give you the privilege to die like a man."

Paralyzed with fright, Stoman didn't move from his knees.

"Yet, you may live," Kil offered, jabbing his dirks back into their scabbards. He removed his weapon belt and draped it over the outstretched arm of the headless gold statue. "All you have to do is defeat me, an unarmed man."

Stoman understood his demise was near. Kil played "cat and mouse" with him. His hand didn't go near his weapon; he'd seen The Warlord destroy enough victims in this brutal game to understand.

Reaching for his sword was the worst mistake he could ever make. Unfortunately for Stoman, not drawing his blade was just as deadly.

"Draw your sword!"

"I cannot. I won't wield my blade against you, my liege."

"Stand you coward! Attack! Or I'll rip your own sword from your own scabbard and slay you with it!"

Stoman shrank back, terror-striken. He hoped Kil was bluffing and all his years of loyal service would prove sufficient to overrule Kil's rage. "I will not, sir."

Stoman's hope died with him. Kil pounced on him. Three quick punches bloodied Stoman's face and sent him sprawling to the floor. The Warlord grabbed a handful of hair and dragged Stoman back to his feet. His open-palmed right hand slammed into Stoman's nose, and the sound of shattered bone echoing throughout the den. Kil let go, and Stoman crumbled to the floor in a lifeless heap.

Kil wiped the blood from his hands on the dead man's clothing, then turned to the silent crowd. "My right-hand man is dead," Kil said. "Throw his body into the street." Two warriors separated from the crowd and dragged Stoman to the secret door. "I will need another," the Warlord said.

The crowd stirred restlessly, nervously. Not one of the assassins had less than superior skills, but they all feared Kil's prowess. The Warlord was a heartless killer, his conscience seared. They knew he'd kill any of them in but a few heartbeats if they stepped out of line. None wished to invoke their leader's wrath.

None wished to be so close to make an easier target.

"Methlon," Kil called.

"I'm here."

"You," Kil said. "You will be my second-in-command."

Several of the assassins snickered privately, smartly holding their peace. For Killion, there was no second-in-command. All authority belonged to him. His "second-in-command" was no more than his personal lackey.

Methlon looked at him dumbly.

"Come forth and stand before the throng, my new right-hand man."

"Right-hand man?" Methlon asked. "I hired you! And I paid a good amount of gold to do it! You're the hireling, not I. I demand my gold returned so my men and I may return to our merchandising."

"You don't know what you say, my newest warrior. The riches are mine."

"What betrayal is this!" Methlon screamed, his hand going for his sword.

"That's not a wise choice," Kil said, nodding to the trail of blood left by Stoman's corpse. He reached for the gold statue and strapped on his belt. His dirks sprung into his hands, and the blades ignited with tongues of fire. Methlon's hand quickly dropped away from his sword's hilt.

"Now," Kil continued. "Regarding you leaving with your men, have you counted your companions since our return? Barely a handful live. Your lieutenants have all been slain in battle. Without your gold and without your band of merchants what life will you have outside The Lurking Shadows?"

"The Lurking Shadows who couldn't even surprise a band of sleeping elves?" Methlon jeered.

Kil's hand snapped out, clutching Methlon's clavicle, squeezing, and driving the man to his knees. Methlon screamed. The incapacitating hold felt like it would snap his collarbone.

"They weren't asleep," Kil growled through Methlon's cries, his hot breath heavy in his face. "We learned from my dead companion they had an informant! Never doubt the prowess of my assassins again!"

"My apologies," Methlon squeaked through gritted teeth.

Kil shoved him to the floor and turned back to his gathered assassins. "These elves haven't seen the last of us. We'll come against them again, but next time, they will be crushed!"

"Arise Methlon and follow me. We must report our failure to The Master. I want you to see your new ruler."

"Master?" Methlon whispered fearfully to himself. "There's someone more evil and powerful that even Kil must answer?" Although every fiber screamed against Methlon's actions, he fell in behind the Warlord, gently nursing his bruised collarbone. He knew his only other option was death, but with the downward spiral his life was taking, death began to sound more and more appealing.

* * * * *

Leaning against a young oak at the border of Verdant Wood, Navarro stared at the million dots of starlight that twinkled over the wide plains. It was late, and he was alone out on the field, the darkness crowding in on him as the funeral pyres died down to nothing more than glowing embers. Everything was calm on the plains, giving Navarro much time to think. He tried to talk to God but this thoughts were too jumbled, the horrible events of the morning incessantly intruding his mind and he found it impossible to push them away.

Although a trained and deadly fighter, Navarro didn't delight in battle. He despised it. He wished somehow all evil could be exterminated and the societies of the nations could live in unbroken peace. An experienced warrior, he realized that dream was impossible. Forlornly, he laughed at an old memory.

When he was several years younger, he was a stalwart lad with an unquenchable fire to vanquish all the wickedness of the world. He thought there was a distinct line between those who were good and those who were evil. With unequaled fervor and with the help of whatever kingdom he aided, he ripped into innumerable ranks of bloodthirsty monsters. He decided he'd eradicate all evil one monster at a time. In his short years as a Paladin, he realized three great mistakes with his intrepid vision.

First, evil never ceased; every nook and every cave forever birthed forth monsters thirsty for blood.

Second, he realized every man had the potential to initiate evil. Through the prophet Jeremiah, God's Word proclaimed the heart of mankind as desperately wicked.

Last, the lines between good and evil were more blurred than he'd at first envisioned. Oftentimes, the adversaries had spies peppered among the forces of goodly folks.

Navarro shook those painful thoughts from his mind, praising God that Candace was in the enemy's camp to overhear their schemes. He was indeed thankful for her warning and Zakili's strategic acumen. Sadly, any celebration for the victory came up empty when his eyes fell on the glowing embers of the twenty-six pyres.

His senses tingled, and he spun away from the tree. Invinitor leapt into his hands. Someone or something closed in from behind, and he stared hard into the dark shadows to discover the approacher.

"It's only me," a voice called out. Although he couldn't see the individual, the voice brought a smile to his face. He dropped his sword back into its scabbard.

"Good evening, Candace," he saluted politely, sweeping low before her.

"Please don't bow to me."

"Very well," he said, shrugging his shoulders. "I pray you feel better after you got some rest. I know the past few days have been exhausting for you, body and soul."

Candace pulled away from the shadows and drew closer, the glow of the stars playing off her golden tresses, causing her hair to glisten surrealistically. "I couldn't sleep."

Navarro chuckled. "That's funny. When we were standing out on the plains I thought you might doze off leaning against my chest."

She smiled, glad the darkness hid the blush of her cheeks. "I was drained, just as I was tired when I laid down in the bed at the housetree, but despite every effort I remained awake. I'm sure you know, when your mind's racing with confusing thoughts, sleep won't come."

"Would you care to share your thoughts?"

She couldn't answer at first, the corners of her mouth drawing up into an amused smile. She simply was unable to get over Navarro's supreme courtesy; inside and out he was the purest gentleman. Never had she met a man quite like him. "It was the battle today," she said, walking closer. "But I noticed you've been out here for a long time looking at the fires. You must be occupied with such thoughts, as well."

Navarro's eyes fell sadly. "It brings me grief that the peace the elves have enjoyed for centuries was shattered so completely. My heart aches for these fallen elves and their families. But thinking of the souls who were lost, those who died rejecting the salvation Jesus freely offers, crushes my spirit. I keep questioning what more I could've done. I should've witnessed longer and harder to the elves before the battle. I should've taken down more enemies on the battlefield..."

"Navarro, you were a one-man army in that battle," Candace interrupted. "You couldn't have done more. And I was there when you shared the gospel with the elves the night before the attack. God used you to proclaim the message of salvation plainly and mightily. Out of that crowd, many were saved!

A number of those who fell had no hope for eternity if you hadn't shared."

"I know Candace. But for those who died without Christ, I would readily trade my own life that they could have theirs back. That they might have a second chance."

"Don't say such a thing! There would be people who would miss you just as desperately as any of the fallen."

"Thank you," Navarro answered, but Candace understood his response was just a brush off.

"You know what I say is true," she argued. "Zakili would not be Zakili without you there to temper him. The Elf King also seems to hold you in high regard." Candace giggled at her next thought. "And from what I've heard, Zakili's sisters would definitely be devastated.

"And I would miss you."

"You barely know me," he said, staring up to the starry night. "Besides, I talk of a hypothetical situation. The past is the past. It cannot be changed."

"How long have you been out here?" she asked, strategically changing the subject.

"Since the memorial. It seems whenever I start reflecting, time escapes me." He looked to the stars. "By the shifting of the constellation it must be well into early morning. I have been out here quite a while."

"But in a time of such tragedy, why do you choose seclusion? You've been out here alone the whole night."

"I can think more clearly when I get alone."

"I'm sorry. I didn't realize I was disturbing you."

"No, you're not. Having you here isn't a distraction at all. In fact, I welcome your visit."

"So why so much privacy? Especially after this horrible incident? I've seen you enjoy your friends' company, and they're encouraged by you. Why do you not gain strength from them and lend your strength in this dark hour? You don't bear the burden of this alone."

"You don't understand, Candace. I'm a Paladin, a warrior whose purpose is to shore up the forces of good when they are in need. Throughout the preparations for the memorial I encouraged the elves and prayed with the grieving. I poured out my soul to those who needed comfort, but now after aiding as much as I could, I exhaust my grief in the way I know best.

"I choose to do this alone. What good would it do if I go back to Elfstay and bring discouragement?

"I feel life is an awesome adventure, but its heartaches can drive me to dejection if I let it. The last thing anyone needs to see is a crestfallen Christian, the one person who should have victory despite the discouraging events of life. I simply needed a brief time to defeat my own sadness so I could be a strength to others."

"The tragedy today grieved my soul as well," Candace confessed. "Maybe that was why I wanted to come out here to see you. After all, iron sharpens iron, the Bible says."

Navarro laughed lightheartedly. "You are quite the encourager, young lady. Listen to you reasoning with me from the Scriptures. I like it.

"And now let me encourage you, Candace. You played probably the most vital role in this victory. Had you not warned us of the coming onslaught, that mighty assassin army unquestionably would've destroyed us all. But cautioning us was only the beginning. I saw you fight. Your swordsmanship was superb. Remind me never to pick a fight with you."

She blushed.

"Just as impressive was your..." he balked, "...your spells."

"Spells?"

Navarro shrugged.

"Oh!" she exclaimed, remembering her preternatural ability to tear the huge viking's sword free of his hands. "That wasn't a spell."

"Really?" Navarro asked. "I would like to hear more."

"I'm not sure how it happened, but I can tell you one way it *did not* was through sorcery. I am born again; I will never venture into the black arts of magic. I sensed the dread in your tone, but you've no need to be concerned. Do you know what I think it is?"

"Please tell."

"You might think this is crazy, but I think it must be some special gift the Lord has given me."

"Interesting."

"Yes. And sending the viking's sword airborne was not the first instance. It seems here in the past few days I have needed the Lord more than ever as I went from one danger to another. Each time there seemed no way out, but when I cried out to God He opened a door of escape or moved the danger far from me."

"Every Christian is given a unique ability from God," Navarro said. "But I have never seen one manifested so tangibly and mightily as yours.

"It seems so mysterious how God equips some of his children with various abilities," he said, winking playfully. "But even though God has given you such a great gift, you're so modest. Yet so potent. I only wish I had a mystery akin to yours to increase my prowess."

"Navarro, it is completely beyond my understanding..." Candace started but let that thought trail away, seeing the opening she sought. "What is your mystery, Navarro?"

"Explain."

"You're a Paladin. Tell me why you chose such a dangerous lifestyle."

"Believe it or not, the choices of my early adult years turned me in a direction completely opposite where the Lord has brought me to now."

Candace moved in closer. "I'm listening."

"The Lord saved me from a hellion lifestyle, Candace. It's a long story."

"I have all night."

Under the starry sky, the two sat down on the plush grassy field, Navarro reclining back and cupping his hands behind his head. Propping herself up on one elbow, Candace lay down and listened intently.

"When I became a man as a teenager, I wanted nothing to do with Jesus or with the church. Reading the Bible was the last thing I would've ever done. Having riotous parties and chasing women was my whole purpose in life.

"And fighting. So for a stint I became a sailor, working alongside my father. He was, and may still be, the captain of his own cargo schooner, the fastest vessel on the seas at the time. The myth of a sailor having a woman in every port was something I made a reality, and I admit that to my own shame.

"But more importantly for me at the time, my travels forged relationships with combat masters. I spent every spare moment learning different fighting styles. With unequaled zeal, I practiced and mastered my skills to a point where I rivaled my mentors. So for several years, my life consisted of nothing but drinking, carousing, and brawling.

"But I'll always remember that in a number of ports we moored, my grandfather would come aboard and visit us. Unfortunately, my father wanted me to have as little contact with him as possible. But an impressive man he was.

"Although aged, his stamina and his physique outshone even Dad. But whenever I got the rare chance of talking with him, he always talked about Jesus, like He was a living person he talked to face-to-face every day.

"His excitement for Christ always captivated me. It seemed so substantial.

"Grandfather was obsessed about God's might and favor, never bragging about himself, which was all I'd ever heard from the other sailors and combat masters. But it was more than his speech--it was his way of life. He was a man of integrity. He never cursed, never got drunk, and even though Grandma passed away, he didn't go to bed with other women. I found all of that inconceivable.

"So I made it a point to learn as much about him as I could. He explained some family history, incessantly shared salvation through Christ and told war stories--many war stories. That's what got my attention. To my surprise some of these war tales happened within the past couple of years, but even more shocking were the allusions he made to battles he would be involved in within the near future. I was amazed. Grandfather was a warrior.

"He was more than a warrior. He was a Paladin, a holy fighter.

"One day, he granted me permission to handle his blade. It was incredible. Flawless. Sharper than anything I ever wielded. He took it back quickly. No one without a pure heart had ever born this weapon. The Sword of the Lord he called it. And although my memory is foggy on what it looked like, it reminds me a lot of Invinitor."

Navarro patted his sheathed blade.

"Go on," Candace said, listening intently.

"Well, one day he told me he was going to give me the Sword of the Lord. He was actually going to give it to me! I was excited at first, until he reached into his pack and pulled out a Bible. 'This is the true Sword of the Lord,' he said, 'more powerful than any blade this world ever forged.' He wanted me to have his Bible, led me to different passages of the Bible where I could begin my exploration, and then told me he'd be praying for me. That was the last time I saw him.

"In deference to him I began reading the Bible. Minimal at first, but the more I read, the more interested I became. I realized I was not alone in this world. I read about God's love for me, I discovered He cared for me and He thought about me all the time.

"Above all, Almighty God became a man in the person of Jesus Christ to die for my sins, then of His own power rose again from the dead three days later. It made me wonder about things beyond this life, particularly what would happen to my soul when I died. I quickly realized the one thing I couldn't defeat was death. Then one day it finally made sense. I was delving into the epistle to the Romans when the Spirit of God convicted me of my sins and my desperate need for Jesus Christ as my Savior.

At that point I really wasn't sure what to do. Faintly, I remembered Grandfather telling me receiving Christ as my Savior was as easy as praying to Him, repenting of my sins, and confessing Jesus with my words, and believing in my heart. And that's what I did!"

Candace beamed. "Praise God! And what a change He has made in your life!"

"Yes He has!"

"But..?" she started, smiling sheepishly.

Navarro raised an eyebrow.

"But what drove *you* to become a Paladin."

"That's the easy part," he laughed. "I've always had the drive to be the best and seek opportunities where I could be useful. The Lord placed that drive in me. I'd used it for corrupt reasons before. He took that same desire and directed me into Christian service. And I think it was no accident the first Christian I met was a man named Salvator, a Paladin who lived with passion for Christ and helped me mature in my faith. Once he thought I was ready, he introduced me to the Brotherhood of Holy Warriors. He knew I earnestly desired to become a paladin, sensed the Lord was calling me and had prepared me. As actively as I possibly could, I wanted to serve the Christ who saved my soul. The best way was to become a Holy Paladin."

"I've heard much about Paladins, but have never met one until you. And until I met you, Paladins never intrigued me. But you being a Paladin is a mystery to me."

"I don't understand."

"Living for the Lord is a vibrant, exciting adventure. I know because I, too, am a Christian. But I also know you're a handsome man. So my question is this: does being a Paladin mean you refrain from relationships with females?"

Navarro's face screwed up oddly, and he laughed. "Zakili sent you out here! He didn't get the answer he wanted from me, obviously, so he sent you to get it for him. You've been talking to Zakili, haven't you?"

Candace smiled gently, seeing the stark embarrassment in The Paladin's eyes, hoping she hadn't humiliated him with her bold question. "No, Zakili didn't say anything. My heart has been talking to me."

* * * * *

"Where are we?" Methlon demanded, his voice coming out in a nervous squawk.

Kil led him down a lonely side corridor within the assassin's lair. At the end of the corridor was a sealed door which the Warlord carefully unlocked and opened, revealing a dark passageway. Kil entered. Methlon grabbed a nearby torch from its sconce for light. Kil slapped it from his hand.

"Follow me," Kil growled.

"What about some light?"

Kil's dirks leaped into his hands. "Follow me now."

The Warlord marched in with Methlon tagging behind apprehensively. The door closed behind them, causing the merchant leader to jump. Darkness enveloped them completely. With arms held out in front of him, Methlon prodded along, advancing cautiously as he listened for the footsteps of his new leader. Understanding the stealthy prowess of the man, he knew Kil could walk without making the slightest noise. The only reason Methlon heard footsteps was because The Warlord purposefully provided them as a beacon.

A long minute passed in that corridor, but they kept walking. By now, Methlon hoped his eyes would've adjusted to the dark, but the blackness was so thick he could see nothing. His heart began to beat faster. Fear closed in. He imagined The Warlord led him into a trap, an act of revenge for offering The Lurking Shadows such a deadly assignment. He had no reason to trust this man Kil who had stolen all his riches and not completed the task he was paid. His steps began to drag.

Why did he continue walking down this unlit corridor with this dangerous

176

Lifespring

assassin? He'd much rather turn around and march out of Kil's lair, and keep on walking out of the town of Senadon. But he knew if he tried, he'd have a knife blade buried in his back. Unless he was willing to accept death, Methlon knew there was no escape from The Lurking Shadows.

"Stop!" Kil ordered, shattering the silence. "We're here."

Methlon didn't question him. He couldn't see a thing. *How did Kil see anything in this dark corridor?* he wondered. Listening for Kil's next move, he heard a sharp rustling noise as if a piece of linen was being yanked away.

The hall was suddenly illumined as a huge rectangle blazed to life. Methlon was happy for the light at first. But when he gazed at the mirror-like device, he shrank back at the sight of the eerie swirling mists. They looked like they'd shatter the glass holding them and spill out into the passageway. He smelled sulfur and reasoned he was staring into the heart of the abyss. His soul grew heavy, almost like it was being crushed by evil-inspired fear.

"No demons," he heard Kil mumble dreadfully under his breath. "Draw near," was the next command Methlon heard, and he obeyed. "What you're looking into is a sorcerer's mirror. Only with this device can we communicate with The Master. Be cautious. When The Master is wroth, his rage can radiate through this instrument. Today the explosion of his anger would likely dispel this entire building."

"Why are we just standing here? Do we just stand around and wait to be dispelled?"

"Silence fool! Prepare to bow before the future despot of the world!"

Methlon did indeed fall speechless and panicked as the mirror flashed brilliantly, then crackled, before being engulfed in complete darkness, blackening the corridor again.

"We didn't have to wait long."

"What happened?" Methlon peeped. Kil didn't answer, forcing him to look back in the direction of the mirror. When he did he nearly fell over in fright. The veil of darkness was pierced as a pair of flaming eyes opened.

"My Master," Kil whispered, falling to one knee.

"Has it been done?" a booming voice asked from the mirror.

"No, my Master."

"WHAT!" the voice exploded, nearly toppling over Kil. If Methlon hadn't been so paralyzed with fear, he would dash down the hall at full speed.

"Don't destroy us, Master. The Lifespring is guarded by an extremely adroit race of elves. Silver Elves they are called. Because of a fatal mistake by one of my men, whom I've already punished with death, the elves were warned of our coming invasion. They were ready for us and defeated us."

"Then why do you still live?"

Kil said nothing. The sorcerer had commanded the capture of the spring. The Warlord knew Zeraktalis didn't accept the claim of defeat from his subordinates until every fighter was dead. Kil and only half the assassins he took with him escaped with their lives. The Warlord had seen the jaws of defeat closing on his

Lurking Shadows and wasn't willing to be cut down in a losing effort. Rather than suffering certain death against the elves, he opted to take his chances with the Dark Sorcerer.

"My forces come shortly," the booming voice announced, shaking Kil from his thoughts. "But you, Warlord Killion, have not been relieved of your responsibilities. Prepare the way for my arrival. Regroup the assassins and enlist more, even if only as fodder. Soon my monsters will emerge in your land. Don't fail me this time!"

The glowing eyes went black. A lightning bolt exploded from the heart of the mirror. Methlon saw it slam into Kil and hurl him through the air, then all was dark in the corridor again.

"Kil?" Methlon whispered, too fearful to move. A flood of thoughts raced through his mind. If Kil was dead, maybe he could escape this town without having to be wary of lurking assassins for the rest of his life.

Another consideration came to mind. Were he to exit this corridor without Kil, The Lurking Shadows might find pleasure in his slow death. He'd seen the looks in their eyes and knew they would enjoy nothing more than torturing the man who hired them for such a failure as Verdant Wood. "Kil?" he called again. "Are you dead?"

The sound of shifting somewhere near him in the darkness signaled to Methlon The Warlord was moving.

"If my fealty were any less, The Master would have disintegrated me. You cannot imagine the pain of his wrath. Next time I must succeed or die. But I have a plan. I know exactly who I can manipulate against those accursed elves!"

* * * * *

His eyes blazing, Zeraktalis turned away from his sorcerer's mirror. "The fool has not secured Lifespring!"

From the shadows of the dark chamber mighty Krylothon emerged. The usurper knew what that meant. With eager flames burning in his spider-like eyes, his leathery wings stretched ominously wide, each wing tip nearly scraping the opposite sides of the chamber.

"The energy of Lifespring is the key to infinite power. It's central to releasing the demon lord Diabolicus from the chains of the abyss. I must have the elves' spring! My plans will have to be modified."

"The creaturesss yet fight among themssselvesss," Krylothon hissed. "The throng growsss ressstlesssss!"

"It's time to unleash them upon the unsuspecting land of Avundar. They'll succeed where the humans have failed. They will destroy the Silver Elves and capture Lifespring, and with its power, we will unchain the mightiest forces of hell!

"Ready the monsters! It's time to turn our army loose on the godly. Finally the brutes' hunger will be sated when they taste the blood of the people of Avundar!"

* 13 *
DRUMS OF DOOM

Lightning ripped the sky in half then boomed into oblivion, shaking the earth below. Baricon the burly giant chieftain with the bald, tattooed head halted his march through the forest suddenly, staring awestruck into the swirling, electrified clouds. Another bolt tore the darkness, followed by an explosion of thunder, knocking leaves into the wind and sending bats flying frantically away from their shaken perches.

"The Master is summonin' power from the Prince of Darkness!" Baricon roared to the clan of giants following him.

"It looks like I am followin' ye to me own destruction!" one giant complained. A branch of lightning ripped across the backside of the mountain, trailed by an earth-shaking explosion, accentuating the behemoth's fear.

"We have been commanded t' come!" Baricon reminded him, sweeping his arm wide to indicate the rest of the giants as well.

"Why do we have t' come runnin' at his bidding?" another giant asked. "Ye're the boss."

Lightning tore the sky again.

"Are ye so dull-brained?" Baricon screamed, charging over and getting in the other giant's face. "Ye saw with yer own two eyes how The Dark Sorcerer rules the slilitroks, and ye watched when he commanded them t' tear Sheklok to pieces! I will obey and live! If ye don't wish t' obey his bidding, ye tell him!"

A mighty gust of wind surged against the chieftain, nearly causing him to stumble. He felt a strange chill as the winds swirled with a wretched, repulsive aura, and he roared in excitement.

"The time has come!"

"What are ye talkin' about, Baricon!"

"This is the season The Dark Sorcerer's promised us years ago!" Baricon roared again, thrusting his huge fist to the sky. "We are soon t' be grinding men's bones with our back teeth. We're soon t' be destroyin'. The Master's preparin' the way for armies o' monsters and demons together to arise and choke out the goodly, so evil shall reign forever!"

"How'll this happen?" one hulking giant asked.

"Look!" Baricon instructed, pointing straight ahead through the branches to their destination. The giants stared beyond the canopies of the twisted trees, at the looming apparition of rocky Mount Gloom. Sprouting from the top of the mountain like some perverted blossom, the Black Fortress, tall and jagged, pierced the flashing maelstrom.

"This is the stronghold of The Dark Sorcerer?" one giant asked as the behemoths continued their trek.

"It's a place o' darkness and evil," Baricon said. The thought of the Black Fortress made even his wicked heart shudder. "I've been there once. The place reeks o' death and demons. Meself couldn't imagine a place more wicked than that."

As the giants cleared the jungle, the majestic and evil splendor of Mount Gloom came into full view, and what a dreadful sight it was. Lightning tore the darkness once and again, illuminating the pointed spires of the Black Fortress. More than one giant who had never witnessed the sorcerer's stronghold stood with mouth agape. Baricon told many a rumor about that place over the years, the most frequent, of its origin. From powerful Zeraktalis' sorcery alone, it was told, the mountain gave birth to the monstrous, multiple-armed Black Fortress. And any of the giants who doubted suddenly became believers when they experienced the fear of the awesome sight.

Drawing closer to the base of the mountain, the clan spotted a sight far more dreadful than the apparition of the Black Fortress itself. Grunts, roars and howls filled their ears. Several of the giants balked, paralyzed with unbelief.

"Goblin guts!" one giant cursed.

Baricon scanned the mountain's foothills, seeing the grounds crawling with activity. "Look at 'em all," he breathed, stunned.

"Goblin guts!" the giant behind him cursed again.

Mighty Baricon waved his clan forward, the fearless giants following his lead cautiously. The giant chieftain was overwhelmed with the power of The Dark Sorcerer who was able to bring this impossible assemblage together. Milling about the foothills were wicked legions of every foul race inhabiting the island Genna Fiendomon. Restlessly, anxiously, the brutes paced about in their respected ranks, all savage and warlike.

Natural enemies of each other, they surged and bowed up, chomping and swiping threateningly. But to Baricon's surprise, they didn't pounce and commence slaughter as should be expected. *What a testimony to the awe-inspiring power of the Dark Sorcerer!* he thought.

When the clan approached and took their place, Baricon scanned the night-shrouded mob again, taking in the impossible sight. Armies of goblins, burly and ferocious, amassed, hooting and arrogantly waving their weapons at the other brutes.

Dangerously close to them was a mob of lesser number but far greater prowess, the tall canine humanoids known as masnevires.

Baricon was again surprised when he spotted a crowd of thick, armor-skinned monstrosities slightly shorter than a masnevire but nearly as stout as they were tall. The powerful creatures had huge, beetle-like heads armed with deadly, crushing mandibles and claws powerful enough to dig through solid rock. They stood unconcerned, oblivious to the chaotic races around them. These were the cave ravagers.

Rustling noises in the jungle reeds far to his left pulled his attention away. The stirring was subtle at first, and with the gusts swirling around the mountain base, Baricon could easily have dismissed it as the wind. But the air quickly took on an eerie feeling and he shook off a sudden chill. The multiplied throngs of monsters grew strangely silent, some nervously sniffing the air while others drew their weapons, eyes darting about warily.

180

Johnny Earl Jones

From the swampy jungle which reached for the base of the foothills, strange noises began to drift into the air. An undercurrent of a crude language echoed back and forth in the dark shadows under the jungle canopies. Along the edges of the trees and tall grasses, shapes gathered in the darkness, deformed and gaunt. Dozens of beaming red eyes glared out of the jungle's shadows, gathering ominously, their numbers increasing by the second. Baricon and the other monsters stared into the jungle, obviously growing uneasy about the hidden creatures in the swamp below.

"What be movin' in the shadows?" one giant asked, his bass voice shaky.

Baricon knew dreadfully well. And his heart dropped. "They are..."

Slilitroks! They burst from the shadows with a vengeance. Howling and drooling, their gangly arms swung and their ridiculously large hands swiped the once-concealing reeds, shredding them to pieces. Dozens, hundreds, emerged.

The closest brutes evacuated from before the charging slilitroks' path, opening a wide swath no monster dared close. Savage and vicious, the gaunt creatures stared at the other armies with their beady eyes. Grinning. Hungry. A threat.

"These are the most feared monsters on the island, always huntin' in great packs 'n nearly impossible to destroy," Baricon said. "The wicked creatures haven't commenced tearin' into the other monsters, but hold back, reluctantly, seemingly kept in check by the fear o' a power greater than their own."

Lightning flashed again, illuminating the sky, and even at the great distance far above, the monsters spotted the minute outline of an imposing figure standing at the pinnacle of a spire, arms reaching to the sky, the wind whipping his cloak furiously. The aura of evil confirmed it. This was who they expected. One monster after another pointed up until all eyes were fixed. The brutes began a chant mixed with fear and excitement.

"Dark Sorcerer!"

* * * * *

Three of Krylothon's fists lashed out in frustration and anger, unleashing a trio of fire streams which slammed into the marble wall of Zeraktalis' chamber, melting the stone until it poured hot onto the floor in molten puddles. He considered for a short moment the holes carved into the bulkhead then threw back his head, an angry roar exploding from his gaping jaws, shaking the walls.

Here he was again in the sorcerer's chambers, this time of his own volition. The first time he'd been summoned. This time he lurked in the darkness, waiting to put an end to the threat to his power and his throne.

Zeraktalis had to be destroyed.

"I am Krylothon!" the burly usurper bellowed. Hearing his own name lent him strength. His six taloned hands clenched in rage. "I am the massster!"

For the last several years, Krylothon alone ruled as sovereign over the island Genna Fiendomon. Every brute on this island had to answer to him until that fateful day, on dragon's wings, The Dark Sorcerer returned, seemingly from the dead, upon one of the many jagged turrets of the Black Fortress.

A contingent of goblin warriors had confronted him there. Years had passed since they'd last seen the sorcerer. The dull-minded brutes didn't recognize him. The monsters never had a chance against him. With the roar of a few arcane words, Zeraktalis summoned dark magic which shredded the battle-hardened brutes.

Zeraktalis' next target for conquest was the usurper's throne. Krylothon had indeed underestimated the power of The Dark Sorcerer. When the usurper barged into the sorcery chamber, the Black Fortress' seat of power, Krylothon was unprepared for the sorcerer's mighty necromantic barrage.

The usurper growled at the thought, recalling the pain, remembering the stench of his own seared hide. Zeraktalis had broken him and took back the seat of power which Krylothon knew rightfully belonged to the mighty usurpers.

His rage boiled. In a matter of days, he was shoved from a position of supremacy to subservience.

"I will be sssecond to no one!" Krylothon roared. "Not even The Dark Sssorcerer! I wasss not prepared the firssst time, but thisss time he will fall."

After the sorcerer's initial victory, Zeraktalis offered a plot which would raze the provinces of mankind and obliterate those warmbloods forever and at first hearing it, the plan brought much excitement.

Krylothon desired the destruction of mankind more than anything. Mankind had been a bane to the demonic since the beginning of time. Although wicked in heart and often used by the demon world to do master Satan's bidding, God's hand was still on these spiritually weak creatures. Somehow, Christ Jesus--Krylothon shivered at the thought of that name--was able to take these humans, these warmbloods, and make an impact in this darkened world through those He had "saved."

God loved these humans and no one in the demonic realm could understand His motives. Strangely enough, God delighted in using these creatures to perform His will.

That's when the humans became dangerous.

They became an extension of the hated presence of God in this world.

Zeraktalis' plan to eradicate all warmbloods would void God's interest in the world. And since all the demonic knew of Christ's final revelation which spelled destruction to all fiends, mankind's extinction would rescue them from God's judgment fires. If all warmbloods were destroyed, God would surely abandon this world, and fiends would rule here forever, thus annulling the threat of the dissolution in the fiery wrath of God.

This all sounded promising, but incredibly, all the usurper could dwell on was his own great pride. He was the most powerful creature on the island of Genna Fiendomon, he convinced himself. And despite Zeraktalis' scheme, Krylothon would rather scrap the project to summon Diabolicus, the devilish creator of the usurpers, and suffer with the existence of the warmbloods than be under another's authority. Krylothon's hands flexed anxiously again at the thought of strangling the sorcerer's throat. Zeraktalis would come through that door sooner or later, not expecting the deadly onslaught which would greet him, but when he did...

He stood upright, proud. "I am the massster!" he hissed to the wide chamber again, the approving echoes like the cheers of a crowd convincing the usurper he was the only rightful ruler of Genna Fiendomon. "Zzzeraktalisss defeated me the firssst time, but he made one fatal error. He didn't dessstroy me. We will classsh again and then there will be only one left ssstanding. I will crusssh the life from him with my bare handsss! He isss a fool if he thinksss I will be hisss ssslave!"

Krylothon looked himself over in the far mirror, admiring his arsenal of deadly weaponry: his mighty talons, razor-sharp teeth and crushing mandibles, and six hands glowing with the fires of deadly sorcery. He was unmatched! The huge usurper flexed arrogantly, muscles bulging, and gloating over his imposing size. "There isss nothing that can withsssstand me!"

He spun suddenly in the direction of left wall, roaring out a string of arcane syllables, his six massive arms thrusting out straight and from his hands six streams of hungry fire poured forth, pounding into the ebony partition and melting another molten pool of marble on to the floor. Krylothon laughed wickedly.

"Impressive," said a booming voice from behind the usurper.

Fearless Krylothon balked, his heart nearly freezing up.

"It's good to see my general is eager for the fight," the voice said.

Krylothon knew who those words belonged to. He spun to the voice, his spiderlike eyes glowing in anger. "Zzzeraktalisss!"

The Dark Sorcerer nodded, apparently unconcerned with the usurper's rage. "I'm pleased you've decided to meet me in my chambers, Krylothon. It'll save the trouble of sending those sniveling goblin slaves after you."

Krylothon wasn't even listening. Summoning his courage, he shrugging off the pressing fear permeating his dark soul. He knew the sensation was inspired by the Dark Sorcerer's wicked persona. It was an overwhelming tide of terror which flooded the surroundings wherever Zeraktalis, The Dark Sorcerer, ventured. The usurper wasn't like any of the sorcerer's enemies nor any of his servants.

Krylothon was mighty. He was unstoppable. He was the sovereign of Genna Fiendomon!

The usurper crouched, poised and deadly, muscular legs bulging, ready to pounce. His mandibles chomped threateningly, talons clenched and unclenched. *How did Zeraktalis get in here?* the imposing monster wondered, but dismissed the question immediately, remembering Zeraktalis had somehow entered the room without using his only door in their other battle as well. A wicked grin crossed his face. If he was to confront the sorcerer it would be on equal footing, power against power. So much the better.

Zeraktalis' fiery eyes glared at the brute, almost seeming to bore into his dark soul. "The usurpers are a mighty race," he stated in deference to the impressive monster. "A powerful race. A proud race. I'd have it no other way! With pride comes power. But don't let that cloud your judgment, my general. It was I who brought your race under subjection to me, and it's I who'll utterly destroy any who oppose me!

"But you're not my slave, mighty Krylothon. None of the usurpers are. Of all the monsters on this island, I consider only the usurpers as equals. Only the usurpers, demon spawns, wield power worthy of such a position. Together we'll rule the world. Together we'll share in the spoils and the triumph of Diabolicus' ascension!"

Krylothon felt himself growing relaxed, acquiescing to what the sorcerer said. Then it noticed the glow of Zeraktalis' fists which signaled the coming onslaught of sorcery. It crouched low again, preparing to spring at Zeraktalis, when the sorcerer spoke something he couldn't quite understand. Suddenly confused, Krylothon shook his head, grunting questionably and defusing its death-promising stance.

"Your army is assembled on the foothills, my general. You'll lead them to victory and prepare the way for my coming. Avundar is our target. It contains the raw power we need to free Diabolicus from his eternal chains."

Krylothon's desire for revenge slowly ebbed away, anger mysteriously replaced by approval, even admiration, for The Dark Sorcerer. He questioned why he ever felt the need for reprisal against the sorcerer at all.

Zeraktalis had returned to dictate the affairs of the island, and as he had incessantly done in the past, The Dark Sorcerer would lead these monsters to a crushing victory over the forces of good. Imbedded deep in every sinew of his mighty body was the desire to wreak catastrophe upon the warmbloods again. And the mighty sorcerer would open the door to the conquest.

The usurper couldn't have fathomed the power of Zeraktalis. While Krylothon dreamt of conquest, the sorcerer had just finished one of his own--against Krylothon. The usurper's new admiration for the sorcerer was actually a suggestion planted in his mind by Zeraktalis himself, every word he had spoken was enchanted, subverting the usurper's rebellion.

"In several days' breath," Zeraktalis went on, "I will send my spy and his army to join ranks with you. He will direct you to Lifespring..."

"A ssspring?" the usurper spat. "For usss to crusssh mankind we depend upon the capture of a natural well?"

"It's like no other spring, great usurper," Zeraktalis continued patiently. Even though he temporarily contorted Krylothon's thinking, his magic had done nothing to quell the usurper's gruffness. "Lifespring is unique. It contains the life energy of an entire land. It is the vital energy of Avundar. For lack of better words, it contains the soul of the land."

"Ssso what?"

"Once the spring is secured," he explained, forcefully holding back the lightning bolt he wanted to pelt Krylothon with, "it'll be imperative that I dissect the energy source from the spring. It won't be easy, but when we force every circumstance into place, I can draw from the knowledge and the power received from my sojourn to the underrealm. Then I'll rip the soul of Avundar from its hold on the land! Victory will be ours!"

"Victory?" Krylothon echoed facetiously. "We'll have the sssoul of a land, but what're we going to do with it?"

"That, my six-armed destroyer, will be exactly what we need to proceed with the plans I learned in the hellish underrealms.

As powerful as the demon Diabolicus is, he's been leashed by the chains of God. Not even he has the strength to break them. But when the mighty source of pure, unadulterated energy from Lifespring is offered as an immolation, the demons and imps of hell will escort it right to the jaws of the demon lord, giving him the added power he needs to break from his bondage, pierce the prison of hell, and ascend back to the surface world to rain down destruction on the forces of good everywhere!"

Krylothon drew forward expectantly, excited about the coming world system, free of warmbloods and finally free from God. He stared at mighty Zeraktalis with a new sense of respectful fealty, one born of his free will, not manufactured by sorcery.

Zeraktalis noted the deference in the usurper's multifaceted, spiderlike eyes and laughed. "Do you no longer wish to challenge me as the only ruler of Genna Fiendomon?"

The giant usurper lost a step, surprised to hear the sorcerer so calmly ask about his treachery. If any others defied Zeraktalis, the sorcerer would blast them into a thousand pieces. Foggy was Krylothon's own ambition to rule, the residue of the sorcerer's spell clinging to his mind. Deep in his dark soul, he still thought himself supreme, and in his mind, he hadn't relinquished his desire to be sovereign of Genna Fiendomon. The diabolical demon spawn decided he would yield to this sorcerer for now. And he would wait. The time would come when he could overpower the sorcerer and regain absolute control, Krylothon told himself, but until then, he'd play this game until the opportunity was ripe. Still, even in pretense, his pride resisted every inch of the way as he bowed before the Dark Sorcerer. "You are the massster." he forced himself to say.

"I'm glad we have that settled. Now arise, my general. Stand tall and imposing as you always are. Our task is before us. We have warmbloods to slaughter. Ultimately, when foul Diabolicus is unleashed, the powers of darkness that will cover all the lands will bury this world in misery like it's never known. And we'll be at the head, directing the evil havoc beside the demon lord!

"Tonight marks the first step to the total annihilation of all mankind. Don't fail me. I am entrusting you to lead the assault, then I'll arrive shortly after. There's still much preparation left to be done here on Genna Fiendomon. Once you arrive, wait for my spy to contact you. You'll know who he is, a man of great prowess leading a formidable army."

"A man?" Krylothon growled incredulously. "Humansss are what we ssseek to dessstroy! We ssseek the power of Lifesssspring to sssummon Diabolicusss and exterminate all warmbloods everywhere! I won't cooperate with a targeted and weak human."

"I'm not to be questioned, mighty Krylothon. Every resource at my disposal shall be used. Remember our battle in this chamber. I should've destroyed you there for your arrogance and insolence, but instead I spared you. You have great capabilities I can use to carry out my plans. In the same respect, this wicked human will be of great use to us, and there's no need for him to know the ultimate designs for which I direct him.

"But I warn you. Don't underestimate this warmblood. He's a flawless assassin who owns an arsenal as deadly as yours. His deftness rivals your own. Don't cross him. You'll find he can be a dangerous adversary."

Predictably, the usurper thrust out his massive chest in defiance. "I fear no man!"

Zeraktalis knew Krylothon and the assassin would be at odds with each other, the whole scenario tantalizingly interesting to him. This would be needed friction to keep the ravenous usurper centered on his task. Zeraktalis knew the usurper's eagerness to kill, coupled with his inclination to enforce his own initiative, could cause trouble. It was critical to keep the usurper's great power and effectiveness focused. Zeraktalis withheld the necessary information from Krylothon so the usurper would have to rely on the cocky warlord to get to his destination. This avoids the possibility the usurper would charge into Verdant Wood and unleash an unplanned, frenzied slaughter.

"What is this human's name?" the usurper asked derisively.

"His name is Kil."

* * * * *

The brutes grew restless in such close proximity to each other, and Baricon had already sent his giants to quiet a few isolated clashes among the gathered forces. So far the slilitroks hadn't started into a frenzy. They simply stood hunched, eyeing the others with savage expressions. They remained inactive. For that the chieftain was thankful. He knew none of his giants would get between the vicious slilitoks and their potential victims.

A powerful gust of wind slammed into him from behind, and he nearly stumbled forward. Strangely, the whole night had been like this. Genna Fiendomon was a humid swampy jungle island where deathly silence accentuated every move and every breath of a nearby victim. But tonight the wind gusts were tumultuous, tossing the wild monsters and agitating them into new heights of savagery. "The sorcerer's behind all this," Baricon guessed. "He's using the wind to keep the army on the edge of violence."

A terrified scream exploded at the far corner of the collection of monsters. Baricon snapped his head in that direction and saw a mangled goblin fly out into the night. The air came alive with wicked cackles from every camp. The giant chieftain wanted to join in the laughter in evil admiration of the goblin's tortured death, but being the new commander, he knew he must lay down the law. The Dark Sorcerer hand-selected him as his force's field marshal, elevating his authority from Chieftain of the Giants to Third-in-Command behind only Zeraktalis and Krylothon.

Baricon shoved out his huge chest and let loose a deep bellow, turning all eyes his way. "The next monster t' kill one o' the Master's forces will be slung into the darkness by me own hand!"

Under the weight of his threat, the brutes calmed themselves. Baricon shoved his tremendous chest out again, this time swelling from his own pride as he considered his greatness. He was a mighty creature, nearly rivaling Krylothon in power.

A fierce screech exploded overhead, piercing the bellows of the tempestuous winds, and shaking Baricon out of his delusions of grandeur. Incited, the brutes from every camp around the mountain base screamed and howled.

Lightning lit up the sky, outlining the gigantic silhouette of a winged, serpentine creature diving down in their direction. The brutes shoved each other to scatter in every direction, fleeing from the descending monstrosity. Above even the howls of the wind, the steady boom! boom! boom! of the huge creature's wings filled the throng's ears. The massive beast drew closer. The booming grew louder, rolling down the sides of the mountain, threatening to crush the brutes underneath it. Some, daring to look up, stared right into the glowing, intimidating eyes of a giant reptilian beast.

"Dragon!" several screamed, each in their own language. Some ran for the cover of the swamp, others bore their weapons, knowing how insignificant they were against a creature of such size.

Lightning tore the sky again and the dragon stopped in mid air, hovering over the brutes. Boom! Boom! Boom! It wings steadily beat the air. A number of goblins yelled out threats and launched spears, thinking doom about to fall on them. The missiles which hit the dragon simply bounced off its hardened scales, but they were enough to aggravate the great beast. It sucked in a lungful of air, its neck lashed out, and a hissing stream of fire poured out on the rear camp of the goblins, leaving a dozen smoldering, stinking mounds where warriors had been.

"Enough!" The Dark Sorcerer's voice roared from somewhere close. The dragon descended, causing the monsters, even the slilitroks, to ebb cautiously away. Riding the mighty flaps of its wings, the dragon lowered itself, its feet slamming down on top of a knoll, sending tremors through the hills, jarring the closest monsters onto their backsides.

With all eyes fixed on the dragon, Zeraktalis majestically rose from the base of the beast's long neck.

"Master," Baricon gulped, overcome.

"Consumman!" Zeraktalis roared and fire leaped to life in his gauntleted palm. With a backfisted throw, he spun a blast of electricity to the ground a dozen yards in front of the dragon. The spell plowed into the base of the hill, and its impact knocked many monsters flat. Black flames roared to life where the bolt struck, burning violently and spreading fast. In every direction, the monsters fled, running for their lives as the flames ran rampantly over the rocky hills.

"Has Zeraktalis summoned us here t' kill us all?" Baricon said angrily. "The flames race like a sweeping tidal wave to the east, threatening to rise and swallow us all."

"Ignooth!" the sorcerer roared, and the flames suddenly snuffed out, leaving only wisps of acrid smoke and fearful screams fizzling into the air. The army was shocked but untouched.

"'The time has come!" Zeraktalis promised. "Behold! The gateway."

The shaken monsters turned as Zeraktalis pointed to the base of the hill where he tossed the spell. There burned a round wall of black flames. The Dark Sorcerer leapt from his high perch, landing squarely in front of the flaming wall.

"Verektof!" he commanded. The dragon responded and leapt into the air, speeding into the night, its long tail whipping behind it with a deafening snap.

A moment later Krylothon swooped down from the darkness and pounded next to the sorcerer.

"I have determined the location where I will release my army," the sorcerer told his usurper general. "To prevent alerting the baronies of Avundar, I will open this passageway in an isolated forest far from any inhabitants until my plans completely crystallize."

"Open it in the cassstle of a fortifed human'sss army!" Krylothon demanded. "Don't hide usss! Let usss dessstroy!"

Zeraktalis' crimson eyes flared angrily. "Never forget! I am your master! I've spoken and you will do what I say without question. I want my army to have as little contact with the inhabitants of Avundar as possible for now."

"We were promisssed the blood of the Avundariansss!"

"And that you will have. But your primary goal is to secure Lifespring. Wait for Warlord Kil and his directions, then you can annihilate the Silver Elves. I must gain the mysterious power of Lifespring. Once that is accomplished, the carnage you reap can be unlimited!"

That announcement raised ghoulish howls from every corner of the gathered camps.

"Let us go to victory!" Zeraktalis roared, pointing to the wall of black flames.

Not a single monster moved. The flames levitating behind the sorcerer leaped and crackled dangerously, the tongues of fire seeming to promise death to any who drew near. Most of the army's creatures had exercised only the basest instincts during Krylothon's rule, a time when they survived for nothing more than to kill and eat. It was that same animal reasoning which wouldn't let them walk freely into the wall of flames.

"This is your gateway into Avundar," Zeraktalis explained, his voice edged with impatience. The brutes began to back away.

"Baricon," he ordered and the giant grabbed the closest fleeing monster, a goblin, and tossed him. The brute bounced across the rocky ground once and skidded to a stop in front of The Dark Sorcerer. Although bruised and bleeding, the terrified goblin got to his feet, one leg leaning out weirdly, and tried to hobble away, but Zeraktalis' arm whipped out, catching the brute by the throat. The poor monsteer thrashed wildly, but one squeeze of Zeraktalis' fist and the goblin no longer squirmed.

"Do I need to make an example out of any others?" he roared, thrusting his arm and the dead goblin into the flames. "You'll do as I say or die like this fool!"

He pulled the goblin out of the fire, neither his arm nor the corpse at all singed.

"Do it now!" was his final warning.

The first creatures to go in were the goblins, not because they were the bravest but the weakest and were thrown in. The next were a pair of usurpers ordered by Krylothon to wait on the other side and organize the ranks as they came through. After a long moment the initial fear dissipated and the remainder of the army eagerly went into the flames, their desire for blood rekindled.

Zeraktalis turned to Krylothon when he was the last one left. "Don't fail me, my general. Obey my instructions. I will arrive soon!"

Krylothon only nodded, turned away and sprang into the flames.

Zeraktalis laughed. He knew what the haughty usurper's intentions were. Until the usurper clashed with the Warlord Kil, he wouldn't follow his directives. The sorcerer would give his bloodthirsty general the freedom to ravage the warmbloods for a short season. Unconcerned about Krylothon's rebellious heart, he was captivated by the intrigue which would develop between a fiery usurper, a bold warlord, and a land unaware of its coming demise.

* * * * *

The stars twinkled brightly in the dark canopy of Avundar's clear night sky. To the east, the crescent sliver of a dawning quarter moon peeked above the mountains, beginning its nightly journey across the constellations. All was calm across the countryside, even the wind was nothing but a hushed whisper.

This was the way Renmore liked it.

He and his companion pushed silently through the tall grasses and crossed into a long and sparsely traveled stretch of forest called the Lonely Woods. Renmore was glad to be among the trees now, where the shadows would block out the revealing illumination of the heavenly lights. Renmore was a hunter, one of the best in Avundar, dressed in dark and worn leather vestments. He ran his fingers through his thick curly hair, shaking his head as his comrade slowly caught up to his long strides.

The hunter had heard tales of this untrafficked grove and suspected the woods must abound with the majestic red deer, hearty animals sought after throughout Avundar and Sheliavon for their delicious venison.

The dark hours were the best for this hunter. Though most avoided hunting at night, he had grown quite adept at it, understanding the animals would be more languid and less skittish, providing him with curiously easy shots. His hypothesis that red deer flocked here was unproven, but he didn't doubt. He had a good feeling about it. He was rarely wrong. Red deer, like most animals, were private creatures and with civilizations expanding at such fast rates throughout the realms, there were few secluded areas remaining. This was one of the rare few.

189

LifespringLifespring

He and his companion traveled several days to reach this spot, a grove only a day's journey from the paradisiacal Verdant Wood of the Silver Elves.

"How're we goin' ta see the anim'ls in the dark?" asked Renmore's companion overly loud.

Slapping his hand over the man's mouth, Renmore shushed him quickly. His comrade was a tall, thin man with a wild beard too big for his face. Renmore had promised a friend he would teach this man, but regrets filled his mind immediately when he considered bringing this amateur to so promising a hunting ground. "You make twice as much noise as the horses we hitched at nightfall. We must be quiet and listen, Cortaz."

Cortaz looked to his mentor incredulously. He wanted to protest Renmore's methods. After all, Cortaz relied more on his sight than on his sense of hearing, and how could they find the animal in the dark even if they could hear it? He slapped himself in the forehead and reminded himself, Renmore was a noted and well-respected hunter. If he wanted to become a skilled hunter like him, he needed to shut up and observe without question.

As they entered, the woods were almost pitch black under the great leafy canopy of the forest. The apprentice wondered how they could traverse the unfamiliar forest in the black of night without smashing face-first into a tree. Cortaz rubbed his eyes trying to get them adjusted to this deeper darkness while staying close behind Renmore, keeping his eyes locked on his outline. To Cortaz' awe, Renmore brushed past tree after tree unerringly, barely making a sound as he walked. Cortaz felt clumsy in the still woods though, leaves crunching under his every step.

After a long uneventful moment of skulking through the woods, he saw Renmore hold up his arm, a signal to stop. Cortaz halted immediately. The hunter backed silently to him.

"A noise to our left," Renmore whispered. "Possibly our first game of the night. Fresh venison, my friend. Now that is a reward worth our long journey to this forest."

Cortaz nodded stupidly, wondering how the hunter could make out any sounds over the crunching of his footsteps.

"Ready your bow," Renmore instructed, "and be attentive. I'm going in after the animal. If my arrow doesn't fell it, I'll need you to strike it down."

Renmore plunged between two bushes, disappearing into the darkness, leaving Cortaz alone with his anxious thoughts. Although eager to test his ability as a bowman, Cortaz prayed that Renmore's shot would take down the deer. The hunter had talked often about his expectations coming to this untapped hunting ground. His expectations were high. Red deer were eagerly sought after and with the number he planned on bringing back with him, the market price would be at his mercy. He had even speculated if the demand was high enough, he would auction the prepared venison to the highest bidder. Renmore was as unshakable about his theory of these woods being a haven for the deer and he was as confident of his own hunting abilities as Cortaz was nervous at that moment. If the hunter's shot was not mortal and the deer darted past him, he feared the possibility of missing the wounded animal and looking like a failure to his mentor.

Sudden, sharp rustling in the distant bushes turned Cortaz. He heard the dull thud of an arrow hitting its target. "Yes," he grunted excitedly, knowing Renmore had found his prey. A hideous squeal cut through the night, sending a violent chill down his spine. That was no deer! The bushes quaked and he heard the noise of something rushing his way. Trembling, he pulled back on his bowstring. Renmore burst back into sight a moment later, and even in the dark, Cortaz could see the hunter's eyes bulging wide.

"What was it?"

"Run!" was Renmore's only answer and he shoved the apprentice into motion.

"What was it?" Cortaz asked again as the two raced through the forest.

"I don't know."

Dangerous rustling resonated from the bushes ahead. The hunter veered to the side, catching his companion's arm and dragging him in the same direction, racing at a feverish pace. Low-hanging branches whipped their faces as they swept by, but the sting hardly slowed them. Renmore veered again, this time in the direction he thought would lead them out of the woods. With fear driving their unrelenting pace, the two raced on, looking for the blanket of celestial dots which would signify their freedom. After several more minutes, the only thing over their heads was the thick canopies of the forest trees. Renmore stopped.

"What're you doin'?" Cortaz demanded, terror in his voice as he tugged on the hunter.

"Silence. We should've cleared the forest by now. I thought I was leading us out, but the detours must have confused my sense of direction. I was confident we were running for the outskirts. Instead we are plunging deeper into the woods." Renmore sucked in a deep breath, trying to calm his heavy breathing and focus his thoughts. Cortaz just stared at him wide-eyed, pacing nervously. After a reflective moment, the hunter let loose with a hearty laugh.

"There's nothing funny," Cortaz complained. "Let's get outta this place."

"We were running from a wild pig," the hunter explained. "Remember the squeal. It must've been from a boar. We were scared of what could've been tomorrow morning's breakfast bacon."

A shaky, relieved titter burst from the apprentice.

"That was our excitement for the night," Renmore said. "Now, let's get back to business."

Loud, rhythmic booming drummed in the night, echoing amid the trees and seeming to come from everywhere, a thick bass thumping which promised death.

"That's no boar," Cortaz cried. "Those are the beats of war drums!"

"This forest is supposed to be uninhabited!" Renmore screamed, panicked.

Numbed by the frightening shock, the hunter couldn't think clearly to discern an escape route. With the sound of the drums beating all around them, a most terrible thought came to mind. They were surrounded!

The hunter popped the strap binding the hilt of his sheathed sword, making the weapon ready for close melee. He notched an arrow on his bow. Noting his mentor's actions, Cortaz likewise armed his bow, drawing strength from Renmore's courage.

The ominous booming of the drums grew louder.

"Face me, you cowards!" Renmore screamed.

Tall bushes shook to his left. Renmore spun and fired off an arrow in that direction. He was rewarded with an unusual grunt which did nothing to ease his trepidation. In quick succession, he fired off four more arrows at the same spot, this time reaping a blood-curdling squeal. Something fell out from behind the bushes, a man-sized silhouette with weirdly distorted features. Not taking time to examine the beast, the hunter notched another arrow, sensing the night shadows closing in. A voluminous roar cut through the rhythm of the drums, immediately signaling to Renmore he couldn't just stand there as an easy target. He had to run. Throwing the bow over his shoulder, he turned to the right and dashed headlong into the night.

"Follow me!" he shouted back to his apprentice whose eyes were transfixed on the corpse of the ugly, tusked brute in front of him. "This way! We'll lose our pursuers!"

Cortaz started running and didn't look back.

Renmore swept past trees and bushes, hearing threatening grunts and rustling closing in around him. Then up ahead he saw stars breaking through the thinning forest canopy, a beacon of hope and escape.

"We've found our way out!"

Renmore dashed hard, his eyes locked on the night sky which promised escape from the eerie situation. He could see the plains now just beyond the trees. He let out an excited shout.

A towering shadow stepped out into the path directly before him. Wicked mandibles opened dangerously wide. Multifaceted eyes stared from a giant insectlike skull. Huge wings stretched wide from its back, blocking out the twinkling stars. Renmore tried to call out to Cortaz, tried to warn him, but the monster's mandibles snapped out with lightning speed, and the hunter was no more.

Cortaz didn't see his mentor's fate. A dozen goblins pounced from the forest shadows, pounding on him and dragging him to the ground. The last he heard was the noise of his own scream.

* * * * *

Kil could hardly believe the request. He had failed to destroy the elves in a well-planned attack, instead losing nearly half his assassins. His military collapse should have cost him his life; Zeraktalis wasn't a merciful master. For some reason, he was spared, but not before the sorcerer branded him with a painful new scar.

Now as The Warlord stood before the sorcerer's mirror, he stoically accepted Zeraktalis' berating and insults pointing out the inferiority of humans. All that didn't matter to him though, not when compared with one consuming obsession. The Master was allowing him to avenge his recent failure against the elves. And avenge it he would! The conflict against the elves had become more than a duty in his unholy alignment with the sorcerer; it was a personal matter now. In his dreams he saw only one face. His thoughts were consumed day and night with this one individual. He hungered to jab his blades into Zakili and watch him die slowly.

"You'll assist in leading the charge against the elves!" a voice thundered from the mirror device, shaking Kil from his contemplation. "The army's already arrived in Avundar. They await directions to Lifespring. You'll work side by side with the usurper Krylothon, but I warn you to watch your back. He's vicious and holds great disdain for humans. However, he'll get the job done. Bring them to Lifespring and secure it."

"And eradicate the elves!" Kil growled to himself, his mind swirling with bitter vengeance from his terrible defeat in Verdant Wood.

"It's imperative you capture the spring for my arrival. Destroying that race is a secondary concern. If the elves are to be engaged, massacre them; however, my monsters will scatter them with ease. As I told Krylothon so I tell you also: the chief objective is nothing more than to procure the spring. Once the task is completed, any killing for sport or enacting of revenge the two armies may do to their hearts' desire."

Kil heard everything the sorcerer said and agreed. He would follow his Master's bidding. In his heart though, all he could think about was taking Verdant Wood and engaging the dangerous Silver Elf, Zakili. Never had he battled an adversary whom he didn't slay, not until they invaded the elven kingdom. His back teeth ground when he thought how the elf not only fended off his attacks, but had him on the defensive more than once.

His pride still stung from the fight. There was no real victor in their personal war. Oh, he burned for a rematch. How he dreamt of carving the elf's heart out with his flaming dirks and holding it before his dying eyes!

"Where do I meet this Krylothon?" Kil asked. But he'd already decided he'd destroy the elves without the help of some foul army and its arrogant general. He was The Warlord of the Lurking Shadows! He needed no assistance, especially not from a mindless throng of brutes.

"At Lonely Forest, not more than a day's journey from the elven woods is where you join the usurper. It's there I have instructed the army to wait for you."

"I know of the place."

"Go to them at once. Those monsters are a reckless group who've not been subject to any form of discipline since my departure years ago. I know without my presence, they will sink back into their anarchic natures, especially with such virgin countryside to ravage.

My army is fierce and ravenous, and unless they are kept focused on their mission, they'll strike out and consume whatever they can get their jaws on."

"But what could I, a mere man, do to curtail their chaotic demeanors?" Kil asked. He pretended humility, but thought the Fangs of Hell would be enough to prevent any monster's agenda. But really, he cared nothing for the monsters, and he was concerned even less with what they did now they were in the land. All that consumed his thoughts was finishing his uncompleted fight with a certain elf who was his fighting equal.

"Don't let them forget their fear of me!" the flaming eyes answered. "Remind them the dangers guaranteed for disobedience! I don't doubt the creatures will stray, even my general is unstable, but the terror of certain death should bring them back under subjection."

"I will do as you command, my Master."

The flaming eyes in the mirror darkened, enveloping the room in blackness.

Zeraktalis turned from his mirror device, evil laughter rumbling from his helm. He had no doubt the strength of his foul army could overrun not only the Silver Elves but all of Avundar. But being the chaotic creature he was he knew his commands to both Kil and Krylothon would certainly pit the two strong-willed leaders against each other. The two would clash. He laughed over the intrigue which would build between The Lurking Shadows and the foul hordes, and more pointedly, the two leaders of the armies--the human and the usurper.

He was unworried whether Lifespring would be captured. His threats were enough to keep either from straying too far from his directives. Besides, he would be coming soon. And when he did, every individual in both armies knew the consequences of failure to follow through with what he commanded.

* 14 *
LIES

"The morning has risen early," Kelt said as he looked to the closed shutters of his window. Sunlight streamed in from every sliver in the veil, illuminating his 'throne room' uncomfortably and forcing him to squint his heavy eyes. He sat up straight in his throne and ran fingers through his tangled hair. Shaking away the fatigue, he tried to rise, but every muscle protested. He hadn't slept in days. Dizzyingly, his thoughts were murmuring and swirling in his mind; however, he found it impossible to grab one and hold on. Finally pushing off from his throne, he got to his feet. He had to summon his strength and continue his search for Candace.

From the moment he discovered Candace had left the safety of the fortress he'd given charge to Simeon and his elite guards to dispatch search parties throughout the regions of Avundar and even into the neighboring kingdom of Sheliavon. Kelt had journeyed with the many parties over the past several days. One group would depart as the morning rose and wouldn't return until the following morning, scouring forests and towns and inquiring in whatever barony they came upon. When one group was relieved so a fresh party could search, Kelt simply requested a fresh horse and went right back out without a moment's reprieve.

Although Avundar hadn't seen war in ages, Kelt understood this land wasn't safe for a woman to ride around in alone. As in every country, there were highwaymen, robbers who preyed on the unsuspecting and the helpless. Candace was hardly helpless. A smirk raised the corners of his mouth. If robbers did come upon her, they'd get more fight than they could ever want. But as good of a fighter as she may be, she was still only one person, and one could easily be overcome by many. For that reason, he couldn't sleep until he had his only girl back at his side. He'd lost his wife. He vowed he wouldn't lose Candace also.

After each group of searchers had returned without Candace, Kelt had grabbed a new cruse of water and gone out with the next fresh explorers. After the fourth day, though he returned without his daughter, he was still determined to continue, but he could barely keep his eyes open or his head from nodding. Under Simeon's advice he dismounted and went to his chamber to rest before starting the search anew. The inactivity and the loneliness of locking himself in his chamber did him no better.

When on horseback, his mind was engaged in locating her. Now with time to think, he still couldn't get to sleep. His thoughts were tortured about what had driven Candace away and what he did to promote it. Strangely, he couldn't remember much. The excitement of a royal suitor, one who finally seemed worthy of her, had overtaken him. He remembered the celebration Prince Killion had begun and the wine he'd reluctantly shared. He hadn't drunk alcohol since before he'd heard the traveling evangelist and had given his life to the Lord... He shook that thought away, ashamed of his spiritual apathy. In honor to the prince he drank, finding himself drinking more and more to the cheers of Killion and his courtiers. Every memory after that was hazy.

"Accursed drink," he spat, looking across the room to the once-elegant silver goblet he'd drunk from which now was dented and battered from his rage and disappointment in his own lack of temperance. "Accursed me."

Groggily, he pushed himself from his throne and shuffled to the window, agonizing over the fact he was unable to remember what he said or what he did to force Candace away. His daughter and he had grown so close in their relationship, they were practically inseparable. What could he have possibly done to force her to flee from the safety and love in her father?

Pushing the shades open, he squinted hard as he came face to face with the sun as it climbed over the mountain range. Looking over the courtyard and past the gigantic wall surrounding his fortress, he absently watched the town of Recqueom coming to life just to the north of his edifice.

This town was established decades ago, shortly after the construction of the impressive fortress was completed. The people of the town had submitted to his rulership as baron and he obligated himself to protect the townsfolk from any harm. How often he and Candace would visit there and regard the wares of the histrionic street merchants, laughing, dining and walking together. Those thoughts made his heart hurt even more.

Turning his eyes away, he looked to the vast forest blanketing the countryside from east to west all about his fortress. Arising like the legendary phoenix to start the new day, the sun washed the forested land in a blond glow. It was days like these he and Candace would travel early to the forest and put her battle skills to the test. He was a deft swordsman, but as Candace became more experienced, he was increasingly hard-pressed to keep up with her attacks, feints, and parries. Kelt growled and pushed that thought away also. Why was he torturing himself? Everything he viewed reminded him of experiences he and his daughter had shared. Downhearted, he turned away from the window.

"Where are you, Candace?" he cried out in frustration. "It's like you've fallen off the face of the world. Night and day as I accompanied the patrols, we have discovered not a single clue, nor have we found anyone who knows anything about your whereabouts. I pray nothing ill has happened to you. It took me years to get over your mother's death. If anything happens to you..." Kelt stopped short, refusing to continue that line of thinking.

"I must go back out," he determined. "I can't rest until I find my daughter." He spun in the direction of the door and began marching across the wide room.

Loud rapping on the outside of the chamber door startled him.

"Who is it?" Kelt demanded, growing suddenly angry as he realized such a knock would have shaken him from his sleep if he had chosen to rest. His last order to his messengers and elite guards was to leave him in peace until he decided to emerge from his solitude.

"Forgive me for disturbing your quiet, my baron," came a voice from the other side of the door. "But you have a visitor who wishes to see you."

"I have no time for guests," Kelt said as he continued his march to the door.

"He says it's extremely important."

"I don't care what he says. I must go find my missing daughter."

"Baron Veldercrantz, it's Prince Killion," Kelt heard as he turned the door handle. "He says he has information about Candace's whereabouts."

The baron threw the door open, staring unbelievingly at the prince. "Please come in," he bade, his voice taking on a more lively tone in the presence of Killion. And he had information about Candace!

Kil walked into the room and quickly bowed to the baron. "We have important matters to--"

"Nay," Kelt protested. "I need bow to you. You are the Prince. Royalty deserves such courtesies."

Kil waved it off.

"Are the troubles with your kingdom diminished?" Kelt asked, taking care to address the prince's concerns before he dwelt on his own.

"Troubles in my kingdom?" Kil balked. "Oh yes. All problems there have been eradicated." He slid up close to Kelt. "But now we face a different problem. I know the fate of your daughter. She must be rescued!"

"Tell me what you know," Kelt urged.

"From my own scouts I've learned she's been captured and is in danger from the wicked imaginations of those who hold her."

"But many rulers throughout this region know of my daughter. Who would treat her so shamefully?"

Kil's head drooped sadly.

"Who is it?" Kelt demanded.

"It's an enemy we would've never suspected. They're a secretive people whom I've heard little about. Now I understand why they're so reclusive and mysterious. Secretly, they're an evil race. The ones who've seized your daughter are the Silver Elves of Verdant Wood!"

Kelt was stunned. He knew of the Silver Elves. Years ago, he'd fought beside many of them when they charged into Sheliavon to rescue that kingdom from The Dark Sorcerer's foul hordes. They were all adept fighters, but he knew little more than that about them. Enigmatic, the elves were fiercely private and completely self-supporting, rarely making contact with other communities. He'd never heard of them being a wicked people, yet here was Prince Killion reporting they'd taken his daughter, his only beloved Candace. "I admit I don't understand their actions, but I'll communicate with them sternly and demand Candace to be returned safely."

"That won't work," Kil informed him. "My men have already penetrated the elves' kingdom to retrieve your daughter, but many were slain at the hands of those wicked elves. The Silver Elves are a fiercely warlike people."

Kelt looked to him suspiciously. How could the prince have vanquished a threatening coup and dispatched a contingent from his kingdom against the elves so quickly? Killion had departed from his fortress only a week ago.

"You look as if you don't believe. Gather your warriors and accompany me to the fringes of Verdant Wood, and see for yourself if they don't have your daughter in their clutches. They wish to use her to fulfill their crude fantasies."

The baron stepped back, rubbing his chin and trying to digest all the information and its implications. If he were to march his army to the edge of the elves' kingdom he'd be inviting war. But if those elves captured her and were using her to satiate their perverse imaginations then he could think of nothing more desirable than wiping out the whole lecherous race. After all, what profit would it be for Killion's army to again face a force that had defeated them once already unless the prince truly desired the safety of his potential bride?

"Well, Baron Kelt Veldercrantz, do you want your daughter back? Do you trust me?"

Kelt grinned maliciously as he cast aside any doubts. "There's only one right answer."

"And I knew you'd choose it. Make haste, baron. In order to get your daughter back safely, we must strike quickly and without mercy."

It took only a few hours for Kelt to gather his warriors once his word was sent out. Soon they were marching toward Verdant Wood as an imposing army. Their numbers swelled as Kil's assassins joined the ranks. With Baron Kelt at the head, Kil leading beside him, the force trudged on grim-faced. "I'm going to have my girl back safely, even if my army and I have to take down every Silver Elf to do it."

"That is exactly what I'm hoping will happen," Kil hissed under his breath. He thirsted to avenge himself from his previous failure. He longed to show The Dark Sorcerer that the Warlord of the Lurking Shadows doesn't need the power of his foul monsters to settle any scores. But above all, he hungered for a final rematch with the adroit Silver Elf named Zakili.

* * * * *

Navarro pushed the door of the housetree open and walked sleepily into the avenue. In his right hand he gripped an instrument which he admitted felt unusual in his grasp. His incessant battles with monsters meant innumerable hours with sword in hand, a weapon of destruction and judgment. How different it felt to be wielding instead of a blade, a hammer.

He, Zakili, and the elves worked feverishly on the battered housetrees of Elfstay yesterday. Although the damage to the homes was minimal, and the work could've waited until after the funeral pyres were lit later last night, The Paladin understood this was how the elves handled their grief. The labor kept the stoic elves focused on completing a task, deadening their sadness over lost loved ones.

He knew he couldn't even begin to understand the depth of their pain. Although he'd seen many good men die young, and grieved for each shortened life, the deaths of the elves seemed even more tragic. Men could attain eight, nine, sometimes even ten decades of life before succumbing to the blackness of death.

But elves could live for centuries. How many hundreds of years were those twenty-six elves cheated out of in The Battle at Verdant Wood? Navarro shook those considerations aside and pressed forward. There were still a number of repairs needed around Elfstay, and he wanted to start early.

"Early?" he questioned. "The sun was out with too much strength for the day to be very early." He had seen every sunrise for the past half a decade, always one who routinely rose with the sun. But today the sun had no interest in waiting for him. Looking up through the canopies of the trees, he noticed the sun climbed toward its zenith. He chuckled. "It's almost noon. I can't believe I slept this late."

With a profound yawn, he stretched. A stream of sunlight broke through the leaves overhead and warmed his broad chest. His unbuttoned shirt hung loosely from his shoulders, and he reached to close it. He and Candace had returned late from their talk out on the plains.

After stretching once again and placing his hand over another large yawn, he scanned the avenue running through Elfstay. All was silent, and nobody was in sight. "The elves are grieving for the fallen," he guessed.

His warrior senses tingled, alerting him to danger. Navarro's sword leaped into his hand, and his eyes turned upward. Crouching on the limb far above him was an elf, his bow trained on him. When the elf noticed it was The Paladin, he eased back his weapon and looked away stern-faced.

"Very unusual," Navarro said. "I've never seen a scout stationed in the Elfstay. And why was he ready to shoot me down? Surely, he should've recognized me." The Paladin wagged his head sadly. "Why should I be surprised? I've been in enough frays to understand the super-sensitivity following such a terrible battle. The elves are taking up posts at every populated area now, no doubt.

"The attack on their forest home was quite a blow to the elves' sense of security. With the peace of decades broken, the elves have become consumed with assuring the safety of their people. But what else could be called for after such a tragedy? The Silver Elves' carefree attitude is gone, turned grave overnight."

"Good morning, Navarro," The Paladin heard from his right, and he turned at the sound of the voice, his glance finding Candace's sparkling blue eyes. He blushed red, hastily buttoned his shirt, and forced himself not to bow at the waist as was his custom. He remembered Candace's request from the night before.

He noticed she wasn't adorned in the elegant, flowing dress and strappy sandals Zakili's sisters gave her. Instead she wore her leather armor, her cutlass at her side. Despite her battle-ready appearance, she still looked lovely.

"Lovely?" he mumbled to himself. "Indeed she is, but who am I to even think such a thing..." He let that train of thought pass. "Very uncommon morning attire," he quipped, turning to her. "Remember, you're among friends here."

"I know," she said, walking over and playfully slapping him on the arm. "But when I woke up this morning I sensed something unusual about this place today. I feel deep tension in the air."

Navarro nodded. "I've reasoned similarly. The elves have even set armed scouts about Elfstay, something never done before."

"Because of the attack yesterday," she said.

"I would have to agree. The battle's changed everything. Elfstay was perpetually filled with laughter and song. Now listen. Only silence."

199

"Give me a shovel, I'll dig my own grave!" a voice roared from high in the trees. The words burst from the canopies, echoed among the branches, and shattered the uncomfortable stillness.

A shape sprung onto a bough, grasped it in both hands, and leaped, flipped once, then landed on both feet in front of Candace and Navarro.

"Another great day!" Zakili said as he smiled at his friends. The elf prince's light attitude and widening smirk nearly convinced The Paladin there was nothing out of the ordinary. Navarro knew his friend well. Zakili had the same insouciant demeanor whether he was in the gravest of dangers or all was well.

"What's going on?" Navarro asked.

"You tell me," the Elf Prince demanded, winking ridiculously. "You two were out together awfully late last night. Sounds to me like we could have a little romance blooming here."

Candace blushed.

"Starting early with the nonsense, are you?" Navarro fired back.

"Remember, it's not that early. Maybe if you two would've been sleeping instead of being wrapped up in each other's company all night, you wouldn't have slept half the day away."

"Enough, my friend," Navarro chuckled, holding his hands up in surrender. "Will you tell us what is taking place about the Elfstay?"

Drawing close, Zakili put his arms about Candace's and Navarro's shoulders, bringing them closer. "Sure I will. Anything for you pining lovebirds," he said.

"You've probably noticed the sentries sprinkled all about Elfstay," he began. "Double the usual number line the perimeters of the forest. It would appear my father has finally heeded our warning--a day too late. His proud assurance has given way to an obsessive paranoia.

"He's ordered that not even an animal may enter into our forest without inspection. That will probably keep quite a few woodland creatures out of our home," Zakili laughed. "They do like their privacy."

"This sounds odd," Navarro said. "I've known you and your father for several years. Never have I seen his judgments swing from one extreme to the other. The King's resolve has always been solid and unshakable. He never made hasty conclusions without evaluating all possibilities. Now he doesn't listen to counsel, and his orders seem like impulsive reactions rather than discerning decisions. Is something ailing him?"

Zakili shrugged his shoulders, his face expressing no emotion. "He's the King. Lately, he's made absolutely sure I knew that. You know, even before the invasion he acted unusual. I don't know if he's sick or if the pressure of the crown weighs him down or what, but I do know this: if being a King makes one bitter and miserable, I think I'll bypass the royal throne.

"Life's not life if you have the royal position but are eaten away by it day after day. For all I care The Circle can halt its growth at me. I care not if I have a ring of oaks spring up to signify my reign. I live to use life to its fullest, not for life to use me!"

"I regret the situation among the elves has gotten so awful," Candace put in, feeling somehow responsible for the troubles among the Silver elves.

"This has nothing to do with you at all," the elf said. "Besides, I was talking foolishness. I'm born to be King one day. I couldn't forsake my people for the sake of my own selfish ambition. Candace, these problems have brewed for months. The breakdown in communication between us has caused a split in the people. It's hard for them, for they are fiercely loyal to the King, yet they appreciate me. I don't talk down to them as a future monarch, but I speak as a friend.

"When Gallatar protests against what he calls the actions of his unruly son, it divides the ranks. That was seen most prominently the morning of the battle. We should've cut down most of the assassins with arrow strikes. But a large company of archers are completely loyal to my father and take orders only from him. That generally isn't a bad thing, but since the King has painted me a troublemaker, they took up posts according to my orders but hesitated to engage in battle until it was already upon us. By then the lines were blurred, and arrow strikes would've brought down our own warriors, as well as the enemies'."

"What brought on this change?" Navarro asked. "As long as I've been acquainted with the Silver Elves, you both have been close, if not inseparable."

This brought a frown to the elf's face. "Old age," he finally offered.

Candace and Navarro looked at him impatiently, thinking his remark more of his sarcasm.

"Honestly, I can think of nothing else. King Gallatar was affable and adventuresome not long ago. If we didn't adventure together, he loved for me to tell of my tales when I returned from my own journeys. He loved to fight, he loved to spar, he loved to eat, and he loved to sing.

"Now he is a gloomy shell of whom he used to be. He never used to be so grim, so serious.

"The only thing I can compare my father's metamorphosis to is the change humans go through when they grow a little over a decade old. I've been studying the old manuscripts and found he's not the first to go through this change. All elf kings are legendary for being delightful until this change which causes them to draw inward.

"You know the outside world's view of the elves of Verdant Wood. We're regarded everywhere as being a private, reclusive race.

"Now tell me, do I act private or reclusive?" He didn't wait for an answer. "However, I've been told by humans that before even their fathers were born the Silver Elves had the same aloof reputation.

"So my father's actions aren't isolated, but inherited. According to our history, the older an elf grows, the less trusting and more suspicious he is of other races. But what's even worse, the elves take on his beliefs, making the Silver Elf nation exactly what the outside world thinks."

"I don't understand what you're saying about the attitudes of the others toward your race," Navarro admitted. "I've heard of none."

"But I have," Candace said. "What Zakili says is correct. Others, my father included, think Silver Elves are a proud, self-sufficient race who could care less if they ever communicated with another society."

"Exactly, but it goes beyond my father's attitude. The elves are infected with his distrust of other heritages. This is not good. The Silver Elves are near total isolation from the world because of the King's anxiety and the elves' acceptance of his perception. And with Gallatar's newest change in attitude, it may grow worse."

"But how does this affect your ailing relationship with him?"

"Who can say? I don't nod my head in agreement with everything he spews forth like a good son should. Maybe he thinks I'm too wild for a Silver Elf Prince. Or does he pull away from a relationship with his people the same way he has from the rest of the world?"

"This is awful," Candace said.

"It's difficult for me to understand. He's my father, the one I've looked up to all my life. Now it seems I can't even find a kind word for him."

Candace nodded, her expression truly empathetic. She understood the letdown. It had happened with Father, the only man she ever admired.

"Is there anyway we can help?" she offered. "I'm willing to abide here interminably if need be. At this moment, I have nowhere else to go."

Zakili's gaze fell sadly. "It would be an honor to have you live here among us. Truly, your presence and your wit complement our race. You're as beautiful as any elf maiden and as friendly as any human I've ever met. Unfortunately, Gallatar's misgivings about outsiders include even you, Candace. One of his advisors informed me, he desires you depart before night falls over this land tonight."

Candace stared in disbelief, her soul suddenly hollow and dejected.

"I can't believe what I'm hearing," Navarro said.

"I couldn't understand it myself. She braved the wrath of The Lurking Shadows, and raced the crucial information to us. Her role was vital in the victory over the assassins. And now she's being tossed away like a piece of refuse."

"Something's terribly wrong, and it must be more than just old age," Navarro said. "This is so unlike anything King Gallatar has ever done."

Backing away, Candace bowed her head despondently. Although she'd never have conceived of dwelling among the Silver Elves before fleeing from her father's fortress, the few days she'd been in Verdant Wood produced many friendships. She felt more like family than a visitor. She knew it was unwise to return to Father and the dangerous warlord, Kil, who masqueraded as a prince. She had hoped this would be the place for her. But no. She was being forced out with nowhere to go.

Navarro gently reached over and put his arm around her, trying to comfort. "Candace, please don't be offended," The Paladin exhorted, misinterpreting her grief. "The command comes from one elf. Don't think the entire Silver Elf race is unappreciative of your great contribution against our enemies. The friendships you forged here will forever be yours."

"I know," she said, forcing a smile, not expounding on her situation. She was a survivor, she told herself. No matter what, she would endure.

* * * * *

The thrashing on the door sent a resounding echo throughout King Gallatar's chamber, and his head snapped in that direction, his eyes narrowing angrily. "Be gone!" he roared.

The door burst open and an elf rushed in.

"Maengh! How dare you intrude into my throne room," The King spoke, rising from his seat.

"Listen, my King," Maengh urged. "There's an army on the horizon pushing toward the forest this very moment. Their banners are held high, and they march in battle positions!"

"The assassins?" Gallatar asked.

"It doesn't seem likely. We destroyed the majority of their forces when they first attacked. Whoever this is doesn't choose subtlety in confronting our kingdom."

"This is foolishness. After the way we massacred the assassins yesterday, who would dare challenge us again?" Gallatar asked, growing concerned and wrathful. "Inform my advisors and commanders to form my elves into battle ranks. I must don the armor. I will lead the elves against this foe. Our attackers will soon learn the mistake of battling the Silver Elf people! Go now Maengh! Tell my military minds to make haste. We will defend our home once again!"

He turned and looked Maengh straight in the eyes. "I expressly demand my son not be notified."

Maengh bowed quickly and rushed out of the room, stopping only once, far from the king's chamber. He leaned against an empty housetree and erupted into a low rumble of evil laughter. "Kil is charging at the elves again! Will nothing stop him? In only a day he has recruited an army to crush these crestfallen elves. What better way to dispose of them than to flush them out and make them play his game? Never have I known a more persistent, resourceful, wicked human!

"Oh, King Gallatar, I will warn your advisors, and they shall rally the elves. Like lambs led to the slaughter, the elves will march out to the field and be destroyed. The Master will have his prize! I, Ironfist, declare it!" Ironfist, in his elven guise, sprinted away toward the advisors' chambers, his wicked laughter polluting the air as he went.

* * * * *

"The elves won't be able to stand against an army as massive and skilled as yours," Kil prodded, provoking Kelt further as they neared Verdant Wood. "Albeit they emerged victorious over my royal army, they suffered considerable losses and scores of injured. With the uniting of our armies, their defeat is assured."

"Those fool elves," Kelt cursed. "Did they actually believe they could practice their perverted ways on my daughter with impunity? Judgment looms over their heads!"

"She's a very lovely woman," Kil said and grinned crookedly, seeing he drew the baron deeper into his web of lies. Soon, The Warlord guessed, the baron would overflow with rage against the elves; his desire to kill all would be insatiable. "I dare to say she's even fairer than the elf maidens. These Silver Elves are lascivious fiends who love the conquest of beautiful human women whenever they can capture them."

Kelt's face reddened.

"Our target is right before us," The Warlord urged. "By annihilating those wicked elves, we can rescue your lovely daughter and prevent this heinous crime from ever happening again."

Kelt growled orders to his field marshals to increase the army's pace as the forest grew closer. Being so visible under the afternoon sun, the baron wouldn't normally have marched his warriors so openly against a force as formidable as the Silver Elves. He would've conducted a covert siege after the setting of the sun, using darkness to veil his fighters.

But with the scenario he faced, this was his only choice. If he were to charge in under the cover of night, the possibility of risking Candace's life drastically increased. This was the best way, Kelt decided. He would demand his daughter's return, then exterminate the elves.

Only a few moments passed under their increased pace before the leading standard bearer bellowed a trumpet blast warning. "Riders headed straight for us!" A cacophony of drawn weapons rang in the afternoon air.

Silver Elves on majestic white stallions poured out of the woods with the intensity of a tidal surge. Their weapons held high, war horns blasted.

"Archers, ready yourselves!" Kelt commanded.

"They come with a vengeance," Kil said. "They'll not give up their prize easily."

"They have no choice!"

"My royal army will melt into your ranks and form a double-strength attack against these villains. Behind the power of both of our armies, we will extinguish this Silver Elf nuisance."

"I wish you to join me in leading the attack," Kelt said. "What better way than to have royalty lead the blows against the enemy?"

"I don't think that would be a wise idea. The elves would recognize my army and their wrath would be invoked to an even higher level of savagery. Confusion is your ally.

"Since they see only your army, there'll be a sense of fear. They know not why you have come to strike them. My warriors will come in from behind once the battle is engaged and fall on the enemy, promising great destruction.

"They suspect they face only one army. Little do they know they have two forces to contend with."

* * * * *

Sitting together in a housetree, the three friends looked helplessly to each other, uncomfortable silence surrounding them for what seemed like an eternity. Zakili's announcement stunned them all, and neither he nor Navarro knew what to say to ease Candace's dejection.

A gentle breeze tumbled a gathering of loose leaves just outside the open door, catching Navarro's attention. In a forest home, the sound of rustling leaves was common, a noise nobody gave a second thought. But today The Paladin noticed how strangely out of place it sounded against the backdrop of deathly silence.

He sprang from the table and rushed to the doorway, sensing something ominous. Candace and Zakili were at his back, obviously sensing it as well.

Instinctively, Navarro glanced in the direction where the lookout was earlier stationed. "No watchman," he stated.

The elf prince nodded, noticing the same thing. "I feel like everybody started the party without us."

"What are you saying?" Candace asked.

"No elves. No lookouts. It could mean only one thing."

Candace gasped. "We were so caught up in our disbelief we didn't even notice--"

The bushes stirred behind them. Navarro spun and his sword leapt into his hand. An elf maiden burst into the open and darted for the friends. Navarro eased down, seeing it was Saranisen, Zakili's youngest sister.

"We have trouble, my brother!"

"I sensed as much. What's occurred? And where have all the elves gone?"

"We have another army on our fringes!" she answered grimly. "King Gallatar has summoned the elves, and they race to meet the advancing army at this moment."

Zakili stared at her hard, puzzled.

Saranisen shrugged, looking just as confused as he. "I don't know what Father was thinking. You're the best fighter among the elves. And he could never rally the warriors as effectively as you can!

"He takes the elves to the open field for battle," she stated, concern in her voice.

"He's doing what!" Zakili demanded. "Our people are not numerous enough to sacrifice many good warriors in open, man-to-man combat. The elves will play right into the enemy's hands. This is strategic suicide on his part!

"Our battlefield is the forest. Here, blending among the trees, we cannot be defeated!"

His gold-flecked eyes narrowed, The Flying Tigers suddenly in his fists, spinning dangerously. "The assassins!" he growled. "They'd not dare venture back into the woods, but are they foolish enough to challenge us again on a battlefield of their choosing? Did Kil actually think he could break our spirits enough to charge back against us in consecutive days?"

"They're not assassins," Saranisen corrected. "It's the army of some neighboring monarch. They ride at the woods as if to wage total warfare."

"Regardless! Our enemies have met their doom! No one attacks my Silver Elves without reaping deadly consequences!"

"Something evil stirs," Navarro reasoned. "Your people have enjoyed peace for centuries, but within the past two days your kingdom has suffered two subsequent challenges."

"I agree," Saranisen said. "Our people are in conflict with no other races. Why would an adjacent monarch want to war with us?"

"If it's not The Lurking Shadows, who could it be?" Candace inquired.

"Who cares? We'll conquer first and ask questions later. My battle-weary elves need every resource they can use against a full-scale army. "Give me a shovel, I'll dig my own grave!" Zakili roared, the war cry echoing through the trees as he sprinted in the direction of the stables.

"He has the right idea. Let's saddle up," Navarro said. "I fear the elves are preparing to fall into a trap, and we are the only ones who will be able to stop them."

* * * * *

Drawing invisible lines, the two armies stood their ground on the plain's grassy field, the remnants of the pyres still smoldering behind the elves, each army waiting impatiently for the next crucial move. The anxious clicking of readying weapons filled the air. All along the leading row of Kelt's army and Gallatar's elves were dozens upon dozens of archers, their bows drawn back, taking a mark on the front line of the opposing warriors. For both sides, the success of the first blow would set the pace for the rest of the battle.

At a standstill, neither force advanced, the heads of both armies understanding the tremendous carnage possible from a hasty open charge. Kelt's force outnumbered the elves nearly two to one, yet the baron's men had a healthy respect for the legendary prowess of the smaller group. Power for power, the armies were equally matched, and King Gallatar and Baron Kelt knew it. A hundred yards apart they held their position in an unannounced standoff.

Gallatar trotted his white stallion back and forth impatiently behind the line of archers, eyeing the person he thought to be the leader of the invaders, an older, straight-backed human with graying beard who appeared to coordinate his men's actions. King Gallatar didn't recognize the man nor the army's standard which flapped in the soft, afternoon breeze, a flag bearing the image of a broad sword crowned about the blade by a diadem. His unfamiliarity with the banner meant little to him. He wasn't acquainted with nor cared to know about the principalities bordering his forest kingdom. He esteemed them as inferior.

The king signaled to his standard bearer. The young warrior lifted his trumpet to his lips and blew out a loud blast.

Kelt's warriors stirred anxiously, held ready their weapons, and thought the moment of battle was upon them; however, the elves didn't charge. Kelt understood the blast to be a prelude to an announcement.

"Here we stand!" Gallatar cried, pointing out the baron. "You've marched to the border of my kingdom with your men armed for battle. We've done nothing to deserve this disrespect! Understand my elves are a peaceful people, peaceful until provoked. You have invaded our domain, and we are prepared to show you the wrath of the Silver Elves! Have you lost heart at the sight of your opponents? We await your attack! Why do you stand around like frightened cowards?"

"Cowards?" several of Kelt's warriors screamed, nearly charging headlong at the elves. Nearly overcome by the insult, Kelt had almost released his men, but instead he held them back with a stern look. How hard it was not to answer that affront. "First we must retrieve my daughter, then we can extinguish these arrogant elves," he placated his men.

"Elf!" Kelt announced. "Meet me in the midst! Alone! Unless you fear!"

"Fear?" the Elf King scoffed. "Of cowards? Let us go now! Immediately Gallatar separated from his army followed by his four advisors.

Likewise, Baron Veldercrantz advanced, flanked by his Elite Guard. Neither side was alarmed. In warfare, no monarch squared off against an enemy leader unless he had his best lieutenants with him. All became silent among the two armies as the leaders plodded toward the "midst," the area of open ground separating the two forces. The archers on both sides trained their bows more intensely. If fighting broke out in the midst, the two armies would collide immediately.

"I command you to release my daughter!" Kelt demanded as soon as he and Gallatar were within several paces of each other.

"Your daughter?" Gallatar questioned impatiently. "I know nothing of your daughter. Don't blame the Silver Elves for the misconduct of your whelp. If she's abandoned your premises, maybe you should reevaluate your abilities as a father and leave my people alone!"

The insult stung deep at the baron's sensibilities, swelling his anger and his shame. He knew his actions, his words, had indeed forced Candace away.

Now, he just wanted his daughter back safely, and he knew the elves had her. Prince Killion had assured him so. "Don't play ignorant with me, deceitful liar! I know your elves captured my girl and hold her prisoner, and I'll kill you all before I allow you to carry through with your lecherous plans for her. This is your last chance to return her to me immediately. If you don't, I'll destroy every last elf to gain her back to my side!"

"I know not what kind of delusion you've dreamt up, human, but I can tell you this: you've come against the last people you want to challenge! If you choose, we'll litter this field with the bodies of your slain men!" Gallatar drew his sword, his advisors pulling into a tight defensive formation around him, swords also drawn.

Kelt unsheathed his double-edged broad sword as his elite guards lined up defensively, swords drawn and faces grim.

To either side of them the armies tensed and weapons clicked in nervous anticipation. There was no time for bravado nor arrogant boasts now, battle was imminent, the dangerous scent of war was in the air.

* * * * *

"It's my father!" Candace screamed from her speeding charger when she spotted the standard of the challenging army.

"This isn't good," Zakili said, shooting an incredulous look her way. "My hope was for a faceless enemy to vent my wrath upon. I was looking forward to a fight!"

"Maybe next time," Navarro said. "Instead we must prevent a fight from breaking out. In Jesus' name, we have to stop them before they clash, or the cost of lives on both sides will be great."

Navarro snapped the reins, lengthening his steed's already hearty stride, and Candace and Zakili followed his lead. With the distance speeding away under the chargers' pounding hoofs, The Paladin tried to formulate a plan, understanding one wrong or misinterpreted movement could unleash terrible bloodshed.

What seemed like an eternity passed by the time the friends rushed onto the scene, and Navarro thanked God the two mighty armies had not yet engaged. They sped past the Silver Elf army and plunged straight into the "midst" where Gallatar and Kelt energetically traded insults and looked as if they'd soon throttle each other.

"Hold!" Zakili roared at the two leaders, understanding the consequences if either monarch struck the other. Both Gallatar and Kelt turned to the unexpected visitors, as did the bowmen of both armies.

The archers held their shots, and Navarro exhaled a relieved sigh. He knew if any one of them had been less than proficient, the friends would've been cut down by the crossfire of flying arrows. The paladin pulled up sharply on Celemonte's reins, turning his steed sideways and effectively barricading Candace's and Zakili's chargers. The armies were ripe to explode into battle, Navarro understood, and an unannounced charge at the opposing monarchs could be the catalyst to unbridled warfare.

An undercurrent of enthusiastic awe and surprise ebbed from the Veldercrantz warriors when they noticed Candace among the newcomers.

"Father! What are you doing?"

Kelt turned, his expression mixed of joy and confusion. The last thing he expected was to see his daughter charging out to meet him when he was about to engage the foe responsible for abducting her.

"This is the whelp you misplaced?" Gallatar asked snidely.

Kelt purposely ignored the jeer. "Did they hurt you in any way, my girl?"

"Who?"

"These... these wicked elves!" he blustered. "Your whereabouts were reported to me. I was told the elves of Verdant Wood abducted you and were abusing you for their own lewd pleasures!"

Candace's brow furrowed in disgust. "Not so at all, Father! The elves are friends of mine, honorable and--"

"I was told you were captured here," Kelt interrupted. "And so the information was true. You're no longer a prisoner. My army has come to liberate you."

"I was never a prisoner. Of my own choice I arrived in these woods to warn the elves of danger. They'd never do me harm. They are a peaceful people."

"Peaceful?" Kelt scoffed, pointing to the elf forces. "Perhaps you didn't see the amassed army flanking your left side, Candace."

"What do you expect?" she protested. "You marched your army to their kingdom's doorstep. How are they supposed to react? You're coming to make war against them."

"I didn't come to make war. I came to rescue my daughter." Once the words left his lips, Kelt realized how ridiculous they sounded. His daughter whom he came to save was right before his eyes.

Gallatar huffed indignantly.

From within the bulk of Kelt Veldercrantz's army a lone rider pushed slowly, unthreateningly toward the "midst." Candace didn't recognize the man and had a strange feeling about him. Navarro and Zakili watched curiously as the man rode up to Kelt and whispered something to him, bringing a revolted expression to the baron's face. The rider dashed back from where he came, disappearing into the baron's gathered warriors.

"What's going on?" Navarro whispered to himself, never in all his battles seeing a face-off quite so unusual.

"You sinister tricksters!" Kelt accused. "To deceive me and to save your miserable hides, you have bewitched my daughter!"

"What!" Gallatar roared.

Candace echoed the Elf King.

Hot-blooded Zakili, enraged by the dishonorable claim, snapped his reins and his charger bolted forward. Navarro's hand whipped out, quickly snatching the horse's harness just as it started off, the strength of his grip forcing the animal into a submissive skid.

"Don't do it," Navarro warned. "You'll surely unleash a war. Remember who we're dealing with."

Zakili took a deep breath, calming himself before glancing shamefully to Candace. Noting her attentions were fully on her father, he was relieved she never saw his sudden burst of rage. *We're here to prevent battle,* he reminded himself. *Not to initiate it.*

"Now I understand why you elves keep your ways so covert," he heard Kelt start up again. "You hide in your Verdant Wood to keep your wicked and diabolical ways secret!"

"You don't know what you're saying!" Candace cried.

"Look at her!" Kelt insisted. "She even defends the people who abducted her and held her against her will. What kind of spell have you cast on her? What illusions have you placed in her mind?"

"You are a fool, human!" Gallatar roared, gripping his sword tightly.

"An insult from a scared rabbit!" Kelt hissed. "Your bravado fooled me at first. To see the great Elf King and his assembled army rushing out to face my forces was an impressive sight. For a moment I feared I might have a small challenge on my hands."

"As well you should!"

"Ha!" Kelt derided him. "I know not what artifice you're trying to create, but you have been found out: staging a big confrontation only to have my spellbound Candace arrive to spare you from annihilation. I'll take my daughter, you deceiver, and she'll be released from your mind-controlling magic. I'll spare you today, but for the good of all, crawl back into your secret forest and never be seen again."

"Where did you get the idea they brainwashed me?" Candace asked, but her father wasn't listening to her.

"I talked to your whelp only briefly and only once, paranoid human," Gallatar said. "She came here freely and without invitation, which means she left your abode just as freely, denying your permission. Take your daughter, your army, and whatever twisted delusion you brought here and carry it back with you. And never lay the blame of the careless upbringing of your child upon my people again!"

Kelt leaped from his horse and lurched at the Elf King. His guards grabbed for his arms, trying to constrain him. Gallatar's flout about Kelt's parenting was like a slap in the face, biting deeper into the baron's heart than the elf could've ever imagined. After his wife's death, he'd taken immense pride in his rearing of Candace. The Baron easily broke free from his Elite Guards and dashed at Gallatar. The Elf King waited for him, his blade held over one shoulder in preparation for a backhand chop. The armies closed in from the sides.

Kil grinned evilly, smelling the scent of war, motioning his assassins to push forward through the ranks, preparing to make the first deadly assault. His plan was proceeding perfectly. Soon the conflict would begin, and then the elves would be outmanned.

Candace leaped from her charger and darted between Gallatar and her father. "Stop this madness! It's ludicrous to fight over my return--"

"Out of my way, girl!"

"Why do you need to fight? I'm right here, and I'm returning home with you. There's no need to fight over my freedom. The elves didn't capture me; I rushed here to warn them of the impending attack of the assassins coming against them."

"This isn't about you any more, my precious daughter."

"Then what's it about? Your pride?"

"I said out of my way!"

"Look at all the men behind you, friends and troops who've been dear to your heart for years. Are you willing to needlessly sacrifice their lives for the sake of your wounded ego?"

"They're murderers!" someone shouted from Kelt's army. "These elves murdered the Prince's men!"

Kil patted the assassin heartily on the shoulder who had yelled the lie.

Candace turned, casting a disdainful gaze in the voice's direction, knowing the accusation to be a falsehood, but Kelt's face reddened in outrage at what he perceived to be the truth. From the corner of her eye, she spotted Kelt navigating around her but she blocked his path with her body, her expression stern and uncompromising. "You have come to retrieve me and here I am. What sense is there in continuing to challenge them?"

"The elves have influenced you, my girl. This wicked race slew scores of the Prince's royal army when he plunged in the elves' forest to save you."

"That's not true!"

"Oh, how they have bewitched you. The only reason I discovered where you were is because the Prince clued me to your whereabouts, saying you were enslaved by these ruthless elves. And he was correct for here you are."

"A prince told you that? What prin--" she choked on her words at a sudden realization. "The Assassin Warlord!" she forced out, her words hardly audible.

"I grow weary of your game, human!" Gallatar announced impatiently. "As your whelp has professed herself, you have retrieved what has escaped you. Now depart from my domain! Leave immediately and no harm will come to you."

"No harm will come to me?" Kelt screamed, echoing the king's threat incredulously. "My army should cut your people down right now to save future generations any troubles from your stinkin'...'"

"Father please!" Candace pleaded, and her pained expression caused Kelt's words to stick in his throat.

The baron roared in frustration and stomped several paces away to cool his anger. Finally he turned to his daughter, drawing close to her and tenderly running his fingers through her golden hair. At that moment she saw the gentle, fatherly love she'd always known.

He tried to say something in this awkward moment, but a sudden cloud crossed his face, contorting his countenance into an angry mask. He looked at her one final time before eyeing the Elf King with open contempt. Without a word, he turned, slammed his blade into his scabbard and left the conflict behind. He mounted his charger.

"Fall back!" Kelt commanded. "Our task here's completed."

"No!" several voices cried from within the ranks. "We must destroy them! A race this evil shouldn't be allowed to live!"

"Who's that, father?" Candace asked.

Kelt stopped, barely hearing his daughter's question. Prince Killion was hidden among the ranks, hungry to pay retribution to the elves who'd prevailed over his royal army. He glanced back uncomfortably, not wanting to disappoint the prince, then turned to Candace, who looked healthy and unharmed, and the heavy weight of indecision fell on his shoulders.

Should he pursue justice and charge the elves, avenging Prince Killion's losses, or would he be wiser to take his daughter, cursed or not, and his men home unscathed? With the jeers of Kil's men in his ears, he felt the pressure mount. Candace looked to him, her sad blue eyes melting his heart.

"We return home!" he called out finally to the army behind him, his tone uncompromising. "I came for my daughter, and now she's restored to me. We depart from this accursed kingdom!"

"And a word of wisdom, Elf King," Kelt began, glaring at Gallatar. "Never let me see your elves around my daughter. If we ever have to meet again, I'll not spare your lives."

Gallatar spat disdainfully, belittling Kelt's threat.

"Let's go, Candace!"

"Give me a moment, Father," she requested, but Baron Veldercrantz never heard her. He was already working his way to the lead position of the army.

"I hope you can forgive my father for this incredible misunderstanding," she pleaded shamefully, waving Navarro and Zakili closer. "You and the Silver Elf people have shown me nothing but acceptance and graciousness these past few days." She turned to the Elf Prince. "Zakili, I could never repay you for your kindness and the friendships I've developed. Your elves didn't deserve any of this. I only wish there was a way to make amends for today's incident."

"Calm yourself," Zakili said softly. "Our thanks is owed to you, a thousand debts of gratitude for risking your life to warn the Silver Elves of the danger. And of the friendships, the privilege has been completely ours."

"Come, Candace!" Kelt's voice called back sternly.

"I guess I'd better leave before I start a war," she said, looking at the elves and backing her horse reluctantly. Monolique, Saranisen, and several others waved to her, their smiles friendly, their eyes full of sadness.

"Remember Candace, you always have a home among the Silver Elves," Zakili declared before glancing slyly in Gallatar's direction. "Despite what my father says."

"I know I do and thank you."

Zakili extended his arm and the two clasped wrists.

She turned to Navarro then, welcomed by his usual contagious smile. Despite her sorrow, she beamed as she pulled up next to him. How often she'd enjoyed seeing his grin their short days together. She realized she would miss him most of all. She looked into his eyes, speechless. What could she say? More mysterious and unsearchable than any man she'd ever met, this uniquely honorable Paladin captivated her.

Watching curiously, Zakili noticed that Candace stared into Navarro's eyes with the same intense concentration he studied hers. He'd never seen anything like this from his friend before. The Elf Prince was intrigued. Even amid the playful flirting of his sisters, females of extreme beauty, The Paladin hadn't given a second glance. But this woman Candace had affected him, and Zakili could easily sense the magnetism between them. They didn't share a word with each other. He didn't think they had to.

"Candace, we are waiting for you!" Kelt's voice bellowed gruffly, shaking Candace from her trance.

"I really must go."

"It's best you do," Navarro said evenly, reaching his arm out. Candace clasped onto his wrist. "Take good care of yourself, Candace. My heart and the hearts of the elves will ever be with you for your bravery."

"She's hooked him," Zakili whispered to himself, smirking as neither made a move to separate, their eyes communicating in a hidden language not even they understood. With a final nod, Navarro pressed his war horse back, his eyes seeming eternally locked with hers as their hands slowly, hesitantly slipped apart. With great effort she looked away, whipped the reins and compelled her charger into a hearty stride.

"Pray for me," she called back. "I sense there's evil at the root of this confrontation."

The Paladin took in the request, concerned. Silently, he watched as she quickly caught up to the Veldercrantz army and melted into it.

Zakili grinned big, and with every ounce of his willpower, he bit back the teasing remark welling up in his throat. "She's a special woman," he finally allowed himself to say.

"Yes she is."

The elf chuckled quietly.

"Don't even get started," Navarro demanded, turning on his friend. "I meant she's an especially... pleasant person."

"Pleasant, huh?"

" I enjoyed her company. She was delightful to be around."

"Ooooh!"

"You know what I mean, elf!"

"Yes, my friend, I know," the elf prince admitted, still smiling big. He knew Navarro was trying valiantly to cover up any hints of sentiment for the courageous woman.

The Paladin peered once more in the direction of Kelt's departing army. The elf understood the unspoken disappointment he felt. Without another word, Navarro turned his charger and galloped after the elves who'd already started back for Verdant Wood. "Come my friend," he called back to Zakili. "We still have a lot of work to do."

The Elf Prince spun his horse about, but before starting back he glanced curiously to the departing army. Baron Veldercrantz, Candace's father, said he was informed by some unnamed prince that elves had abducted Candace. No human prince had ventured into the wood, Zakili knew, therefore one could never have known Candace was among the elves. She'd admitted she'd no predetermined design to seek the elves out; she acted when she discovered they'd come under attack. So, who'd pushed the baron to the brink of war against the elves? Candace suspected Kil. Zakili didn't doubt her supposition.

He stayed a moment longer, watching the baron's army ride toward the horizon. To his surprise, the rear of the army broke away and rode off from the main group. He stared for a long time, puzzled, as the two groups faded into the distance, putting more and more distance between themselves. *What kind of evil is at work?* he wondered.

* 15 *
UNEXPECTED TURNS

A week had passed since Candace's departure. Navarro glanced around quickly, surveying the woodland and scanning the canopies to make certain he wasn't followed. He needed some isolation, some time to think and sort things out in his mind, and to focus his will in overcoming this new, unexpected, torturous emotion.

With all appearing clear, Navarro slipped the bundle of looped rope off his shoulder and cut the wire which bound it together. Finding one end of the rope, he dragged it to a fallen tree, slipped the end under it, tied the rope around its girth, and fastened a tight knot. The log was only about eight feet long, obviously broken from the rest of the tree when it collapsed. The wood had petrified, making it fantastically hard.

He walked the other end to a thick bough, hanging about twelve feet off the ground, and tossed it over, the rope dangling from its perch. Grabbing hold, Navarro heaved, marching in the opposite direction of the log, straining against the resistance at the other end. Refusing to stop for even a second, he trudged on, and using the leverage the bough gave him as well as his momentum, he pulled the heavy log until it stood upright just below the bough. He pressed to the nearest tree, looped the rope around twice, tightened a knot and secured the log in its upright position.

He turned to the log, walking up to it casually, eyeing the object up and down, then his sword leapt into his hands, and he burst into furious action, his blade hacking across, withdrawing, twirling, and jabbing the thick log. He dodged to the left and pounded his target with a backhand chop which sent the log teetering. He lunged in once, then again, always landing a lethal strike, his blade hacking and carving into the petrified wood, sending chunks and splinters flying.

The lifeless faces of the fallen elves forced their way into his mind, increasing his fury. His sword flashed across again and again, the log disintegrating under his merciless blows. He speared the log viciously, turning sharply and came around with a spinning backhand chop which axed into the wood, nearly cutting it in half. The images of carnage and destruction attacked his sensibilities. He leaped and snap-kicked the damaged log, sending it twirling in tight circles.

The shrill cry of a loon echoed from somewhere in the forest, shaking Navarro from his sparring match with the log, and he smiled through labored breaths, thankful for the distraction. With great effort, he forced his troubled thoughts down. Then surprisingly, like light through the darkness, the image of smiling Candace brightened his thoughts. But a scowl etched onto his face immediately for that image now troubled him, too. He shook his head, trying to lose that memory, but unlike the visions of war, the images of Candace couldn't be shaken.

He spotted a number of squirrels staring down at him from a high branch and imagined they were admiring his attacks against his wooden foe. Their furry tails curled wildly behind them as if they were applauding his performance. He laughed.

The week since Candace's departure had been a busy one for him. He and the elves devoted all their energies to repairing the damage caused by the assassins' assault, and the monumental task seemed to whisk by in an instant. The playful, talkative mood of the elves never awoke through those days; instead they worked feverishly, their speech laconic, their faces somber.

The Paladin had seen this before, endless times, throughout his campaigns in the aftermath of victory against evil. The Silver Elves suffered great loss. Twenty-six of them were now nothing more than memories, and the elves, in their own way, tried to adjust to the vacuum their deaths created.

Zakili had assured the Paladin the Silver Elves were a resilient people, saying they don't mourn openly for long; whatever it takes, they will adjust. They'd miss those lost, the Elf Prince said, but elves are stoic and utterly realistic.

Nevertheless, Navarro's heart ached over the cloud of grief and sadness overshadowing this valiant race of people.

Placing things in perspective, he'd a gnawing feeling in his stomach every time he remembered the Dark Sorcerer. His focus returned to the danger promising to be many times worse than The Lurking Shadows.

He returned late last night from the Preacher Johansen's church and shared the warning of Zeraktalis' coming, but the congregation was unmoved. He prayed with the pastor, his long time friend, about the apathy of the people. None of them considered seriously any threat to the land of Avundar. It was practically unheard of.

The Christians of that church were a relatively young, middle-aged group. Located in the town of Pebblefist, nearly in Avundar's center, the church's congregation made up of a cross-section of all Avundar's baronies, including several influential men. None of them had heard the first instance of conflict in the recent history of Avundar's baronies. Navarro understood why serious doubt could arise. Admittedly, even his own grandfather recounted how blessed this land was to have never suffered war. But how short this generation's memory had become.

Did they not recall what happened in Sheliavon, the adjacent kingdom? The Dark Sorcerer had nearly destroyed that kingdom 5 years ago, and if it could so easily be laid waste, not-so-far-away Avundar wouldn't escape similar devastation. Besides, Navarro saw The Dark Sorcerer stand on Avundarian soil, breathing out threats against the entirety of mankind. Together, he and Johansen fell to their knees, seeking the Lord's wisdom and guidance against a yet unseen menace. They also sought for God to heat up the church's lukewarm lethargy before it was too late.

He glanced back to the log, battered, the bottom half hanging weirdly due to the damage he inflicted. Seeking to alleviate his tension bottled up from the conflict and the escalating emotional battles, he'd come out here in seclusion to funnel his frustrations into arduous, physical activity. This was a common ritual for him after every battle.

If he didn't somehow find relief from the perpetual heartache of seeing so many friends and amiable countrymen killed when defending their homeland, he admitted he would probably fall into deep depression. The amount of death he saw regularly would destroy the average man, and Navarro knew it was only by God's grace he had the power to continually press forward despite the endless savagery he

Johnny Earl Jones

witnessed.

As a young paladin, he often experienced recurring nightmares from the horrors he saw. He still battled with macabre day visions sneaking into his thoughts, but throughout the years he enforced disciplined willpower to counteract their intrusion.

He gained victory over war visions, but why couldn't he now deny this new emotion? It caused him to turn restlessly in the dark of night and made his sensibilities do weird somersaults. Throughout the week, he outwardly focused on the repair work in Elfstay, but inwardly he wrestled with feelings he just couldn't shake, and that troubled him more than any intruding visions of war ever could.

In everything he did or considered, he trusted the Lord's guidance, his only vice being his pride on being self-controlled; however, this new emotion was something he just couldn't get a grip on. It eluded his mental inspection and clouded his ability to view objectively. Candace relentlessly filled his thoughts, as she had for the entire week.

Turning in the direction of the plains, his mind drifted, recalling the night on the edge of the woods talking with her, watching the stars, swapping testimonies of how God had awesomely changed their lives. How enthralled he was by her words, and how fascinated she seemed by his tales as they reclined under the night sky.

So much more pleasant, and memorable, was their innocuous conversation compared to the lecherous escapades he'd experienced before Jesus saved him. In his unredeemed life, with so beautiful a woman as Candace... He cast that lewd thought down before it ever had a chance to be seen by his mind's eye.

As a brawling sailor he was led about by his own lusts, never hindered by sentimental feelings. So why was he struggling with them now? He'd consecrated himself to remain free from all romantic relationships.

Cutting through all the confusion and denial, he had to admit she captivated him.

Now it was time to get over it.

"Admiring the forest?"

Surprised, Navarro spun in the direction of the voice, his sword raised. He was horrified he hadn't recognized somebody approaching. His concerns had him so mired he hadn't sensed a presence behind him. It was Zakili. In mock alarm, the elf's daggers went spinning in his hands.

"What're you doing sneaking up on me?"

"Sneaking up?" the elf echoed. "I didn't think anybody could sneak up on..." he let that thought trail away. "I just didn't see you around Elfstay. I was in a bad mood and wanted someone to beat up on, so I came here looking for you."

They shared a laugh.

"I knew I'd find you out here in these woods. If I didn't know better I'd think you were half-elf the way you're enamored with our forest. The first time I met you, you were reposing by Lifespring, and it seems whenever you want to get away, you isolate yourself among the trees. You say the God you worship is named Jesus, but I think you really come out here to worship nature."

"No, only the God who created this nature," Navarro said with a laugh, dismissing the elf's joking supposition.

A grin split Zakili's face. "All right. I concede you may never be a tree lover, but I think you've got some elf in your heart, if not in your personality. Sometimes it seems you're among the forest more than my kin."

"I'm here only for brief seasons at a time," The Paladin said. "I've got to soak up as much of this as I can before a new adventure springs up and sends me on my way."

Zakili discerned his friend's impatient tone, understanding the man wanted to be alone to stew in his own thoughts. Judging himself to be a good friend, he determined to pester a more revealing conversation from him. He looked to the battered log. "It looks like you got out some frustration."

"Just getting some exercise."

"You could've called me for that. If you want some exercise, you know I'll wear you out."

Navarro shook his head, chuckling.

"So why did you come all the way out here to beat up an old dead log?"

"I needed to get away. I just wanted to think," The Paladin answered, not wishing to make his concerns known. "And just soak in the day. As you said: admiring the forest."

"Admiring the forest?" the elf pried.

"That is correct."

"And indeed, this is a great morning to be doing such. Look around. Isn't this forest just as beautiful as the first day you saw it?"

"It is," Navarro said, always cautious about what path Zakili was taking with his line of questions.

"And a great reason to let the day slip by, hiding out here, beating up logs and thinking about the forest. You did say you came out here simply to consider the forest, right?"

"Yes."

Zakili turned and gazed up into a sudden break in the canopy as a breeze rushed through the woods, watching the streams of sunlight filter to the fertile earth below.

"Liar," he mumbled just loud enough for Navarro to hear.

"What!" The Paladin exclaimed, turning fully on his friend.

"What?" the elf asked, acting blameless.

"I heard what you said."

Zakili shrugged helplessly.

"You called me a liar."

"Me?"

"Yes. Why?"

"What? Would I do something like that?"

Navarro stared sternly.

"Oooh, now I remember. Well let me put it this way: I know you better than you think you do."

"Which means?"

"You have more than tranquil thoughts about Verdant Wood on your mind."

Navarro's silence shouted more than any words could say. The Paladin had always enjoyed the camaraderie between him and the Elf Prince. He never grown tired fighting side by side with him, but as great of friends as they were, he was unwilling to dump his concerns and his struggles into anyone else's life. The turmoil in his spirit was one he had to fight alone...

"I think there is something else consuming your thoughts," Zakili said, interrupting Navarro's contemplations. The elf grinned with an all-teeth-showing smile.

"There is nothing," Navarro answered tersely, untruthfully.

"Liar."

"What is your problem?"

"You're lying again."

"How? About what?"

"I don't think it's about what. It's about who."

"About who?" Navarro echoed in exasperation.

"You tell me," Zakili suggested playfully.

"Did you just come out here to harass me? This game's getting kind of tiring."

"What game?"

Navarro threw his hands up in an exaggerated surrender, laughing about his friend's persistency. "You never have been the one to give up on anything. You just don't quit until you have finally conquered whatever is standing in your way. This time you have sniffed out a challenge that doesn't exist."

"How long have we been friends?"

Navarro narrowed his eyes curiously. What direction was Zakili taking him now? "I cannot recall exactly. Maybe too long."

The elf laughed. "Being companions for so long, do you think I cannot read the emotions in your face? I'm no novice to the game of life, my friend..."

Navarro raised an eyebrow, smirking at the elf's fatherly tone.

"...I have sensed from many a man the quandary you now find in yourself. And as your closest friend, I can't let you go through this on your own without pestering the problem out of you."

Navarro smiled at his friend's unique sense of humor and genuine concern. But what could he say? He was the type to carry his burdens solely and privately. He'd decided early on he would live as an encourager. He refused speak anything which would cause concern or discouragement. The last thing he wanted to do was burden someone else. But could it be that as hard as he was trying to disguise his inner turmoil, it could still be read by the expressions on his face?

"It's Candace, isn't it?"

The bluntness of the question nearly knocked Navarro flat.

"Sir Navarro!" a voice called from among some nearby trees, turning the two friends.

"How did you find us here?" Zakili asked, seeing several elves pick their way quickly through the trees.

"We've been looking for The Paladin all morning, my Prince."

"Speak on, Zatrus."

The elf turned to Navarro. "I'm not sure what I'm feeling right now, but I do know I needed to find you. One of our elves, Baliesto, told me something when he came to my rescue during the battle, and it has consumed my thoughts from that day on. I tried to ignore it during the week, but it won't go away.

"He confessed he'd received this Jesus you always talk about as Savior and said he knew he'd go to live with Him in a place called heaven if he were to die. He said it with such confidence and assurance I couldn't deny the veracity of his words. But he also said my eternity was doomed without Jesus..."

Navarro listened patiently, thankful for what he heard. At the same time, he silently prayed the Lord would settle his thoughts in order to share the message of hope with the elf.

"...and although I avoided your Christian meetings, from others I heard much about what you spoke and about the Bible from which you read. Now, my heart beats fast whenever I think about this Jesus or when I consider the fate of my soul. I just speak for myself. But these elves have also joined my search for you, seeking the truth about what they've heard.

"Navarro, I want to know how I can have this Jesus as my Savior. What must I do to be saved?"

High in the treetops, an invisible demon hissed at the sound of that holy name. It sprung away, catching a breeze, and soared to the north, back in the direction of Genna Fiendomon.

* * * * *

For nearly three days he had ridden horseback to this place called Lonely Forest, three days of long and meticulous inspection of himself and the situation he had been forced into. A couple of weeks ago he'd been the leader of a lucrative merchant band, living comfortably and quite safely among his team of warrior-merchants. His entire life ordered so securely he needed nothing. Too late, he realized his downfall. He desired everything. He coveted riches, fame, and recognition. As leader of his merchant troupe, Methlon had received all three.

But he had to have more. He wanted to be rich, famous and adored forever. And he thought to achieve it meant capturing the Silver Elves' Lifespring and its life-giving waters for himself. That was his worst mistake. This new lifestyle as an assassin was the consequence of his obsessions. Methlon spat at the bitter turn. Was he locked into this dark existence for life? In his anger, he whacked his steed's backside, causing the animal to step up its pace.

The assassins nearest Methlon eyed him, sneering, and the merchant tried to shrug off the weight of their stares. Their animosity had been vocalized throughout the journey, not to him directly, but could be heard in the undercurrents of their conversations. These men, among the land's most notorious killers, were enraged that he, a former merchant, was given charge over them. Second-in-command was how Kil told them to address Methlon, who was filling the vacancy left by Stoman. From his eavesdropping, he knew the assassins didn't have apprehensions with his predecessor Stoman, because he was a Lurking Shadow as long as they'd known him. But now he was dead.

Kil had destroyed him, and his death was a surprise to all. He'd been Kil's favorite, but his carelessness had brought about his demise. All The Lurking Shadows understood if loyal Stoman was not immune to Kil's wrath, none of them were.

Methlon proudly stuck out his chest. Because of the fear Kil inspired, the assassins remained submissive to him, like it or not.

"Finally, we're at these accursed woods!" Methlon mumbled several hours later as the troupe pulled up to their destination. Glad the long, uneventful journey was finished, he longed to get his sore backside out of the saddle. Then the tremendous magnitude of his travel hit him. His concern over the long ride and the despair of his failed life blew away in the breeze when he considered the reason he was here.

He was to make contact with a throng of bloodthirsty monsters!

A vicious chill raced down his spine, just as it had when Kil initially informed him of this task. Methlon hadn't dared refuse or even balk at his liege's command; the Fangs of Hell were held comfortably in Kil's hands.

"Follow a safe distance behind me," Methlon ordered the assassins, trying hard to quell the nervous shaking in his voice.

As was customary with The Lurking Shadows, Kil's secondary man was to meet with any group before the Warlord paid a visit. Remembering the process it took for him to enlist the assassin's services he recalled this was how he met Stoman that night alone. "What a fateful turn of events that was," he groaned.

The Lurking Shadows nodded obediently, laughing wickedly under their breath. Methlon didn't like these men, but he did feel safer approaching an army of unspeakable brutes with trained killers watching his back.

Methlon's troupe entered the quiet forest slowly, their horses' hooves barely a whisper on the grassy sod. Aside from the Lurking Shadows' goblin slaves, Methlon had never encountered a monster. He trembled at the thought of encountering not only one, but a whole throng of the brutes. Desperately, he tried to recall the points Kil had outlined when he met them, but he struggled to pierce the fog of fear which clouded his mind.

Given no specific direction or destination, he pressed forward aimlessly, every snap of a twig or rustle of the leaves turning him nervously. His eyes darted in the direction of every swaying shadow. With his assassin companions riding a couple dozen yards back, he felt alone and vulnerable and afraid. After a tense half hour, no monster had showed itself, and Methlon hoped they'd already left forever.

He feared encountering the monsters, near to the point of fleeing and never returning to Avundar again. Kil had a long arm though, and Methlon knew if he deserted The Lurking Shadows he'd have to skulk around in the shadows for the rest of his existence if he wanted to stay unseen and alive. He didn't like that idea. He continued on.

Reflectively, Methlon judged the woods quite peaceful and lovely, hardly seeming like the haunt of bloodthirsty monsters.

A bizarre hoot off to the side jolted Methlon, and he instinctively reached for his sword. Nervously, he glanced around. Sharp rustling sounded in some bushes to his right. He spun in that direction, cravenly pointing his sword, his heart beating fast. He saw nothing. From the corner of his eye, he noted a shadow dashing from behind a bush to the cover of a nearby copse of trees. He turned to get a look at it, but it was simply too fast. He could hear his heart beating in his ears now, his hands trembled, and he wiped his sweaty palms on his tunic. He sat up straight and unmoving in his saddle for a long time, carefully scanning the trees.

Potential death at the claws of monsters or certain death at the hand of Kil? Methlon weighed. Which was worse? He groaned. *What were those points Kil had instructed him to use when facing these monsters?* He put his hand to his head as a sudden headache pulsed in his temples. Growling in frustration, he pushed aside his swirling thoughts and took in a deep breath. He had to do something, sensing monsters gathering all around him among the shadows. He seemed hopelessly trapped in a situation with no door for escape.

"Don't fear," Methlon called to the shadow, attempting the hardiest tone he could muster.

"Fear?" a deep baritone voice questioned, rumbling in Methlon's eardrums like the boom of thunder.

Shrinking down in his saddle, he realized the foolishness of his statement. He was the one gripped with fear. He drew in another deep breath, trying to stop the visible trembling of his sword arm.

"We should tears him to pieces," a screeching voice suggested from somewhere in the shadows.

"I hunger for the taste of warmblood flesh," another barked. "The first two were hardly enough to whets my appetite!"

"I come..." Methlon tried to shout, his voice coming out in a squeak. He quickly cleared his throat. "I've come to meet with Krylothon!" he roared, sounding as ominous as possible. He remembered Kil informing him that to show fear before the monsters was inviting doom.

"Krylothon will haves the first bite," the high-pitched voice proclaimed.

Methlon's heart felt heavy. His eyes filled with dread. He would soon be monster bait!

An ugly head poked out from behind a tree. The beast's skin was mud-colored, its beady eyes stared at him, and its oversized jaw grumbled. Its large canine teeth overlapped its upper lip. The brute danced out in front of Methlon's horse, thick and humanoid in appearance, and was summarily joined by a dozen more

Johnny Earl Jones

who spilled out of the shadows, grunting and hooting and pointing their weapons threateningly.

The trees shook to Methlon's left and his eyes darted in that direction. He felt and heard the boom of one footstep then another then another. He felt the blood drain from his face. One more booming footstep pounded before the boughs were pushed aside, a gargantuan humanoid stomping into the clearing, swatting away the closest goblin with one swipe of his hand.

"A gi..gi.. giant," Methlon stuttered, swallowing hard as he looked up at the monster standing four times his own height.

"I want to crunch yer bones between me teeth," the giant offered in a throaty baritone rumble.

Methlon froze in paralyzing terror, his steed backed away nervously.

"Dinner," the giant suggested dumbly.

"Breakfast," a goblin protested, but the giant dropped its colossal fist on his head.

"I come in the name of The Dark Sorcerer!" Methlon cried, his desperation rooting up the trump Kil guaranteed would prevail if all other reasoning failed.

"The Dark Sorcerer?" all the monsters mumbled in fearful unison, backing respectfully away.

Methlon, always having more pride than common sense, gloated about the power he now wielded. With mere words, he'd held at bay a mob of hungry monsters.

"I'll watch him rip each one of you to shreds for your folly!" he continued, testing his new weapon further. The goblins trembled in response, and the giant threw his arm before his eyes to ward off the terrible threat.

His overwhelming sensation of fear fled, and in his bravado, he poked out his chest as he continued to berate the brutes with threat after threat. Single-handedly, he was pulling these monsters' strings. Never had he wielded such absolute power. He controlled even these mighty monsters. Maybe life as a Lurking Shadow wouldn't be so bad after all, he mused.

Methlon's arrogance was short lived.

He heard the sound of cracking wood, and looked over in time to see a young healthy tree lean, then begin falling in his direction. Methlon snapped the reins wildly, but his horse really needed no such prompting; it was already skittering off to the side and just did get out of the way as the tree crashed to the ground where they'd been standing.

A hideous, hulking brute stepped over the fallen trunk into the clearing, and Methlon nearly fell off his horse from fright. The creature stomped forward threateningly, towering over Methlon and his steed, his bulbous, multifaceted eyes fastening on him, vice-like mandibles clamping and gaping jaws dripping saliva from between triangular, serrated teeth. Methlon gasped dreadfully as the creature's six corded arms whipped out wide and its leathery wings unfurled and stretched out behind it.

It looked several times more frightening than the worst visions of his nightmares. He thought at any moment the behemoth would propel itself at him and tear him apart.

Methlon's horse turned and started to run until Methlon shook himself from his fear and brought the animal back under control. Why was he letting this monster terrorize him, especially when he knew the name to bring this beast under his control.

"I come in the name of The Dark Sorcerer!" Methlon yelled, but nearly overwhelmed with fear, his proclamation didn't come out with much conviction.

To his surprise the monster halted its charge and studied him, its fierce insect-like head pivoting from side to side curiously.

A superior smirk turned up the corners of Methlon's lips. The name could stop even this monstrosity!

"I come in the name of The Dark Sorcerer!" he cried again, this time with more authority.

"Ssso what!" the muscular brute hissed then advanced again.

"Halt! Or I'll be sure the sorcerer destroys you slowly!"

The monster did stop, but only long enough to double over in mocking laughter. "You mussst be the pathetic assssasssssin Zzzeraktalissss told me about."

"I've come to meet with Krylothon. Take me to him."

"That isss who you faccce, puny warmblood!"

Methlon tried to keep up his calloused facade, but his face paled, and his breath was stolen away by the majesty of the frightening beast before him.

"How pitiful," the towering monster Krylothon spat derisively. "I expected a much more impresssssive ssspecccimen. Zzzeraktalisss talked highly of you, Kil. What an error he hasss made. You are no greater than any other sssniveling warmblood human I've had the pleasssure to dessstroy. I ssshould break you in half right now and fly your piecccesss back to the Dark Sssorcccereer to ssshow him the error of presssuming ssso much of a cowardly human."

The usurper stepped forward. Methlon felt a tremendous lump in his throat.

"I'm not Kil," he squeaked.

"What did you sssay?"

"I'm not Kil. I'm Methlon, his second-in-command."

"Then we can devour you right now," the usurper decided, his words drawing the giant and the goblins in closer, licking their big lips.

"You cannot!" Methlon exclaimed, his voice coming out as a fearful squeak.

"We cannot?" Krylothon echoed. "You don't undersssstand the appetite of my army. Sssix moonsss have ssset sssinccce a handful of my minionsss tasssted warmblood flesssh. The lasssst two humansss didn't go far amid an army of ravenousss monstersss. Multiplied thousssandsss ssstill wait to whet their palate. You wouldn't deny them of that pleasssure, now would you? Could you sssay no to facesss like these?" Krylothon waved his arm wide in deference to all of the slobbering monsters before clamping its own dangerous mandibles hungrily.

"I'm Kil's messenger," he breathed. "Without me, there's no contacting him."

"Sssurely, if you are consssumed, he'll sssend othersss."

Krylothon's presumption caused the brutes to wipe the eager saliva from their mouths and draw in yet closer.

"No! He will not!" Methlon screamed, knowing in truth any other could easily take his place. "Kil's a hard and unforgiving man. He'll not take lightly his messenger being eaten."

"Very well," Krylothon agreed, seemingly too easily for Methlon. "Tell Kil to sssend no more lackeysss. We've already waited in thessse woodsssss for too long! Assssure him if he doesss not come quickly, my army will begin itsss march on thisss land without him!"

"He will come," Methlon promised, barely able to get the words past the lump in his throat. He turned his steed, holding in the tremendous sigh of relief, thankful he was escaping with his life.

"One more quesssstion before I allow you to return to your masssster. Did you come alone asss wasss the arrangement?"

Methlon's heart beat a vicious drumbeat against his ribcage, his face breaking out in a sweat. "I did," he lied.

"We feassst then!" Krylothon roared.

Methlon thought he was dead.

"Capture the intrudersss!"

A swarm of monsters sprung from behind trees and bushes and out of shadows and washed over the Lurking Shadows who had been trailing far behind. Methlon heard the clash of swords, knowing those vicious assassins wouldn't go down without a fight. Several dying screams echoed through the forest as the lives of a couple of monsters were forever ended.

"Get out of my sssight!" Krylothon growled.

Methlon started to protest, but remembered easily enough how much worth he placed on his own hide. Those assassins didn't care for him anyway, he decided. He snapped the reins and sped away. With the screams of the men now filling his ears, he could only imagine the fate of those poor assassins. He wanted to see nothing of it.

* * * * *

"Thank you, Lord," she praised under her breath. She wanted to shout it from the housetops. She slipped through the wide courtyard of Castle Veldercrantz and
out the open portcullis at the high wall.

The watching eyes of all in the castle had tracked her for days. She had timed her "escape" perfectly. This was the hour of the midday feast and few rarely missed it, especially her father's ravenous warriors. Thus, for a brief moment, no one was shadowing her or hiding behind doors to watch her every move. The only difficulty was getting past the gates, but today two young warriors stood guard. Two she knew were enamored with her, so she charmed her way past and rode Elyion into the surrounding Maribowam forest.

Ever since returning from the mystical home of the Silver Elves, her father had behaved strangely toward her. Habitually, he was overly loving, thus overly protective of her. Throughout the years she'd often threatened to share with his warriors how tenderhearted their tough warrior-baron really was. But now things were different. Instead of being the protective father she'd always known, he behaved as a jailer, as if she was some kind of notorious villain. She felt like a caged animal.

Aside from the war in Sheliavon, she couldn't remember a day since the departure of her mother when she and Father had not gone into the Maribowam forest and sparred. They shared time alone together, swapped stories and told each other their dreams. She loved her father, but he acted so strangely, so completely unlike ever before.

Early during the week she tried numerous times to influence him to go out to the woods and spar, but his continual response was one of suspicion. Normally, she could play the strings of her father's heart. She was his pride and joy, he'd often told her, and she could talk him into anything. But not now.

He was under the delusion the Silver Elves bewitched her with some kind of magical spell. In his uncharacteristic paranoia, he feared she was going to turn on him and open the castle up for attack to the Silver Elves.

She couldn't help but compare the way he acted with the attitude of Zakili's father, Gallatar. And she empathized with the Elf Prince's frustration.

Even more disturbing than Father's distant reactions was his violent attitude. Her father was normally a gentle, thoughtful man who held no grudges and entertained no prejudices. Since their return from Verdant Wood, he actively verbalized his budding hatred for the elves and that venom infected his warriors' attitudes as well.

Her shoulders drooped in discouragement. After living with the Silver Elves for several days, she understood them to be a goodly race, certainly undeserving of the slander they suffered from her father.

They'd done nothing evil to him.

Immediately, she pushed all those thoughts aside, feeling a small headache coming on. She pressed her horse onward, her mind racing with insatiable curiosity. The great Maribowam forest was practically at the doorstep of the castle's outer walls and surrounded it on nearly all sides. Off to the north was the town of Recqueom, nestled down in a quiet valley, which relied on the baron for its defenses. She cast it a passing glance, then continued unerringly to the trees. She loved this forest. It was tranquil, unpolluted by the debris of wayfaring merchants or passing travelers. A place of peace and solitude, Kelt had maintained the forest as a sanctuary since before he took over the barony.

Slipping in among the trees, she was careful to scan behind to be sure she wasn't being watched or followed. Satisfied she was in the clear, she pushed deeper, her curiosity burning like a raging fire. Since returning to the fortress, she longed for a private moment to test her unpredictable power to move physical objects, but Father had a guard posted at her opened door night and day, leaving her no solitude.

She couldn't even bathe alone! But thank God her father displayed the decency to not allow any men nearby; instead, one of the unfortunate maidservants was given the task of watching her, the whole time wearing an apologetic expression on her face.

Candace took a deep breath. This was the escape she needed, not only to test her power, but also to get out from the weight of suspicious eyes.

"Has someone replaced my father with an evil double?" she quipped, giggling bitter-sweetly.

Candace didn't have to travel far to find a testing ground. Just a couple of yards ahead laid a fist-sized rock. Quickly she slipped down from Elyion, went to one knee, and looked at the rock nervously. Her last attempt to move a similar stone in Verdant Wood was an utter failure.

She locked her eyes on the stone, probing its contours and angular surface. She studied its size and guessed its weight. In retrospect, when she tried to prove her mental powers in the elves' woods, she had simply bid the object move. The three times her powers had surfaced, she was so emotionally involved in the situation she couldn't remember what particular action or thought initiated the object's movements.

Complete and total concentration must be the key, she decided, remembering in each instance she knew exactly what object she wanted moved and that alone was displaced. Besides, concentration had been the key to success in every endeavor she'd ever been involved, be it her rugged exercise routines or her training in weapon mastery. Gaining control of her mental faculties couldn't be much more different.

With her thoughts locked on the stone, she raised an open palm. "Come to me."

After a long, uneventful moment, the rock remained unmoved.

Candace shifted, shaking away the frustration welling within. In a final fit of aggravation she ran her fingers quickly through her golden tresses before facing the rock again, her expression serious.

She focused, calculating its weigh again, exploring its jagged texture with her eyes. "Sit in my hand," she ordered this time, thinking the stone needed more direct instruction. She urged the stone intently, thinking she could actually see it begin to quiver ever so slightly as it awoke to movement.

But it was all her imagination. The stone didn't budge.

She growled in frustration. After several long breaths she tried again, focusing harder and longer than the previous two times.

But once more, nothing happened.

Stomping away from the stone, she waved the whole attempt away as a complete failure. She could never do it, she grumbled, crestfallen, then immediately corrected herself. She had done it before. Three times her unusual ability had saved her, the most vivid instance being when the huge viking's weapon plummeted toward her skull. Somehow, when she was down and defenseless, her powers cast the heavy weapon away, sparing her life.

"Thank you, Lord," she exclaimed, "that Navarro, despite being in the heat of battle, warned me of the viking's charge."

The thought of Navarro made her beam, causing her to forget about the unsuccessful episode with the stone. Over the past week, she thought often about The Paladin. Since her childhood, she always dreamt of meeting a man who was virtuous, brave, and godly. Although she'd been introduced to a myriad of men from every class and walk of life, she never encountered any who lived up to her "fairy tale" expectations.

Until now. How different this Paladin was from the countless number of suitors who'd invaded her life. Navarro was gentle, selfless.

And yet, so alien.

He seemed untouchable, beyond the evil influences of man or the world. This seemed more incredible after he had shared his testimony with her, explaining his past lifestyle compared to the way the Lord had transformed him and changed the direction of his life.

At first, she was strangely jealous of his discipline. He embodied the composure and self-control she'd always longed for during her years of weapon mastery and combat training. Her skills had been honed for over a decade, but The Paladin operated a caliber above any she'd seen, not only in his fighting ability but also in his private life. He was a man of integrity, she decided, smiling. And he was truly magnanimous, majestic far beyond the pretense royal monarchy clothed themselves. Noble both in word and in deed.

She had implied her interest enough times, she remembered shamefully. Yet he didn't take advantage of her. During their time with each other, especially when they were completely alone, he could've taken her. She felt her cheeks flush in private embarrassment then she shook that last thought away, knowing neither of them would have submitted to the heat of passion.

The act would have fit neither of their characters, nor would they have shamed God in such a way. Candace straightened proudly, shrugging off her embarrassment. Neither she nor Navarro would fail Christ.

She giggled quietly when she recalled the first time she saw him, his hair wet and soaked, his thin shirt clinging to his muscles. She remembered gawking, but how much more delightful he proved to be when she discovered his personality.

She admitted she missed him.

"Lord, if that rock were Navarro..." she didn't miss the allusion to the paladin's steadfastness, "I'd ask it to fly into my arms."

Why didn't she pursue him when he was in arm's length? she berated herself.

She broke from her thoughts when she spotted the stone spinning toward her.

"Stop," she screamed, instinctively dodging to one side. To her amazement, the stone halted in midair and dropped. For a brief moment she knelt, took in a deep breath, and heard the rapid pounding of her heart. Once the shock wore off, she scanned the woods, looking for assailants.

She saw nobody. She heard only the chatter of birds and the gentle whistle of the wind.

Then she glanced over to the stone she was concentrating on.

It wasn't there.

She looked down at the rock, which had fallen close to her boot, and picked it up, inspecting it. This was the same one.

"How is this happening?" she whispered awestruck.

She nearly screamed excitedly when, like the last piece of a puzzle completing a full image, her mind made a final connection which showed her the source of her powers.

"Lord, you said our faith can move mountains, but I didn't know my prayers can move objects!

"When I declared I wished this rock would fly into my arms as if it were Navarro, it went airborne. My thoughts were on The Paladin. My eyes were on the stone. It was the inadvertent inert object of my supplication."

Continuing that same train of thought made her laugh outloud. "When the viking came in on me with his huge axe, I prayed out in desperation, and the weapon was ripped from his grasp. The same thing happened with that bough as I charged into Verdant Wood. And how about the door when I was trapped in the den of The Lurking Shadows?

"God, my powers are not fueled by focused thought," she prayed aloud. "They're a gift through the power of prayer."

"Candace, the magicians have come," a voice announced from behind, jolting her from her considerations. Her hand reached instinctively for her cutlass, but all she found was her weaponless hip. She had neglected to bring her blade!

She sighed in relief when seeing the visitors were not assassins but her father and his elite guards.

"The magicians have come," Baron Kelt reiterated.

"Magicians?" she questioned. "You know I don't care much for magic tricks."

Kelt smiled at her dry humor before becoming suddenly grave. "They're here to remove the elven curse from you."

* 16 *
THE FACE OF DEATH

"We cannot!" one usurper argued, then promptly and wisely stepped out of his fierce commander's striking range. This usurper, seven-feet tall and powerful, had the strength to rip a young tree up by the roots and had the arsenal to eliminate a mob of goblins single-handedly in a matter of moments, but his might paled in comparison to his intimidating leader, Krylothon.

Under the luminescence of the quarter moon, Krylothon's glowing, multifaceted eyes shimmered, intensifying his threatening stare as he locked gazes with his subordinate. His massive muscles twitching under his scaly hide when his taloned hands gripped and loosened rhythmically. Easily translating his leaders actions, the usurper took an extra step back. Krylothon didn't like being second guessed.

"The Dark Sssorcccerer would dessstroy usss all for our disssobediencce," the second of Krylothon's lieutenants sibilated.

"You dare quesstion me?" Krylothon roared, staring down the two usurpers, his voice echoing into the night. His army, hidden throughout the dark forest, shifted uncomfortably.

"I wasss there when the sssorcccerer returned," the second usurper replied respectfully. "I have ssseen hisss anger and hisss power!"

"I have felt hisss power!" mighty Krylothon roared.

"The sssorcccerer commanded usss not to move againsst the elvesss until Kil'sss army hasss linked with oursss," the first usurper reminded.

Krylothon guffawed at the statement, his mandibles clicking together noisily. The two usurpers stepped back further, not knowing what to expect from their unpredictable leader.

"Of coursse we cannot foolsss," he agreed. "You came to me to argue that point? We won't know the location of the elvesss until the human disssclosssesss that to usss."

The two lesser usurpers stared at each other, confused.

"I don't propossse to attack the elvesss. What I demand isss a feassst!"

"But the sssorcccerer..." the first started. With a sudden lurch, Krylothon was at the brute. His burly arm lashed out and backhanded his lesser across the jaw, launching him against a wide oak, jarring the huge tree and sending a resounding boom into the night. The behemoth peeled himself off in a fury, spitting out broken teeth, and with rage in his spider-like eyes, he opened his mandibles threateningly wide, his toothy jaws gnashing dangerously. Usurpers were proud creatures, and this one wasn't going to let the assault go unchallenged.

It charged.

Krylothon turned fully on the brute, displaying his own deadly arsenal, his wings unfurling and his six deadly talons coming to bear. Gaping mandibles and several rows of serrated teeth promised certain destruction.

The lesser usurper knew he stared death in the face. Cooling his rage, the brute skidded to a halt. He was sorely overmatched. With great effort, the proud brute eased down humbly before mightier Krylothon, willing to accept the slap and live than to defend his pride and die.

"The sssorcccereer'sss order wasss not to ravage thisss land until we have sssecured Lifessspring," Krylthon finished the usurper's statement. "I'm not sssuggesssting to unleasssh our throng on thisss countryssside jussst yet. But my monsssstersss long for blood! And thisss human asssasssin hasss chosssen to play gamesss. It isss time for usss to take mattersss into our own handsss until he recognizzzesss the foolissshnessss of hisss delay. My army hasss consssumed all the animal life in this foressst. They desssire more. They long for the flesssh of warmbloodsss!"

"How will we be able to sssatisssfy the bloodlussstsss of sssuch a masssive army without exposssing oursssselvesss?" the second usurper asked.

"Over the passst few daysss we have learned few warmbloodsss venturre into thessse woodsss," Krylothon explained. "Happensssstanccce will bring usss no victimsss. We mussst invite oursssselvesss to the feassst! Ssscoutsss have already been dissspatched to explore the regionsss and expossse the areasss ripe for conquessst!"

"You have sssent out sssscoutsss?" both asked incredulously.

"Before the moon fallsss behind the mountainsss tomorrow, we'll know the location of our next victimsss. Go now! Sssselect a raiding contingent, an assssemblage of the most battle-hardened goblinsss and masssneviresss we have. Ssset Baricon and the giantsss as field commandersss over them. The raidersss will ssstrike under our command, according to the reportsss of our returning sssscoutsss, and they will return with warmblood flesssh to sssatiate my ravenousss army. The remaining ssshall linger in thessse woodsss. We can't allow oursssselvesss to be dissscovered by the Avundariansss until the time for the asssault againssst the elvesss!"

The lesser usurpers rushed away to follow their commander's order.

"Thisss isss only the beginning," Krylothon said to himself, sneering. "I'll have conquered thisss entire land before the arrogant sssorccceror even departsss from Genna Fiendomon. Where he couldn't sssuccccceed in Sssheliavon, I'll prove victoriousss in a much greater land!"

* * * * *

"Incredible," Saranisen whispered in the night from the tree bough some thirty feet above the forest floor.

"Incredibly ugly," her older sister Monolique corrected, viewing the same sight.

"How many of them in all?" Monolique asked the sentry, Jorab, who had initially spotted the intruders and signaled for a representative from the king. The two sisters had come in response.

"Only three."

Curious, they watched the three burly invaders carefully skulk around the trees, trying to remain unseen. They were oblivious to the fact they were being watched the entire time. Saranisen nearly laughed at the irony, but she was a curious type, so she silently slipped to a lower bough to examine them more closely. These were creatures she'd never seen before: burly, man-shaped brutes wearing helmets and leather armor over their mud-colored skin, and she strained her memory trying to recall their ilk. "Hunched, big ears, bald pates, really ugly," she listed aloud, hoping the verbal inventory would give her a clue, but after thorough contemplation she drew a blank. "I can't think of any community in Avundar with such ugly humans."

Older than her sister by a decade and being more worldly wise, Monolique understood gravely what these intruders were. "Those aren't humans at all. Those are goblins!"

"Goblins!" Saranisen gasped, almost too loud. She slapped her hand over her mouth to muffle the volume and gazed below, hoping they hadn't heard her.

The goblins continued on unaware.

"I thought father said monsters wouldn't dare enter our woods or the land of Avundar," Saranisen called to her sister in the sing-songy voice the elves used in secretive conversation.

"So did I," Monolique replied. "And I wish that was true, but these beasts are real and wicked. I can sense the evil waft from them like a foul stench, polluting our beautiful forest."

"These creatures have to be stopped. I'll allow them to proceed no further," Jorab decided, knowing on his watch, this quadrant of the forest was his responsibility to defend.

"You're correct. They can no longer be allowed to wander freely through our forest home," Monolique said. "You must inform the advisors about these monsters. Saranisen and I are going to have a little fun with these bold invaders." A mischievous smile crossed he lips and was mirrored by her sister.

"Go back and miss out on the sport?" Jorab protested. "I think not, ladies. Besides, the king would have my head for leaving his daughters alone to tangle with a pack of monsters. He'll want these ones alive to question, so I'm staying around to protect them from you two."

"Very well," Monolique laughed. "Then you'll get to join in on the entertainment as well."

"Whyses do we continue on?" one goblin complained. "We've traveled through this place since the moon was high. There is no warmbloods here to eats."

"Shuts up!" the largest goblin commanded. "Krylothon sended us here to finds the location of victims. Thats isses what we must come back with."

"Yes, commander Trock," the complaining goblin said, bowing in mock humility.

Trock abruptly slapped him on the head and knocked off his helmet.

"We continueses on," the goblin commander ordered. "The next incident wills be reported to Krylothon. His punishment wills be worse than a smack across yer head."

The other two goblins sobered immediately. Chills coursed down their spines as they considered Krylothon's torturous form of penal discipline.

From the corner of his eye, Trock noticed movement and turned, a hungry snarl twisting his lips. He wiped the sudden saliva from the side of his mouth as a small, furry animal with long ears emerged from its hole in the ground.

"Gets it, Rast!" Trock called to the goblin nearest the animal.

Rast sprang, but the little beast darted to the side. The goblin took up the chase, hands swinging clumsily in an attempt to snatch it up. Propelled by its long hind legs, the animal skittered about in a quick, half circle, putting distance between it and the frustrated goblin. With long ears sticking straight up, it stopped and peered at the vile creatures who intruded on its sanctuary.

"Catches it! Thats wills be dinner!" the commander screamed to both of his lessers. They scrambled after the little furball, and again the chase was on. The hare was small, barely enough to satisfy one of them, certainly not all three.

But individually, each goblins imagined once caught, the rabbit would be shoved into his mouth before his companions could do anything about it.

Sensing certain danger, the small rabbit found an opening and raced for it, but Rast, his reactions quite keen, dove and snatched the hind legs just as the rabbit's body disappeared under the ground. "It'ses mine," he yelled as he quickly lifted it to his tusked jaws.

"You should pick on somebody your own size," a voice suggested from the darkness, turning all three goblins. Shocked, Rast dropped the rabbit.

The hare hit the ground running and escaped down the hole. The two goblins yanked their curved-blade scimitars from their scabbards.

Trock drew his long sword from the scabbard secured to his back, his eyes darting around looking for the speaker. Grumbling to himself about his own carelessness, he remembered Krylothon's threats of destruction to any scouts spotted. He scanned the darkness. He wanted the speaker on the end of his blade.

Several moments passed with tensed silence.

"Where isses the enemy?" Rast finally asked, his heat-sensing vision locating no one.

"Enemy?" the voice spoke again. "It's you who are the enemy."

The brutes spun in the direction of the voice and saw two slender silhouettes fan out from behind the broad oak. Stunned, the lesser goblins stumbled back and kept their weapons between them and the personages.

Leaning in closer, Trock inspected the figures. Subtle curves defined their bodies and radiant beauty their faces. From the moonlight seeping through the trees, their raven tresses glistened surreal sparkles. Trock followed their graceful advance, his lips smacking hungrily. "Female warmbloods," the goblin leader said. "Females will make a sweet meal," he decided. "And an easy capture."

"Is that right?" one of the two silhouettes protested.

"What isses you waitin' fer?" Trock asked his lessers. "This is what we've come fer. These is warmbloods!

The goblins charged, bounding the short distance between them and their victims. The silhouettes wore long flowing gowns and appeared weaponless. Wicked smiles split the goblins' faces. Goblin scimitars went overhead, and the brutes unleashed the cruel blades at a downward arc aimed to cut their victims at the waist.

Each elegant silhouette spun back and out of range from the overconfident assault. The blades ripped nothing but air.

Saranisen giggled at the all-too-serious situation. She trained for decades in battle techniques and often sparred with her older brother, Zakili, but she'd never stood toe-to-toe against an actual monster eager to take her life.

"What's so funny?" Monolique asked, hoping her younger sister's naivety wouldn't allow her to think this some kind of game.

"Battling a real, live monster," she said. "It's so invigorating!"

Monolique rolled her eyes. "Well, I'm going to make this a little more interesting. Are you ready to step up the fun?"

"Yes!"

Reaching into the concealing folds of their gowns, each sister extracted a thin sword. Saranisen bounced around and kicked her legs out wide, barely able to control her excitement. Monolique glanced over curiously. Her sister's sandals tumbled to a stop at a nearby tree, her toes peeking out from under her gown.

She was barefoot.

"You definitely are the spritely one, now aren't you?"

Saranisen tittered excitedly.

As Trock watched, the goblins charged again, their blades swiping in wide, wild arcs. Saranisen sprang off to the side, drawing one goblin in chase. Monolique stood her ground, her blade slicing across swiftly to deflect the strike. The burly goblin didn't slow his momentum, reversed the angle of his blade, and plunged it side-armed. The elf slammed her blade downward, intercepted the scimitar, and locked it up with her sword's hilt.

Weighing twice as much as the elf woman, the goblin churned forward, using his bulk to drive her back. Quickly, she freed her weapon and spun away. The goblin stumbled a few steps before righting himself and eyed her hungrily.

Not far away, Saranisen danced around her opponent. The goblin slashed at her time and again with his curved blade and tried to keep up with her intricate movements. Several minutes of pursuit and vicious slashes, the goblin still hadn't gotten close. The frustrated brute lunged, swiping down hard. With a graceful leap and spin, she floated away from the attack, letting her sword trail to force the ring of metal as the blade tips clapped. The goblin cursed and took chase once more. The elf maiden darted sideways, then backward, and spun a wide circuit around the dangerous brute.

The goblin halted his tiring pursuit, hurling curses.

"What a foul mouth," she said, stopping cold and staring into the goblin's bloodshot eyes. "Somebody needs to teach you some manners!" She feigned a lunge, forcing the brute to react with a wild swipe of his blade. In that split second, his empty strike sent his sword arm sailing wide. Saranisen saw an opening for an easy attack, but changed her mind. She snickered mischievously. The brute charged again, but she danced away in a circular pattern, forcing the goblin to abruptly change directions. Saranisen leaned in, blade leading, but the brute stumbled back and batted away the attack with an unfocused swing. She continued her dance, feigned a lunge and pulled out suddenly, feigned another lunge and pulled out, keeping the monster on the defensive and unsure when the real attack would come.

Predictably he lashed out wildly with his blade, the attack coming up empty. Breathing heavily, the goblin came at her again. His sword slashed out and again missed his mark. The spritely elf dashed in behind the sword arm, and plucked a greasy whisker off the goblin's chin with an immediate retreat.

"This is so fun!" she squealed.

Trock stomped in the direction of the fray, sword in hand, eager to end this foolishness.

"You're forgetting somebody," a voice called from behind.

He spun about to discover a male elf this time. The unusually brave goblin growled and charged at his adversary. Several bounding steps brought the elf into range, as the goblin's sword sliced across then dropped in a vicious chop, aimed to cut the elf in half. The elf, Jorab, back-stepped quickly and escaped with only a stinging gash against his hip. Jorab came at the goblin with a vengeance, his sword cutting high to low at the goblin. Trock blocked the attack with his broad sword and countered immediately, throwing all his body weight behind a vicious chop.

The lithe elf ducked the blade. He quickly sprang in behind the sword's momentum and behind the goblin. His sword's hilt slammed onto the unbalanced monster's skull. Trock crumbled to the ground in an unconscious heap.

Nearby, Monolique pressed in. Her sword clashed noisily with the goblin's curved blade. She quick-stepped to the side. This time her blade came across in a backhand chop. The brute parried the attack. He rushed her. Monolique spun, took a new angle, unleashed another sword strike, and again allowed the goblin only enough time to get up his defenses.

Her sword swung up as if to make an overhead chop. The goblin's eyes and scimitar followed. Suddenly revising her attack, her blade path abruptly arced in a wide loop and jabbed straight at the goblin. The brute reacted quickly. His weapon crashed against the elf blade, defeating the attack.

"Don't kill them," Jorab instruct. "We need to interrogate these brutes."

Monolique glanced back at the elf standing over his fallen monster. "What have you done with yours, Jorab?" she asked accusingly.

"He sleeps."

Monolique's opponent suddenly charged, scimitar swinging wildly, and he forced Monolique back on her heels. Taking her focus off the goblin gave him time to regroup and now he was pressing her hard. She had forfeited her advantage. Snarling viciously, the goblin swiped out and grabbed hold of her gown, stopping her retreat. The goblin raised his weapon high to finish her. A sharp whistle sounded, and the goblin jerked strangely and collapsed to the ground. She heard another rapid whistle, a dull thud, and the fallen brute twitched viciously.

Then went still.

Saranisen's opponent went down next with a similar whistle, but the spritely elf was so caught up in her fighting dance she didn't stop to question. Instead she argued, trying to coax it from the ground. A sudden whistle and a thud later left the goblin writhing in death throes. Unnerved, she bent down and looked at the dead goblin. Protruding from the brute's back was a long black arrow. A second had pierced his skull.

"What's going on?" Saranisen asked before hearing another dull thud, this time from the direction of Jorab's downed monster.

"Somebody's killed them!" Monolique said, finding the same macabre evidence on her goblin.

"Those monsters were essential to discovering the origin of the goblin nest hidden here in Avundar!" Jorab fumed, his countenance twisting more in rage than in confusion. "Who's done this?"

"It is I," a voice said from the darkness.

They all turned to see a bow-wielding elf step out from behind a tree.

"Maengh?" Jorab questioned, recognizing the person. "Why have you killed them? We could've interrogated them and discovered the hidden lair of these vermin."

"Things were beginning to look perilous," Maengh explained. "I feared for the safety of the King's daughters."

"The King's daughters were not in danger," Saranisen said.

Maengh bowed in apology. "That's not what I saw. And as King Gallatar's guard, one of my prime responsibilities is to insure the well-being of his girls."

"The King must be told of this intrusion," Jorab reasoned, drawing agreement from the sisters.

"That wouldn't be a good idea," Maengh blurted.

The others looked to him, unbelieving.

"These might be creatures lost and wandering."

"More likely, they're scouts for a much larger force," Monolique argued.

"Possibly, but what could be the chances? Goblins haven't invaded Verdant Wood in a millennium, and no tribe of goblinoids dwells within Avundar.

"Besides, think of your father," he continued. "His heart is still heavy for the lost elves and the burden of mending peace among the suffering families of those war casualties. With all the other burdens weighing on the King, he has much more important things to worry about than a roving band of lost monsters. He already gets more than enough problems from his troublesome son."

Saranisen raised a suspicious eyebrow. She'd known Maengh all her life. He and Zakili had always been kindred spirits, wild and unorthodox, sharing a friendship since she was a child. But lately, Maengh acted unusual: plotting, calculated and surreptitious.

This was the first time she'd ever heard him speak ill of Zakili. She thought it strangely out of character for an elf claiming to be a friend. She tucked that away, and broke from her musing to hear her sister and Maengh negotiate what they should do next.

"But why should we cause your father to be concerned over an incident that may mean nothing?" Maengh argued.

"This goes beyond Father. I'm concerned for the welfare of all the elves of Verdant Wood. Have you so quickly forgotten the battle with the assassins? We lost twenty-six precious souls that day. Who would've foreseen that attack? The only reason we didn't lose more was because we were prepared for the onslaught."

"But Monolique, are you suggesting an army of monsters has bulled into Avundar without anyone's knowledge? Verdant Wood is surrounded on three sides by the open Ormantict plains and backs right up to the Soaring Mounts. Do you actually think an army of monsters could scale those mountains, dragging supplies with them, and not be noticed? And would there be a possibility a throng of brutes could march through this goodly land and attack our home without catching the notice of the baronies they pass through? With your father's fiery mindset, could you imagine his wrath at time wasted with such illogical conclusions?

And all this based upon three wandering goblins?"

Monolique started to protest, but after considering, only nodded her head. Maengh was absolutely correct about Father. She was painfully familiar with his new disposition. Only a year ago, she enjoyed her father's presence, listening to his tales, delighting in his fond attention, and loving the private moments they shared on father-daughter adventures. Even though she was the third child, she relished the fact he gave her as much attention as any of her siblings. She absolutely loved Father, but with the fading of the old year into the new came the unexpected change of his character. How argumentative and spiteful he'd become. The slightest problem sent him into an uproar. She didn't understand what could have transformed him into such a bitter wretch.

Sadly, she'd forced herself to keep her distance until whatever ailed him had passed. Coming to his Throne Room and informing him of three dead goblins, then suggesting a possible invasion would surely stir his ire. Especially since it would disrupt his work about Elfstay. He had so much on his mind already.

"What do you propose?"

"Since I'm one of your father's guards, I'm close to him, very close. We must remain silent for his peace of mind. If anything greater occurs, inform me immediately. I'm trusted by the King, and after the incident with Zakili and the King's advisors, I think he has rested more confidence upon me. I'll relay the message to him, explaining it in detail."

The reasoning seemed sound to Monolique, who agreed and released Jorab back to his lookout station. Monolique departed. Saranisen started away also, but not without a suspicious glare Maengh's way.

Left alone in the darkness, Maengh's smile widened hideously, nearly taking in his ears--much too large and canine for an elf. But Maengh was no elf. He was a creature of darkness, a creature of evil, and a servant of The Dark Sorcerer. Understanding the implications of finding these goblins forced up evil laughter.

Zeraktalis' forces were ready to march. The onslaught would soon begin. Maengh looked at the three dead goblins he'd silenced to protect the secrecy of the attack. The elves would've made the brutes talk. Maengh had to kill them. He felt no sorrow. There were thousands more where these came from.

He planned his next move. Although he'd silenced the goblins, their corpses would still cause disturbance among the elves and draw the attention of Zakili and his Paladin friend. He didn't want them involved. They'd not be so easily quieted.

Ridding himself of these bodies would be tricky; he had to remain unseen. Knowing the routes of the lookouts, he calculated the path he needed to take out of Verdant Wood to the ashes of the funeral pyres. There he'd incinerate the brutes.

In the likeness of the elf Maengh, each goblin outweighed Ironfist by a hundred pounds. Ironfist still possessed the great strength to carry them, but how awkward these dead weights would be. He desired to transform into the broad-shouldered form of the viking he most preferred, but that would draw eyes his direction before he could even get halfway through this forest. He picked up one corpse by the back of the tunic and tossed it over his shoulder. Slowly bending next to the other, he grabbed a fistful of its chain mail armor and slung it over his other shoulder and started off into the night.

Barefooted Saranisen came dancing around a copse of trees far behind the jothenac, scanning the plush grass for the shoes she'd kicked off. She spotted the elf from the corner of her eye and turned, seeing what she thought to be two burly goblins, one draped over each shoulder, as he packed them off into the darkness! Her mouth fell agape.

* * * * *

"Monsters! Terrible monsters!" Methlon cried. "Creatures more horrible than anything I could've imagined!"

Kil stood and listened, surprisingly calm, waiting for the frightened man to fall silent. For two days, Methlon had raced away from Lonely Wood, his fear gnawing at his nerves. The Assassin Warlord knew if Methlon didn't spill it all out, his heart would burst from bottled-up fright. Several stammering whines and complaints later Methlon quieted, his strength drained.

"It's good they still wait," Kil said. "The Master informed me they were a chaotic bunch with little restraint. Perhaps the power of the monsters' dread of The Dark Sorcerer is stronger than the Master thought."

"That insect monster Krylothon said you better come quickly," Methlon whined, his face pale from fright. "If not, he said he'd launch his own assault on this land!"

"The sorcerer warned me against arrogant Krylothon. That fool! He's bluffing! He can't locate the Lifespring without my guidance. The master had foresight not to disclose that information to the volatile usurper."

"Whether it finds Lifespring or not matters little to him, I'd guess. I think he just wants to start killing! Wh... what're we going to do?" Methlon stammered.

Johnny Earl Jones

"We'll join up with them," Kil stated calmly, causing Methlon to wince. "But the usurper's arrogance has become a problem already." The Warlord pondered for a moment. "Yes, we'll meet with the monsters and their usurper commander. But we'll allow the usurper's fiery swagger to cool. Not until several moons have risen shall we journey out to meet this army. This'll give him time to consider how he should demand anything from The Warlord of the Lurking Shadows!"

"But d... didn't the sorcerer want you to act immediately?"

"The plans are being modified. I must extinguish Krylothon's haughtiness first then we can proceed. If I were to arrive as at his commad, then he'll think he controls my actions. He'll think he controls this quest!" Kil lifted his dirks, the blades burning with unnatural fire. "No one, not even a usurper, will tread upon me!"

Methlon backed away slowly. Despite enjoying the power he wielded briefly in the Lonely Wood days ago, he quickly concluded being a Lurking Shadow wasn't such a good thing. At that moment it was a deadly thing. Planning to attack the formidable elves again was dangerous enough, but to force a pact with evil, ravenous monsters was like enlisting more adversaries.

Methlon guessed Kil's pride wouldn't yield nor would that of the horrible behemoth, Krylothon. The play for power was set in motion.

* * * * *

"We have trouble, Master," the ghastly spirit said, hovering in the darkness of Zeraktalis' chambers.

Ominously, The Dark Sorcerer turned, fiery eyes staring fiercely at the demon. "Speak."

"I've returned from Verdant Wood after overhearing conversation among the inhabitants. Within the midst of the elves is a God-fearer, and he actively shares the Christ's plan of salvation with them. Do you know what that means? The God-fearers there'll grow more numerous and--"

"God-fearer?" the Dark Sorcerer interrupted. "What did he look like?"

"An unusual sight, my liege. The man was of imposing stature resembling a long-haired, island man. But I could sense the power of God in his life and in his speech, and discerned he was a Holy Warrior. Distinguishing no fear or area of his life that wasn't yielded to Christ, I could find no weakness to construct a stronghold in his mind. Every facet of his life is submitted to the Lordship of Christ.

"Those kind of Christians can be dangerous. And hard to overcome."

"He'll be destroyed like the rest!" Zeraktalis said with confident finality. The demon spirit bowed and departed.

"You're still alive," Zeraktalis growled, reflecting back to the episode on the meadow several weeks ago where this God-fearing Paladin challenged him. He'd exhausted some powerful sorcery before stepping through the rip in reality and leaving The Paladin to an inescapable demise. But somehow, the paladin had cheated death.

Zeraktalis hadn't made provisions for such a power-filled Christian to stand in the way of evil's ultimate victory. Pondering on this troubling insight for a moment, he finally decided The Paladin was of no consequence.

"After all, he was just one man. And what difference could one man make?"

* * * * *

The magicians stood befuddled. They looked to their ineffective wands, then into Kelt's impatient expression.

"What more will it take for you to trust me again, Father?" asked Candace.

Baron Veldercrantz shook his head incredulously. "The curse may be stronger than we originally thought," he told the magicians, not acknowledging his daughter.

"They've tried every trick in their ridiculous spell books," Candace said. "Maybe the reason it seems nothing has been removed is because there was no curse there to begin with."

"Candace," Kelt said softly, moving in closer and looking her in the eyes. "I love you, girl. I prize you more than my own life. After your mother died, you were the only remnant of hope I had left. My vow from that day forth was I'd never let any harm befall you, and above any other promise, I'll make certain that one is fulfilled.

"No matter how subtle and seemingly innocuous a magical curse may seem, it eventually has fatal effects. Somehow, some way, I'll have this thing removed before it's too late--"

"Father, I have no curse! I wasn't cursed by the elves; I'm not cursed now and I've never been cursed in my entire life! I'm not cursed!"

Again, Kelt shook his head sadly. "You don't even know you've been deceived. Whatever spell the Silver Elves have placed on you isn't retreating without a fight."

Quick-witted Candace jumped lines of thought, perceiving she may be able to gain more ground by reasoning with Father than by arguing with him. "Why do you think I'm under a curse?" she asked, her tone calm.

"We've been over this before."

"Then it won't hurt to discuss it one more time. After all, if I am truly cursed, I have nothing but time to burn while these magicians try to dig up another supposed cure."

Kelt huffed in frustration.

"Please Father."

"To start with, you defend the enemy. You refuse to accept the fact the elves kidnapped you, instead saying you came to them with some kind of warning."

"But it's so."

"I received information to the contrary. The Prince told me you were indeed captured by the Silver Elves to be exploited for their own wicked pleasures. He even sent a detachment into Verdant Wood after you, but the warlike elves wanted you so badly they brought all their forces to bear against the Prince's men and defeated them.

Many, many of those men were slain, yet you still defend those wicked elves.

"The only reason they released you was because they feared the size of my army. Now explain how that information could be untrue. I found you in the location he told me you'd be?"

"The elves never battled against any royal army. They defeated a throng of assassins who invaded them. What prince are you talking..."

Her face blanched. "Prince Killion?" she asked horror-striken. "The Assassin Warlord masquerading as a prince. Is he who you refer to?"

"Forget it, Candace," Kelt said. "This gets us nowhere. Your curse even has you confusing who the real nemesis is."

"Kil is no prince! He's the Warlord of The Lurking Shadows!"

"Enough! This curse has overwhelmed you and has twisted your understanding. The elves are the enemy, and for me, they are the most despicable kind, because they corrupted who I loved the most. Although I have you back in body, they have warped your mind."

"Listen to what you're saying--"

"Say nothing more! Your only hope now is that these spellcasters can release you from your delusion..." she heard Father saying, but her thoughts turned inward, lamenting for her father's lack of discernment.

He'd been deceived into thinking she was accursed by whoever that messenger was on the plains outside Verdant Wood. Could that have been an assassin planted among her father's army? Her heart beat fast as she considered that Kil's wicked hand was still pulling the strings on events going on around her.

Additionally perplexing was how Father had completely abandoned the faith he once held dear. Now he allowed magicians, workers of dark magic, into his home. She looked to the robed men suspiciously, maintained her composure, and prayed the Lord would bring Father back to his spiritual senses.

"I just want my dear daughter back," she heard him say.

"And I want the father I've always loved back," she mumbled under her breath.

* * * * *

"Baron Veldercrantz will be pleased to hear our report," the warrior said to his companion. They rode through the quiet forest under the power of their chargers' easy gallop.

"I agree. He's been concerned those wicked elves would invade his barony and abduct Candace ever since he rescued her from the elven forest. It'll put him at ease to learn his borders are free of any Silver Elf sightings."

"Those fiends make me want to spit! Candace is the only family Baron Kelt has left. A proclamation has gone throughout Avundar and to neighboring kingdoms. If any wizard or magician is able to remove this curse from his daughter he'll pay them handsomely. He's sparing no amount of wealth as a reward."

"I'm saddened by this turn of events, friend. Kelt was never inclined to the dark arts of wizardry, but his daughter's condition has turned him to such desperate measures. I hope she's cured soon."

"As do I."

Easily guiding their horses through the last stretch of shadowy Maribowam Forest, they spotted the distant, towering fortress walls through the leafy branches. The night was warm, and a constant gentle breeze wove through the trees. It was a great evening to ride, so the warriors slowed their horses to a saunter, breathing deep to take in the forest's sweet aromas.

Their relaxing ride didn't last long. Frantically, the horses sniffed the air, tread in defensive circles, and whinnied in deep, panicked breaths. The first rider pulled up on the reins and patted his steed's muscular neck, trying to calm the animal. His companion's horse reared, whinnying in fright, and when its front legs hit the ground it bolted forward. The warrior could do nothing but hold on.

"What is it, boy?" the first rider asked, securing himself as his charger darted forward.

"It must be the elves! The horses can sense the evil around us! Those elves have infiltrated our Maribowam Forest!"

With wide, bloodshot eyes, they peered at the two riders and grinned wickedly. Separating from the shadows, they wiped eager saliva from their lips and watched the men flee.

"Those isses what we has comes for!" one gnarled goblin cried, drawing a punch across the jaw from his comrade.

"Be quiets," the punching brute growled, pointing to the high walls surrounding the fortress. "Can'ts you see how close we isses to their lair? Imagine all the enemies that den may hold? They'd obliterate us without hesitation if they found out we was here."

"True," the third monster put in. "But as Gorkin hasses said, those isses what we were sents to find. Warmbloods! And we found a entire castle filled with 'em! Krylothon will be pleased to hear our news."

"Sees," Gorkin complained, rubbing his sore jaw. His fist jabbed out, punching the other goblin in the eye. That goblin roared and retaliated, his forearm batting Gorkin on the side of the skull. Gorkin stammered back, shaking his head to get his bearings. A moment later he charged, bowling over the other goblin. The two went down in a jumble of fists and feet, roaring, cursing, and biting.

The third goblin kicked at the combatants, hoping vainly to break up the battle before they attracted attention from the castle. His prodding merely spurred the beasts to fight harder, each thinking the blow came from the other.

"I wills not die before I tastes the flesh of a warmblood!" the third goblin screamed, but the two goblins warred on.

"Then I will returns without you," he threatened, "and I wills gain the praises for bringing the glorious news of the warmblood victims' location to Krylothon."

He looked to the walls and saw the sudden bustling among the towers. The goblins weren't deep inside the treeline of the forest.

"The warmbloods musts hasses spotted us, and they will come soon!" the goblin warned. The beasts fought on.

Hardly caring for the fate of his companions, he turned to escape, but he bristled at the thought of venturing back on his own in this unfamiliar land. One final glance back to the frantically moving lookouts solidified his decision. His desire to live outweighed his cowardice.

Leaving his comrades behind, he slipped deep into the forest. With as much speed as his bowed legs could muster, he ran toward Lonely Forest and his waiting commander.

* * * * *

"Let them die!" Zeraktalis roared. The walls shook and several, mighty usurpers cautiously backed away. With eyes like minute volcanoes under his horned helmet, Zeraktalis stared into his sorcerer's mirror to spy on his minions. Watching the stupid goblins wrestle on the outskirts of a human fortress, he longed to blast the brutes to dust for their foolishness.

He could only stand back and observe as a squad of calvary charged the area, running the creatures through with their spears.

Waving his arm before the mirror, the glass became opaque. "They should never have been there! Krylothon sent them against my will! I'm The Dark Sorcerer and no one disobeys me. No one! Not without devastating consequences. Not even mighty Krylothon shall escape. And where's Kil? He should've arrived to quell the usurper's arrogance!"

The usurpers behind him grew wary. The Sorcerer's volatile fits of rage had shred many a mighty monster with his preternatural sorcery. They didn't doubt Zeraktalis might turn on them. The usurpers were fearless and powerful. They wouldn't go down without a fight; however, they understood frightfully well here in the Black Fortress, the heart of The Dark Sorcerer's power, that they'd little chance against him.

Strangely, The Sorcerer exploded into laughter, the bellows echoing around the black marble walls, making the usurpers even more cautious. Several called upon their innate magical abilities, fire and lightning burning tenaciously in their taloned hands.

"I'd not foreseen this magnitude of intrigue among my commanders!" Zeraktalis cried. "Such games my underlings play in my absence. An arrogant warlord against a stubborn usurper; the confrontation should prove to be explosive.

"They made this conquest entertaining, even at the expense of disregarding my commands. But did I really expect anything less from two such chaotic personalities?

"Kil hasn't joined with the monsters yet. For if he had, Krylothon wouldn't have dared send out those scouts."

Zeraktalis' laughter peeled against the walls like claps of thunder.

"The two must have already gotten a taste of each other. But Kil will come soon. He knows the consequences if he does not. I will allow time for their power struggle.

However, if they don't become focused soon, I shall destroy them both!"

* 17 *
THOSE WHO LIVE BY THE SWORD...

"This is what I feared," Navarro said as he and Zakili stormed across the plains on their magnificent chargers.

"I can't believe Maengh told my sisters to keep this news silent!" the Elf Prince roared. "Who does he think he is to determine what information Father can handle? His actions are suspicious, unlike the wild elf warrior I've always known. I'll have to keep him close and keep an eye on him."

"Thank God for your baby sister Saranisen's tenacity. Had she not discounted Maengh's advice, we still might not know about the goblins which penetrated your forest home."

"Goblins!" Zakili roared, a look of disgust distorting his features. "It's sickening. Those evil beasts polluted our forest with their stinkin' presence! How could they've gotten all the way to Verdant Wood without being spotted or shot down?

"What's worse, goblin scouts guarantee a goblin army hidden somewhere in Avundar! When I ran across the goblins in the Dolunar Forest along the outer edges of Avundar's borders, I discovered how they got into our land without being seen," Navarro said. "That was where I saw The Dark Sorcerer Zeraktalis, and it's the same place he nearly destroyed me.

"When I followed a party of goblins, they unknowingly led me to a meadow where the sorcerer ripped a hole in reality. He and those goblins traveled there through that portal."

"Do we expect to find a goblin army in that forest?"

"I'm not sure, but that would seem the only lead we have to go by right now."

"Godspeed to us then," Zakili decided. "We have wicked monsters to dispel."

"Indeed," Navarro concurred, smiling at the elf's use of Christian vernacular. "Godspeed to us."

* * * * *

"This is such a majestic land," Shimre said. He was a middle-aged man with a stern jaw and eyes displaying decades of traveling experience. From the driver's seat of his wagon, he led his caravan leisurely across the wide plains, flanked on either side by endless reaches of forest. "I have heard so much about this land, Avundar, so many awe-inspiring stories. But to see it first hand makes any tale seem dull in comparison."

"Indeed, you are correct," said his wagon partner, a rugged old man with a face as tight and weather-beaten as an aged saddle. "But I have heard more than a fair number of merchant caravans travelin' through the baronies displayin' their wares."

"Gimshaw, that's what I like about you. You always keep me in correct perspective. To match my supreme optimism, you have the same degree of pessimism."

"I'm just statin' a fact, boss," the older man defended himself, flashing a smile missing a few teeth. "As you inferred, this place is a paradise and tends to draw quite a few folks, especially merchant caravans like ours."

"How do you hear about all these things?" Shimre asked, teasing the nosy old man.

"I keep my ears close to the ones who flap their jaws. Much useful, free information can be gained that way."

"So I see. You don't lack free useful information about many things."

Gimshaw stuck out his skinny chest, thinking he just received a compliment.

"Since you've heard so much," Shimre continued, "tell me about the information you acquired. How friendly is this land toward raising a family?"

Gimshaw sat up straight and serious like an orator and cleared his throat, perpetually eager to share his thoughts. "The interestin' fact about this land is it has no king over it. The land is made up o' a republic o' baronies and townships. No one single ruler makes the laws for all. Instead each barony is its own sovereign state, as is each township. Amazingly, they all work well together through periodic meetings of barons and town counselors called the Council of Rulers. Indeed, this land is quite unique..."

"Families, Gimshaw. I want to find out about the atmosphere for families; after all, we do have ours, and those of the merchants working with us, traveling in our wagons."

"Well boss, each barony is ruled by a particular family which protects its subjects in return for their services in the military. Really quite an equal trade: the families supply the warriors, the warriors protect the families. But this is where the information gets interesting.

"There hasn't been a war inside Avundar for generations. This land is as peaceful and secure as any we've ever visited.

"But why a question like that? Yer not thinkin' about settin' down roots are ya?"

"One can never tell," Shimre admitted. "Always being on the road is no way to bring up a family especially with my wife's recent birth of twins."

"An outpost then," Gimshaw said excitedly.

"That's an option."

A horse rider galloped alongside their lead wagon. "Sir Shimre," the rider said urgently, "we have a score of shapes racing for us from the woods."

"From the woods?"

"Could be a pack of woodsman, spotting our caravan and hankerin' for some new supplies and rations," Gimshaw suggested hopefully.

Shimre stood in his seat and turned where the rider indicated. He easily spotted them. The burly shapes moved quickly in the tall grass and looked more like a pack of animals than a gang of hungry woodsman.

"I don't feel good about this," Shimre admitted. "Let's keep the caravan moving. Inform the other wagoneers to follow and increase their pace."

The rider nodded and the spun to the wagons. Shimre snapped the reins, urging the horses into a faster stride.

"What's happening?" Ginshaw asked, more than a little concerned.

"I'm not quite sure," Shimre said. "We'll keep straight and travel as fast as we can. We have a forest to our left and a rise topped by another forest to our right.

"Dig into that useful information of yours Ginshaw and tell me about the history of marauders here in Avundar."

"There is none."

He looked back and saw the shapes draw closer.

"Then what is coming after us? Even with our increased pace, the shapes continue to close on us!"

"Sir Shimre!" the horse rider's cried frantically. "The shapes have gained on us! They're not far away!"

"Who are they?"

"Not who, what!" the wide-eyed horse rider said as he pulled even to Shimre's wagon. "We are caught in an ambush by monsters! More come from the other side."

"Monsters?" he echoed fearfully. "Blow the trumpet! Everyone to arms!"

The horse rider snatched his horn from his side and put it to his lips.

The trumpet blast never came.

Shimre turned to discover why, only to see the rider propelled off his steed. Landing awkwardly on his side, a spear protruded from the unfortunate man's back.

"Call to arms!" Shimre yelled, yanking his sword from the floorboard of the wagon.

"A call to yer death!" he heard.

A muscular, hairy hand reached around the side of the wagon and grabbed his tunic. A huge fist pummeled his face once then again and again, crunching his nose and welling stinging tears in his eyes. Shimre was battered and bloody, but he wasn't going to give up. Not when the lives of his wife and babies were at stake. He beat on the beast's arm and jabbed at the creature's face. The tall, muscular, canine monster shook him viciously, holding tight to Shimre's tunic.

"This one here has some fight 'n 'im," the masnevire declared, laughing mockingly. His comrades weren't as interested in toying with their prey.

The noise of battle decreased with every second, Shimre noted, heavy-hearted. He heard one or two dying screams from the monsters his men must have slain. But more often, the anguished cries came from his overwhelmed and dying men. He lashed out with another punch, aimed for the brute's face but didn't connect. The masnevire held him at arm's length, and the brute's reach was far greater than his. Another fist slammed into Shimre's jaw, snapping his head to the side.

"Ye are goin' t' die, puny human!" the masnevire promised.

"Not before you feel my sting!" Shimre roared, springing forward and kicking the brute in the gut. The monster's grip loosened as it doubled over and Shimre pulled away, racing for his fallen sword. He felt the weight of many glares and knew the brutes would soon be on him. But if he could get to his sword, maybe he could take a beast or two down and buy enough time for his wife to grab the twins and flee to safety.

He snatched up his blade and turned on the advancing brutes. Everything blurred through his one, teary eye, the other was blackened and swollen shut.

He could hear swordplay by a wagon a dozen feet beyond him, then a victorious "Got her!" He heard the defiant yelling of his wife.

"Shimre!" she screamed. In terror, he knew his family was doomed. He wanted to vomit.

"Rebeena!" he called back desperately. "If you hurt her..."

"So this female is yers, is she?" said the masnevire who had pounded on him, pushing his way past the others to stand in plain sight of Shimre. "Bring her to me!"

Two masnevires dragged the woman, kicking and screaming, through the pack of monsters and up to the front, next to their leader. "Here's yer woman, Lunitak," one masnevire answered.

"Human, shall I beat her before yer eyes?" the masnevire asked, turning to Shimre. "Or can ye get through all o' us to rescue her?"

Lunitak grabbed her by her long, red hair, pulling her head back and exposing her throat to his cruel blade. Teasingly, he ran the dagger's point along her neck and under her chin. "What do ye say, human?" the masnevire commander asked. "Yer life fer yer female's life?"

"Don't do it, Shimre! They're goin' to kill us all anyway!"

He heard what Rebeena said, but his mind was desperate, not reasoning. *If they would let my wife and children live, he thought, I would gladly give my life.*

"Drop yer sword, human, and yer woman can walk away."

Shimre looked down to his blade, but from the corner of his eye he saw shapes advance. "Get back!" he ordered.

"Look at yerself. Ye are beaten. There be more than a score o' us and only one o' ye. What chance do ye stand?"

Shimre heard the piercing sound of his sons' cries, and he turned back to the wagons.

"We found two whelps!" a masnevire declared hungrily.

"Our babies!" Shimre cried desperately, his strength draining away under the hopelessness of the situation. All his men were dead, his wife and twins were in the clutches of monsters, and he was pitted against unbeatable odds.

"Time to die, human!" Lunitak declared, pushing Rebeena into the grasp of the nearest masnevires and stalking in, wielding a sword as tall as Shimre. With a roar the monster lunged, his sword slicing across viciously. Shimre got his sword up but knew he could never stop the attack's momentum or his imminent death.

A metallic clang later and the masnevire's sword careened into the grassy earth.

"What?" the masnevire asked skeptically, seeing a short, stout knife blade lying on the ground.

"A small change of direction," a commanding voice explained, and when the masnevire turned he saw the racing figures of a horse and rider. His final sight was the gleaming of a long sword speeding at his head.

Shimre gawked as the monster's head bounced at his feet. His rescuer rode past.

"Let's move!" Navarro advised. "We've got monsters to fight!"

One masnevire turned fully on The Paladin, thrusting a spear aimed for his heart, but Invinitor lashed across, snapping the spear in half. It flew away like a busted boomerang.

"Get him, Celemonte," Navarro told his warhorse then jumped from his saddle, pulling down one of the masnevires who held Rebeena. A quick jab of his sword in the brute's ribcage ended that one's life, and The Paladin leapt up, intent on the other masnevire which grabbed the struggling Rebeena around the throat.

Navarro came in confidently. The monster yanked out a dagger and stuck the tip at the base of her skull. The Paladin stalked around the monster in a half-circle.

The brute shifted, keeping Navarro in his sight. The masnevire pressed the dagger against Rebeena's exposed neck, drawing a scream when the point pierced her skin. He shook her torturously as he glared at Navarro. "Back away! Or next time she dies."

Navarro jammed his sword into its scabbard, and backed away, hands up in resignation. The woman looked pleadingly, but The Paladin only winked. The monster cocked his head in confusion at his action. A second later, Celemonte's back hooves bolted up and caved in the back of the monster's skull.

"Fine job," Navarro complemented his charger, receiving an excited whinny in return.

As Navarro looked to the side, he saw a small explosion send a masnevire crashing to the ground in flames. "It's about time you got here, Zakili!"

"I wouldn't miss it for the world!"

A spear wielder came at Navarro from the side, the weapon jabbing in to skewer him, but Invinitor swept across, smacking the spear aside with the flat of his blade. Two masnevires charged in from behind, swords drawn. Navarro sensed them coming and spun, Invinitor whipping across and cutting through the two attacking swords like butter. A minute and sudden adjustment of his grip reversed the angle of his sword and sent it jabbing into one monster's heart.

Navarro's senses tingled again, and he ducked just in time as a spear flew over his head. Turning slightly with Invinitor in hand, he jabbed, his blade disappearing into the spear wielder's gut.

An agonized cry turned him the other way. The masnevire with the destroyed sword fell to the ground with a monster's spear buried in his chest.

Shimre battled over to his wife's side, snatching up a sword along the way and placing it in her hands. Together they battled back a taunting masnevire, smacking away the monster's sword repeatedly, but neither had the prowess of their rescuers and did well just to keep their opponent at bay.

"The babies?" Rebeena asked. "Are they safe?"

A flaming, screaming masnevire stumbled away to the side of them.

"Your children are safe now and tucked in tight," Zakili informed from the wagon.

"What sport is there if I just shoot 'em all down?" the Elf Prince complained to himself, throwing the bow over his shoulders. His daggers, the Flying Tigers, leapt into his hands.

A masnevire turned fully on the elf with a loaded crossbow.

"Great! What a time to put away my bow."

The elf dodged to the left. The crossbow followed. He dodged back to the right. The masnevire kept him in his sights. Zakili charged forward suddenly then stopped, but the brute still hadn't pulled the trigger. "A steady shot are you? If you won't flinch at my feints..."

A second masnevire stepped up, also holding a crossbow.

"Well, this is getting interesting." The elf shifted from one foot to the other, his blades spinning in his palms.

A third masnevire stomped up, this one with a battle axe and a severe snarl on its canine face.

"Stop playing around Zakili," Navarro urged against the background noise of another dying brute. "We're outnumbered, and these monsters are more skilled than goblins!"

"You always take the fun out of it."

Zakili spun toward the axe wielder, tensing him up, then dove and rolled, forcing the snarling masnevire to turn and face him, making the brute an effective block against the crossbowmen.

With the flick of Zakili's wrist, one dagger soared from his hand and lodged in the throat of the axe wielder. "One, two…" the elf counted then tossed his other dagger. The first masnevire fell off to the side, and the second dagger whistled end-over-end past the brute. The Flying Tiger struck mortally into the first crossbowman's face.

Zakili dove and rolled again and snatched up a dagger as his momentum carried him back to his feet. He dove toward the other downed brute. Predictably, he heard the clicking of the crossbow trigger. Impossibly fast, he yanked free the other dagger from the dead brute and in mid roll somehow got both daggers up in time to careen the crossbow bolt to the side.

As he got to his feet, he dove and rolled again in the direction of the masnevire. The brute threw his empty crossbow aside and grabbed for his sword. He never made it. Zakili's sprung back to his feet, and before the masnevire could prepare his defenses, the elf drove both daggers through the masnevire's rib cage and into its heart.

Navarro spun, slashing out with his blade and knocking away a vicious sword strike from his right. Another masnevire lunged in, sword going for The

Paladin's throat. The Paladin planted his right foot stopping his swift turn. His sword angled up diagonally and slammed the brute's sword harmlessly away.

From behind a masnevire rushed him, thinking he had an easy kill, his sword lifted overhead in both hands. Navarro's preternatural sixth sense warned him, and The Paladin's foot snapped out, slammed into the masnevire's solar plexus, catching the monster by surprise, and blasted the air from his lungs. The Paladin's sword swiped hard and sliced through the brute's chest, then sliced back once, and again, deadly accurate. The masnevire fell over dead. Navarro turned and sent Invinitor overhead, then arcing across in time to mow down another masnevire who recklessly charged.

The Paladin looked to the pair of humans they rescued. They kept the single masnevire at arms' length, but now a few more brutes were working their way behind the couple. Cruel blades drawn, they moved in like a pack of wolves.

"You have enemies at your back!" Navarro warned. Shimre spun in that direction. He could see the stark fear on the man's face as multiplied enemies stalked him and his wife. Navarro knew that the couple, who were merchants, held no chance against the bloodthirsty gang. Navarro dashed toward them.

The brutes closed in. One masnevire charged suddenly and aggressively, its sword hacking across low to cut the merchant's legs out from under him.

Shimre barely thrust his blade down in time to parry the weapon. The power of the creature's attack drove him back. From the corner of his eye he spotted another masnevire closing. This one bore down on him with a spiked club.

Down the masnevire's weapon plunged. Instinctively, Shimre's thrust his thin sword up to block and he braced for the impact, knowing his parry would be futile. The club blew apart in a fiery explosion before it finished half its arc down, throwing flaming splinters into the air.

Surprised but still aggressive, the masnevire rushed in anyway, tossing aside its blasted weapon. The monster grabbed hold of the man's shoulder and slammed him to the ground.

"Help Shimre!" his wife screamed, but he was helpless to do anything. A heavy boot stomped onto his shoulder and pinned him to the ground. When Shimre looked up with his one good eye, he saw the masnevire with sword overhead. It was going to decapitate him!

A loud explosion rocked Shimre's eardrums and, he protectively closed his eyes. Suddenly he didn't feel the masnevire holding him down any more. Shimre leapt to his feet and turned in his wife's direction in time to see a brilliant sword punch through the back of the slobbering monster which was strangling her. Navarro kicked the dying brute off his sword and clashed with another attacking masnevire.

Shimre looked to the lifeless corpse of the aggressive masnevire which tried to decapitate him, a grotesque burn mark burrowed all the way to its dark heart. He looked off to the side and received a quick bow from the black-clad elf.

"Thank God for you both," he breathed in awe as the two warriors with breath-taking skill battled and parried the fierce canine humanoids. Invinitor slashed and blocked masnevire strikes and sliced down the tall monsters at every turn.

Zakili's daggers did their death-dealing dance and ended the lives of just as many. Celemonte and the elf's charger fought just as aggressively, doing their share of pounding brutes into the ground.

The last two monsters, seeing the rest of their contingent destroyed by the two warriors, fled at high speed toward the forest.

"This is an advance strike force," Navarro said. "If these two get away, or they'll warn the main army."

"Consider them eliminated," Zakili assured, raising his bow and taking aim. He pulled back on the silvery bowstring and from nothing appeared a crackling energy arrow. He released the first lightning arrow. He didn't even wait to see the results. He pulled back on his bowstring again. Another energy arrow electified. He launched it.

Then there were no more masnevires.

Navarro and Zakili waded their way through the bodies to the two merchants.

"We are forever in your debt, brave rescuers," Rebeena said and she hugged close to her husband.

"No amount of thanks could express our gratitude. We are heart-broken for the good men slain. But I praise God for you sparing the lives of my wife and my infants."

"I only wish we could've been here sooner," Zakili said. "Maybe we could've prevented this slaughter."

The elf walked away, checking the downed men.

"You have many terrible wounds," Navarro said as he looked over Shimre. "Sit here on this wagon. You need healing."

"Healing?" the man asked questionably.

"God can do the impossible," Navarro explained. "I'm a Paladin of Christ." Shimre's smile grew wide.

"We have one who still breaths!" Zakili called.

Shimre looked, seeing the elf kneeling next to an older, thin man. "Gimshaw, my friend. You're still alive!"

* * * * *

"Beware warrior, the wicked will burst from cave and from den,
in earnest to free the demons and bring mankind to an end."

Navarro remembered that image like yesterday. One of the mysterious blind men sitting by the bonfire warned him of a worldwide monster uprising. The creatures' main quest, some powerful energy source which would unleash the mightiest demons Christ Jesus had chained in the bottomless pit.

With Zeraktalis, who appeared to command the monsters searching for this power, Navarro understood the sudden urgency not only for Avundar but for every land. If the monsters succeeded in releasing the vilest of demons, they would seek out and destroy every soul in every land.

Now it appeared The Dark Sorcerer's monster hordes were beginning to focus their sights on the land of Avundar as the origin of this powerful energy source. Navarro was concerned when he heard the incredible news of goblin scouts venturing even into Verdant Wood, but he was shocked when he saw more than a score of brutes attacking Shimre's merchant caravan.

The foul horde of The Dark Sorcerer was mobilizing. The evidence was overwhelming. A monster army hid somewhere in Avundar!

Navarro and Zakili escorted the merchants to a small town called Pebblefist, where dwelt many an adept warrior. The two friends regretted they had to lay Shimre's fallen merchants and their families in shallow graves. Times were urgent. They piled the bodies of the slain masnevires in a ransacked wagon, and Zakili ignited a raging bonfire to consume the evidence of their demise.

As they departed from the small town of Pebblefist, Navarro noticed the ominous signs of distant, billowing, smoke plumes. The Paladin looked to his friend who returned an equally dreadful gaze.

"The horde has struck its first town."

* * * * *

A tear rolled down his cheek, and he forced himself not to look away despite how his stomach turned and somersaulted. Navarro felt sick.

He felt like he wanted to get sick.

Zakili looked to the ground, disgusted at the sight he just turned from.

The western sky washed red against the darkening canvas of evening, shedding an eerie huc on the bowl-shaped valley below. From the top of the precipice, they saw the rural town Lunumdra.

What was left.

Black wisps of smoke slithered into the sky as flames ate home after home from one end of the town to the next.

Navarro scanned the devastation. He spotted no movement, no life at all, among the ruin.

"We're too late," Navarro lamented. "The town is destroyed. Apparently taken completely unaware."

"When Saranisen told us about the goblin scouts in Verdant Wood, I grew concerned for my elves. But I fear the monster scouts must've been dispatched throughout Avundar to locate targets," battle-hardened Zakili said, his heart angry and saddened at the horrible sight.

He made acquaintance with several of the humans who lived in this town, men of character and formidable fighting prowess. Now they were gone, their town flattened and burned in one evening.

He never imagined this could happen in Avundar.

Looking past the ruined, smoking town, Navarro spotted the distant, dissipating billows where he knew another town stood.

"Look," he said somberly, pointing to the rising smoke. "The town of Garrison Walls has been sacked and destroyed also. By the thinning of the smoke billows, it must have fallen victim before Lunumdra."

"The horde is systematically destroying every township it passes," Zakili said.

"We must return quickly and warn the elves. Then we send word out to the baronies and townships," Navarro said, "but I don't feel we can leave just yet. I sense there's something we need to discover in the town below."

* 18 *
GIANT PROBLEMS

The sun was creeping below the mountain ranges by the time Navarro and Zakili reached the town and began to investigate the tragedy. The stench of the smoldering village assaulted The Paladin's nostrils. The flickering tongues of flame cast a golden glow throughout the cluttered streets and onto the wooded inclines of the shallow valley. Long eerie shadows stretched off into thedarkness.

"Goblins and masnevires," Navarro said grimly, pulling away from the telltale footprints left in the dirt. "There doesn't seem to be much sign of melee. The foul throng appears to have pounced quickly, catching the men of the village almost totally off-guard."

Among the burning rubble he spotted several uprooted trees thrown upon homes, obviously to flush out any groups of resistance which may have developed. "And giants. Those behemoths specialize in throwing boulders and heavy missiles with amazing accuracy."

"All this devastation," Zakili said, "but I find nothing but bloodied streets, not a single body could I discover among the ruins."

Navarro turned.

"I wager they didn't take prisoners."

"Goblinoids don't take prisoners. Their driving force is to destroy. No, I fear a more foul reason they snatched up the townsfolk."

The elf acknowledged with a sour scowl.

"And my guess would be the ruins of the town sacked before Lunumdra look similar."

"This doesn't make any sense. How did a horde of monsters press into the heart of Avundar without any notice? Surely, a throng huge enough to effectively wipe out two towns had to raise alarm no matter *where* it entered this land."

"I have no answer for that," Navarro admitted. "What concerns me is the coordination behind these brutes' movements. It's too organized. I assume first they sent out scouts to various parts of the land to measure its strengths, as they tried in Verdant Wood, then they struck quickly. This is all hauntingly familiar to the war in Sheliavon so many years ago."

"With the addition of one thing."

"I know," The Paladin agreed.

"Those creatures favor the blood of men and elves. In Sheliavon, the armies I warred alongside busted up many a grotesque feast.

"But never did I see them clear a field of *all* the fallen."

"Hiding somewhere in Avundar there is a great army to feed," Navarro guessed, "and they systematically crush town after town without the masses of Avundar's baronies even aware."

"Surprise is their ally. Nobody in Avundar would ever expect to wake up one morning to a horde of monsters swarming over their town."

"That advantage is now stripped away. We know they're in Avundar. We must solidify the forces of Avundar against them." The Paladin lost his breath at a sudden thought. "If this horde continues its swath, Castle Veldercrantz stands next in their path. Before we can warn the rest of the land, Baron Kelt's defenses must be shored up against the imminent onslaught."

The Paladin stared into the distance, his mind dizzy with concern and dread. Zakili knew his friend worried about the safety of Candace and her father. The elf omitted his usual sarcastic comment about The Paladin's affections toward the woman. Bravely and determinedly, Navarro chose to never seek Candace out again when she departed from Verdant Wood. The elf understood the emotional struggle of his friend (although The Paladin would admit none); for this woman, this Christian woman, had deeply touched his heart in a way Zakili had never seen before.

Now he feared this woman who had forever secured a place in Navarro's heart might be mauled by a swarm of monsters.

"We must be on our way," Navarro said. "Night has fallen in full. We have no time to pursue the horde; although, they surely must be slowed by the weight of their grim trophies. My guess is they will cart their victims away to their den and carry on with the momentum of their bloodlust. I have battled enough of these brutes to understand their ravenous frenzy once they've begun killing."

"Back to Verdant Wood then to retrieve more warriors?" Zakili asked.

"Indeed," The Paladin agreed, but his face went suddenly grim, and Invinitor's ruby heart glowed fiercely.

"Danger?" the Elf Prince guessed by the look on his friend's face.

"I sense it's very near in the darkness... Run!"

Zakili zipped away to the side, Navarro right on his heels. They hadn't gotten more than twenty feet before a thunderous boom echoed behind them, and the earth shook under their feet. The Paladin turned quickly. An uprooted tree lay sidelong where the friends had just stood. Its boughs and roots still rocked from the impact.

"Turn and flee," The Paladin shouted again, dashing away to his left as he sensed another missile flying their way. Zakili was right with him. They felt the displacement of air just barely over their heads before a booming crash thundered again where they had just been standing. Navarro knew it was another launched tree.

"Get down!" he whispered, dropping to his belly. "Now get quickly to the tree."

The friends pressed close to the fallen tree's trunk, searching the dark bowl-shaped valley for enemies.

"Had I not sensed the danger, we would both be under a tree. I'll give you one guess who hasn't left the valley yet."

"Stinkin' giants," Zakili said.

Navarro nodded.

"I remember battling against armies of those evil, destructive creatures in Sheliavon. They're powerful, vicious, and hard to kill.

"Especially so when they hide in the dark and throw trees at you!"

255

Johnny Earl Jones

The Paladin scanned the sloping descent which led to the level ground where the town lay. Trees grew tall in every stretch of the decline aside from the path into the town and up the tall, rocky precipice where the friends had viewed the town before making their way down. Navarro quickly eliminated the precipice as the giants' hiding spot. If they had been in that rocky area, they would throw their more preferred missiles--boulders. No, they were hidden among the trees, but where? He turned to his friend, who could see much better in the dark with his elven eyes. "What do you see?"

"Nothing yet," Zakili answered. "No movement. Yet. I'm sure that will change soon. Giants are not the most patient creatures."

A thundering boom sounded deeper in the village behind them.

"Another tree," Navarro said. "It appears a few stayed behind and encircled the valley. They are throwing volleys from different directions. They too can see well in the dark, but when there's no movement, they can't pinpoint a hidden target. They're throwing blindly."

"They have a lot of trees to throw," the elf said. "I don't know the wisdom of just staying still and letting them bombard this place. We can't see these trees fly in the darkness, and one might get off a lucky shot and pound us."

A loud crash sounded in the darkness--a home crunched under a thrown tree.

"Time will run out if they keep us on the defensive and locked into this valley. We need to get out of here and warn Baron Veldercrantz of the imminent attack."

"It's time to draw them out," Zakili decided.

"Bring 'em to us," Navarro agreed, Invinitor leaping into his hand. "It's time to cut some evil giants down to size."

The Elf Prince sprang to his feet, pulled back on his ivory bow, and fired an energy arrow. The arrow sailed over the town in the valley pathway's direction.

"Dive!" Navarro said and sprang to the other side of the tree. The brief sound of whistling leaves broke the night's silence then a tree crashed down on the one where they had been hiding. Branches, bark, and splinters sprayed into the air. The Paladin evaluated the direction of the noise and the momentum of the tree. He spun about and saw the distant glow of heat-seeking eyes among the trees.

"There!" Navarro indicated. "Fire now!"

Zakili spun and fired a quick volley of lightning arrows into that section of trees.

"Charge!" Navarro urged. Both friends leapt the tree trunk and raced for the incline, hearing the pained grunt of their hidden attacker ahead. Another tree slammed down a few steps behind them, again shaking the earth under their feet. The warriors didn't hesitate. In a brief moment they were at the treeline. Before The Paladin plunged in, he blew three short, shrill whistles then ascended the wooded incline.

"We no longer need fear a tree falling on our heads," Navarro said lightly, understanding they were hardly out of danger. Now, more dangerous, they had to face the physical threat of a towering giant.

Stopping behind a thick tree, the two listened, trying to discern movement in the even darker, shadowy night of the forest. Several loud crunching noises and heavy grunts sounded not far to their left.

"Let's get 'em." Navarro and Zakili said simultaneously, nodded and dashed off in that direction. But the friends could now hear pounding footsteps approaching from a distance.

"There's more than one here," Navarro related to his friend.

Navarro barely saw the large hole and he nearly stumbled into it. A giant had been here, The Paladin knew. This hole once held a living tree. He veered around the pit and raced onward.

Zakili, who was lighter and faster on his feet, made his way quickly around it and Navarro, but skidded to a halt, raising his hand as a signal to stop. Quickly alongside his friend, The Paladin's ears were assaulted by a barrage of vulgarity from one of the giants hidden in the dark. Peering around a tree, Navarro spotted one burly giant. Stung by one Zakili's arrows, the giant clutched his wounded chest. Two other club-wielding giants broke into the clearing and spotted their comrad.

"Twice our height," Zakili evaluated.

"Five times our weight," Navarro guessed. "And powerful."

"When I find 'em, I will crush those warmbloods for woundin' me in me chest," the giant threatened. "No, even better, I will make one watch as I rip the other from limb to limb as I did with those villagers!"

Navarro's eyes narrowed at the thought of these giants slowly and torturously killing people slowly in front of their own families. His sword spun eagerly in his hand.

"It's time to take them down," he declared. Before he leapt into battle, he felt an evil presence at his back.

Navarro spun about just as a gigantic axe swung sidelong at him. There was no way to escape the speeding weapon. He quickly twirled in the direction of the wielding giant. This effectively took Navarro out of the axehead's path, but not of the thick handle.

Invinitor chopped down swiftly and the blade cut cleanly through the handle. The axehead looped into the darkness and landed with a loud crash against a nearby tree.

"What was that?" the injured giant demanded. A cacophony followed. The other giants stirred.

At that urgent moment, it was a distant thought for Navarro. The thick, headless axe handle plummeted down at him like a club.

With no other option, he leapt in the direction of the giant and rolled on one shoulder, coming to his feet between the giant's massive legs just as the handle's end burst into flames.

"Beware of your own safety!" Navarro yelled to Zakili, understanding the elf's energy arrow had ignited the weapon. "This one picked a fight with me. I'm going to take him down!"

"As you wish," Zakili said and fired an energy arrow in the other giants' direction.

In the distance, Navarro heard the howls of other behemoths.

The giant threw aside the flaming handle and turned to respond to his agile opponent. Navarro stepped back and Invinitor slashed deep across the back of the brute's leg, hamstringing the monster. With an agonizing cry which left The Paladin's ears ringing, the giant swiped back with one huge hand. Navarro already anticipated that and fled out of range.

The behemoth turned, snarling in rage, and snapped off the nearest tree bough. "I will crunch ye fer stingin' me with yer nasty little sword, warmblood!"

The giant slammed the bough down at the paladin, but agile Navarro dove and rolled just as the bough pounded his footprints into oblivion. Navarro's momentum carried him to his feet, and he caught a tree branch and held on to stop his roll down the slope.

"Your master Zeraktalis made a grave error by bringing you to this land!" Navarro said. "I won't allow your kind to spread over Avundar and destroy our communities."

"There is nothin' ye can do!" the giant spat back.

"This land's not like Sheliavon. Your sorcerer won't lead an army of giants and goblins in victory over the people of this land."

The giant bellowed thunderous laughter. "We have already begun t' crush the inhabitants o' this land. And our army consists o' more than just giants and goblins."

"Such as?"

"I am not here t' banter with ye! I am here t' crush ye!" The giant chopped at him with the huge limb. Slipping behind the closest tree, Navarro avoided the hit. The makeshift club slammed into the tree's trunk instead. He could feel the tremendous vibrations under his feet from the impact.

He stuck his head around the tree. "You're no match for me, giant. If you really thought you could crush me, you wouldn't be afraid to tell me about the strength of your army. If you actually thought you would win, you would fill my heart with fear for the people of this land, and I would have to take that to the grave with me."

"I needn't tell ye anything, puny warmblood!"

Navarro sprinted away from the tree, tracing a quarter circle away from the giant and stopping behind another tree. He understood most giants were not smart creatures. They were essentially huge, powerful bullies. If he could taunt the giant enough, the challenge wouldn't go unanswered. The violent crashing off to the side drew The Paladin's attention and he understood more giants were moving in.

A blood-chilling scream reverberated through the forest followed by a flood of profanity. "That warmblood blew half my ear off!" a behemoth roared. Navarro knew his friend had scored with his powerful bow.

"Your allies will come soon to help you, slow one," Navarro said condescendingly to the brute. "Do you need help destroying a solitary human?"

He saw the giant's face redden, the huge veins in its neck bulge, and he knew

258

the giant's temper was quickly getting to his boiling point. Knowing the injured giant wouldn't be able to move fast enough to catch him, The Paladin stepped away from the tree and into the open. "Are you scared, giant? Do you fear to tell me what your army consists of? After all, you said there is nothing the people of Avundar can do to prevail against you."

"Warmblood, we have in our throng monsters ye cannot kill!"

"I refuse to believe that. I've never met a monster that will not die."

"Ye have never met any like these," it said with a crooked smile.

"Like what?" he asked, but his senses screamed danger. He felt the ground shake under his feet once.

Then again.

"There's a giant behind me," he said, understanding the tremors he felt were footsteps.

He spun suddenly, and under the darkness of the moonlit sky, he spotted the towering, hulking shape of one of the most terrifying giants he'd ever seen. Grabbing hold of two young trees which stood in his path, the giant pushed them in opposing directions, forcefully uprooting the firs and allowing more moonlight to accentuate its monstrous features. The giant was bald, with swirling patterns tattooed on its skull. Its eyes burned with the reddish glow of nocturnal vision. Burly muscles rippled as he reached over his shoulder to extract a thick club from a back holster.

"That one looks too thick for even Invinitor to cut through," Navarro evaluated as he tried to figure out how he would get out of this predicament. He couldn't possibly stand against the brute strength of so many powerful giants, and the longer he and Zakili were pinned down on the valley slope, the more giants seemed to appear. They had fallen into a trap, he realized.

After the monsters had leveled the town and moved on, the giants had stayed and positioned themselves around the bowl-shaped valley slopes to destroy any who came to investigate the smoking town's demise. Looks like we were the first to pay a visit.

He turned and stared the bald giant in the eyes, listening for the other giant at his back, but knowing it could move only slowly with its hamstrung leg.

"What are you cowardly giants doing in my land?" Navarro questioned. Taunted. "I didn't give you permission to set foot in Avundar!"

The bald giant's brow furled angrily, his fist tightening around the club. "Tiny gnat, I need permission from nobody, especially not ye! I am Baricon the Great!"

"Baricon the what?" Navarro asked, knowing he played a deadly game but hoping he could extract some more information. He knew giants were easily angered, and when their wrath was aroused, they boasted information they normally shouldn't. The downside to that plan was that giants often devolved into a mindless rampage as well. If he could outwit his opponent he could defeat him, if not he'd be destroyed.

"Baricon the Great!" the giant roared again, his face flushing with fury that could be seen easily even in the dark. A giant club chopped down swiftly, and Navarro spun away, barely escaping the impact of the club as it crashed into the earth, forcing dust flying into the air, and sent shudders through the ground. The Paladin slipped behind a tree. He was amazed by the behemoth's speed.

"You tell your sorcerer Zeraktalis that once again he has sent you creatures into a battle which will spell your demise!"

Baricon laughed. "Yer land won't be razed by an army o' simple brute killers as Sheliavon was. All of Avundar will be crushed by the greatest horde this world has ever known!

"And if this town is any indication o' the resistance we will face, yer land will be conquered afore the sorcerer even emerges from Genna Fiendomon!"

Navarro didn't know what a Genna Fiendomon was, but he was intrigued by the hint that the sorcerer wasn't even guiding these monsters' actions yet. "So who's telling you what to do?"

"Nobody's telling me what to do!" Baricon roared in outrage.

Navarro doubted that claim but continued this line of conversation, seeking what other information he could discover from this strange encounter. "My respect for you has increased a hundred-fold, great giant. I'm impressed. You are the leader of the monster army which has infiltrated this land of Avundar?"

"I am the Chieftain of the Giants, the strongest of the monsters! Krylothon commands the weaker races," the giant said in a superior tone.

The Paladin remembered suddenly that not only do giants anger easily, but they are also swollen with racist pride. But who is this Krylothon? "Do you rule over Krylothon, Great One?"

To that question, Baricon's thick brows furrowed. Navarro had his answer.

Behind him, the clumsy noise of pounding feet told him the other giant lumbered from behind. He discerned he had a moment before the brute was upon him. He stuck his head out from behind the tree. "Hey, Baricon the Late! Do you think you can hit me this time?"

Baricon roared and predictably charged up the slope. Navarro looked back quickly and saw the other giant was closer than he suspected, its tree limb club raised overhead for a finishing blow.

Bending quickly, the paladin snatched up a fist-sized rock and hurled it. The stone slammed close to the giant's eye and wrenched a painful cry. Intrepidly, Navarro ran toward it.

Baricon bounded after The Paladin, his club sweeping across low to mow down the fleeing man. The furious Baricon hardly noticed the man run between the other giant's thick legs. His focus was solely on the taunting human. The club slammed across. Navarro fled at full speed, hearing the thunderous snapping of bone as rampaging Baricon's club crashed into the unsuspecting giant's shins. The Paladin glanced back quickly and watched the giant crumble toward Baricon, but the chieftain tossed the shattered giant aside, sending him in a headlong roll down the steep slope.

Continuing his sprint, Navarro dodged from tree to tree, trying to keep himself out of Baricon's sight as much as possible. Placing his fingers to his lips, he released three long whistles into the night. From the distance below, he heard a commotion and understood yet another giant pushed his way up the slope.

"Zakili! I think we have worn out our welcome here."

"You're not kidding," the Elf Prince's responded close in the darkness.

"And it sounds like the rest of the family comes to kick us out."

"Our only escape lies in fleeing to the base of the valley."

"That makes us easy targets for flying trees."

"Trust me on this one," the Paladin said.

Behind him, Navarro heard the pounding, sliding footsteps of Baricon as he tried to keep up pursuit on the steep slope.

"We're running out of time. We must make our move now," Navarro said.

Zakili burst into the open and came alongside his paladin friend. "I'll race you there."

A giant axehead slammed into the tree just behind them.

"Last one there..." Zakili challenged.

The two warriors darted down the decline, sliding more than running and often times grabbing hold of trees to prevent from plunging headlong. From behind them and higher up they heard trees splinter and feet pound as the giants took up pursuit. The noises came from everywhere, and Navarro wondered how many giants hid in this single valley. The one thing to their advantage, they were much smaller than their foes and able to hide among the trees as they escaped. But how long would that last? The stride of the giants was nearly three times their gait, Navarro knew, and if the creatures could locate them, they would close ground quickly.

Through the trees, the paladin spotted the ruins of Lunumdra not far below. In his peripheral vision he saw the shadow of the Elf Prince keeping stride with his own feverish pace.

With the storming giants at his back, Navarro bounded down the slope in reckless leaps, each heel digging in just enough to keep him from tumbling into a dangerous roll. Although he heard the giants draw closer, he knew he and Zakili made good speed and prayed they could break free of the trees before the giants caught them.

He saw the tree line several strides away! They would make it!

Two bounding strides then a third brought the friends to level ground.

But just as they broke free of the trees, Navarro's senses and the ruby heart of Invinitor fired up! The Paladin stopped then jumped back. A club smashed down, barely missing him. Aggressively, Navarro attacked, his sword slicing down just as the club was retracted, cutting cleanly through the weapon's handle and taking several fingers with it. The giant roared in anguish, its booted foot kicking at Navarro. Navarro spun aside, turned, and plunged Invinitor into the giant's knee, wrenching a flood of profanity from his thick lips.

Behind Navarro, the sound of battle had begun. A second giant challenged Zakili.

Time is running out, the paladin thought. The whole clan of giants would be upon them soon. Then there would be no escape. But an even more dreadful thought came to mind. The longer they were held here, the closer the foul horde got to Kelt's fortress and to Candace.

Navarro's senses tingled again, and he dove for the ground just as a tree swept close overhead. The loud of snapping bones and an ear-shattering scream later, Navarro's adversary collapsed, the tree crashing into the giant's knees, shattering his legs.

The Paladin raced toward the second giant which his friend still battled, exhaling two loud whistles into the night as he ran.

"What're the whistles for?" Zakili asked and he pulled back on his bow.

"I'm signaling our help."

The giant turned, seeing another opponent challenging him. Zakili fired off an energy arrow, but this giant had a colossal shield and quickly ducked behind it. The impact of the arrow exploding into the shield merely forced the giant back a step.

"We have no time to play," Navarro said.

"That's easy for you to say," Zakili argued as he raced out of the way of a spiked club. "The other giants finished off your monster for you."

"We must flee. The others are converging. And..."

"And you fear for Candace's safety," the elf finished.

"Correct," he admitted as he arced to the side of the giant. The behemoth was quite keen, angling himself to keep The Paladin in his sight.

Zakili dashed to the opposing side of the powerful, shaggy-headed giant, firing off another energy arrow. The giant shifted the shield and effectively defeated the missile, and roared in evil laughter. "Ye puny warmbloods, ye don't know who yer dealing with! I am Maxicon the great!"

"Any relation to Baricon the great?" Navarro asked mordantly, stealing the thunder from the proud brute's proclamation.

"I will crunch ye between me teeth while ye yet live," the giant threatened.

"If ye yet live," The Paladin responded, mocking Maxicon's speech.

The giant picked its teeth, pulling free something soggy and flipped it at the man. Navarro looked coldly at the blood-stained remains of a little girls' dress.

"Me latest victim," he boasted, laughing. "The whelp's parents thought they could defeat me too. I snapped them in half and the last thing their dying eyes saw was their screaming whelp being dropped into me mouth."

"We've got interesting news for you, Maxicon. We will be the last thing your dying eyes ever see."

Navarro charged. The giant, shocked by The Paladin's boldness, balked before sending his spiked club looping down at The Paladin. Navarro easily dove and rolled to the side and the huge weapon bludgeoned the grassy earth. Quickly back to his feet, Navarro barely lost stride. The shield swept in front of him, but Invinitor shaved a chunk of it away. The paladin spun to the outside and behind the huge barrier.

Three strides later, his sword sliced across, hacking through the tough hide of the giant's boot then his flesh, and digging into his shin. Maxicon roared and tried to swat the warrior, but he was on the opposite side of the giant's club hand and the shield arm provided an effective blind spot. The powerful giant lifted his huge foot instead and tried to stomp his aggressor.

"Hey, Maxi!" came a call and the giant looked over wide-eyed. A split second after he thought of raising his shield in defense an energy arrow exploded against his wide chest, sending the giant staggering backward. Navarro, already positioned, threw his shoulder and all his weight at the back of the giant's knee. Maxicon stumbled and collapsed over, landing hard on his back, the collision shaking the earth.

The tree line splintered as several rampaging giants spilled onto level ground, their footsteps sending tremors through the ground.

"Delay them, Zakili," Navarro requested.

"My pleasure," the elf responded and pulled back on his bow.

Navarro leaped onto the shaken giant's chest. Predictably, a huge hand swatted across, but The Paladin had already sprung, somersaulting in the air and coming down hard on the giant's solar plexus--blasting the breath from his lungs.

"This is for the family you destroyed, evil one!" Navarro said, and Invinitor drove down hard, plunging into the giant's chest and piercing its dark heart.

The sound of several more giants crashing onto the scene brought The Paladin's attention to the mounting danger. He put his fingers to his lips and let out one loud piercing whistle.

"I won't be able to keep all these behemoths back much longer," Zakili said, firing arrow after arrow at the growing clan of giants.

"Run!" Navarro cried, sending the elf into a wild sprint.

An uprooted tree slammed down.

"Now we're dodging giants and trees," Zakili said impatiently.

As his senses tingled Navarro spun away to the side, barely avoiding a thrown tree. Looking to the tree line at the base of the valley's slope, he spotted several giants ripping trees from the ground and hurling them.

Zakili fired once and again, but the mob of giants pressed closer.

Navarro sprinted away again as another tree crashed down.

"Move this way, quick," The paladin warned, and the elf dashed his direction just in time to miss being crushed by a tree.

"If you're able to sense those things without having to see them, I'm sticking close to you."

"Stick really close."

Navarro dashed forward, Zakili at his side, and a tree crashed down close behind. The Paladin darted off to his right suddenly, avoiding another tossed tree. To the side, he noticed the looming shapes of the powerful giants growing closer.

Baricon burst through the treeline, slowly, deliberately, and looked to the downed giant. "Ye killed me brother!" He reached over and pulled a tree from the ground with one mighty hand. "It is time to die, warmblood!" He hurled the tree end-over-end.

"Destroy them now," Navarro heard the giant's surly command, sending the

Johnny Earl Jones

huge brutes into a wild sprint. The Paladin dashed away and Zakili followed close as Baricon's hurled tree slammed down close and went into a wild end-over-end tumble.

Zakili pulled back on his bow once then again, launching energy arrow after energy arrow at the closing mob. The missiles pounded painfully into a couple behemoths and slowed them considerably. As the elf readied to fire again he was grabbed by the collar and pulled back. It was Navarro. The ground shook under his feet a moment later as another tree pounded down uncomfortably close.

The giants fanned out, spreading like an ensnaring net.

Navarro blew out three short whistles.

The giants rushed in.

Grim-faced, Zakili launched energy arrow after energy arrow. One missile took a giant in the face and dropped it to the ground. "We'll fight them to the end," the elf promised.

"The end is not yet," Navarro's said, and from the direction of the downed giant came two charging shapes, both brilliantly white under the surreal glow of the stars. "Good boy, Celemonte!"

The pounding hooves of the chargers outdistanced the racing giants, and the animals plunged in the direction of the warriors, slowing only enough for Navarro and Zakili to latch onto their respective charger and swing themselves into their saddles.

"Charge out of this accursed valley and back to Verdant Wood," Navarro commanded, and Celemonte's pace increased exponentially, leaving in their wake a mob of cursing and roaring giants.

* 19 *
TALL, DARK AND UGLY

"Avundar faces destruction far greater than Sheliavon experienced," Navarro said. He and Zakili had raced across the plains on their chargers and came upon a long stretch of trees which stood sentry for miles along the winding Languid River.

"What have you learned?" the elf asked now their pace decreased. With reins tightly in hand, he led his horse through the maze of trees to where the water flowed. Leaping from his steed, he petted his horse's neck gently as the beast lowered his mouth and thirstily lapped the water. Celemonte pulled up alongside to quench his own dryness as The Paladin dismounted.

"Those giants are extremely arrogant or very stupid. Baricon revealed a force fiercer than Sheliavon's giant and goblin army is on the march. These giants are larger and stronger than the ones we defeated years ago. They are swifter and more cognizant than any giant I've ever faced. I fear for the baronies and townships of our land. The horde thoroughly leveled Lunumdra. Undoubtedly Garrison Walls, attacked previously, shared the same fate."

"When we led the Silver Elves into Sheliavon, there were tales that the Dark Sorcerer somehow possessed the giants and goblins," Zakili said. "He endowed them with fighting ability beyond their natural capacity.

"Could another group of possessed brutes have infiltrated Avundar's borders?"

"No." Navarro answered. Those brutes are not led by The Sorcerer at all right now."

"Excuse me?" Zakili asked in unbelief.

"The giant said The Sorcerer is in some place called Genna Fiendomon and hadn't even left from there to join his monsters yet."

"So who's leading this mixed horde?"

"Someone named Krylothon."

"The Sorcerer's apprentice?"

"I don't know. In my adventures I've never heard that name. Whoever it is must be powerful. When I asked Baricon if he ruled over this Krylothon the proud giant showed disdain."

"Giants were the field marshals and strongest of the forces in Sheliavon. The future of Avundar is grim if even mightier creatures lead this horde's forces. Avundar's lived in peace for so long, I don't know if the baronies could unite effectively enough to stave off a full-scale onslaught," the elf admitted.

Navarro nodded. "One more disconcerting thought of which a different giant boasted. He said the army is composed of monsters which do not die."

"Impressive claim," Zakili ridiculed. "Only problem is, the creatures we faced went down to death like any other foul monster we've defeated before."

The Paladin waved off the whole improbable thought. "You're right, my friend. There is nothing alive that won't taste death, and no evil which good cannot overcome in the end. I just hate monsters' boasts. I never know what kind of evil surprise awaits."

"I know what awaits them!" Zakili said. With an all-teeth grin, his twin daggers sprung into his hands.

"Excellent point," Navarro agreed, drawing out his mighty sword.

"Two excellent points," the elf corrected, sending both daggers into a dangerous spin.

"The horses have drunk and we have no time to let them rest further," The Paladin decided. "We must proceed to Verdant Wood. The horizon begins to lighten."

"We ride then," Zakili said, striding to his charger. He stopped suddenly. Hunched shapes milled in the shadows on the other side of the shallow river.

Navarro's senses radiated warning, as did Invinitor's ruby heart. The elf prince pointed to the gathering shadows. A hundred red-dot, beady eyes peered through the darkness at the two warriors. "Evil gathers."

"Looks like trouble has found us again," Zakili said.

The shapes shifted strategically among the trees. Gathering like a vicious pack, they grew in mass.

"With time against us, we have only two options--we either back out and ride around, hoping these creatures won't mirror our route, or..."

"Or we break straight through them," Zakili finished, knowing the only other choice.

Celemonte stood tall and straight. Snorting anxiously, the charger stared at the shapes ahead, then looked to his master, wagging his head.

"Ready to take them on, boy," The Paladin asked, patting the horse. "You've been my companion through many a bloody fray. Your courage never lets up.

"I don't know what these monsters are ahead of us, but we will overcome them as we have all others. Christ Jesus already proclaimed us as more than conquerors."

With a bounding leap, The Paladin was in his saddle. "The stretch of trees is not deep. Once we battle our way past them, we have the open plains ahead of us all the way to Verdant Wood."

Zakili was up on his horse then, jabbing his blades into their scabbards. "Then I'll blaze the trail," he said and pulled his ivory bow off his shoulder.

Kicking his charger's flanks, the elf set his horse into a charge, holding tightly with his knees as he pulled back on his bow. Navarro and Celemonte took up the chase right behind him. Both chargers hurriedly splashed through the mild currents and emerging on the river's other bank in full stride.

Zakili noted the multitude of red eyes peered at him from both flanks. They weren't drawing closer and that troubled him. His charger raced on, nearing the trees.

Johnny Earl Jones

By this time he'd expected the mob to converge on him, but still the eyes only stared.

"Looks like they don't want anything to do with us," Zakili called back. But just as the words left his mouth, a pack of tall gangly slilitroks rushed out of the shadows to create a living wall of monsters, their deformed mouths howling weirdly.

"Too easy," Zakili said. He pulled back on his bowstring and fired an energy arrow at the closest monster. The missile knocked the creature backward, stumbling and screaming in an eerie, high-pitched wail. The rest of the wall held its ground. Navarro gripped his blade securely as they drove closer. Zakili fired another shot, blasting one more of the gangly creatures off its feet, loosing yet another eerie scream.

Suddenly the copse of trees was alive with screeches and howls. Zakili hit the wall of monsters first. Several trampled underfoot and nearly tripped his charger. The elf fired once, twice, sending two more creatures flying away, screaming into the darkness. The others rushed in fearlessly from the sides, swiping with the dagger-like nails on their huge hands. Many grabbed for the lethal bow which sent several of their companions to their doom.

"They were herding us into their trap," Navarro said, his blade hacking and slashing mightily. Long, exaggerated arms and distorted heads flew into the night.

Zakili managed to draw back on his bow again and fire an energy arrow down the throat of one monster that lunged at him.

More and more slilitroks poured out of the shadows, charging in from every side, long claws raking across, tearing into leather armor and horse flesh. The chargers pressed on, now slow and weighed down as monsters pressed on every side.

The Elf Prince fumbled to keep his bow out of the monsters' reach more than he was able to shoot it. Slamming it over his shoulders, he whipped out his daggers, sent them into a deadly spin, and sliced off fingers and hands when they got too close. Several monsters fell away with a gauged eye or a fatally gashed throat.

Relentlessly, Navarro mowed down monsters on each side with his long blade. The slilitroks seemed endless. Every time he cut one down, another took its place. But to The Paladin's horror, he saw many of the monsters he had dismembered or decapitated simply replace their severed limb or head. Navarro watched slimy tendrils reach out and reattach the parts back to the monster.

"My friend, I think we have run into those monsters the giant described: the ones who can't be killed," Navarro said with growing aggravation.

"It's time to change that!" Zakili offered, his blades whipping back and forth, taking down slilitroks on one side then the other.

Bracing tightly to his horse, Navarro slashed Invinitor left and right, clearing wide swaths, cutting down two, sometimes three slilitroks at a time with his keen blade.

From behind every bush and every tree, more and more slilitroks rampaged at the friends, the beasts salivating and screeching from the depths of their throats as they clawed forward to get an angle on the warriors. Those slilitroks who were cut and beginning to mend were tossed aside by the able-bodied.

Their bloodlust hit a fever pitch.

The warriors raged onward, blades stabbing and slicing, chopping and cutting creatures to pieces. Celemonte and Zakili's charger added their own blows to the fray, kicking and stomping the brutes as they pressed on.

But Navarro knew the odds in this battle were overwhelmingly against them: four against a hundred or more. And he knew the majority of the brutes hadn't entered the fray yet, still awaiting their opportunity. He and Zakili had tremendous ability and stamina, but how long could they keep up this frenzied pace, especially against monsters endless and regenerating?

"I hate to say this, my friend, but this is a battle we're going to have to flee!" The Paladin said. Invinitor swept across, cleaving through three monsters on his right side.

"That'll be twice in one night we had to run," Zakili said, his slashing blades taking the hands off of a reaching slilitrok. "This is a bad trend we started."

"This is a battle I would rather fight on my terms and without Candace's life hanging in the balance!"

"Point well taken," the Prince said, slicing down another slilitrok. "Any suggestions on how to get out of this pack?"

"There's no easy way about it," The Paladin decided, his blade dropping onto a slilitrok's collar bone and crunching it to the ground. "The most efficient way is going to be the hard way!"

"Are you suggesting what I think you are?"

"It'll be our only way to break free."

"Let's do it!"

Navarro leaped from his saddle, pounding feet first onto the nearest slilitrok, stomping it to the ground under his boots. Long arms and clawed hands reached in eagerly as monsters converged on him, but Invinitor whipped across then reversed angles and sliced across again, sending limbs airborne. One brute leapt, its jaws open wide, beady eyes on The Paladin. Navarro charged it, and Invinitor jabbed straight up, driving into the soaring brute's chest. Using its momentum, Navarro launched the slilitrok overhead and into a pair of on-rushers.

Zakili too sprang from his armored stallion, his blades twirling in a dangerous dance which sent grotesque body parts spinning in every direction. But onward the slilitroks came, some minus fingers and hands, straining their necks to get their distorted jaws, which were armed with dangerous teeth, on the elf's flesh. Zakili kicked one monster in the chest, standing him up straight. The elf spun and kicked again, sending it stumbling back, effectively blocking the approach of several others. Away he danced in his reckless style, spinning close to the monsters, his blades twirled and slashed.

Both chargers, free of their riders, trampled creatures rushing from the front and mule-kicked those sneaking in from behind, sometimes sending the brutes flying into the throng, other times breaking bones or crushing skulls.

Johnny Earl Jones

Seeing the pack press in more heavily, Navarro took Celemonte by the bridle with one hand, driving the warhorse forward, carving and chopping through the swiping, clawing slilitroks. The brutes continuously dropped off to the side, dismembered or decapitated, but no matter how many The Paladin left in his wake there was little cause to celebrate. Each downed monster was quickly replaced by another eager and ravenous slilitrok. The injured ones simply reattached their severed body parts until the creature was whole again and could rejoin the fray. Faithful Celemonte, having fought beside The Paladin for so many years, understood Navarro's lead and strove forward to gain ground.

"We must break free of the copse!" Navarro yelled over the screeches of the slilitroks and the noise of battle. He received a vicious slash on his arm from his blindside. Invinitor whipped across and sliced that beast in half at the waist. "Our only hope is to get to the open plains!"

"I'm taking them down as fast as they come," Zakili said, "but there seems to be no end to them."

One slilitrok reached in as if to capture the elf in its deadly embrace. The Flying Tigers sliced apart fingers and opened arm arteries, disabling the dangerous claws. The elf's foot shot out and slammed into a slilitrok's gut. It doubled over. Zakili's knee flew up and smashed into its chin, putting its ugly face in perfect range. Both daggers dove forward and popped out the creature's eyes. The slilitrok wailed like a wicked siren but was soon trampled over by others of its bloodthirsty kin.

"The fight is going to be long and tough," Navarro said through labored breaths. "Unless..." A slilitrok rushed in, its long dirty nails swiping at The Paladin's skull. Navarro ducked and sliced a leg out from under the slilitrok. It collapsed into the pack. Another dove in, hands swiping and distorted jaws gnashing hungrily. Invinitor jabbed forward into the monster's mouth and out the back of its head. Navarro kicked the flailing creature off his blade.

"I know what you're suggesting," Zakili answered, "but in a melee this close and fast-paced, my bow won't be as effective as my blades!"

"It may be our only chance! We can't keep up this pace. We are taking too many hits, and our enemy does not tire!"

Zakili sliced off a pair of hands reaching for him. Another monster came in from behind, but with a slight turn, his stallion double-kicked and sent it flying into the night.

Another slilitrok gnashed at Zakili. The elf ducked the bite, then slashed the slilitrok's neck. Black blood squirted and its head hung by tendrils. Zakili's punched the creature's head off, and it rolled between a jumble of monster legs.

"Don't lose your head," Zakili exhorted the stumbling monster.

"Every moment we linger draws all people closer to jeopardy," Navarro called.

A slilitrok's hand swiped down from overhead, but Invinitor sliced it off at the forearm. The disembodied hand spun forward onto The Paladin's shoulder, where it grabbed on and inched toward his throat. The one-armed slilitrok came in

269

Lifespring

again for another swipe. Navarro spun away, and the creature stumbled forward. It righted itself and came back in. Just as the dismembered hand was about to dig its claws into Navarro's throat, The Paladin snatched it and hurled it onto the slilitrok's face. "Need a hand?" he quipped, then kicked the monster away.

The duo and their chargers made some headway, but many slilitroks remained between them and the opening onto the plains.

"Zakili?" Navarro questioned, breathing hard and bleeding from multiple wounds.

"I'm working on it," he answered as he slashed at the approaching brutes with one dagger and released his bow with the other. The slilitroks swiped at the bow, focusing their attacks on the weapon rather than the elf. "They really don't like this bow."

With one wide swipe, the elf cleared a narrow swath in front of him, plunged his daggers into the scabbards, and pulled back on the bowstring. An energy arrow formed just as a slilitrok latched onto the bow. Zakili released the bowstring and the energy arrow rocketed into the monster's chest, igniting the creature into a flailing, screaming, stumbling fire.

The slilitroks closest scattered. One couldn't get away and flames began to consume its tall, gangly body.

The creatures closest to Zakili attacked fiercely, swiping and slapping at the ivory-colored bow. The elf tried to fire off another arrow but one slilitrok smacked the stock, nearly wrenching it out of his hands.

The elf heard a pained cry from his stallion. The horse was tough and hadn't shown the pain from his other gashes. Zakili knew this time the charger had suffered a terrible strike from one of the monsters.

A jagged blow tore a shallow gash in his shoulder. The Elf Prince had to act quickly. Feeling his arms grow heavy, he knew his endurance in this fast-paced battle couldn't keep up against the scores from the multiple foes.

With a vengeance, the slilitroks stormed him, swiping wildly with their wide hands. Zakili tried to fire back but the crowding monsters pressed in too close, and he was forced to use his bow more as a club than for shooting arrows. Long nails ripped a gash into his thigh and he gave an agonized grunt. One claw went for his head which he successfully ducked, then he felt the tug against his bow. One brute had latched with both hands! Zakili pulled the bowstring and fired, blasting the slilitrok back into the pack, flaming.

The slilitroks stampeded from every side, long gangly arms swiping, mouths of sharp, crooked teeth gnashing. Zakili took another hit on his already injured shoulder.

"Enough!" he roared, leaping onto the back of his stallion. "Give me a shovel, I'll dig my own grave!"

Navarro chopped down another of the resilient brutes, smiling when he heard the elf's unusual war cry. "I was wondering when you were going to start getting fired up enough!"

Johnny Earl Jones

In rapid-fire fashion, the elf pulled back and fired, pulled back and fired, blasting away one slilitrok, then another. He fired again and again, sending brutes flying away into the crowd, each consumed with flames.

"Back to Elfstay?" Navarro suggested, not seeing the damage his friend wreaked but definitely hearing the sound of demolition.

"Back to Elfstay!" the elf cried, leaping to the ground between the two chargers, his arm a blur as he pulled back and fired repeatedly, blazing a path through the slilitroks ahead of them.

Curiously, Navarro noticed the smoldering carcasses didn't rise again, nor did they regenerate. He had no time to ponder this, as slilitroks still rushed from every side. Invinitor chopped and slashed, taking down slilitroks at every turn.

The Paladin pushed farther in front of his charger, his blade aiding his friend's firepower as they cut through the mob. With the trees slowly moving behind them and the starry sky showing overhead, they cleared the copse and the open plains were ahead. Finally, the slilitrok mob began to thin out.

"It's time to charge out of here!" The Paladin exclaimed.

"I'm with you!" Zakili agreed.

Navarro latched onto his charger, his sword coming across and splitting the face of a rushing slilitrok. He sprang into his saddle.

Waiting on the other side of the horse was a slilitrok, its filthy claws swiping at The Paladin's head. Adroitly, he slashed across and Invinitor sent the creature's hands flying out into the night. His blade repositioned, and he thrust it through the slilirok's distorted skull and into its wicked brain. Kicking the beast away, he ripped the blade free, snapped his reins and bolted forward on Celemonte, leaving a pack of howling slilitroks far behind.

"It's about time you caught up," the elf said a moment later as The Paladin pulled alongside.

"We need some healing and fresh chargers," Navarro decided. "And a band of fearless warriors."

Zakili nodded. "It will be difficult to convince Baron Kelt of the impending danger. He thinks the Silver Elves are the true enemies."

"We must try. Whether he heeds our warning or not, he'll soon discover the reality. A monster horde bears down on him.

"And his daughter."

* 20 *
UNCOMMON ADVERSARIES

Kil knew he tread dangerous ground with The Dark Sorcerer by hesitating several days before meeting with the usurper Krylothon. His strategy spelled death if his Master ever discovered, but in The Warlord's mind, it was necessary.

When Methlon returned and babbled out the entire tale about the monsters he encountered in the forest, Kil was hardly concerned. But when his lieutenant carried on about their leader's boasts, that was almost more than he could stand. The Warlord had pretended to be calm, but inwardly he fumed. Proud Krylothon denied his authority, and even more foolishly, the usurper ordered him to come at once.

Several times during Methlon's narrative, Kil wished to slay the whining man as he repeated Krylothon's demands. But he knew it would be his own frustration at not being able to destroy the insolent usurper instead. Engaged in a battle of minds and wills, he knew if he lost restraint, the usurper already won. He decided to play the waiting game instead, giving Krylothon time to contemplate his arrogance to demand anything from the Warlord of The Lurking Shadows.

But The Dark Sorcerer's overriding command was that he and Krylothon join forces and seize Lifespring. Thus he had trekked with a large contingent of his assassin warriors across the plains to the outskirts of Lonely Forest. Pulling up on the reins, he halted his demon charger. On cue his warriors fanned out beside him. The forest shadows hid a vast army of monsters, he knew.

So close to his imperious ally, he felt a battle rage within, and he tried to check his disdain for the arrogant usurper. Thinking past the intrigue, Kil understood clearly they were intertwined in something much larger than their battle of wills. The Dark Sorcerer's mysterious plan to use the Spring's energy source was the overriding motivation for both he and the usurper. Zeraktalis never disclosed to him the need for this mystic spring, and Kil really didn't care. He was the Warlord of the most notorious band of assassins anywhere. Whatever power plays The Sorcerer and his foul horde wanted to make was of little consequence. His only desire concerning this Lifespring was to get it into Zeraktalis' hands. With The Dark Sorcerer's hunger for power sated, then, perhaps, The Dark One would let him run his guild without constant interference. Then, maybe, he'd be freed from the pact made years ago in the Kingdom of Sheliavon.

Kil punched his left fist in the air, followed by his right. He watched as his imposing assassins on either side drew their weapons and filled the air with the hiss of steel. When Krylothon emerged to face him, Kil wanted his forces to appear as formidable as possible. In a war of minds, every pretense counted. Methlon told how Krylothlon ordered the murder of his assassin escorts. The Warlord understood he'd have to accept that insult. Although those men were of little value, slaying Kil's men was meant as an insult. One meant to dishearten him and force him into subjection. Kil smirked. Krylothon had no clue. Kil was not some easily-defeated adversary whose confidence could be shattered. He was the Warlord of The Lurking

Shadows!

Facing the woods, Kil pulled a long horn from his saddlebag. "It is time for you to come to me," he growled before lifting the trumpet to his lips.

BAH-BAHBAAAAAH!

A long moment passed. Nothing. The battle-hardened assassins shifted uncomfortably, waiting for an imminent assault.

But Kil sat leisurely in his saddle, watching for any movement among the trees. He wasn't as troubled by a sudden charge of monsters as he was about Krylothon's first impression of his forces.

Another long moment passed. Kil felt the tension among his warriors, and was not surprised the usurper didn't heed the first call. In this war of wills, neither would yield readily to the other. He forced himself to retain his relaxed position, biting back the frustration clawing at his mind.

His perpetual solution to those who opposed him was to destroy the problem. But now his opposition was a creature he was forced to ally with.

Sucking in a lungful of breath, he reminded himself he would emerge victorious. Placing the horn to his lips again, he vented another blast, this one longer and louder.

BAH-BAHBAAAAAAAAH!

"Come to me!" he demanded.

In response, two winged shapes exploded through the trees into the bright sky. They swooped down and dove in low, scattering the assassin formation, but not before several crossbow bolts and daggers were launched.

Unharmed, the pair wheeled about for another pass.

"Shoot them down!" Kil ordered.

"That won't be asss easssy asss you think!" a thunderous voice hissed from somewhere within the forest shadows.

Kil glared in the direction of the ominous voice, searching for its source. Dozens of arrows took flight behind him. He heard the disbelieving cries of his men a moment later above the deafening beating of wings. His heart plummeted.

"The arrows won't penetrate their hide!" one assassin archer cried.

A blood-chilling scream spun Kil in time to see a warrior ripped from his saddle as one of the fast-flying monsters zoomed by and lashed out. With eyes narrowed in rage, he swung his gaze back to the woods. Krylothon had ordered his forces to attack The Lurking Shadow army!

"Face me, cowardly worm!"

Silence.

"Stand before your better! Must you send your lessers to do your work for you? Or do you fear me so?"

"I FEAR NOTHING!" a voice exploded from the shadows and shook the trees. Even Kil shrank from that colossal roar.

Within the forest a loud crack echoed then a thunderous crash. Kil patted the Fangs of Hell hanging from his waist. He would need their deadly power to defeat this incredible opponent. Another loud snap echoed through the forest followed shortly by a booming crash. The Warlord shifted uncomfortably. It sounded like live trees were being forced over.

Then Kil saw a shape blacker than the shadows advance slowly through the tangle of trees. Stray light beams bent and twisted on the creature's massive six-armed torso.

"How terrifying is that?" he said, awed. "Is this Krylothon?"

His demon steed backed away. A chorus of troubled whispers sang into the air as the assassins pointed and stared at the emerging monster. Kil could feel himself caught in the terror of this horrible creature. Then he stopped, grabbed the reins of his horse firmly and yanked the creature back in line.

"I am the master here!" he growled, unwilling to let the monster's mere presence dominate the meeting. To fear was to lose the upper hand. "Well, do we finally face Krylothon or another of his lackeys?"

One of the monster's arms snapped out, its huge fist splintering a young oak and sending it toppling to the side. As the tree fell away, the afternoon rays revealed a beast more frightening than any nightmare could unleash. Man and demon-steed alike backed away in deference to the imposing creature.

The usurper roared. The warriors clamped their ears in pain. From behind the monster's back, membranous wings unfolded, wide and ominous. His six-talon-like claws flexed, causing thick muscles to writhe. Jaws opened like a ferocious lion, exhibiting rows of serrated teeth.

Kil studied the usurper, awed and repulsed at the same time. The creature looked like the crossbreed of a dragon and a gigantic spider. Multifaceted eyes stared back icily. Without question, Kil knew this was Krylothon.

"You are late!" the huge usurper growled, his spider eyes glaring at The Warlord.

"We arrived as soon as possible," Kil lied. Forcing himself to ease back in the saddle, he pretended to be unimpressed by the creature.

Krylothon advanced slowly. Ominously. Eyeing him. Silent.

Noticing his palms growing moist, Kil took in a deep breath and steadied his nerves. He could feel the aura of fear pressing in on him. The more imposing monsters naturally radiated this strange emanation which would intimidate most warriors. But he wasn't like most warriors. Shaking off the anxiety, he stared into those cold eyes, trying to discern what the beast might be thinking. He gathered no information. Silently, The Warlord applauded Krylothon for his lack of weakness.

"I have come by command of The Dark Sorcerer to lead your army against the Silver Elves," Kil finally said.

"You are late!" Krylothon repeated, drawing an unyielding glare from The Warlord.

"You have destroyed one of my men!" Kil accused, feeling his patience fade quickly in the face of this arrogant monster.

Krylothon guffawed, throwing his head back in exaggeration. At that moment Kil wanted nothing more than to snap his dirks into the usurper's heart, but he understood the importance of this alliance.

Zeraktalis had ordered it.

"If you're concccerned over the death of one sssoldier you're not fit to lead at all!"

"Well said," Kil responded, pretending humility. His accusation was supposed to put the usurper on the defensive, but the monster turned it against him. Discerning this was an intelligent creature, he rifled through his thoughts and tried to pull out reasoning which would neutralize the arrogant usurper.

"The death of one of mine is equal to the death of one of yours," he finally answered. "From now on we are not two armies but one. We are to work in unison and follow the Dark Sorcerer's commands. We are but pawns for the greater plan of our master, Zeraktalis."

"Our master?" the usurper growled derisively. Obviously, Krylothon didn't agree. In truth, neither did Kil, but he wouldn't openly admit it, especially not to a volatile monster. "And our master foresaw the need to withhold Lifespring's location from you in order for the Lurking Shadows to lead you to it.

"I will lead you," Kil said, stressing each pronoun.

Krylothon laughed long, unconcerned. "I've dissscovered sssomething much more important to my hungry monstersss. We have a feassst!"

Kil's dirks leapt into his hands, and he sat up alert in his saddle. He took the usurper's words as an open threat.

The six-armed usurper threw his head back and laughed hideously again. "Fear not, human. I won't devour you. Not yet. But your delay hasss cossst you more than you could afford. My horde hasss already crussshed two of your land'sss townsss, returning with warmbloodsss for my ravenousss army to feassst on."

Kil didn't flinch about the gory information. Death did not bother him. He was a trained killer. Death was his business.

"But now my horde will march on and conquer until thisss whole land isss a giant ssslaughtering field. Then at my leisssure, we will find thisss Lifesssspring."

* * * * *

"If we stay concealed much longer, I fear the townsfolk will begin to grow suspicious," Zakili said. The elves and Navarro walked the bustling streets of Requeom, the town on the outskirts of Castle Veldercrantz. "Baron Veldercrantz considers the Silver Elves his nemeses. If we are discovered, our welcome won't be friendly."

"Look over there," Navarro said, pointing to a pair of merchants loudly proclaiming the benefits of their wares. "The townspeople are used to strangers in their midst. I'm sure a troupe of cloaked figures walking the streets will no more alarm them than these boisterous merchants. Besides, my gleaming armor attracts more glances than a number of cloaked figures."

The Paladin looked back at the disguised elves which walked casually through the crowds, spreading out loosely so they covered both ends of the street. Each wore a long cloak which hid their weapons and a hood pulled over their heads to conceal their heritage.

When he and Zakili broke free of the slilitroks early that morning, they raced to Verdant Wood. There the Prince quietly recruited some of his best warriors to join in warning the baron and fighting beside him, if need be.

The Elf Prince replaced his charger, but brave and stubborn Celemonte, bruised and slashed by the slilitroks, refused to leave Navarro's side. Navarro fought many battles beside Celemonte. And although The Paladin felt guilty racing his horse back across the plains to Baron Veldercrantz, he knew Celemonte wouldn't rest while Navarro charged into battle without him. So Navarro laid hands on the horse, calling upon the Lord to heal the beast's wounds and give him added endurance.

Zakili's sisters answered the call for warriors, but The Prince wouldn't let them accompany his party. With a narrowed-eyed, tight-lipped gaze, his youngest sister watched the elves ride onto the plains.

"Saranisen was incensed you wouldn't let her come with us," Navarro said, trying to lighten up the mood.

"She'll get over it," the Elf Prince said. "As the oldest brother, even though I have trained my sisters to fight well, I will not put their lives in danger."

Navarro laughed.

"What's so funny, Paladin?"

"Your sisters were critical in battle against The Lurking Shadow siege. They looked death in the eye and came out victorious. All your sisters are adept fighters and don't need to be sheltered. They know how to handle danger.

"But your youngest sister, Saranisen, has that extra tenacity that sets her apart. She has a lot of her older brother in her."

Zakili turned a smile Navarro's way. "That's why I'm concerned about her the most. She's just as reckless as I."

Navarro laughed lightheartedly. It seemed like weeks since he had. Danger and death had kept him, and the frolicsome elves, in a grim mood. The peril hadn't waned, however; it was just beginning.

Hearing the titter of children, The Paladin turned. A group of boys raced from on house to the other trying to avoid a single boy who took up chase, tagging as many as he could. When the untagged boys reached the other house, each gave a victorious shout. Those tagged joined the single boy between the houses and targeted a tag victim as the uncaptured boys raced back to the wall of the first house.

"How peaceful, how carefree," The Paladin said. "How wonderful the innocence of youth. Not a care in the world. No enemies to be found." Navarro glanced to the heavens. "Lord, I pray for Your favor on these little ones. Protect them from the harm battle will bring upon this innocent town. Protect them from this ravenous horde which invaded this land and may, even now, march in their direction.

"And Lord, most of all, protect their hearts from the deceit and prejudice which has placed such hatred between the elves and Kelt's men."

"Wow! Can you believe it?" a little voice asked. Navarro looked in that direction and spotted a boy pointing at him. "It's a Pal-e-dine!"

The boys forsook the tag game en masse and charged Navarro's way.

Bending down on one knee, Navarro smiled as the curious, excited boys surrounded him, inquiring about his name and asking to touch his armor.

In a friendly voice he told them he was Navarro Silvinton. One by one, he asked the names of each boy who delightfully screamed it out to him. One boy even braved asking if he could see Navarro's sword.

"Step back while I draw my mighty blade," Navarro said in a dramatic voice.

The boys did, willingly, their stared locked on him.

Navarro gripped Invinitor's handle and with a metallic ring, the sword appeared. The afternoon sun reflected off the hilt and silver blade. Brilliant sparkles danced along the sword.

A hushed awe covered the mesmerized gang. Navarro smiled at the children's simple curiosity, than beamed even more when he saw other children stream from houses and side streets to see him.

"How cool? Look at that awesome sword!" one boy cried. "Can I touch it?"

"Be careful. It's sharp."

Tentatively, the boy reached over and touched the blade, quickly pulling his hand away and giggling. The other children received the boy back to the gang like some kind of hero.

"Have you ever fought a dragon with your sword?" a dark-haired girl asked, staring up at him with big, brown eyes.

"What's your name, young lady?" Navarro asked.

"I'm Chezney, and I like swords."

"Do you?" Navarro asked with a smile. "Well, Chezney, yes, I have fought a dragon with this very sword."

She gawked at him, her eyes wide. "Did you live?"

He laughed at her nervous question. "Thank God, yes, I did survive that encounter."

The girl slapped her forehead histrionically. "Of course, you lived. I'm so silly."

"That is quite all right. It's good encouragement to have someone remind me I'm still alive."

He glanced at all the kids. Grabbing their attention with a soft voice, he told them to run off and have fun. Excitedly, the children complied. Some bragged about touching his armor. One boy boasted of touching his sword. And little Chezney crowed about the dragon question. Smiling, Navarro stood to his feet.

"Well, if you ever decide you're tired of being a Paladin," Zakili quipped, "you can always be a nanny."

"Yes, you are the funny one," Navarro responded, smiling.

All around them, the streets bustled. People shuffled from house to shop, from one side of the street to the other, and Navarro admired their lack of concern. But he knew a storm headed their way in the shape of a ravenous horde.

He glanced about this town of one-story buildings. The towering wall

Johnny Earl Jones

around Castle Veldercrantz was a comfortable distance from the outskirts of town. Stationed along the perimeters of this small town were tall watchtowers manned by armed soldiers. Surrounding both the town and Castle Veldercrantz was the great Maribowan Forest. The Paladin tried to picture scenarios of possible attack, measuring the potential effectiveness of the watch posts and the townsfolk's ability to repel an onslaught.

After witnessing the complete devastation of Lunumdra, he feared the horde too big and too organized to be staved off without all soldiers on high alert. He had to get into Castle Veldercrantz and warn Baron Kelt.

As he passed the front porch of a quaint log house, Navarro overheard the mention of elves between a small group of elder gentlemen relaxing in wooden chairs. He slowed his pace, even bent down and pretended to look at something in the grass while eavesdropping.

"...I just think the baron must be desperate to cure his daughter Candace, you know what I mean Harbel?"

"But it doesn't make any sense, Yomik. We have a church right here in the village, and he can ask the pastor and us to pray for a cure. But he chooses to use magic wielders to break the curse the elves placed on Candace."

"Well, if you remember," Yomik explained, "Baron Kelt avoided church since his wife's murder many years ago. If he can remove the elves' curse with magicians, what will it hurt? At least, she'll be free from the evil magic of those forest dwellers."

"That's just it. All magic is evil, not just that of the wicked elves. No matter how harmless or helpful it may seem, we have to remember the source.

"If magic becomes an accepted practice, it'll reap devilish consequences."

"Amen," Navarro whispered.

"I don't believe all magic comes from the devil," Yomik said. "Besides, a troupe of experienced magicians come this afternoon to answer Kelt's plea for help. The Baron's promised to pay them handsomely for their abilities. We'll see how beneficial magic can be."

Navarro had heard enough and moved on. *What was Candace being subjected to?* Deeply concerned, he could barely believe magic-users were not just walking free here, but invited. How deceived Kelt was to believe the elves bewitched her. How tragic Candace's own father was afflicting her.

When Navarro looked to the sky and noticed the position of the sun those thoughts flew away. In this darkest hour of Avundar's history, how had the allegiances become so splintered? Now, two of the republic's prominent rulers were violently alienated. They'd be unable to unite against the deadly foes who threaten to swallow them all. The day had grown late, and he still hadn't warned Kelt of the danger which threatened his barony. But how could he get the elves in with him to solidify the dire warning?

Replaying Harbel and Yomik's conversation in his mind, he began to formulate an idea. But time was running out. They still had much to do before trekking to the castle gates. In a few hours, the sun would sleep behind the horizon

and darkness would fall.
And night was when monsters come out to hunt.

* 21 *
FRIEND OR FOE?

"I am not sure this is a good idea," Leminek the elf said. The small elven troupe led by Navarro and Zakili rode up to the gate-like iron portcullis, the only entrance through the great wall surrounding Castle Veldercrantz.

"We are the only ones standing between them and destruction," Navarro said, laying an encouraging hand on Leminek's shoulder, then turning to the other elves. He motioned for them to pull their cowls lower over their faces.

"Why should we warn these men of the danger? They proclaimed their hatred for the elves," Navarro heard someone say from behind, starting an undercurrent of grumbling. "What business is it of ours?"

"The foul monster horde marches this direction. They have already destroyed two villages. The townsfolk of Requeom and the warriors of the fortress will be crushed unless they prepare for the attack. I understand there is still much bitterness, but I refuse to repay evil for the evil they wished on the Silver Elves. I hope we're bigger than that," Navarro answered, silencing the murmurs.

Despite the urgency of warning Baron Kelt, The Paladin was concerned. Entering the baron's home with the elves so shortly after their standoff, with emotions volatile on both sides, Navarro feared a clash could erupt. But he saw no other choice than to brave the friction between man and elf to give the barony a fighting chance against the monster horde.

Navarro spotted two armed guards approaching the portcullis from the inner courtyard. Both eyed Navarro's troupe as it inched closer in the dark, moonless night. Navarro was the only one not wearing a cowl. He had instructed the elves conceal their faces so they could receive an audience with the baron. The tower guards would've shot them all down if they knew Silver Elves drew near.

"Let them die. They're no allies of ours. They came against the Silver elves in an effort to annihilate us. We owe no allegiance or friendship to these fools!"

Navarro turned, his golden platemail glistening in the flickering light of the guards' distant torches. "Speak no more, Maengh!" he commanded, pointing at the elf. "This meeting will be tenuous at best. Don't ignite tempers already heated.

"They may not be friends, but they're our fellow warriors and neighboring Avundarians. And they need our help."

"Helping our enemies?" Maengh huffed. "Why don't we just fall on our own swords?"

Navarro spun his charger about to get in Maengh's face, but Zakili beat him there. "The horde is our adversary, not these men. But if you can't rid yourself of that attitude, remove yourself and head back to Verdant Wood.

"Or stay here and cause contention, And I'll consider you an enemy. Then I'll destroy you."

"My apologies, my Prince," Maengh placated, bowing his head low. "Being so close to our enemy's fortress has brought me to the edge of my patience."

"These men are not enemies," Zakili said, placing a hand on the elf's shoulder. "We're here to forge some sort of amity. With a monster horde on the rampage through Avundar, the last thing the people of this land need is to be divided."

"Identify yourselves," one of the guards called as the elves drew close to the portcullis.

"Navarro Silvinton and his troupe."

With stern scowls, the guards looked over the group, eyeing each individual carefully, suspiciously.

"You're a Paladin," one guard said, recognizing the golden armor unique to holy warriors. Navarro nodded and asked the names of the two sentinels. Normally, he chose not to wear armor unless at war, but the peoples of Avundar held Paladins in high regard and the plate mail armor was a holy warrior's most commonly identifiable icon. Certainly the baron would be familiar with the reputation of a Paladin. Navarro hoped his alliance with the elves might build a bridge conducive to peace.

"What brings a holy warrior to the baron's fortress at so late an hour?"

"We heard there's a terrible crisis, and we have come here to help."

"Paladin, who are your companions?"

"They're my friends who have also come to see your baron."

"Why are they hidden beneath the shadow of their hoods under the darkness of night?"

"They're a private group," Navarro answered vaguely, his mind racing for some sort of explanation. If he told the sentinels the plain truth, they'd never be let through.

"Tell them to remove their cowls," a sentinel instructed.

"We will not," one of the hooded riders said. Navarro recognized the voice as Zakili.

"Unless we see the faces of our baron's visitors we cannot let you pass. We are wary of an attack by a wicked race. You can understand our orders I am sure, Paladin. We must see their faces."

"You don't want to see their faces. They are scarred and ugly beyond belief. They prefer not to have any man look upon their countenance. None of them even possess a looking glass, because they don't wish to see themselves."

"We understand that, holy warrior. But we have strict orders. We must see them, or they won't pass by us."

"They're wizards," Navarro lied. The false words felt like bile in his throat. Since the baron sought help from magic-users to cure Candace from her curse, he pulled that trump, hoping to get past these guards. He knew lies, like vicious dogs, turned against their user, but he prayed this one would not. "I have escorted them to cure the baron's daughter of her mystic ailment."

"It's good you have brought them," the once-surly guard said. "Perhaps

Johnny Earl Jones

their powers will prevail where the tricks of the magicians have proven useless."

"This is our hope also," Navarro said, though he was troubled by the spiritual ignorance of these men. A holy warrior leading a troupe of dark-art sorcerers was inconsistent, at best.

Without another question, the guards rushed to the cranks and energetically rotated the handles, slowly lifting the portcullis.

"I will lead you to the baron's throne room," the first guard offered once all were in the courtyard.

"Will he be awake at this hour?"

"Baron Veldercrantz rarely sleeps anymore. Almost all his time and energy goes to seek help for his daughter. He adores his girl and won't rest until she's cured. Candace is loved by the townsfolk and all in the fortress.

"We want this wicked elf curse removed from her as soon as possible."

As the guard led them in, he expounded on the events of the past several days. From Candace's rescue from the cowardly elves to the daily visitations of boastful magicians who without exception failed to rid Kelt's daughter of the powerful, elven mind curse. Navarro listened carefully to his continuous monologue, noting the disdain and unabashed hatred for the Silver Elves this man probably never met. Just how deep and contagious was the baron's slanderous loath of the Silver Elves that it produced such hatred among his subjects?

"This is the reason we are here," Navarro interrupted, cutting short the man's racist remarks. "We hope to remove the curse from her and from this land."

* * * * *

"Remove yourselves from my sight!" Kelt screamed at the befuddled magicians.
"Leave my chambers, take the fee I paid, and never let me see you fraudulent workers in my barony ever again!"

Candace reclined comfortably in a plush chair, her legs draped over one of its arms. She smiled as Father hurled his explosive tirade. She'd witnessed this scene several times. Various groups strutted into his chambers only to leave like scolded dogs.

"We've exhausted the entire night using every spell accessible by our powers," one magician spoke up, shrugging helplessly.

"Maybe your magic wasn't strong enough," Kelt said in a dismissive tone.

"Indeed, our magic contained much power," the offended magician rebutted. "If we couldn't remove the curse from your daughter with our casting repertoire, then perhaps there's no curse to be removed from her at all."

Kelt turned to his daughter. "Candace, did the elves abduct you?"

"No sir," she answered, placing her hand over her wide yawn. "But it is getting very late."

"What do you say to that?" Kelt roared as he swung back toward the magicians. "She is held in bondage to this elven curse, and your powers aren't enough to break its chains."

"She probably needs no help," a different flustered and indignant magician

dared to comment. "If none of our spells worked, the reason is clear. There's no curse to work against. She's an adult, and she's told you she's not cursed. Maybe you should listen."

"Get out!" Kelt screamed, shoving the back-talking magician toward the door. "All you miserable failures flee and never appear in my domain again or I will personally cut you down!"

Immediately, Kelt's elite guards were in the room to escort the magicians out by the arm. Once the last was gone, Kelt slammed the door and dropped down on his throne.

"It was a good try," Candace admitted, trying hard to hold back her giggles.

"Silence, insolent girl!" Kelt grunted in frustration.

"I really don't have a curse on me," Candace explained, her voice sincere and soft.

"I've raised you most of your life, Candace. I know your stubborn spirit and your fierce independence. Under no circumstances would you defend your kidnappers unless you were magically charmed. You would've fought and kicked against them the entire time."

"You're absolutely correct. I would've resisted them to the end and badmouthed them after my escape. But all that only proves my point, Father. The elves did nothing but befriend me. And fight valiantly beside me. I owe them my gratitude, not my distrust."

"You're blinded to what the curse has done to you, girl. You deny the truth and instead defend the lecherous devils who intended to abuse you as they willed. Don't you remember any of that?"

"I can't remember what never happened."

"My poor girl. The Prince was right about the elf charm. But it's even more powerful than he had suspected."

"Listen to me, Father," she demanded. "Killion is not a prince. He's the Warlord of the Lurking Shadow assassins..."

"Enough, Candace! It's the curse which causes such delusions in your mind. Prince Killion attempted to save you from those fiends, but his forces were defeated. How else could he have known you were in Verdant Wood?"

Candace's legs swung off the chair arm and her feet landed firmly on the rug floor. She looked her father in the eyes, her expression serious. "He knew where I was because he waged war against the Silver Elves, and I was there to see his defeat."

Loud knocking on the chamber door echoed in the room, breaking their unyielding stare as both Candace and Kelt turned.

"Sire, it is Simeon," a voice called from the other side of the door.

"Speak."

Johnny Earl Jones

"One of the gate guards has escorted visitors who wish to see you."

"It's hours past sundown. Who dares come this late to seek me? Send them away and advise them to come back when the sun awakens."

"Yes si..." he heard Simeon begin, before he suddenly went silent. A moment later he spoke up again. "They say if we wait until sunrise, it may be too late."

"Who are they?"

"These men say they have heard of the trouble with your daughter. They've come to assist in any way possible…"

Candace groaned and sunk deep into the chair. "Not again."

"...Sire, they're wizards."

Kelt trudged to the door, wiping his sleepy eyes, and swung the door wide, staring into Simeon's aged but alert eyes. Behind him were several mysterious-looking figures and one longish-haired warrior adorned with the most magnificent suit of golden plate mail he'd ever seen.

"Sir Paladin," Kelt acknowledged respectfully, looking the handsome man in the eyes. He balked for a second. "Do I know you? You look strangely familiar to me."

"I travel constantly, Baron Veldercrantz," Navarro answered, bowing reverently. "Perhaps we have crossed paths somewhere along life's journey. Navarro Silvinton is my name. I'm pleased to be at your service."

Kelt laughed. "Forgive me if we've met and I can't remember. Over the years my memory has begun to dim. I refuse to call myself old, though. I prefer to use the word 'experienced.' Unfortunately, the more experienced I get, the more my recollection seems to fade."

Navarro smiled warmly, raising Kelt's smile in response.

"Come in," he invited, holding the door open for the visitors. "You're an answer to prayer," Kelt continued once all the hooded visitors and Simeon entered his Throne Room. "You've come at my plea to deliver my daughter from the mind-bending spell. What kind of fee do you require for your abilities?"

"No fee. In my duty as a Paladin and in the mighty name of Jesus Christ, I will exhaust all the power I have to help. I serve to prevail against the plague which threatens to swallow not only your daughter, but all of Avundar. I come urgently this evening."

"I know nothing of a pestilence threatening Avundar. The only curse I'm aware of is the one placed on my daughter by those wicked Silver Elves."

"And for that reason my friends accompany me."

"Wizards," Simeon explained to his Baron, although his tone was void of excitement.

Navarro winced at the false description.

"Excellent," Kelt decided, turning to Candace. "Do you hear that, my daughter? We have fellows able to cure you after all. Those magicians knew only children's spells. Wizards have real power."

He looked at her, waiting for a reaction, at the least her common quip used every time he talked about her curse. "Wizards have arrived to cure you," he reiterated, but there was no response. Instead he saw her stare wide-eyed at the armored fighter.

"It's wonderful to see you again, Candace Veldercrantz," Navarro said, addressing her in a stately manner, walking up and extending his hand.

She grasped his hand and pulled herself to her feet, then threw her arms around his neck. "Navarro," she whispered into his ear, sudden tears coursing down her cheeks and wetting his face. "I feel like a prisoner in my own home. My father treats me like I'm an enemy. And worst of all, I missed seeing that contagious smile of yours. You being here is like the sun cutting through a black and stormy week." She hugged him tight.

"Do you know this Paladin?" Kelt asked suspiciously.

"This Paladin?" she balked, slipping slowly away from him. "I, uh..."

Navarro stepped in. "A week ago, I came to her aid and warned her of an adversary who prepared to deliver a death blow to her. After my cry, she brought her attention back to her enemy in time to thwart his attack and dispatch him altogether. It appears she's still particularly grateful."

She looked up to Navarro, receiving a furtive wink. She understood he was up to something. She glanced around behind him, looking curiously at the hooded men who filed back to form a living barrier in front of the entranceway, not knowing what to think of these mysterious characters. Hearing Navarro and Kelt talk again, she came out of her thoughts to listen.

"...not one of their spells seemed to have an affect on her. But you've brought wizards! They should be able to succeed against the curse where the puny powers of the magicians failed."

"Ah, yes, the curse," Navarro said ponderously, turning back to Candace and locking gazes with her crystal-blue eyes. Kelt watched curiously as they stared, sensing a strange magnetism between them. "This curse," The Paladin started again, hesitantly tearing his gaze away from Candace. "It may be something totally unlike anything which has afflicted this land. It's one which will have terrible consequences for all the inhabitants of Avundar unless we can pull together."

Kelt stared at him questionably. "What do you speak of? I seek your help because the elves have placed an arcane charm on my girl."

"The elves have done nothing to your daughter. In fact, they're our main allies in facing the plague threatening to overrun our peaceful land."

"What're you saying?" Kelt growled, his brow furrowing suspiciously. "You came into my fortress with a troupe of wizards using the story you come to cure my daughter. Now you say nothing ails her, but instead you purport the real problem is an imminent plague on this land. And you pronounce those wretched Silver Elves as our hope to quell it?"

"Has anything unusual occurred around your fortress?" Navarro asked, ignoring the baron's argumentative questions. "Has anyone seen anything out of the

Johnny Earl Jones

ordinary?"

"No," Kelt answered too quickly.

"Are you absolutely sure? No one is immune to the pestilence which I have already seen afflict parts of Avundar," Navarro said. He hated this cryptic speech, but needed perfect timing to spring his dreaded news on the baron. "Your cooperation could save the lives of those who rely on you."

"Being a Paladin, a holy warrior of the Living God, you undoubtedly feel responsible for the lives of all people," Kelt said. "I know it must get burdensome to steer danger from us. Navarro, I respect you for your courage, your diligence, and your oft thankless duty.

"But honestly, I have no interest in whatever quest you're on. I only want my girl cured of whatever curse those elves placed on her!"

Navarro smiled warmly, his eyes growing soft. Kelt's impatience, frustration, and pain existed because he thought his daughter was in danger. The Paladin sighed inwardly. He knew the baron's great love for Candace pushed him toward solutions he never would've enlisted before. Navarro knew the curse didn't exist. And the more time they wasted, the heavier the urgency to tell Kelt of the advancing monster horde.

He had an idea.

"Let's do what the baron requests. Use your powers to defeat this delusion," Navarro said, motioning for a cloaked figure to glide over next to him.

The "wizard" lifted his arms, pointing his fingers toward Candace. Kelt stared anxiously. A long, pregnant silence filled the room. Moments passed in slow motion to Kelt as he waited for the result.

"What do you say about this elf curse?" Navarro asked, breaking the silence.

"There is no curse," the cloaked one answered, drawing an incredulous, mouth-gaping stare from the baron.

"No curse!" he screamed. "She still proclaims the race which abducted her is blameless. She's too strong-willed to believe such a lie unless she'd been magically violated!"

"Why don't we ask her if there is veracity to your accusation against the elves?" the cloaked one asked.

"That's nonsense! If she were charmed, she couldn't speak the truth, no matter how many times we asked."

"But would she tell the truth if it really was the truth?" Navarro asked.

"Of course she would. From a young age she was raised to live by godly standards. Integrity was a virtue I emphasized incessantly throughout her childhood, and since she was young, she held resolutely to her honesty."

"Good. Now the question is: Would you believe her if she was really telling you the truth?"

Kelt started to fire back an answer but stalled when he took in the magnitude of the question. He pondered for a moment. "I would believe her if there was any truth to what she said. However, I know there's not."

"You do?" Navarro asked, his tone curious. "How can you tell?"

"The fact is if I didn't know better, I would believe what she says. She sounds convincing. However, a reliable source shared information with me to the contrary."

"A reliable source?"

"A prince."

"I see," Navarro's said. He glanced to Candace, who returned a troubled look. "And what did this prince say which would override the words of your own daughter?"

"Listen, Paladin. I don't know who you think you are to come into my fortress and question me. I make the judgments here, and I discern truth from falsehood. I don't need a warrior to question my conclusions."

"Forgive me, Baron Veldercrantz," Navarro apologized. "But all of us were in Verdant Wood when Candace arrived. If not for Candace's warning of impending attack by the assassin army, none of us, not even Candace, would stand here now.

"She was not a victim of the Silver Elves. She was nearly a victim of the assassins. And she was a valuable ally who fought alongside us to defeat that wicked force."

Kelt shook his head. "That's a lie. The Prince sent his own forces into Verdant Wood to rescue Candace."

"I assure you, the army who attacked was not a royal army."

"The Lurking Shadow Assassins attacked Verdant Wood," the cloaked figure stated.

"I refuse to believe Prince Killion would hire such an infamous group to assault the elves."

"Kil," the cloaked figure said coolly.

"What?" Kelt asked, his eyes narrowing at the "wizard's" pronunciation of that name, his hand heading for his sword.

"Kil," the pretend spellcaster said again. "Your Prince Killion is none other than Kil, The Warlord of the Lurking Shadows."

The Lurking Shadows? Kelt was stunned. A blur of memories rushed through his mind as he tried to assimilate this. When The Prince first came to the fortress, he displayed all the charisma and royal niceties of a monarch confident and comfortable with his position. None could have pretended nobility so successfully, could they?

Upon his initial meeting with Candace he jokingly shortened his name to the abbreviation "Kill" to his drunken guards' laughter. Had a Lurking Shadow actually infiltrated his home without him discerning it? He'd heard horror stories of those assassins infiltrating kingdoms, assuming an identity, and gaining the sovereign's trust through deceptive ploys. They then opened the door for an army of Lurking Shadows to sneak in unchecked, consequently destroying that dynasty.

The Baron shook the thought from his mind. He was a skilled judge of character. He could never be tricked by the pretenses of a masquerading assassin.

Johnny Earl Jones

"That's impossible," he said. "Prince Killion couldn't be an assassin."

"It's true, father," Candace piped in, refraining no longer from the conversation. "When I ran from home, I was concerned for my survival. After much mental anguish, I judged I would earn my living as a mercenary, thus Senadon became my destination.

"The same day I arrived, I was visited by a man who said he was a Lurking Shadow and invited me back to his lair. My only other option was death. Following him into a shadowy den I saw Kil, or, as you call him, Prince Killion. After hearing his plans to annihilate the elves, I escaped, hoping to warn them of impending assault. Your supposed prince is a murderer, not a monarch."

"Why should I believe any of this?" Kelt demanded, defensive again. "For all I know, the elves could have charmed you while in the woods."

"That's unlikely for two reasons," Navarro explained, locking his gaze with Kelt. Any attempts at reasoning with this man would fail and waste precious time. And time was not a luxury they had. "First, the Silver elves possess no magical capabilities. Second, even if they were spellcasters, they wouldn't deceive themselves."

The "wizards" all threw back their cowls, revealing their true heritage.

"Zakili!" Candace cried, excited to see another of her friends from Verdant Wood.

Recognizing the elves, Kelt yanked his sword from his scabbard. "Silver Elves! You Deceivers!"

Simeon swooped to Kelt's side, his weapon drawn as well.

"These are your peaceful elves," Kelt roared in Candace's direction. "They've come here in revenge for losing their precious toy!" He turned and glared at the elves. "Understand you won't slay us without great loses to yourselves!"

"The elves haven't come to harm you," Navarro promised, his strong voice prevailing over Kelt's boisterous cries. "We have come to warn you of a looming danger."

"The threat is within my own chamber! Have you too been deceived by these wicked elves, Paladin? Surely, you cannot..." Kelt stopped and stared hard at The Paladin, his memory suddenly prompted.

"Wait! I recognize you now. You were with the elves on the Ormantict Plains. You're in league with them!"

"A couple of days ago, we discovered the remains of some goblin scouts who infiltrated Verdant Wood," Navarro began, choosing to ignore the baron's frantic accusations. He must warn the baron before the dialogue broke down completely. The Paladin didn't miss the sounds of Maengh stirring uncomfortably in the background. "What is that to me? Could an army of elves not dispense of a few rogue goblins?"

Navarro understood the inconsistency in the man's words. Any mention of goblins in Avundar should raise alarm. Why did Kelt seem so indifferent to this trouble?

"I sense those goblins were sent to spy out the terrain and search for victims ripe for their army to attack.

"Zakili and I traced the destructive path of an immense contingent of brutes. They already destroyed the towns of Garrison Walls and Lunumdra."

Kelt's eyes narrowed suspiciously. A quiet gasp from Simeon signaled he had friends in those towns.

"The fiends are on the march, leveling towns and killing anyone who gets in their path. And giants are among them, bigger and more powerful than the ones we faced five years ago. It feels like Sheliavon relived.

"But I don't believe that throng could've picked apart those towns so thoroughly unless they first scouted out and marked weaknesses. My theory is each town had monster spies evaluate the targets before attack. Their destructive swath promises continued northern advance. This places Castle Veldercrantz directly in their path.

"This leads me again to an extremely important question. Have you discovered anything unusual in your domain?"

"Nothing unusual and no monster spies," Kelt said, glaring hatefully at the Paladin.

Navarro accepted the answer, noticing Kelt's guard look incredulous.

Heavy banging on the outside of the Throne Room door reverberated within the chamber. Several gruff voices demanded what transpired in the room.

"My guards have arrived to escort you out!" Kelt said. "If you resist, they will surely slay you where you stand!"

"I exhort you to bolster your defenses," Navarro pleaded as he walked to the door and disengaged the lock. "The army heads north, crushing every settlement in its path. If it continues on that same path, your barony will be the next to come under attack."

"More deception, Paladin? More lies? Are you trying to provide a smoke screen to cloud my eyes from the vile work of your cohorts?"

The door burst open and a score of warriors poured into the room, swords drawn and faces grim.

"I should kill you all for what you have done to Candace! You could never have tortured me in a worse way than to afflict my daughter so. But I promise you, she'll be freed from your trickery! I see no good reason to spare your lives, but I'm too weary to destroy you all this night. I grant you mercy this once and let you pass unharmed. But be certain the next time I'm forced to see your faces, you'll be shot down without question."

Navarro swept into a respectful bow. "Very well. I see it's time for us to depart. Baron Veldercrantz, please don't let the warning go unheeded. If you won't listen to me for any other reason, hearken for the sake of your daughter's safety."

Kelt cast a concerned glance back to her.

Navarro too turned his eyes toward Candace, noticing that in the midst of this crowded room, she looked so alone. Here in her own home, under the authority of her father whom she loved so much, she looked like a forlorn, caged animal. Her pensive expression grieved his heart. What he wouldn't do to push through Kelt's guards, comfort her with a friendly hug, and whisper Christ's promises and love to her?

But he understood that would cause more conflict than peace. Candace stared back at him and forced a smile, but her eyes were joyless. Just days ago, she was so vivacious, so full of life. Now without a single word, her sad countenance spoke volumes and broke Navarro's heart.

"Jesus loves you," he mouthed silently, perking her up. "He's still in control." He flashed a contagious smile, forcing her to grin.

The guards ushered him to the door once all the elves had been escorted out.

Candace dropped into the cushioned chair, staring at the empty doorway. Time seemed to stand still, and all her mind could hold was Navarro. After Verdant Wood, she thought she'd never see him again, yet he burst back into her life briefly, only to walk back out while she sat helpless. Her head dropped into her hands, and a tear raced down her cheek.

* * * * *

It took little time for Navarro's party to traverse the winding passageways to the courtyard. Burly warriors gathered along the sides of their path in increasing numbers, cursing and jeering them the entire way. Stoically, the Silver Elves pressed onward, not looking back and not answering a single slander. Navarro glanced over at volatile Zakili. His friend wore a tight-lipped smile. He could sense the tension boiling within the Elf Prince. Zakili was never the type to let an affront go unanswered, yet he refrained from violence.

Navarro admired the Elf Prince's self-control. He knew as well-trained as Kelt's warriors might be, one-on-one they wouldn't have a chance against this fiery elf. Zakili's restraint set an unspoken example for the rest of the frustrated elves.

Navarro stayed close to unpredictable Maengh.

"It's time to crawl back into your holes, lying worms!" the gateman shouted once the friends arrived at the portcullis, the courtyard now bright from the multiple torches of the gathering mob that shadowed the elves.

Navarro bowed respectfully to the insulter, and the man stared, his face growing red with fury when he realized he would receive no emotional outburst. Stomping over to the crank, the gateman and his partner churned the handles, slowing drawing up the heavy iron grating.

Untethering their chargers, the friends mounted and headed for the gate.

"Wait, Paladin!" someone called from behind. "I have disturbing information I must share with you."

Looking back, Navarro saw a warrior push through the mob and sprint toward him. He recognized Simeon, the older guard who led them into Kelt's Throne Room. He steered his horse around and trotted back into the courtyard, meeting

Simeon halfway.

"Your questions about the goblins," Simeon started, trying to catch his breath.

"Yes, what about them?"

"Baron Veldercrantz didn't convey the truth. Just days ago, the tower watchmen spotted a group of goblins in the woods very close to our fortress. The Baron sent out a detachment immediately, and two monsters were slain. But the warriors said even after a lengthy search, they couldn't find the third. He got away."

"But why would Kelt not reveal such significant information? Those evil creatures were near his home. How dreadful that would seem in light of the news they'd already crushed two towns? Surely, he'd desire allies against such a potential threat."

"He would never consider your elf friends allies. In fact, he has insinuated the Silver Elves are behind the goblin presence in the Maribowam forest. He says the goblins are elven spies, and thus associates the elves with the side of darkness.

"I'm not sure if that's true or not. I had apprehensions about even coming out here to divulge this information to you."

"What caused you to decide in our favor?"

"I'm concerned for Candace's safety. Aside from Baron Veldercrantz, I'm possibly her closest and most trusted ally. And I love that girl with all my heart."

Navarro smiled, empathizing.

"Since she was a youngster, I've been endeared to her. Like she was my own daughter.

"Now look at her. She's grown up to be a confident, spirited woman. And I'd be crushed if harm ever befell her. When she was abducted... I mean, when she left the fortress, I was with the patrols day and night looking for her. Many urged me to rest, but I couldn't. Now with Candace in potential danger..."

Navarro smiled as he listened to this seasoned warrior. The man's emotions overflowed from his true, heartfelt love, and it brought incredible comfort to The Paladin. The only woman who ever affected his heart was surrounded by many who loved her.

"...the threat of a goblin army is fearful," Navarro heard him continue. "Being a Paladin and having battled their kind in countless struggles, you know how vicious these brutes can be. When we journeyed to Sheliavon several years back, I saw the terrible desolation these creatures left in their wake.

"Goblins have never entered our peaceful domain before, and just like Lunumdra, I fear no town or barony will believe a ravenous monster horde has invaded until they attack.

"Then it will be too late.

"But overriding it all, I fear for Candace's well-being if they attack this fortress and prevail."

"And so do I," Navarro agreed. "So do I."

* 22 *
MONSTERS

"Why do we camp so close to the baron's fortress instead of returning to Elfstay?" Jorab asked. He nervously peeped through the tree limbs, watching the commotion of the torch-bearing warriors on the wall and the watchtowers. "Baron Kelt was emphatic about us departing from his home and his domain."

After being ushered out of the castle, Navarro and the elves mounted their steeds and disappeared into the woods. But less than half a mile away under the darkness of the trees, Navarro and Zakili stopped the troupe.

"We should have struck him down when we had the chance," Maengh grumbled, drawing an unbelieving stare from Zakili and The Paladin. "We all understand the disdain he has for Silver Elves. His hatred stems from a crime we never perpetrated."

"The Silver Elf race would forever be known as murderers if we forced our way into his home and took his life," Zakili corrected.

"He'll continue to be a threat to us!"

"The Silver Elves never knew him until Candace arrived in our forest with the warning of the assassins. You heard yourself that he was misled into thinking we'd captured her. That lie was explained, and his daughter is returned. Logic dictates we'll never see him again."

"Then why do we waste our time here--" Maengh started scornfully, but the Elf Prince was in his face, a frightfully calm, yet deadly, look in his eyes. Zakili had felt his own temper boil at the undeserved insults as they traversed the halls of the fortress; however, his ire hadn't risen to where he'd take the baron's life. It seemed Maengh grew more distant and dangerous by the day. Zakili had once counted this elf as a friend, but now he no longer knew him. This wasn't the Maengh he'd known all his life.

"Why then do we camp here in his forest, so close to his fortress?" the elf Reuben asked respectfully.

"I feel there will be trouble," Navarro answered, turning all eyes his way.

"Trouble?" several elves asked, the word echoing quickly through the camp. The Paladin's amplified sixth sense, his ability to discern unseen enemies was well known to the elves of Verdant Wood. They had seen it in a mock battle between he and Zakili in the Avenue. They witnessed Navarro sense, spin, and knock away strikes which would have taken down the most adroit fighters. And many saw it at work in the terrible battle against The Lurking Shadows.

"What do you perceive?" one of the still-cloaked elves asked, warily drawing out his blades.

"I'm not certain, but I feel there'll be evil about this place tonight."

"The baron saw no monsters spying around his forest," Maengh said. "He didn't tell us the truth. And it seems obvious enough why. We tricked our way into his fortress, and he thinks we're responsible for abducting his daughter and placing some mythical curse on her," Navarro said. "But as we departed beyond the portcullis, the elite guard who intercepted me informed me otherwise.

"Days before we arrived, the watchtower sentries spotted a group of goblins among the forest shadows. They managed to slay two, but the third escaped."

Navarro didn't miss the disgusted scowl on Maengh's face as he turned.

"This is disturbing news," Reuben said. "Not even legends of old tell of goblins warring in this land. The presence of just one monster should be enough to alarm the whole countryside."

"That's a concern for a later day. For now, I suspect evil will fall upon this place, and we must be ready. It's harrowing to think foul scouts ventured into Verdant Wood, but to imagine probes dispatched to the different regions of Avundar trumpets horrible tidings. Two towns are already soundly crushed by the foul horde. Castle Veldercrantz is next. This is where their march of terror must cease."

"And if they don't come as you suspect?" Maengh asked sharply.

"If not, we can say we had a nice night under the stars and leave with the first light of dawn."

In the darkness of night the watches were assigned, the first two elves taking their post close to the forest's tree line, giving them a clear view of the fortress. The other elves settled into their impromptu, lightless camp and tried to find rest. The anxiety of fighting vile monsters kept most awake, lying on their backs, and staring at the stars. Navarro broke away briefly to pray, but soon reunited with the elves. He saw their anxiety, but his attention was curiously drawn to the center of the camp where Zakili laid comfortably, arms crossed and snoring contentedly. The sight forced a smile on the concerned Paladin's face. With darkness fallen and the myriad constellations visible in the wide firmament, all the troup could do was watch and wait.

"Do not fear," Navarro called out, encouraging the warriors. "The Lord is on our side."

* * * * *

Kelt slipped down into a sitting position, leaning against the parapet of the unmanned tower. He could hear the excited voices of the watchmen he'd relieved from their duties as they descended the tower stairwell. Feeling shaken by the earlier intrusion of the elves, the baron desired a place of solitude to sort out the confusing events of the past couple of days and particularly of that night. He could barely remember what was said, his rage blocking out almost all memory of their conversation. Vaguely, he recalled some talk of goblins. The watchmen had spotted a few skulking in the woods days earlier.

Reclining, his fatigue suddenly struck. Kelt tried to resist, but before he knew it, he was defeated. His heavy eyelids pressed down, and visions of monsters became blurry swirls as his sleepless nights caught up to him and dragged him into the land of unconsciousness.

Much time had passed when he finally woke up. He rubbed his neck which had grown sore from his leaning against the parapet. Gazing up, he noticed the constellations had shifted, and he wondered how long he'd been asleep. He sat up rigidly when he remembered the pressing issues which had driven him to the tower. Silver Elves! Goblins! Enemies seemed to press in from every side! Then there was Candace. One of the few things he recalled the elves saying was that she had no malady. She, too, professed adamantly she wasn't accursed, but the words of Prince Killion belied all of that. To add to the confusion, The Paladin cast doubt on the prince himself. Baron Kelt grabbed his head in both hands, feeling a terrible headache coming on. Taking a deep breath, he eased his head back against the stone and stared at the constellations, unblinking, trying to clear his mind.

A smile spread across his face at a sudden thought. This tower had been his and Candace's favorite evening respite since she was a little one. Kelt had specifically designed this one lookout to be without roofing. How many times they had released the lookouts in this tower from their duties in order to just spread out a blanket and look at the stars together. They pointed out constellations and even made up names of their own. He chuckled as he again identified *Nestar's Mug*, a constellation Candace had named "Slinky the Wiggle-Worm" when she was only ten. To this day, that was still what that grouping of stars was called by them. Kelt felt himself relax as he recalled his girl throughout the years. The image of Candace when she was four replayed. He could see her try in vain to wield her daddy's sword as she fought an imaginary dragon. She could always get the hilt off the ground, but his blade incessantly scraped the floor as she tried to swing. Then he remembered her as a young teen, wiry and full of energy. Stronger and more adept with the sword, she constantly tripped over her feet, which she hadn't grown into yet.

And now at twenty, she had blossomed into a beautiful young lady, having the same delicate features and eyes as her mother. His head dipped sadly. Oh, how he missed his wife. How much *more* Candace must miss her mother.

He poured himself into his daughter once he got over Celeste's death, placing his time with her as a priority over any barony concerns. Painstakingly, he instructed her in deference and manners, raising her up as a respectful child. After his wife's death, he refused to talk to God, but he understood the importance of her relationship with Christ, so he entrusted Simeon to train her in faith areas.

Most importantly, he trained her for the past ten years in combat training. He was pleased to see her gain an immediate interest in it, and consequently, she excelled in every area he trained her. He was confident in her fighting ability, knowing she was prepared for any dangerous situation. He couldn't bear it if she fell to a fate similar to her mother's. Without hesitation, he tossed that morbid thought aside.

But how curious it was that he felt more protective about her now as a grown woman than he did when she was a child. *She was entering a different world,* he told himself. His cute little girl was now a woman of stunning beauty. He wanted the best for her. In the truest intent, he desired her life to be better than his. He wanted her to live in the comfort of royalty.

Guilt pressed in on him as he considered those thoughts. The woman whom he dreamt to be a princess was the one he imprisoned like a dangerous criminal for the past several days. But she was still controlled by that wicked elven curse! Or was she? All doubts fled away in a moment. Oh, how he loved her! A sudden thought sent his head wagging sadly. Since her return, he hadn't demonstrated that love. He'd not wished her one good night's rest.

His eyes dropped to the floor, and his heart filled with shame. With his wife gone, Candace was all he had. How could he have acted so stern and heartless toward her? He was all she had, but because of his aloofness, she had no one to comfort her. Even when she attempted to talk with him, he wouldn't listen. How isolated she must feel. How lonely.

Kelt rose to his feet and straightened his shoulders, lifting his chin. He had to go to Candace. He had to reassure her of his love. Elven curse or not, he refused to let his concern slowly be choked away. It was his responsibility to love her. It was his privilege. With a spring in his step, he made for the ladder and climbed down. He hoped it wasn't too late. He needed to make amends.

Little time passed as Kelt traversed the corridors, his healthy stride moving him along with the strength of almost forgotten youth. He turned down a familar corridor, cut a sharp corner, and pressed on until he reached a wide door carved with beautiful etchings. Candace's creation, Kelt considered absently. There he stood at the door of his daughter's chamber, the final obstacle. He pulled out his key and moved it toward the keyhole, his hand trembling. Then he froze.

What right did he have to barge into his daughter's room and ask restitution? He had dealt shamefully with her. The seemingly endless nights of subjecting her to unsuccessful magicians came to mind, dropping the key farther from the hole. He hated to think he had alienated her in the name of a fictitious malediction.

What if she rejects me? he worried. What a selfish consideration, he evaluated immediately. It was he who had neglected her feelings and kept her caged and isolated the past several days. The responsibility rested upon him to set their relationship aright. If she did turn a shoulder to him, it was what he deserved. His duty as a father was to love her no matter what. He lifted the key once more, but again couldn't will himself to unlock the door.

His shame stole his courage.

* * * * *

"The night has been uneventful," Dalamisen, the elf watchstander whispered in a sing-songy voice nearly identical to the whistles of a forest bird. This type of communication was introduced by the elves of ancient times and had been perfected throughout the generations to use in covert operations. "The other two pairs of scouts reported seeing no movements outside the trembling of a leaf. I think this whole thing is a waste of time."

"We are the last watch before morning," Baliesto, the other elf said. "If there's no activity around the castle when the sun peaks over the mountains, we will break camp and go home. Lord willing, we won't see any harm come to the baron or his servants and warriors. We'll just have to wait it out and see."

"But why?" Dalamisen asked, his voice growing sharp. "Doesn't it seem peculiar we follow the instincts of a human, a member of the race which plotted to destroy us?"

"That comparison is unworthy of Navarro's character. He's not favoring this baron because they are of the same race. The Paladin is above that. I don't know Navarro well, but from all I heard from Zakili and others who do, he is honorable. And he is devoted to eliminating the plague of evil and defending the innocent."

"Well, if he's so honorable, if he's not biased toward his own race, how would he justify his actions in the Battle of Verdant Wood? He didn't put the sword to any of the invading assassins. And they were all human!" The elf scout slapped his hand over his mouth, his agitation forcing his last sentence out in his normal voice.

"Yes, I heard that, too," Baliesto agreed, drawing a concerned stare from his suspicious companion. "Although he failed to take any enemy lives, he incapacitated a great number of them, and even assisted those elves who were overwhelmed by a mob of assassins, myself included. Because Navarro is a Paladin, he is forbidden to destroy human life. But don't be deceived Dalamisen. Only Zakili took down as many of The Lurking Shadows as Navarro did."

"But King Gallatar distrusts the human race as a whole, labeling them all as greedy and lewd. Surely if he's suspicious of every act perpetrated by that race, his people should be too. And Navarro is among that race."

"The King has no qualms with The Paladin. He is as trusted as any of the elves in the wood. Ease your mind, Dalamisen. Navarro is fully on our side. We have nothing to fear from him."

"But Maengh said..." Dalamisen began to complain again, but his words trailed off when he heard sharp distant whistling and saw Baliesto stare intently toward the fortress. His eyes followed and spotted unusual shadows skulking close to the fortress walls. The first shadows seemed man-shaped but more and more arrived quickly, the shadows becoming broader, and in many cases, taller.

"What is that?"

"It is just as Navarro had suspected. The enemy has arrived," Baliesto said grimly as he watched the gathering shadows press close to the wall, their numbers increasing exponentially. His sharp eyes looked to the many towers closest to the shadows. Why weren't the lookouts sounding an alarm? The first tower looked unmanned. So did the second. From the third, he saw a warrior fallen across the parapet, an arrow protruding from his lifeless body. "They shot down the lookouts on this side of the walled city-fortress. The attack has begun!"

"We must warn the others!"

Baliesto turned to his companion, his visage stern. "You go alert the others. I must stay and help against the invaders however I can."

"But the humans won't accept your assistance. And you'll be no match against an army of wicked monsters."

"Warn Navarro and Zakili," Baliesto ordered, "before it's too late for any of us to do any good!"

* * * * *

Kelt rejected the doorknob again, his hand trembling as his mind replayed the past days' events and how shamefully he had dealt with his only daughter. Would his efforts be in vain now? Had he treated her so despicably she was beyond granting him any kind of absolution? Or would she prove to be the magnanimous, forgiving person he'd raised her up to be and had know her to be all her life? All those considerations buzzed through his mind in a dizzying swirl of fear and hope. He would never discover the answer to those myriad questions standing outside the room staring at the doorknob, he knew. He took a deep breath and willed himself to grab hold of the doorknob and turn the key. How she reacted this morning to his intrusion no longer mattered to him. Even if she did despise him, and rightfully so, at least she would know he still cared.

Gently he opened the door, pushing it with barely a whisper of noise. The illumination from a lantern hung in the passageway flooded into the dark room. And there in the soft light, he saw Candace lying in her bed, her golden tresses flowing over the blankets and around her face. She had one foot poking outside the covers just like she had slept since she was a little girl. She was already asleep! Kelt cursed himself, not wanting to wake her. His head drooped, and slowly, reluctantly he began to pull the door closed.

Candace stirred though, sleepily pushed her hair from her face, and tried to focus her squinting eyes. Kelt smiled at her innocence. Oh, how he loved his girl! He fought back the urge to run over, scoop her up, and hug her close.

"Father?" she asked.

"It is I."

"More magicians have come?" she asked dreadfully, pulling her blankets defensively about her. "Have you awakened me to be tested again?"

Kelt's heart nearly broke and he felt tears well up in his eyes. How could he have mistreated and shamed his girl the way he had? He poured his whole life and all his love into her only to humiliate her and incriminate her in the end. "No Candace," he finally said. "No magicians."

Slowly he approached and sat down on the side of her bed as Candace pulled herself up into a seated position. Putting his finger under her chin, he gently lifted her gaze and looked into her azure eyes. She looked back curiously, indifferently. He opened his mouth to say something, but he didn't know how to start. Silence reigned for a long time.

"You know, I'm really not cursed," she said, finally shattering the awkward moment.

Kelt hugged her close. "You don't know how sorry I am for the way I've afflicted you," he said, his voice quivering. "I'm unsure how to even begin to ask for your forgiveness." He took a deep breath, bringing her back out to arms length to look into her eyes again. "Candace, you're all the family I have since the decease of your mother. And because of that, I admit I've been overprotective of you at times--"

Candace laughed at the statement, cutting his words short. "At times? I think you mean you've been overprotective of me all the time! You never even wanted me to get a scrape on my knee and when I did, oh did you fret!"

Kelt smiled wide, not at all minding the interruption. His girl was laughing again even after all these past dark days.

"Please forgive me for neglecting you and caging you like some diseased animal. When you returned, I thought I was doing the right thing bringing in the magicians. I presumed I was helping. I'm ashamed my faith has slipped to the point where I placed my hope in those who practice the dark arts of magic. Oh Candace, I should've listened to you."

"I know," she answered playfully.

"My girl, the last thing I ever wanted to do was hurt you."

She smiled graciously. "We can't live life without being hurt every now and then."

"Then you forgive me?" he asked hopefully.

"That all depends," she haggled, giving him a sly look. "Do you still think I'm under some imaginary curse?"

Kelt raised his hand to his chin and looked contemplative, the hesitation drawing an irritable huff from Candace. "Of course, I don't. I just wanted to see your reaction. I know for certain you can't be spellbound; no amount of sorcery can duplicate your impatience."

Candace hugged her father and laughed. Kelt chimed in, but his was inspired more by relief than mirth. Kelt rose from the bed and looked at his daughter. She was back. A surge of guilt coursed over him. She'd never left. He was the one who changed.

His daughter threw off the covers and trotted over to him, a spring in her step. The white gown she wore flowed surrealistically with every step, the hem waving low, ebbing back and forth across her toes. The garment perfectly complemented her shapely figure. Kelt imagined he saw an angelic vision as his girl stepped up to him. Then he realized he'd never seen her adorned in this gown before, although it looked familiar. *Where had he seen this..?* he wondered before wiping a sudden tear from his eye.

"It was mother's favorite," she said, seeming to read his thoughts. "I recall she always wore it for you during the evening hours. When I thought you'd given up on me, I put it on to at least have her close to me, even if it was only in my heart."

Kelt snatched her up and hugged her close. "What I would do to have those spent days back to correct all of my wrongs. Never have you deserved such ill manners from me. I'd give anything to go back and take away every last bit of pain I caused you. I am so, so sorry, Candace."

"I know," she whispered, kissing him on the cheek. "Despite it all, you're still the best father any girl could hope to have."

Kelt beamed and hugged her tighter.

Frantic steps echoed in the corridor, catching Kelt's attention and shifting him in the direction of the noise.

"Sir, sir," he heard a messenger cry out urgently as he skid to a stop before Candace's doorway. "I think we have trouble. The watchmen on the far wall towers spotted an elf just beyond the trees, waving his arms and pointing to the other lookout towers!"

"A decoy!" Kelt growled. "And a bad one at that. The elves obviously plan to flank us while distracting us with this bait elf. We'll not fall for it. These forest warriors have a lot to learn about real combat. Send word to general Baracus to ready the men for battle!

Kelt shot a suspicious gaze Candace's way after the messenger's departure. He suspected she'd concoct some excuse for the elves' behavior, but the truly befuddled look on her face extinguished his fury. "We must protect ourselves," he said in an almost apologetic tone.

"The walls have been breached!" another cry resounded in the room as three elite guards rushed down the corridor, Simeon leading. "We're under attack!"

"Why are the elves doing this?" Candace asked, shocked.

Kelt's brow narrowed angrily as he considered how those fools took advantage of Candace's naivety, but he grew more enraged when he recalled having the unassuming elves, the real enemies, in his home the day before. How foolish of him not to assume the elves had entered to scope out weaknesses within his fortification. "What damage has been done?" he demanded. "And what is the position of those wicked elves?"

"The outer wall has been penetrated, and the armory wall adjacent to the warriors' sleeping quarters has been leveled. But it's not elves who assault us; it's a horde of vile monsters!"

"Have we engaged the brutes?"

"The majority of our warriors are trapped within their sleeping quarters," Simeon said, trying hard to push away the despair on his visage. "Only the watchstanders are free to counterattack, but they're few and heavily outnumbered."

"Why do we stand here then?" the furious baron asked. "Despite the odds, we must assist the troops!"

Drawing his sword, Kelt turned and ran for the doorway, his men in pursuit. But just as he drew near, a hulking, two-legged, armored insectoid lumbered from the corridor, obstructing the room's only exit and eclipsing the glow of the lantern. Before the baron could formulate an attack plan, a second brute arrived, this one not as wide as the first, but taller and hairy. Its wolf jowls wet with eager drool, it spotted the five humans.

"Warmbloods," it howled as the brutes pressed into the room. "We have more warmblood victims to add to our feast!"

Kelt's sword cut a threatening circuit through the air. "Think again, dog face!"

The wolf monster glared at the proud human. "I am Howluuusin the masnevire," the brute howled, "third field commander of this detachment. I delight in ripping insolent warmbloods to pieces. And as for this one," it pointed to the massive, insect-headed brute, "this is a cave ravager. His claws can slice through your armor and your flesh as easily as its kin tore through your stone walls."

In demonstration of its strength, the ravager's claw swiped back, tearing a chunk from the doorway.

The commotion drew a dozen more monsters to the entrance of the chamber, the brutes gathering behind the two bigger monsters.

"Goblins!" Kelt spat, noticing the ugly creatures hungrily smack their big jaws.

"Cast down your weapons," Howlusin ordered Kelt and his men. "The more you resist the more agonizing I will make your deaths!"

"Begin imagining your tactics," Kelt dared, his anger overpowering all fear. "We're not laying down our weapons until all of you lie dead on the floor!"

* * * * *

"Disperse!" Navarro ordered as his band hit the outskirts of the Castle Veldercrantz's forest. He now wore his leather armor. The plate mail clanged too noisily for their quick-paced, covert movements. The elves took up their positions along the tree line.

Zakili stayed close to Navarro, informing his friend of all enemy movement. Although The Paladin's eyes had adjusted to the darkness, Navarro understood the value of an elf's keen ability to view even the most subtle of movements in the dark of night.

"No more than a score of goblins stand their posts at the breached wall," the Elf Prince accounted. "None in the lookout towers, at least, not yet."

"The elves have their bows ready," Navarro said confidently. He had sketched out a strategy when Dalamisen had returned with news of the invasion. From the size of the horde which flattened Lunumdra, The Paladin estimated the attacking army as huge. His own band was not many, but the Silver Elves were masterful archers and Navarro understood a missile attack imperative when matched against so many adversaries. His intent was not to defeat the army with his warriors, but to shore up Kelt's fighters as they fought the brutes. However, the near silence amid the fortress troubled him deeply. *Where were Kelt's warriors, and why couldn't he hear them fight back? Had they already been destroyed by this ravenous horde?* Navarro resisted those thoughts and decided that somehow they must still be alive.

Turning back to the fortress, Navarro spotted the many dark silhouettes milling about the outer wall's huge cavity. The overconfident brutes seemed little concerned about the possibility of attack from outside. They guarded that post solely to keep warriors from fleeing from the fortress, The Paladin guessed.

"There's evil in our land," Navarro said. "Let's get rid of it."

Zakili slid his gold-veined, ivory bow from his shoulder and took mark at the creatures with an imaginary arrow. "Sounds fun! It's elimination time!"

"Do it now!" Navarro ordered before sprinting away from the trees. He kept

his body low to the ground as he sped for the curve of the wall which would hide him from the goblin's wary eyes. A goblin could see in the night as good as any elf, so he moved quickly and carefully. Behind him, several soft bird calls sounded, and he recognized them as the elves' covert language. In the still of the night, he didn't hear their advance but knew the elves could be silent as death. He sensed their nearby presence clearly enough.

Without incident, Navarro made it to the wall and quickly inched forward, the rounded grade of the wall shielding him from the goblins' vision until he nearly crept up on the brutes.

"Did you come expecting an easy meal?" he said, drawing all the goblins' attention his way.

"There isses one o' those warmbloods!" a goblin shouted, its expression a mix of shock and bloodthirsty hunger.

"Don't lets him get away," a different goblin ordered. "We will snacks on him before da horde captures da rest o' the feast."

Frenzied, the goblins brought their weapons to bear, staring hungrily at the sole warrior. But as Navarro continued to stalk forward, seemingly unconcerned with the troop in front of him, the craven brutes became unnerved.

"Gets him!" the order rang out, but the brutes started reluctantly.

"Ye heared what Griklon sayed," another surly voice rang out. "Gets him."

A half dozen broke away from camp and rushed Navarro.

Invinitor leapt into The Paladin's hands in time to smack aside an iron spear launched at him. His sword reversed angles and came in low, piercing the wielder's solar plexus. Navarro kicked the dying brute away and surged to the side, slicing across to parry away a blade speeding for his neck. He had no time to retaliate.

In his peripheral vision, a goblin charged him with pike extended. With a subtle sidestep The Paladin avoided the pike, and the charging goblin. Not expecting such a deft maneuver, the goblin rampaged harmlessly past.

Almost.

Navarro's leg whipped across in a front-to-back hook-kick motion. His heel slammed into the brute's gut, stopped him in mid-stride, and bent it over at the waist. Invinitor sliced down and finished the task, the goblin's head rolling toward the camp. Navarro heaved his sword into a backhand chop, parrying a blind side sword attack. Navarro turned, and Invinitor retaliated, cutting a wide swath and sending two goblins scurrying away.

The brutes, thinking they were at a safe distance, mocked him.

"Resists while you may, warmblood. You isses outnumbered, and you will falls under the blow of our many swords!"

"Bring it on!" Navarro challenged, his blood pumping fast.

What the brutes could not know was The Paladin had positioned them perfectly for his next strike. Navarro drove forward and with one vicious slice, then a potent jab, the two goblin lives were ended forever.

A spearwielder, suddenly cautious and a good distance away, launched his

missile. His aim true.
Johnny Earl Jones

But Navarro, too adroit and too alert, batted the weapon out of the air. A master of all weapons, he jammed his sword in his scabbard, snatched the goblin's spear, and returned it to its owner. The missile drove through the monster's chest, knocked him off his feet, and pinned him to the ground.

The others fled to the camp, any eagerness to battle this man vanquished. Navarro noticed several goblins with trumpets. Those concerned him. If they escaped, their trumpet blasts would warn of the elves' approach.

"Three trumpet blowers," The Paladin called out as he charged the camp. The goblins, not knowing who he was talking to, stared at him strangely.

"He isses only one!" Griklon growled. "Kills him!"

Several whistles cut the air, then thuds and dying grunts sounded in the darkness.

"Gets up!" Griklon ordered a goblin which went down next to him. He cursed at him, kicking him, trying vainly to make him rise. But on closer examination, he noticed a shaft protruding from his skull. The goblin was quite dead. "Yarka hasses been shot dead!"

"So hasses Hairlip," another cried.

"Scarpate too," called one more.

"The enemy isses all around us," a different goblin bellowed, although it could see no adversaries other than the attacking warmblood.

Attacking warmblood!

Navarro blitzed into the camp, his blade streaking silver. The confused, distracted goblins foolishly split their attention between the rampaging paladin and the unseen archers. A backhand chop dropped one particularly hideous goblin with long sharp teeth. The Paladin's senses tingled suddenly. He spun and threw Invinitor. The sword pierced through the heart of a battle axe-wielding goblin. Navarro ducked a sword attack, mule-kicked the goblin, then sprang toward the dead axe-wielder. He retrieved Invinitor just as an axe arced for his skull. Invinitor intercepted the attack, stopping the axe in mid-swing. It thrust forward, jabbing into the goblin's gut, eliminating that savage adversary. Another goblin charged from behind. The brute's cruel blade hacked down. Shifting slightly, Navarro swept Invinitor across. The Paladin's sword pounded hard against the goblin's weapon and sent it careening into the night. Invinitor swiftly dove in and finished the brute.

The elves had played their part, Navarro knew. Two of the trumpet blowers lay prostrate in the grass. Undoubtedly, Zakili led the elves to the courtyard into the castle proper. Navarro understood the responsibility for finishing the assault was his. He spotted the last trumpet blower dashing for the huge cavity in the wall. Two additional goblins remained, but The Paladin dashed straight for the hole, ignoring the others, intent on bringing down the trumpet-bearing brute. He ran past one slain goblin and tore a dagger loose from its shoulder harness. The fleeing goblin put the trumpet to his lips. Navarro tossed the dagger. The trumpet blower dodged at the last moment and the dagger missed, instead slamming against the trumpet, sending it spinning away into the night.

The other two goblins were on him then, a polearm coming in low at his

knees. He hurtled over the oncoming polearm blade. And when he came down, he planted his lead foot, stopped his momentum and lunged back at the polearm wielder. Before the goblin could bring his heavy weapon back into play, Navarro's blade slipped between two ribs and pierced the monster's dark heart.

The other goblin charged in fearlessly, a hand axe in each fist. Navarro engaged the brute. He grew suddenly distracted when he spotted the other goblin snatch up its trumpet again.

The axewielder came in aggressively, chopping with both axes, forcing The Paladin to swiftly block one blow only to shift and block the other strike. The elementary one-two chop assault would play itself out quickly, but Navarro feared this goblin would still hack away as the other got the horn to his mouth.

The hand axe drove down again, but instead of parrying the attack Navarro let it come in unhindered. When the axe chopped down, it hit nothing but air. Navarro had quickly spun to the side. Just as he expected, the other axe drove across at his exposed back. The goblin's arm reached to make the blow, baited. The Paladin knew the brute couldn't resist such a seemingly easy target. He spun toward the goblin, Invinitor whipping across and severing the brute's arm at the elbow. The arm and the axe dropped to the ground.

The trumpet blower put the horn to its lips.

Navarro snatched up the fallen axe and took mark. With one long stride to gain momentum, he sent the weapon spinning. The first blast of the horn sounded, but was immediately drowned by a dying shriek. The axe cut down the goblin. Navarro turned and finished the axewielder.

* * * * *

With a mighty swat, the masnevire slammed the chamber door shut. Candace's bedroom was his personal arena. It pushed past the wide cave ravager and started for Kelt. Simeon and the other guards came in defensively to their leader's side, weapons drawn. In response the troupe of goblins yanked their weapons free and leered menacingly at the men.

Howlusin the masnevire grinned haughtily at the outnumbered humans.

Candace started toward her father's side to fight with him. She measured up the masnevire as it approached, noting the wolf monster was not only burly but stood a head above the tallest warrior. As imposing as this monster appeared, she had to wonder, how deft was it with a weapon? Her father was pure warrior, and she believed one-on-one the monster didn't stand a chance. But the restless goblin soldiers and the inert ravager tipped the odds heavily in the monsters' favor. She felt her stomach churning from dread.

Arrogant Howlusin stalked up to the men, eying Kelt. "I may give ye the privilege o' being the last one t' see yer death! How dare you still oppose the great Howluuusin! I will kill yer kin before yer eyes, before I rip you to pieces personally."

Kelt stood unmoving.

"Do ye fear, warmblood? Do ye stand paralyzed in the presence of the great Howluuusin?" the masnevire swiped out with his hand, mockingly batting Kelt's sword point to the ground, but stars filled his eyes as the baron lunged forward and immediately backfisted the brute in his canine nose. Howlusin stumbled back howling.

"Are you ready to die?" Kelt mocked.

"Kill them!" Howlusin shouted, and the goblins surged forward. Kelt and his guards didn't wait; they attacked head on. Swords crashed and rang out as the two forces collided, the din of clashing weapons filling the room.

Candace turned to the back wall where her armor and sword hung. Weaponless and clad in only a nightgown, she felt helpless with no way to assist the valiant men fighting against the monsters. A creature's scream pierced the air and a goblin fell dead. She nodded grimly. The prowess of these men may actually defeat the odds.

But she couldn't just stand by and watch. Somehow she had to help.

From the corner of her eye, she noticed a large shape gravitate toward her. She snapped her head in that direction.

The masnevire.

He stalked her like a jackal cornering its helpless prey. Dangerously, he licked his furry jowls, the hideous monster more grotesque as bubbling saliva edged his black lips. Oh, how helpless she felt without her armor and blade! The only weapons she had were her bare fists and feet.

How effective would they be against this formidable monster?

Candace backed away, matching every step of the masnevire with a backward step of her own. Her retreat was short-lived. When she backed up against her bed, she ran out of room and out of time.

Another goblin scream echoed in the chamber. One more down.

Howlusin came in relentlessly, a glassy, hungry stare in his eyes.

Quick-witted Candace hopped on her bed. She'd studied canines--and certainly, this monster resembled a large, two-legged dog. To show fear meant quick death. She fixed her eyes on the brute and ordered, "Stop!" To her surprise, he balked.

But only briefly.

"Devouring ye will be a delight which I hadn't expected from this simple raid. So much the better! I so enjoy multiple conquests!"

"What have you done with the men of the fortress!" she demanded courageously, not expecting an answer, doing whatever she could to hide her fear and distract this brute. The wolf monster sniggered at her question, and Candace worried her intrepid display was in vain.

To her surprise, the creature answered. "The warmbloods awaits their fates in our horde's bellies. They huddle trembling in the same chamber where we will throw the bodies o' your companions once they lay slumped on the points o' our swords!"

Candace understood the brute referred to Father and the Elite guards, but

another cry from a slain goblin emptied the masnevire's threat.

"Maybe we'll throw your dead bodies in that chamber instead," she retorted, drawing a vicious snarl from the brute. The masnevire swiped at her with his clawed fingers, but Candace leapt, somersaulted in the air, and landed feet first on her bed. Her fist shot out and blasted the brute on the snout. Howlusin backed, clutching his nose, eyes narrowed dangerously. Drawing a dagger from his sheath, he marched back in.

"Dare to try it again?" she asked.

"Indeed warmblood," he growled, grinning wickedly. "It matters not hooow I will take ye, whether it be alive or dead. I will prove victorious."

With an agonizing screech, another goblin's life ended.

Candace leapt from the bed. Her feet hit the floor running and she dashed for her sword. The mighty masnevire skid the bed across the room and sprang at her. Candace dashed the final few feet to her scabbard and grabbed for her cutlass, but all went black in a moment as sharp agony pierced her neck.

The masnevire's claws dug in right below the base of her skull. In his clutches, her flight halted, her mouth open in a silent scream of pain.

"Now it is time to play, warmblood," the masnevire threatened, his jaws close to her ear.

"Candace!" she heard Father's worried cry but was unable to do anything. The brute squeezed the back of her neck, digging his nails in deeper, intensifying the pain. She heard the dying squeal of a goblin foolish enough to get into her Father's path. With an aggravated growl, the masnevire's claws sunk in yet deeper, ripping a scream from her again. "Destroy them!" Howlusin roared to the cave ravager. "Destroy them all!"

Through her pain, she heard the sudden, loud crashes and the dull thump of swords falling on some ungiving substance. The Ravager had attacked. The cheers of the goblins filled her room, and her heart dropped when she heard several of the men cry, "Our swords cannot penetrate its armor!"

"Now, where were we?" the masnevire mocked, his face so close to Candace's, she was overwhelmed by his rancid breath. Teasingly, he traced a line across her throat with his dagger. "I think I'll bleed ye fer all yer trouble, slowly and painfully." He squeezed on the back of her neck again, making her wince, and all the time she was agonizingly listening to the defeated groans and cries of the men as the ravager beat them down.

"You are such a pain in the neck," she managed to growl through the agony, shoving the dagger away with both hands, then reaching up and punching the monster across the jaw.

The masnevire growled angrily. His jaws snapped out and ripped into her shoulder. She nearly screamed but she forced herself to muffle it, not wanting to give the brute the satisfaction of hearing her agony.

Tightening his squeeze on her neck, he shook her viciously, intensifying her torture and dropping her to her knees. Howlusin brought the dagger point back under

her chin. "I've had me fill o' trouble from ye, warmblood lassy! 'Tis time to die!"
Johnny Earl Jones

A thunderous echo resonated through the room. The door burst free of its
hinges and slid into the chamber. All eyes turned to see standing in the doorway the
silhouette of a man wielding a mighty sword.

"Navarro!" Candace cried hopefully.

"It's time to evict some unwanted guests," the paladin said sternly as he
stepped into the room.

"Destroy him!" Howlusin ordered. The cave ravager turned from Kelt's
battered men and charged the newcomer. Candace watched fearfully as the armor-
skinned monster pumped its mighty legs and sped in Navarro's direction. The
Paladin stared the insectoid beast in the eyes as it gained speed and momentum. At
the last second, Navarro spun away into the hall and the ravager zoomed by.

Smashing face first into the corridor wall and busting it to pieces, the
ravager was buried by an avalanche of bricks and mortar.

Candace started to cheer as her captor stared dumbfounded. The brick pile
shuddered violently and the ravager tore out with a vengeance. Navarro bobbed to
the side, ducking as a three-fingered claw swiped at his head. The monster came up
empty. The paladin swept back in, whipping his blade across at the flailing monster's
other arm, the sword smacking hard against the ravager's armored forearm and
bouncing off harmlessly. "This beast has extremely thick skin if even Invinitor won't
penetrate it."

Throwing off the rest of the brick pile, the ravager pumped its mighty legs
and stormed The Paladin again. Navarro rushed back in the room. Quickly glancing
around, he noticed the savage goblins surging in on Kelt and his men. One warrior
was down, a terrible gash torn in his chest, obviously the work of the ravager. He
had to get to the downed man soon if he were to have any chance to survive.

But first there was the problem of the cave ravager. Navarro highstepped
backward, taunting the ravager and placing his back dangerously close to the furious
battle with the goblins. Churning its legs and bulling in at him, the ravager's arms
extended wide to snatch up the paladin and crush him. Navarro stood still, daring the
beast forward.

In response, the ravager lowered its head, coming in hard and fast.

Navarro dove to the side just as the ravager's thick arms constricted, its
deadly hug coming up empty, The Paladin rolling on his shoulder and coming to his
feet several yards away. The rushing ravager couldn't stop; it collided with an
unsuspecting goblin and splattered it against the wall.

The ravager turned. Angry, he shook the gore off its forehead. Navarro was
there before the beast could even begin to look for him, his sword chopping and
slashing viciously. The beast guffawed as the blade cut a few nicks and carved a
shallow furrow across his armored chest, doing no real damage. The ravager's
mandibles snapped out suddenly, but The Paladin ducked, the vice-like clamps just
barely missing the top of his head.

Invinitor jabbed the brute's gut, but it was armored as well and the blade
merely cut away a chunk of its exoskeleton. The ravager's huge fist swept across.

Navarro pulled back, but couldn't get completely out of the way. The powerful

punch clipped the side of his jaw and sent him sprawling. The ravager drove in immediately, mandibles stretched wide and a mouth full of needlelike teeth agape.

Howlusin turned from the battle. He thought it over. Grinning wickedly, he pulled Candace to her feet with his imbedded nails.

"Hungry?" Navarro asked, getting his feet underneath him as the ravager closed in. "Eat this!"

Invinitor plunged into the brute's carnivorous mouth, shattering teeth, piercing through the monster's palate and driving up into his brain. The mandibles shuttered violently, and the ravager's thick arm heaved back to make another blow. But any of the creature's strength slipped away in a moment. His legs buckled and the monster dropped heavily to the floor.

Navarro tore his sword from the beast's head and turned his gaze toward the tall, hairy monster terrorizing Candace. "Release her now!" he commanded, his strong voice echoing throughout the chamber. The masnevire turned in surprise, staring incredulously from The Paladin to the dead ravager.

"The cave ravager, ye killed it?" Howlusin asked nervously, more to himself than to Navarro.

"I did. And you're next."

The masnevire pulled Candace in front of him, placing the dagger to her throat.

Navarro slid Invinitor into its scabbard and pulled the bow off his shoulder. Snatching an arrow from a small quiver strapped tightly to his back, he notched the arrow and took a mark on the brute.

"Put yer weapon down! One wrong mooove will cost her life."

Navarro stared coldly into his black eyes.

"Did ye hear me? She will die!" Howlusin screamed over the din of the still battling men and goblins.

The Paladin took a step forward and read the courage in Candace's eyes, which told him not to give in to the monster's demands.

"If she dies, you will follow shortly after."

The brute looked past Navarro to the doorway, smiling wickedly. "Destroy him! Come in here and cut him down!"

Navarro didn't flinch or take his eyes off the crouching monster. He knew the monster's cries to newly-arrived allies was only a ruse. He sensed the presence of no monsters at his back. The Paladin took another step forward, his strong arms holding the bowstring taut.

"I'll rip her to pieces!" the masnevire threatened, shaking her by the neck, the claws imbedded in the back of her neck wrenching out an agonized cry. Navarro stopped.

That action didn't go unnoticed by the masnevire. He shook his hostage violently again, teasing The Paladin. Pain contorted Candace's face. The brute smiled smugly, thinking he had firm control of the situation now. "Ye warmbloods are weak! Never would I put the life o' another before the consummation o' the

mission!" Ducking behind Candace for protection from the dangerous paladin's bow,
Johnny Earl Jones

he pushed her forward, inching her toward the door and his escape.

The monster made a foolish error though. The expression on Candace's face showed Navarro she'd had enough. A knowing grin raised the corners of his lips. She was not some victim to terrorize. She was warrior.

Navarro took aim. The monster shook her again. Candace screamed in pain and anger.

Candace would take no more. She slammed her heel hard on top of the monster's booted foot, wrenching an agonized howl from the brute. With her right hand she held Howlusin's dagger at bay, and she spun as best she could, ignoring the piercing pain in her neck, and launched her elbow into the ducking monster's windpipe. The masnevire straightened reflexively, gasping to get air down his bruised throat.

That was the last mistake it would ever make.

Candace heard a sharp whistle pass her ear then she felt the monster tug her backward. She pushed the dagger arm away. To her surprise the grip on the weapon loosened and it fell to the floor with a sharp clang. But with the monster still griping her neck, she lost her footing and fell, landing on her back. Waves of pain rolled across her as the claws slid in deeper. Steeling herself against the pain, she beat furiously on the arm and pulled loose, backing away frantically into the arms of another assailant. She launched her elbow up to where she knew the face might be, but it was blocked. She spun away, with fists raised defensively, and stared at her new attacker only to find she was not sparing against a monster. She locked her gaze with the emerald eyes of Navarro Silvinton. Her eyes softened, and her fists dropped. Looking back, she spotted the wicked masnevire supine on the floor, an arrow protruding from between his eyes like a miniature flagpole.

"Hold still," he told her quietly, and he prayed, laying his hands on the bleeding wounds on the back of her neck and shoulder. "In the powerful name of Jesus, I beseech you Lord, heal every wound inflicted upon Candace by this evil monster. In Your mighty name I pray. Amen!"

Candace stood amazed, in awe, as the pure power of the Lord's healing touch. She felt a river of renewing energy flow over her, washing away the pain, and closing her wounds. A moment later, Navarro released his hand, and Candace felt the back of her neck. The wounds were gone, her skin smooth. She looked at him, her eyes full of wonder.

"We are far from finished," Navarro said, looking over to Kelt and his men. With a wink to Candace, he dashed away, his sword leaping into his hands just as a spear-totting goblin turned to him, a wicked snarl on his face. The brute's spear thrust out straight for The Paladin's belly, but Invinitor lopped the spear head off. The Paladin lunged forward, his sword driving in hard, piercing armor, bone, and finally the goblin's black heart.

One of Kelt's guards was motionless on the ground, but the others fought back valiantly, encouraged by The Paladin's appearance in the fray. Invinitor looped down in a wide chop, cutting down one of two goblins bearing down on a single Elite

Guard. The other goblin spun on The Paladin, dropped his sword, and withdrew a

pair of knives from a shoulder holster lined with blades. With a flick of both wrists, the knives spun Navarro's way. The Paladin sidestepped one and batted the other to the side with his mighty sword. In came two more. He ducked the first and snatched the second out of the air with his right hand.

"I have something of yours," Navarro told the goblin. "Catch." The dagger spun back at the goblin a second later. And he caught the blade. Right in his chest.

Candace streaked past, still barefooted, but now wielding a sword, coming to Father's side and driving back the foul monsters.

The fighting lasted only a few moments longer, the re-energized warriors summarily cutting down the remaining goblins.

Navarro rushed to the downed warrior. The bloody chest gash from the cave ravager must be treated. Getting close to the warrior, Navarro could still hear very shallow breathing.

"Is he alive?" Kelt asked, concerned.

"Just barely," The Paladin said matter-of-factly, his calm tone surprising to the baron.

Navarro asked everyone to stand back as he placed his hands over the man's gory wound. Closing his eyes, he lifted his face toward heaven and called for the Lord's miraculous healing power to flow through him. A moment later, he felt the streams of the Christ's regenerating energy course down his arms, into his hands, and through his fingers--released into the body of the prone warrior.

Only seconds passed, but to Candace, Kelt and the others mesmerized by the supernal action, their amazement replayed over and over again in their mind. The Paladin stepped away, thanking the Lord for his mercy, as the guard began to stir.

"How do you feel?" Kelt asked, rushing to his side.

The man stretched, yawned, and leapt to his feet. "Never felt better!"

"That's good," Navarro said, "because beyond this chamber looms a horde of vile monsters. They're bloodthirsty. They're fearless. And realistically, chances are any one of us, or all of us, could lose our lives out there."

The men looked to him grimly.

"Personally, I don't plan on going down to some stinkin' monster," The Paladin reassured. "But if something does happen to me, the Bible says I'll immediately see Christ in Heaven.

"Are you men born again?"

"We have no time for religion. We must fight!" one warrior said.

"You're right. There is no time for religion. Religion hasn't gotten a single person to heaven. Only the Lord Jesus Christ can do that. If any of you die in your sins without Jesus, no matter how noble the cause, your fate after death will be infinitely worse than your demise here.

"Jesus Christ is your most dire need." The men listened intently as Navarro shared the saving gospel of Jesus Christ and invited them to pray to receive Jesus as their Lord and Savior. The two guards fell on their knees, and Navarro bowed with them.

Kelt looked on, fully convicted and shamed his repressed Christian beliefs
Johnny Earl Jones

had made no difference in anyone else's life. He felt jealous of Navarro's vibrant relationship with God, but at the same time, he was proud of the young man for standing on his convictions.

When Navarro and the guards rose to their feet, The Paladin turned to Kelt.

"It's imperative we release your warriors if any of us are to get out of here alive."

* 23 *
DANGER ALL AROUND

"They're everywhere!" Kelt roared.

Navarro swatted away the goblin's sword when the creature sprung out of the darkness. He had no time to counterattack. A spearhead from a different monster thrust straight for his throat. Invinitor swept across, slicing through the spear like candle wax, and that goblin retreated back into the mob.

"We can't have these at our back when we clash with the monsters barracking your warriors," Navarro told Kelt, who cut down a goblin before nodding in agreement. "They all must be finished here!"

"Twenty against six," Candace cried. "No problem!"

Navarro smiled. "I love your unquenchable optimism."

Four goblins surrounded Navarro on three sides hoping to distract him enough to gain an opening. "If we destroys this warmblood, the rests will falls," one brute said.

"You won't defeat me! And you won't defeat us. Christ is on our side!"

His last sentence brought the snarling brutes in ferociously, swords slashing wildly and curses spitting out of their foul mouths. Invinitor cut across, blocking two sword blows simultaneously. Navarro, shifting his feet ever so subtly, used the blocked goblins to shield him from the coordinated attack of the other two. A second later, Navarro kicked one goblin away, then pounded the other in the gut with a crippling side kick. Invinitor finished the brute.

Navarro came hard at the brutes, his sword a silver-streaked fury. The Paladin blitzed in, sword driving across, he forced a goblin to awkwardly block the attack, and the impact sent the monster stumbling backward. Twirling sideways and hacking with a backhand chop, the paladin severed one retreating goblin's arm at the elbow. The brute wailed, his cries echoing throughout the intersecting corridors. Invinitor silenced it with a swift jab. In came Navarro again, sword chopping and thrusting, the frantic goblins on their heels as they cursed the raging Paladin. "Curse your God!" one brute spat. The others chimed in.

"My God is too good and too awesome to curse, evil ones! No, you're the accursed ones, and only everlasting darkness awaits you!" Invinitor jabbed right through one goblin's defenses, pierced his armor, and drove into his chest. Another goblin charged from the right, curved scimitar arcing toward Navarro's skull. No time to yank his sword free, Navarro released it and spun to the side. The goblin's weapon missed and the goblin charged by, but The Paladin's fist shot out, blasting the monster on the back of the skull. The goblin stumbled, disoriented, into a pack of brutes battling Kelt's elite guards. The men picked off those distracted brutes easily.

Navarro spun back to the impaled goblin, dead on the floor, and yanked his sword free. He sensed a brute storm in from behind and whirled about. Invinitor darted upward as battle axe dropped. Invinitor smacked the axehead aside. Navarro spun and Invinitor sliced across the goblin's exposed torso, carving a diagonal line through the brute's armor and through its flesh.

Invinitor jabbed to the right, driving into a huge, slobbering goblin who attacked from his side, putting an end to that one's evil life. The Paladin's senses tingled, and with sword in both hands, he thrust overhead and back. Invinitor's tip found resistance as it struck. Letting go with one hand, Navarro turned and looked into the dying eyes of a scarred and gruesome goblin. Twin blades fell from the slain brute's grip. Navarro ripped his sword free and turn to face any other brutes. But Kelt and his men were finishing off the last of the ravenous monsters.

"With all that noise, I hope we haven't signaled all the monsters in the fortress to our location," Dellis, an elite guard, groaned.

"Bring them on," Candace cried, wiping black blood from her sword onto the tunic of a dead goblin. "I would face any danger without fear by Navarro's side."

Navarro smiled apologetically to her father for the compliment but didn't miss the admiration on her father's face.

"All of our lessons made you into quite a fighter, young lady," the baron said, a wide smile crossing his face.

"You and your elite guards are masters with your weapons, as well," Navarro said in deference to the fighting prowess of the men. "But we must move quickly now. Dellis was not far wrong. We may have brought undo attention our way. I don't know what kind of monsters wait at the door of the trapped warriors, but we must burst through them and free the men before the wrath of the monster army falls upon us."

"What about your elves? How will they fare?"

"Their role is not a surreptitious one like ours. They openly show themselves to the monsters, leading as many away from our direction as possible."

"Reports from the scouts have accounted for an overwhelming number of monsters. How many elves did you bring with you?"

"The twelve I brought into your chambers."

"They will be vastly outnumbered!"

* * * * *

Zakili raced up the stairs to the top level of the fortress followed by his elves. On one side they were hemmed in by the high walls of spires and turrets. On the other, the parapets lined the outside wall--the only obstacle between the walkway and a far drop into the courtyard far below.

"Follow me," he instructed and dashed ahead into the darkness. A few seconds later the elves heard the monstrous roars and pounding footsteps as the monsters clambered up the stairs the elves just climbed.

Two elves broke away from the main group and stayed behind, pulling their bows off their shoulders and snatching arrows from their quivers. The first monster to rise from the opening was a hulking, wolf-headed masnevire. Jorab's arrow took flight, struck the monster hard in the chest and unleashed an earsplitting roar. The other elf, Leminek, unleashed his arrow, the missile striking the monster's face and toppling it over. Three others rose swiftly as the first masnevire fell. Jorab and Leminek sent their arrows again, one glancing off a well-armored brute, the other diving into a bare-armed monster's bicep, slowing him. A surge of slobbering masnevires pushed the balking monster over the parapet to fall to his doom.

The two elves fired off several more arrows each, felling the lead masnevire and crippling the next monster, effectively slowing the brutes' surge.

"We'll run out of arrows soon," Jorab said. "We must catch up to Zakili if we hope to stand any chance at all." The two sprang away into the darkness, the red glowing eyes of the masnevires gaining speed once the merciless brutes tossed the injured over the side and out of their way.

* * * * *

"Perhaps we have forced our hand in odds we cannot hope to overcome," Maengh said when they rounded a gentle curve to find a mob of masnevires and goblins blocking any further progress. "Monsters in front and monsters in back. It would seem we're finished."

"If you think so, fall on your sword!" Zakili growled through clenched teeth. "The elves and I fight until none are left standing!"

The Elf Prince raised his ivory bow to the sky and let a blazing lightning arrow soar. It carved a dazzling arch into the night.

"That arrow will alert all the monsters to our whereabouts," Maengh complained.

"And..?" Zakili asked, unimpressed.

Jorab and Leminek caught up to the group. "A swarm of monsters rushes us from behind!" Jorab warned. "They were too many to hold back with our depleted arrows."

"Let's see what they are made of!" Zakili cried, rallying the elves. "Baliesto and I will engage the monsters before us. The rest of you take down those following!"

Five elves bent on their knees and the other five stood tall, bows in hand, as the monsters stampeded toward them down the wide walkway.

"Steady," Jorab instructed. "Hold your fire until I give the command."

The masnevires crowded in closer, closer, their red glowing eyes hateful. The brutes cursed, howled, and derided the elves.

"Hold your fire."

"Why do we let them so near?" one elf asked.

"We have limited arrows. Each hit must count."

In the masnevires came, hooting, weapons waving.

"Now!"

A swarm of arrows took flight, stinging the leading monsters. Several dropped. Those following scrambled over the dead, but another volley of arrows cut down several more. Some ravenous monsters tossed their dying comrades over the wall to clear a path. Others paired up with a dead body to use as a shield. Again the elves notched their arrows and took aim. A few monsters went down, but several valuable arrows were lost on the lifeless shields preceding the mob.

"I only have a handful of arrows left," Leminek said, hoping he was the exception, but several others nodded grimly. Their quivers were close to empty as well. "How many of you Christian-types do we have here?"

To his surprise, the majority of them answered up. "Well, you better do like Navarro does and start praying. We're going to need it."

"We have been," Jorab said.

* * * * *

"They come at us hard and without concern for their lives!" Baliesto said.

"So be it," Zakili answered. "For I have no concern for their lives either."

Relentlessly, the elves launched volleys at the charging brutes. Goblin and masnevire fell dead to arrow and lightning.

"Lord, renew my strength like the eagle," Zakili heard Baliesto pray as he fired arrow after arrow. The Elf Prince knew his troupe was winded. They fought and ran for more than an hour now without reprieve--mercilessly chased by the bloodthirsty monsters. Zakili pulled back on his bow again, and let a lightning arrow fly. The missile cut through the air then cut through the leading masnevire, throwing him back into his compatriots.

Still they came.

"They have no fear," Baliesto said. "And slowly they inch forward despite the numbers dead."

"More troubling, is there seems to be no end to the horde."

Always aggressive, always optimistic Zakili had to agree with the elf's assessment. But what could he do? Just lie down and let the monsters run over him? No way!

From his memory, Navarro's words emerged. *When you don't know what to do, look up.*

"What good's that going to do me?" Zakili asked himself. "I'm no Christian." He understood what those words meant. God helps His children when in need.

Zakili fired and fired again, blowing one evil brute over the wall and felling another to the floor. Baliesto notched his arrow, fired, and cut down a goblin before reaching back into his quiver for yet another arrow. The elf sang out even as he felt only a couple arrows left.

"My help!" Baliesto's melodic voice sung out.

"O, My help! My help!

"All of my help cometh from the Lord!"

Look up, Navarro's words sounded gently in Zakili's mind.

"Prince! We have nearly extinguished all our arrows," an elf said from behind.

Zakili roared, firing off another lightning arrow which ripped viciously through one goblin and pounded the masnevire behind it in the chest. Both fell over dead. Still, innumerable brutes with red, glowing eyes charged forward to take their place.

Look up, came the calm words again in his thoughts.

With a huff, Zakili lifted his eyes. He saw nothing in the darkness but the overhanging brick turret of an empty lookout post overhead about twenty feet in front of their position. He tore his focus away, enraged and disillusioned. He hadn't seen anything helpful. Zakili loosed another lightning arrow into the mob.

The lookout tower!

"Keep the monsters back as best you can," Zakili instructed, and Baliesto grabbed his next arrow with a knowing smile.

Zakili pulled back on the bowstring and a lightning arrow formed. The newest lead monsters balked for just a moment at the sight of it. The Prince aimed upward. His lightning arrow zipped through the air and slammed against the base of the turret. Mortar and chunks of brick rained down on the brutes below but did little to stop their momentum. Zakili fired again, blasting away a greater chunk, just under the rounded construction of the tower's base. Several monsters covered their heads as bricks tumbled down. But their march continued.

"I've got one arrow left," Baliesto announced.

"Use it well," the Elf Prince said, and another lightning arrow rocked the base of the turret.

"It is done!" Baliesto stated grimly after shooting down a closing brute.

Grinding and cracking sounded above him.

"And so is this!" Zakili answered as another energy arrow streaked from his bow and blasted the bricks once again. The Prince retreated, grabbing his partner by the shoulder and pulling him back. He heaved on his bowstring and fired, then fired again and again, launching lightning into the foul mob.

The cracking, grinding sound grew louder until finally the weight of the small tower collapsed its crumbling foundation and it plummeted down. Zakili fired off another arrow to keep the brutes attention until the brick tower crashed side long onto their walkway. Deafening, the tower crushed dozens of monsters before crumpling the parapets, that section of the walkway, and plunging into the courtyard below. Zakili and Baliesto struggled to keep their balance against the shockwaves of the hit, but the unsuspecting elves and monsters at their back lost their footing and sprawled to the floor.

"One group of monsters and their access way to us is destroyed," Zakili said. He turned to face the mob coming from the other direction.

"But this group is just as endless," Baliesto said. "And this time with no turret to send down upon them."

"Fight like the mighty elves you are," Zakili commanded the now risen elves. "And if we die, we'll die like warriors!"

* * * * *

"The corridor empties out into the armory hall," Kelt explained. "The door on the other side of the wide hall leads into the warriors' sleeping quarters."

"So we have an army of men who have no weapons," Navarro said, his mind racing. *How could he get weapons and armor into the hands of those men?* "Our troupe and the elves could win the smaller skirmishes, but without the assistance of Kelt's warriors, we won't prove victorious over this huge throng. When I scouted the corridor I noticed the outside wall is caved in, and a large number of monsters were milling about. Goblins and masnevires guard the door, but the most disturbing sight was the Cave Ravagers and the two giants."

"Two giants," one guard echoed unnerved.

"Cave Ravagers," the other grunted, nearly experiencing death at the claws of one earlier.

Navarro understood their troubled feelings and quickly encouraged them, sharing his plan of how to free the warriors. "If God be for us, who can be against us?" he quoted. "I will clear the corridor of any wandering monsters. A few moments afterward, take to the corridor and meet up with me. Then we will start the distraction and follow the plan." Navarro dashed into the dark corridor, leaving Candace, Kelt, and the guards behind.

"Impressive young man," Kelt said. The two guards Navarro had healed agreed.

"He's unlike any man I've ever met," Candace said softly to herself.

Overhearing, Kelt glanced furtively in her direction, and he understood the emotions swirling in her heart.

* * * * *

As he pulled up close to the high-ceiling armory, Navarro noticed the beasts seemed distracted. A fire had been lit in the middle of the armory floor, and the monsters stood in a wide circle around it. The Paladin squeezed up close to the corridor wall. The brutes suddenly cheered and the doorway into the armory from the sleeping chambers was opened. Two masnevires and a cave ravager dragged a reluctant man into the midst of the circle before slamming the door. The man was barefoot and dressed in only a night shirt, Navarro noticed. A well-armored goblin wielding a two-handed sword approached him. The unarmed man backed away. The monsters' cheering was a prelude to a one-sided duel. Shoved in the back by a goblin in the surrounding circle, the man stumbled forward, dangerously close to the stalking goblin. Chopping across viciously, the goblin nearly took the man's head off, but the unarmed warrior ducked and scampered off to the side.

"You will die, warmblood!" the goblin roared.

"Give me a weapon, you dog! Then we'll see how well you really fight!"

The monsters hissed and spat at the man, jabbing at him with long spears. The armored goblin laughed derisively.

Navarro had all of this he could stand. Silently, he sneaked into the armory, concealed in the flickering shadows close to the walls. His choice was simple: forfeit the element of surprise by saving this man or keep the advantage of an unexpected attack at the cost of not intervening for this man's life. For the altruistic Paladin the decision was already made. He remembered the Lord's Word saying if he was faithful with little, he would bless him with much. How many circumstances that could apply to? Most pointedly, it meant helping this doomed man right now.

As Navarro traversed the circumference of the huge circular room, he noticed the different suits of armor, chainmail and platemail, all varying in size. They lined the walls, as well as weapons ranging from battle axes to swords and spears to... daggers.

He stopped, quietly pulling the dagger from its pegs, then turned to the monsters and tried to visually measure the distance between he and the armored goblin. He heaved back his throwing arm and launched the weapon spinning into the midst of the circle. Navarro knew the dagger would do no real damage from that distance, but it would buy the man some time. The dagger whistled hilt over blade, arching down and bouncing off the back of the goblin's head. The unsuspecting monster stumbled forward, crashing down at the feet of the unarmed warrior. The goblin tried to get up quickly, but the warrior kicked it in the head with his heel before yanking the sword free from its grip. The goblin's sword dove into his own back. Navarro struck then, bow in his hand as he fired arrow after arrow, mowing down a line of brutes.

The man in the circle raced in the direction of his rescuer, the confusion of the moment preventing him from being cut down by any frothing monsters. He easily spotted the path The Paladin had cleared out for him and ran toward Navarro. The Paladin's quiver was still ample. He only used one arrow before entering this room and that was to shoot down the masnevire threatening Candace. So with abandon, he pulled arrow after arrow from his quiver and let fly, downing masnevires and goblins at every turn. It took only seconds for the half-frightened, half-furious warrior to make it to The Paladin's side.

"Don't just stand there!" Navarro commanded with a grin. "Don your armor and grab your weapons! We've got monsters to defeat! I'll hold them off!" He notched another arrow, firing it, and bringing down a burly masnevire.

"What kind of mess have you started?" he heard a voice call from the corridor, a voice he could recognize anywhere. Candace.

"Hopefully, nothing we can't handle." Arrow after arrow launched from his bow, biting into the monsters' numbers, but he realized quickly that the monsters were beginning to organize their ranks. He was swiftly running low on shafts. Something else troubled him. He had heard a crash outside the fortress walls while he was yet in the corridor and wondered if that had anything to do with the fact there were no giants and only a few cave ravagers now in the armory.

Navarro heard the clash of weapons close to the corridor. Kelt and his men!

The Paladin exhausted all his arrows but two, shooting down several bloodthirsty monsters before hanging the bow diagonally across his shoulders. Invinitor leaped into his hands, and he charged, cutting a path through the masnevires and goblins streaming in at him. Invinitor sliced and backhand-chopped through the dangerous throng. He hacked through tempered-steel weapons and carved through armor to cut the dark souls out of the closest monsters.

His progress was slow but steady toward the door, but after several minutes, he began to feel his momentum slipping. His arms grew heavy and screamed for reprieve. The Paladin willed himself onward, rejecting the fatigue.

But by this time he'd drawn the attention of the monstrous mob. They swarmed around him, apparently understanding he was their most dangerous bane. The Paladin went into a deadly dance, his sword whirling and slicing any who got too close.

The sea of snarling brutes pressed in on him. Reality said he couldn't exterminate them all. But he refused to give up hope. His muscles ached with a thousand, tiny needle pricks as he fought on, beyond exhaustion now.

He ducked suddenly as a dagger flew past his head, its point slamming into a masnevire's face, sending it howling off to the side. He couldn't believe they threw blades in such close melee! Invinitor sliced low, cutting the legs out from under a goblin. His senses tingled and he spun about, his sword arcing out wide and taking the head off a charging masnevire. His senses tingled again and he spun, stepping aside as a spear narrowly missed him and jabbed into the belly of a monster with sword arm raised to attack The Paladin. The increasing danger energized Navarro, and he forgot about his tired arms and shoulders. A sword flew by, nearly nicked his cheek, and stabbed into yet another brute.

"Sorry!" Candace yelled. He realized suddenly the weapons weren't being thrown at him by monsters; somehow, Candace was willing the weapons to take flight at the brutes.

The rescued warrior cut his way to Navarro then, one by one stabbing into the turned monsters' backs. Navarro pointed him in the direction of the shut door. Kelt and his elite guards fought their way out of the corridor and into the wide room. Candace continued to pray, driving the armory weapons into the heart of the monster throng.

The bodies of monsters lay scattered all about the floor, tripping up attacking foes. Around Navarro, the corpses began to pile up and the attacks came in less frequently. The Paladin, breathing hard, was able to catch a breath and rest his arms for a second before resuming his deadly, whirling dance with his blade. Seeing Candace from the corner of his eye, he quickly sliced down a goblin, and motioned for her to concentrate her efforts toward the warrior dashing for the door. Kelt and his men saw the signal as well and fought in that direction.

Navarro stepped up his attacks, biting into the brutes ferociously with Invinitor, suffering a nick from a glancing blow and the beginning of a jab before he quickly parried it away, his sword jabbing suddenly and eliminating the attacker. "Lord! You are my strength!" he cried, encouraging himself. "And You said I am more than a conqueror! Only You can give us victory in this impossible situation."

A spear thrust at him, but Invinitor cut it in half, and The Paladin sent his blade arcing wide, separating the spear-wielder's hand from his wrist. In the distance he saw several monsters sprawl to the floor who blitzed toward the warrior running for the door. Blades protruded from vital areas.

"Good shot, Candace." Navarro said. His smile grew wider as Kelt and his guards caught up to the lone warrior, and together they fought toward the door.

The sound of weapons clashing off to his right turned him suddenly. What he saw filled his heart with dread. Candace was alone against an onslaught of monsters! Navarro leaped over the barricade of corpse and carved his way through the monsters, slicing, jabbing, parrying, spinning, and slicing again, dropping dying brutes in his wake. Among the horde, he saw her battle desperately, her sword cutting and parrying furiously against the attacks of several raging monsters. Navarro burst through the sea of brutes. His sword hacked across once then reversed angles and cut back viciously again, dropping two of Candace's attackers to the floor.

"I was wondering if you'd ever get over here," she joked through labored breaths, ducking under a sword slice and running her blade into an exposed goblin's belly. Two more slices from Invinitor and Navarro stood by her side, his blade twirling and slicing and seeming to flicker and mesmerize as it reflected the flames at the room's center.

"It seems these brutes have us backed into the corridor and locked out of the fight. When they turn on Kelt and his men, the baron won't stand a chance. We have to cut through this mob and assist them."

"Can you keep these monsters occupied?" Candace asked.

"I've been able to keep their attention so far," he said, parrying away an axe swing and jabbing out with his sword.

"Keep them back a moment while I cut us an opening."

With no time to look back and ask how she could do it, Navarro sent his sword into a whirlwind, slapping away attack after attack. The monsters came in furiously, sensing The Paladin trapped. Navarro worked his blade, blocking, parrying but only rarely getting in a jab or a slice against the onslaught. One masnevire angled its battle axe perfectly and with a mighty huff spun it Navarro's direction. Not missing a beat in his swordplay, The Paladin chopped it out of the air.

A phantom dagger knocked that monster to the ground a moment later. In flew a battle hammer skipping off the skull of one wicked beast and slamming into the face of another. A javelin darted through the air and pierced a snarling goblin. Several more airborne weapons spun into the mob, taking down monsters and throwing them into confusion. Weapons clashed, and the brutes, in their confusion, began hacking away with their swords and axes, cutting down one another.

"This is our chance," Navarro said, extending his hand to Candace. "This opportunity will close quickly, so let's hurry!"

She grabbed hold of his hand and kept pace with the racing paladin, still praying aloud and sending missiles spinning at the monsters. The brutes' self-destructive massacre only lasted a few seconds, but it was long enough for the pair to join Kelt and the others.

"They sealed the door with a deep-driven wedge," Kelt explained in frustration.

"Form a perimeter around the door," Navarro instructed.

Candace began praying again, fell on her knees, and cried out in the name of Jesus. The armor and loose weaponry around the room began to shake, then in rapid succession flew toward the door.

With three chops of his sword, the door was cut free of the hinges. Navarro speared the thick wood and pulled it away from the door frame.

"Move aside!" he called to the warriors on the other side as weapons and armor skidded into the room. "The light from the fire should be enough to see by," he said, turning to fight along side Kelt. Both tried desperately not to be distracted by flying armor and blades.

The monsters vastly outnumbered the men but came in more warily, slowing the feverish pace of fighting. To Navarro's delight, the longer the moments passed, the greater his troupe became as warriors poured out of their prison, armed and with an eager fire in their eyes. Blades clashed, the perimeter widened, and the tide of battle slowly began to ebb in the warriors' direction.

But from the corner of his eye, Navarro spotted two huge dark shapes eclipse the caved in wall.

The others spotted them as well.

"Giants!"

* * * * *

"Next ones, lead in!" Zakili commanded as his whirling blades, the Flying Tigers, carved, parried, and dropped monsters on every side. The walkway was only four shoulder-widths across, so he rotated his warriors against the monsters. The prowess of his lightweight elves enabled them to hold their ground against the brutal, undisciplined assault of the horde's soldiers. The elves slowly gave ground against the constant onslaught, but the goblin and masnevire corpses began to litter the walkway. The brutes had to trudge over the fallen to get to the elves. One elf had been taken down in battle thus far and was carried behind the line of battle. He was alive but bleeding badly, and the elves off-rotations set about binding his wounds.

At one point a pair of giants trudged out into the courtyard, looking up and observing the battle. They laughed at the doomed elves as the monsters continued to stream at them.

But Zakili thanked Navarro's God the giants didn't join in the battle and toss chunks of the battered tower at them. They were obviously too amused to bother.

As for the dead brutes tossed into the courtyard, the giants just shrugged.

"There is more where they came from," one giant boomed. Both laughed, and bored with the battle, soon walked off.

Another elf went down.

"Get him back!" the Prince ordered, and two elves dragged him away while two more elves rushed to join in the fray.

"How much longer can we keep this up?" Jorab asked, parrying away the jab of a masnevire spear.

320

Johnny Earl Jones

"As long as it takes to clear these things out of the fortress!" Zakili said, and his daggers became a blur and metal scraped metal as the blades parried away sword and spear and lunged in to find throats and guts. Brutes clutched at sudden, mortal wounds. One masnevire sent its sword lopping across wildly. Zakili ducked, jabbed the brute in the ribs, and using the momentum of the swing, pushed it over a parapet.

"The goblin stream seems endless," one elf cried, but those words only added to the Prince's frenzy. He heard a painful yell to the side. Another elf had gone down.

"Lord, we need you now!" Baliesto screamed to the heavens. He parried a sword jab and countered with a jab of his own, piercing the masnevire's hairy arm.

Zakili roared and rushed the monsters, his daggers sweeping left and right, cutting arms and slicing exposed necks and ribs. He dropped monsters right and left, but his kills seemed futile. A fresh monster arose to replace every downed one. The horde pressed in harder, seeing they were beginning to tire the valiant elves.

A goblin rampaged in, his spear thrusting straight for Zakili's heart. With a double chop of his daggers, he batted the spear to the floor. But before he could slip in and finish the beast, the goblin straightened suddenly and fell over the parapet to the courtyard below.

A sharp whistling noise sounded through the chaos. Another monster fell dead. Several more whistles cut the air. Then like a sudden epidemic, the monsters closest to the elves began to collapse. More sharp, short whistles and dull thuds sounded followed by the collapse of one monster, then another, and another.

"That's why you sent a lightning arrow into the night sky earlier," Baliesto said to Zakili, smiling. He turned his eyes heavenward. "Thank you, Lord!"

More whistles cut the air. More brutes were cut down.

"The elves from Recqueom!" Jorab cried ecstatically.

"Victory is ours!" Zakili cried. "Did any of you doubt?"

* * * * *

Navarro sprinted near to the wall, closing on the gigantic shadows as the warriors eager for battle filed out. The giants pushed into the room, one wielding a tree trunk club, the other picking up a chunk of collapsed wall. The giant heaved his arm back, taking aim with the colossal brick.

The Paladin understood the great danger of a giant's incredible aim. If the giant started launching those chunks, many warriors would be crushed. The Paladin whipped the bow off his shoulders, over his head, and tore free one of his two remaining arrows. He fired the missile and it pierced the wrist of the giant's throwing hand. The behemoth roared in agony and dropped the chunk.

But to The Paladin's amazement, the bricks stop in midair and hurtled at the back of the other giant. Navarro turned, seeing Candace praying hard. "That's my girl!"

The hit knocked the giant stumbling forward, inadvertently crushing a few of his lessers under his huge boots. He righted himself easily enough, his eyes angrily slits as he turned. He swung his massive club and smashed the other giant's jaw, sending it crashing to the ground. With glassy eyes, the fallen giant stared up at his companion, spitting teeth and cursing. He yanked his own huge club from his belt and swiped at the standing giant's legs.

Navarro glanced over and briefly observed the confusion. The quick tempers of the giants would be their own undoing. He watched the heated exchange between the two behemoths, the glassy-eyed giant screaming that it didn't throw the boulder. There would be no better time to strike the giants. Navarro notched his arrow, took aim and fired, the arrow plunging into the giant's wide mouth and lodging deep into the back of his throat. The giant fell away, clutching his neck.

A mob of masnevires rushed The Paladin from the side. Navarro yanked a throwing axe from the wall and tossed it, eliminating one. Then he clashed with them. His sword sliced in low, but was deftly blocked by a masnevire blade. But with the weapon down low and with a slight shift of his feet, Navarro snapped his heel into the brute's chest and sent it stumbling backward. A blade came in high at Navarro, but he ducked, and Invinitor lashed out, cutting the life out of the sword-wielder. He spun again, sword hacking through another monster's polearm weapon and beyond, severing its wolf head.

"Kill the warmbloods!" the remaining giant roared. From behind him scurried in the thick, armored cave ravagers who pierced through the mobs and went straight for the warriors.

"This isn't good," The Paladin decided, diving back into the thick of the battle. "Concentrate on the goblins and masnevires," he cried, "and be wary of the ravagers. There's not many, but they're hard to kill!"

He sided with the group closest to him and went straight for the attacking ravagers. Three armored insectiods ganged up on these warriors. With the swipe of one clawed hand, a ravager knocked a warrior sprawling to the ground. Navarro dashed forward, his sword chopping down on its thick arm, but the blade simply bounced off the stubborn, insectoid armor.

The ravager swiped out at him, but The Paladin dropped under the attack then he lurched, his blade cutting across its bulbous insect eye. The creature roared in pain and rage, its thick arm swinging wildly, but Navarro ducked and Invinitor's point dove hard, piercing through its exoskeleton and into its heart. On came the next one, and Navarro was ready.

"Go for the eyes!" Navarro said.

The fighting grew more vicious as the armies evened out, the warriors biting into the horde's numbers. Battle lines between armies blurred, especially when the brutes began to turn on each other.

Navarro took full advantage of the confusion, navigating through frays to exterminate the handful of ravagers running loose. Then there was the giant, barking out orders and a greater menace as it advanced, swinging its club and batting warriors against the wall.

Jamming Invinitor back in its scabbard, Navarro pulled loose an arrow protruding from a monster corpse and raced around the giant. He notched the shaft and sent it flying into the behemoth's shoulder blade.

"Over here!" Navarro yelled, daring the monster his direction. "Do you think you can triumph over a single warmblood?"

"Metorok has waited years to grind yer kind on me back teeth!" the giant said, stomping in his direction.

Navarro raced for the colossal hole in the wall, not quite sure how he'd stop this formidable giant. His paramount concern was pulling the behemoth away from the fight. With all the warriors engaged in battle, this giant could simply stomp in and crush the men at will if not halted now.

In full sprint, Navarro leaped over a chunk of fallen wall and continued racing into the wide courtyard. The giant burst through the caved-in wall, bounding onto the grassy grounds where Navarro stood defiantly. Unnerved, the behemoth stopped and eyed the man. The Paladin flashed a victorious smile. He had diverted this dangerous giant away from Kelt's warriors.

"Do you fear, not-so-mighty giant," The Paladin taunted.

"Fear ye, puny warmblood? Ha!"

"Then why do I stand and you do nothing about it?"

"Ye have made yer last mistake!" Metorok roared, surging in and slamming his massive club down at The Paladin. The heavy weapon pounded into the earth, but Navarro was no longer there. He dove forward, rolling on one shoulder between the behemoth's legs and came back to his feet behind the giant. His sword whipped across, slicing open the back of the monster's knee.

Screaming, the giant hobbled around, launching his club in a sidelong swipe. Navarro dropped and flattened to the ground, and the dangerous club swept close. The Paladin felt the gust of the speeding weapon. He leapt up immediately, sword in hand, and chopped at the giant's trailing arm, stinging his wrist.

"Ye shall be ripped apart bit by bit fer that!" the giant roared. His club dropped fast at The Paladin, forcing him to leap off to the side.

Navarro heard the fighting in the armory grow more intense, monsters hooting and roaring ferociously. The giant's last strike against Kelt's warriors renewed the ravenous brutes' fervor and energized them to battle harder. Navarro knew he had to destroy this giant quickly. The behemoth's presence alone motivated the brutes. That feat was easier said then done, for thus far he struggled to get past the furious giant's defenses. Metorok stomped in, swatting his club across. The Paladin back-flipped out of range. Gaining his footing, Navarro flipped his mighty sword in the air, caught it by the blade, and turned to the giant, taking his mark.

"I know you can swing your club well, and I've heard your kind can throw boulders with some measure of accuracy. But how good are you at catching?" Navarro launched his sword, looping it hilt over blade. "Lord, guide my blade like you guided David's stone against Goliath."

The giant heaved back his club for another strike and stared evilly at The Paladin. Suddenly, he noticed in the darkness the blade twirling straight at him. He tried to block. It was too late. The blade dove straight between his eyes and drove through his thick skull. The behemoth jerked and became suddenly still. Slowly, like a chopped tree, the behemoth swayed, focusing a hateful stare on The Paladin for one last moment before his eyes rolled back into his head. He toppled over, falling, falling, and finally crashing down onto his back, quite dead. The reverberation of the crash sounded like an ominous death knell to the monsters inside.

Navarro noticed a band of lithe shapes rush his direction from the dark courtyard. The elves had come! He yanked Invinitor from the giant's skull and waved them on, leading them through the caved-in wall and into the battle. The elves who still had arrows fired feverishly, raining down destruction on the brutes. The others drew their blades and joined in the melee, following The Paladin's charge.

The battle was on!

* 24 *
AGAINST THE FACE OF DEATH

"Behind you, Paladin!" a voice warn, but Navarro had already sensed the brute charging from his blind side. He feigned a slice toward the masnevire who had him locked in combat. The brute reacted with a wild swing, meant to knock away his attack, but The Paladin's sword wasn't there. The force of the brute's swing carried his blade too far. He couldn't parry the true attack as Invinitor jabbed in, penetrating armor and piercing deep into the brute's ribcage, collapsing a lung.

Navarro spun, fading a step away and arching backward, barely evading a spear thrust by the charging goblin he'd sensed behind him. The speeding goblin tripped over Navarro's leg and stumbled past. Invinitor slashed across and took that one's life.

"The fury of these creatures hasn't diminished even with my army now free to fight!" Kelt yelled to The Paladin as the two warriors fought through the fray, nearly standing side by side. "They usually turn coward when the odds begin to even up."

"It's frightening," Navarro admitted, parrying away a masnevire's sword thrust. "It reminds me of the prowess of the brutes we battled in Sheliavon."

"Candace dreamed several weeks ago that she was pursued by The Dark Sorcerer," Kelt said. "Her dreams have proved to be prophetic throughout the years. I fear the sorcerer is still alive and may be possessing these creatures now."

Navarro found a crease in his opponent's defenses and drove his sword forward, the blade diving into a masnevire's chest up to the sword's hilt. He yanked Invinitor free and kicked the wicked beast away. "The Sorcerer's not possessing these monsters," he said. "At least, not yet."

"What do you mean?" Kelt asked, after he downed a charging goblin.

"Zakili and I happened upon a clan of giants who lay wait in the pummeled town of Lunumdra. While dueling with one, it inadvertently revealed the monster army was not being led by The Sorcerer, but by a different creature." He ducked a vicious chop from a goblin and drove his sword into the rampaging brute's gut. "However, The Dark Sorcerer is coming."

"How can you know such a thing?" Kelt demanded, his sword piercing his wily goblin opponent. "How do you know he's alive?"

"I've seen him in a not so distant forest. He nearly destroyed me there. He's alive."

Navarro saw Kelt's shoulders droop. "I was hoping what Candace dreamt was only a nightmare, nothing more. How dreadful to think something that evil still exists."

"Lift up your head, Baron Veldercrantz! He's still alive, but so are we! And I won't go down to a pack of stinkin' monsters!" Navarro drove forward, Kelt taking his flank, and a number of Kelt's warriors and some elves formed a wedge. Together they cut into the bulging throng of monsters.

"Rotate!" Navarro ordered every several minutes from his position at the point of the wedge. He tried to keep fresh warriors on the edges of the formation while the wounded were carried back, and the others rested briefly for their next rotation.

Masnevires and goblins fell by the dozens, although ferocious, they couldn't overcome the coordinated attacks of the men and elves, nor, in the chaotic fighting establish a unified formation of their own.

Roars, war cries, the ringing of swords resounded all around them. Navarro's wedge continued to advance, cutting into the swarming monster army like an axehead driving through new wood. They left a wake of destruction behind, but not without cost. His contingent, though extremely effective, was small. Every hit they took brought down a much-needed warrior.

Navarro knew his formation couldn't hold much longer. He was losing too many fighters, several slain at the end of a monster's blade. Others were too injured to fight on. Although stung by a few glancing hits, The Paladin turned back many of the wounded who desired to keep fighting even if it cost their lives. He wouldn't permit it and asked Kelt to have the wounded help other wounded away from the raging battle.

"The moral of these brutes should've been broken by now," Kelt told Navarro. "What's driving them?"

Before Navarro could respond, the ground collapsed underneath the baron and he fell waist deep into a crater. Navarro rushed for him immediately, grabbed his hand and yanked him up.

A wide claw burst from the ground and grabbed hold of Kelt's knee. Relentlessly, it pulled downward, crumbling the baron to the ground. Navarro hacked at the thick forearm with his sword but to no avail. The blade couldn't penetrate the creature's armored skin. The hand continued to pull on Kelt, who was forced onto his side, the hand descending through the ground.

"It's going to snap my leg!" Kelt yelled.

Quickly, Navarro evaluated where the subterranean cave ravager's head might be and jammed his sword into the earth. A hideous cry later, the hand released and quickly descended. One of Kelt's elite guards helped his liege to his feet.

"Can you fight on?" Navarro asked, noting the baron's wounded leg.

"I will fight on!"

The wedge marched forward.

Along the eastern horizon, the sky around the mountain peaks began to grow pink and orange. The morning was dawning, renewing the hope of the fighting men. Still the monsters didn't relent. They collided against the warriors insanely, recklessly, crushing small pockets of the defenders' resistance with their sheer number.

Navarro had fought in enough battles to understand these evil brutes wouldn't continue to fight in a battle they couldn't win. The field commanders, the giants, had been slain, leaving them with no leaders. Only the underling invaders remained, and although they outnumbered the men and elves, they fell swiftly to the push of the defenders. Without a commander to force them to continue, their self-preservation instincts would have each providing for his own survival. But they fought on.

Something was out there still commanding them. But who?

In his peripheral vision, Navarro noticed the downward chop of a battle axe and reacted quickly, Invinitor slicing up in a tight arc and severing the axehead. He reversed directions quickly, his elbow flying high and slamming the attacking masnevire in his wolf nose, briefly stunning him. Navarro's blade thrust forward, ending his wicked life.

"Two more giants have separated from the forest!" a warrior cried.

"More field commanders," Navarro said dreadfully to Kelt. "With the fighting already fierce, I don't think these warriors can hold up under the burden of such imposing foes."

"What do you propose?"

"Are you able to lead this contingent?" Navarro asked, nodding at Kelt's injured leg, his sword lashing out and taking the life of a wildly charging goblin.

"That's just a flesh wound. I've led these warriors for years. I'm not going to let a few scrapes stop me now."

"Good. I'm going to break away and engage those giants." The ground burst apart under Navarro's feet, but he deftly leapt to the side and thrust his blade into the earth. An otherworldly dying scream resonated from the ground then went silent.

"Two giants are more than a match for any man."

"They might be, but I've got to distract them before they move in and start slaughtering our already overwhelmed fighters."

"You can't go taking all the big kills for yourself!" a voice called from across the courtyard. He glanced over and saw Zakili leading a troupe of warriors. A smile broadened Navarro's face.

"And I'm not staying behind while you take on that danger," another voice cried over the battle. Parrying away a high sword attack, then reversing his blade and thrusting it into a brute's heart, The Paladin turned. Candace worked her way toward him from another battling contingent of men and elves. His smile grew even wider.

A distant scream caught Navarro's attention, and he looked in time to see a warrior hurtling through the sky. Tracing the man's flight with his eyes, he spotted the two giants. They'd just pushed through the collapsed outer wall. One behemoth guffawed and pointed to the dark stain on his massive club. The other, with a club of its own, sent his weapon into motion, swiping into a jumble of fighting men and monsters. As the men tried to flee, the giants swatted two warriors flying into the air. The goblins and masnevires capitalized on the chaos and took down several men whose attention was divided between the giants and the horde.

"We have to stop the giants! They will turn the tide of this battle if we don't cut them down now!"

"Let's start chopping!" Zakili said.

Navarro slashed furiously into the throng, felling monsters left and right.

Zakili, even though in close melee, began launching lightning arrows with painstaking accuracy so as not to shoot down men or elves. The warriors wisely cleared away once the streaking arrows began to fly, allowing Zakili freedom to mow the brutes down at will. He blazed a path first toward Candace, then back toward Navarro, who was already cutting a swath in the giant's direction.

Several more screams echoed from the direction of the club-wielding behemoths and Navarro spotted another hurtling warrior.

"Lord, every moment we're stalled by these brutes, more men and elves will perish," Navarro prayed as he cut methodically through the wicked throng. "Christ Jesus, we need Your help. We need You to get us to those behemoths quickly."

The battle raged on.

"The reinforcements have arrived," Zakili said and blasted his way to his friend's side. Candace took up his other flank.

"Let's blaze a trail!" The Paladin roared, Invinitor slashing and jabbing. Streaking arrows rocketed from Zakili's bow. Candace alternated between her sword and prayer that the slain monsters' weapons hurl into the attacking brutes.

Another dying scream, then another, pierced Navarro's heart. The giants were picking off the men! "Lord, thank You for the help, but this is not fast enough."

A loud crumbling sound echoed through the courtyard ahead. Curious, The Paladin tried to look, but the battle raged too fierce around him in a flood of goblins and masnevires. A spear jabbed in. Invinitor chopped it in half. Navarro lashed back across in time to swat away a sword strike. His blade twirled once in his hand, and he thrust it forward, taking that brute in the gut. More goblins stepped up to take its place. His blade went into a flurry, slashing across, parrying, thrusting and slashing some more. Fortunately for him, the brutes were packed in so tight, their numbers hindered them from fleeing or backing from many of his attacks, leaving many a dead or dying monster falling in his wake.

Ahead he noticed more monsters, some standing on what he thought, at first, was a small hillock in the courtyard. "Vicious monsters on higher ground will not bode well for us," The Paladin knew.

The cry of another dying warrior wrenched a frustrated roar out of Navarro. The Paladin saw a sea of monsters between him and the giants who continued to pommel the warriors. "Lord Jesus, make a way!"

"We're getting close to where I brought down that turret on a mob of masnevires," Zakili said.

Now the paladin understood how the goblins had gained high ground. They were standing on the remains of the turret which had fallen into the courtyard. With bows in hand, the brutes notched arrows and began firing at the friends.

Zakili fired a lightning arrow, knocking one missile out of the air while Candace ducked, allowing the arrow to fly past and slam into a monster trailing her. Navarro's blade whipped across twice, batting the arrows into the dirt. Several monsters cried out, pierced by errant shots.

The mighty crumbling and cracking sound echoed through the courtyard again.

Zakili fired, downing one goblin before it could replace its spent arrow. Navarro slashed into a wild-eyed masnevire and prepared to charge the goblin archers, but his senses warned him to stay back. The goblins placed their arrows on their bows and pulled back in unison, each smiling wickedly. They never noticed their doom.

A huge slab of the castle wall caved in at the base, the sturdiness of the bulkhead compromised by the turret which collapsed upon it earlier. A section broke loose and dropped into the courtyard just as the goblin archers took aim. It crushed those brutes, as well as a gang of adjacent monsters.

"Thank you, Lord!" Navarro praised, leaping onto the fallen stone even before the dust settled and raced toward the giants.

Zakili glanced over to Candace. "Hey, he's going to try to take all the fun!" Off the two companions raced after him.

The fallen section of wall wasn't huge, only about thirty feet, but The Paladin cleared it in seconds and drove into the confused mob on the other side. His sword jabbed and sliced into wicked brutes, Invinitor's keen blade ending monster lives with every slash, often decapitating them or piercing vital organs. But Navarro noticed he was still a considerable distance from the dangerous giants.

A streak of energy flew past him and blew a masnevire off to the side. A spearhead twirled through the air and caught a goblin full in the face. His companions were back at his side, Navarro knew, but heard another anguished dying cry. The limp figure of a warrior spun into the air. Navarro's rage turned fully on the two behemoths.

With a quick, determined prayer, Navarro drove into the horde. One foolish masnevire shield-rushed him, but Invinitor drove through the shield, the brute's forearm, and into his chest. The Paladin slammed into him shoulder-first, knocking the dying beast off to the side, but was quickly met by the swing of a spiked club. His sword lashed back with the flat of the blade leading, his weapon colliding against the club and halting its dangerous arc. Navarro's foot snapped out, catching that goblin in the gut. But before the brute could catch his breath, Invinitor had cleaved his clavicle in half.

A goblin to the side went flying back into the throng, his chest alive with fire. "Good shot, Zakili!"

"There's more where that came from!"

A sword hacked at Navarro's hip. Invinitor chopped down swiftly, severing the blade. Invinitor punched out and drove through that brute's heart. The Paladin slashed across in a backhanded swing, taking out a bold masnevire sword-wielder.

The ringing of blades on either side and to the rear told him his friends tore into the throng's numbers as well. Candace with her cutlass and Zakili with his powerful bow.

"We're drawing closer," Navarro cried.

"Closer to bigger danger," Zakili said. "I like the way you think, Paladin!"

Navarro couldn't help but smile. Coming from Zakili, that was a compliment.

"Eprercto eathero finise!" a giant thundered.

Invinitor slashed across, taking down another brute. His blade jabbed forward and toppled a tall masnevire. Navarro drove forward but the throng fled from him, leaving his path to the giants clear. The booming command he heard must have ordered the monsters to clear away from the bold challengers.

"You don't know the mistake you just made," Navarro said under his breath.

"Ye fleas are workin' yer way to get at us?" the haughty giant asked, laughing. "Ye indeed are some bold ones. All others run from us. But ye have come to stare yer deaths right 'n the face!"

"How are we going to do this?" the elf asked.

"I'll take the big-mouth. You and Candace take the other."

"Hey!" the elf complained. "Why do I have to share mine?"

One giant stomped forward, its club arcing overhead.

Navarro spun aside, and the club rocked the earth were he'd been. Navarro sprinted at the giant. Keeping the club in sight as he rushed, Navarro became suddenly aware this was no ignorant brute. The club was not overly thick and bulky like most giant clubs. Instead its girth was barely wider than Navarro's waist. For a monster double The Paladin's size, this was thin. The creature could strike and withdraw quickly. There was no opportunity for a quick attack like Navarro had planned, the club swung sidelong for him again. Unable to change his direction quickly enough, he hurdled over the speeding club. Airborne, he cringed at the damage the club would have made if it connected. The Paladin landed lightly, his charge not slowed a bit.

This time the giant couldn't react in time to interrupt the attack. Invinitor lashed out and dove into the giant's leg, slicing through thick leather boots and biting into his calf. The giant had already started stepping back though, or Invinitor would've caused more damage. The club chopped down viciously. Navarro spun to the side, and barely missed being crushed. The Paladin charged back in, but sensed danger from behind and swiftly darted away again. The ground exploded in a fiery eruption where he'd just stood.

"What was that!" Navarro demanded. Glancing back, he saw a shape speed through the sky above him, tall, burly, reptilian, and with the head of a spider. Its membranous wings rocketed it high into the air and it wheeled about to make another pass.

His senses tingled again, and he leaped head first as a club chopped down, slamming an indention in the ground where he'd been just a second ago.

Quickly rolling to his feet, Navarro spotted the four-armed flying monster speeding his direction. One of the creature's arms wound back to throw a ball of flames it held in one hand. The giant stepped in at him from the other side, his club speeding forward in a mighty, two-handed swing.

* * * * *

Zakili and Candace weren't doing much better. The other giant, wielding a huge shield had blocked most of the elf's lightning arrows. Only a few slipped through his defenses and blasted his tough hide. The behemoth used his shield well to block the attacks and any charges by the friends. His club beat down repeatedly at the warrior and kept them from getting too close. More dangerous, masnevires and goblins swept at the friends from behind. The elf had to turn away several times to pick off brutes who attempted a craven charge at their backs.

Spinning back around again, Zakili let loose another lightning arrow which, of course, the giant deflected with his huge shield. But the impact knocked him back a step. Candace pulled a dagger from the hilt of a downed masnevire, flipped it in the air once, caught it by the blade, and tossed it at the giant. The blade lodged into the giant's bare thigh. With the swat of his hand, he knocked the dagger away, drawing a thin line of black blood.

"That is but a sting, ye little gnat," the giant roared, unleashing his thick club. Candace anticipated the attack and sprang quickly out of the way, leaving the weapon nothing but earth. The behemoth turned to the waiting horde. "Destroy them!"

Ravenous, bloodthirsty cries filled the air as the goblins and masnevires charged, waving swords and leading with spears.

"Candace, it looks like the giant is yours. I've got a mob of uglies to keep off our back!" Zakili cried back to her, pulling back on his bowstring rapidly, unleashing lightning arrow after lightning arrow. Strategically, the elf cut down the leading spear-runners first. Undaunted by the swarming mob, he fired again and again. With the lead monsters going down, the throng slowed slightly as the brutes tripped over dead bodies or tangled their legs in the spears of the fallen. Zakili fired his inexhaustible supply of energy arrows again and again, taking down a monster with every shot, but the mob continued to make slow progress. "Things could get interesting real soon!" he warned.

Candace stopped and, to the giant's amazement, prayed. Seeing such an easy target, the behemoth raised his club high to finish her. Just as his club descended, he pulled back suddenly and ducked behind his huge shield as spears and swords hurled forward and pelted his shield.

"Ye witch!" the brute roared. "I will crush ye!" The giant swiped across low.

Sprinting forward, Candace raced toward the giant and dove. Barely missed by the club, her legs were clipped by the giant's forearm. She tumbled to the ground, landing painfully on her shoulder. Looking up, she saw the yellow teeth of the giant's wicked grin as he raised one huge boot to stomp her.

* * * * *

Furiously, Zakili fired off lightning arrow after lightning arrow. One monster then another was pounded by the missiles, sending them flying back into the press, but the mob surged stubbornly forward. He was losing too much ground. The brutes were coming in from all three sides, and with the giant at his back, they would

331

be upon the friends soon enough.

A spear soared through the air, heading his direction. Zakili lifted his bow and pulled back the string and fired. A lightning arrow rocketed forward and blasted it out of the sky, spraying smoking splinters everywhere. Another spear took flight. Turning, the elf pulled back again and fired. The brutes charged from all sides. Zakili knew there was no possibility of shooting them all down, but he knew if he didn't hold them back, they would sweep over Candace then Navarro next, and the heart of resistance would be crushed! "It looks like doom may be about to fall on us," he admitted. "But now is as good of a time as any to put Navarro's claims to the test. If this Jesus Christ he worships is real, I want to see Him pull hope out of hopelessness!"

With wild fury in his eyes, he stared at the charging brutes. "Give me a shovel, I'll dig my own grave!"

* * * * *

With the usurper swooping in from one side and the giant's club sweeping across from the other, Navarro's situation seemed hopeless.

"Lord Jesus, You are my hope," Navarro proclaimed confidently. With barely a second to consider his move, he reacted, dashing toward the speeding club. The giant laughed. The club came in to splatter his midsection. With his running start, Navarro's leap catapulted him over the speeding club!

He landed in a shoulder roll and tumbled back to his feet. Turning swiftly toward the diving usurper, he only had time to instinctively send his sword slashing across as a black fireball hurtled at him. His blade hacked into the sorcery, but the power of the sorcery slammed hard into the sword and knocked The Paladin on his back.

Quickly, regaining his composure, he realized he didn't hear an explosion from the diverted magic. The Paladin glanced about, fearing he would struggle against sorcery similar to that the Dark Sorcerer used.

He saw nothing.

The tremendous boom of a collision had him ducking reflexively, but he turned in the direction of the sound to see the usurper knocked away by the swing of the giant's club. The weapon unintentionally slammed the demonspawn, who had gotten too close.

The usurper flapped his wings furiously, stopping his backward momentum and shrieked at the muscular behemoth. After roaring a mystical sentence, a sphere of black flame burst to life in his taloned hand. The usurper pitched the flaming sphere at the giant, blasting him in the shoulder and sending it stumbling backward.

"Evil shall destroy the wicked," Navarro said, recalling a verse from the Book of Proverbs. "These nefarious beasts will trade blow for blow with anyone no matter ally or enemy."

With the sound of the battling behemoths in his ears, he turned to his friends. They were in trouble! He sprinted in their direction, his mind racing. How could they overcome these tremendous odds?

"Christ help us!"

Two masnevires rushed up to intercept him, polearms leveled. Invinitor slashed across then back, clipping the long weapons in half. The Paladin didn't slow his stride. His blade chopped viciously into one monster, then reversed angles and cut down the other.

* * * * *

The huge woolly boot came above her head. Pieces of crushed skulls were embedded in the soles, promising death. The giant's foot stomped down. Thinking quickly, Candace thrust her cutlass into the top of the other foot. Using that as leverage, she pulled herself out of harm's way. The booted foot slammed down, pounding a deep, harmless impression in the earth. Withdrawing her weapon, she fled.

Candace heard the elf's furious cry behind her and knew he was in a dire situation. Seeing fallen monsters strewn about the battlefield, she prayed ardently. Just as the giant took a huge stride toward her, a barrage of spears and swords bolted from the ground and hurled at the behemoth. Defensively, the giant lurched away, swinging its massive club to ward off the dangerous torrent--just as she had hoped.

She spun in Zakili's direction, gasping at the innumerable horde rampaging toward her and the Elf Prince.

Although Zakili was firing his lightning arrows with abandon, taking down brutes on every side, she saw there was no way to hold back the flood. He would be overrun in moments! She had to help.

Noticing the dozens upon dozens of slain monsters the horde was clambering over, she focused her eyes and her prayers on the dead ones' weapons. "...Lord, let their own evil destroy these wicked ones!"

Zakili, breathing hard and firing his missiles into the mob like a wild man, heard the sharp and metallic singing of weapons emanate from the mob. Continuing to shoot repeatedly, he braced himself, unsure of what these monsters would unleash next.

"Please, do it now, Lord!" Candace roared to the heavens.

The ringing of weapons, a whoosh of air, and the anguished cries of scores of monsters filled the air as dozens of unmanned weapons sprang from the ground. The entire front line of the rushing throng collapsed, tumbling to the ground as the lead monsters were slain. The surging brutes slowed almost to a stop. Mounds of bodies littered the ground. *The victory might be short-lived,* the elf knew, *but it bought the friends some more time.*

"Good job, girl!" Zakili roared, shooting off a few more lightning arrows before turning to praise her. "The whole front line is destroyed!"

When he turned an approving smile her way, his face blanched in horror.

"Behind you, Candace!" the elf screamed.

Navarro raced toward her, pointing and yelling. As Candace turned, she saw a huge club speed at her low and from behind. In desperation, she sprang, trying to back-somersault over the giant club.

"Candace!" Navarro and Zakili cried.

The huge weapon slammed into her legs and back, and Candace screamed. She spiraled awkwardly through the air and landed in a heap a short distance away.

"Noooo!" Navarro roared, wanting with all his soul to go straight to Candace, but the giant turned to him. The Paladin's eyes blurred with pained tears. His heart ached as if pierced with a dagger. He could barely swallow past the terrified lump in his throat. "Lord, please don't let Candace die! Don't let her die!"

With tears streaming down his cheeks, he charged the giant.

"More hittin' practice," the giant laughed, swinging his club in low as if to bat The Paladin into the sky.

Navarro didn't slow. In his rage, he unleashed Invinitor, the blade chopping down mightily and severing the huge club as it came in at him. The giant stared in disbelief.

But to The Paladin's dismay, the blade quivered violently, black energy sparking and dancing about the blade. "The usurper's sorcery has infected the sword!" Navarro growled.

His pace took him close to the giant. He held onto the hilt tighter. The behemoth lifted a foot to stomp him, but Invinitor lashed across in a swift arc into the other leg, chopping through the giant's woolly leather boot and then through his tough flesh, all the way to the massive bone.

The giant's other foot slammed down for support—rather than to crush The Paladin. With a pained scream thundering from his throat, the behemoth's hand slapped down swiftly at The Paladin. "I will crush ye!"

Mighty Invinitor lashed out, sending disembodied fingers flying onto the battlefield. Another thunderous scream assaulted Navarro's ears, and the giant stumbled back. The sword quaked viciously, the black energy sparking again.

Navarro glanced Candace's way. She lay motionless. He had to get to her.

* * * * *

The masnevires and goblins streamed in, the barricade of dead monsters not holding them for long.

"Do you smell victory, you stinkin' dogs?" Zakili roared. "Do you smell the end? It is your own doom you sense, not ours!"

The elf shouldered his bow, and his twin daggers leaped into his hands as the monsters stormed in at him. His daggers, the Flying Tigers, whipped across, slashing and cutting and taking down brutes on every side. He took several minor hits, but the monsters could hardly keep up. How much longer? he wondered. His strength was waning and he was bleeding from a dozen wounds. One thought of Candace flipping through the sky dismissed those hopeless thoughts. He and Navarro were the only ones who could help. Kelt and the other fighters were still engaged with the horde, unable to aid her. But surrounded by a swarm of monsters, how could he get to her? He roared and slashed out again and again.

* * * * *

Heaving back his half-club, the wild-eyed giant stared down at Navarro. The giant swung his arm forward, but Navarro sprung to the side. The throw was just a balk to make The Paladin wary. The giant laughed.

Navarro didn't think it was funny. Candace lay dying not far away. His heart felt torn in two. All the years he lived as a godless sailor, conquering women at every port, he hadn't considered their emotions. He had no standards. He didn't know love; he knew only how to fulfill his lusts. But when the Lord saved him, he chose to abstain from female relationships for fear of being drawn back into that old sin. But Candace, a woman having moral fiber and a strong relationship with Jesus, inadvertently captured his heart and filled his sensibilities with emotions he'd never experienced before.

Now she lay still on the ground after the horrible strike of this evil giant. She needed him, but the behemoth stood as an obstacle.

The giant heaved the club back again, and tossed it. Navarro grabbed his gleaming sword like a javelin, rushed forward several steps, and though the massive club spun straight at him, he launched his weapon. He dove for the ground and barely escaped the missile which spiraled close to his skull.

Navarro jumped back to his feet immediately. Invinitor pierced into the giant's chest. The blade buried all the way to the hilt. A mighty, muffled explosion boomed inside the giant, the behemoth's chest ballooning suddenly then smoking. The huge giant roared, but only smoke rolled out his mouth. The giant's eyes rolled back in his head and he toppled over.

Wasting no time, The Paladin leaped on the dead giant and yanked his sword free. The blade was unscathed, and no longer vibrating violently. "Invinitor wasn't affected by the usurper's sorcery," Navarro rejoiced. "It consumed it and then unleashed that sorcery into the giant, destroying him!"

Navarro looked to Candace, then to Zakili who fought for his life against a flood of monsters. *Which friend should he save?*

"Go to her!" Zakili cried, answering The Paladin's thoughts. "These brutes picked a fight with me. I'm taking 'em down. Go!"

In the background, he could still hear the colossal battle between the usurper and the giant. Navarro turned and dashed toward Candace. Invinitor carved a swath of carnage through those brutes fooling enough to get in his way.

"Give me a shovel, I'll dig my own grave!" the two friends heard from behind them.

"Hey, that's my war cry!" Zakili protested. He turned slightly to see dozens of white stallions charging through the breach in the fortress' wall, an elven archer on each one, Saranisen and her older sisters leading the way! Scores of dull thuds strummed the air and arrows rained down on the brutes, dropping masnevires and goblins dozens at a time.

"I thought I told you, you couldn't come!" Zakili argued as he cut down advancing monsters. "It's too dangerous out here!"

"I guess I have too much of my older brother in me!" Saranisen answered.

"Well, in that case. Give me a shovel, I'll dig my own grave!" Zakili roared throwing himself at the now scattering brutes.

Covered in his own blood and the black blood of the monsters, Navarro slashed his way to Candace's side, gently laying her crumbled form out so she was lying flat on her back. He could hear her singing weakly, her eyes closed.

"You are my strength, O Lord.
You are the hope I cling to.
I give my life to you.
As a living sacrifice for you.
O Lord, be pleased with who I am in Christ.
It's all I have to offer You."

"Candace. It is I, Navarro."

Slowly, her eyelids opened, and she stared at him with her piercing, crystal-blue eyes. "Navarro," she said, a huge smile spreading across her face. With a quivering hand, she slowly reached up and touched the side of his face. "I thought I would never... see you again," she said, then started to choke and gasp.

Navarro looked to her terrified, reaching to her. She quickly calmed and looked into his eyes. "I hear... the noise of battle. The elves and men are still in danger. Do not linger here with me, Navarro..."

"I can't leave you like this. I can heal you."

A fiery explosion then a tremendous crash boomed off to the side. The Paladin looked up and saw the usurper standing victoriously over the marred and blasted giant he had been fighting. He pointed at Navarro.

"Time to die, Paladin of Chrissst!"

A tear raced from the corner of Candace's eye. "They need you. They can't prevail without you. Win the day. Defeat this evil... for me."

Navarro's chin quivered and his eyes grew blurry with tears.

"Navarro," she said in a weak voice. "I love you."

Tears streamed down his face and dropped softly on her cheeks. Navarro stroked her hair gently, a confusion of whirling emotions and questions spinning through his mind, his soul torn. Her injuries severe, she was dying. He had the power to bring healing to her fading soul. But with battle raging all around him, and with the demonic usurper stalking forward menacingly, he had no time to remain.

"Please Lord," he prayed fervently. "Don't let death take her."

Pulling hesitantly away from her, he rose to his feet and looked the usurper in the eyes. He was the only one who could destroy this monstrosity. The usurper had absorbed several blows from the giant with little, if any, damage. He doubted anything the men or elves could do would stop it. He had to put an end to this demonspawn. If he didn't, the hope for all would be gone.

The usurper grinned wickedly. "Not even your God can help you now,

Paladin of Chrissst!"

Navarro stormed the usurper's direction. A masnevire rushed at him from the side. Invinitor whipped across, beheading the brute before it could initiate its first attack sequence.

"You're the one leading this horde," Navarro accused. "You're the one responsible for all this carnage."

The usurper laughed in its otherworldly, hissing voice. "I am a demonssspawn, you fool! It isss of my innermosssst exxxissstenccce to kill and dessstroy. But what you sssee here isss nothing compared to what isss about to be unleassshed on thisss world. "And you have no clue what isss about to be unleassshed on you!"

Springing into the air, the usurper soared at the paladin, its four mighty arms outstretched and talons bared.

Navarro stood his ground.

The usurper's mandibles opened, and its mouth gaped, unleashing a loud, piercing roar.

"Is that supposed to unnerve me?" The Paladin said, undaunted, his feelings beyond fear. Righteous indignation mingled with anguish over Candace dulled any anxieties.

The usurper swooped in, its wide hands swiping. Adroit Navarro dove into a roll, but claws shredded his armor and carved lines of blood down his shoulder. The Paladin growled away the pain and sprang up just as the demonspawn swept by. Invinitor lashed out and took several inches off his trailing tail.

Cursing, the usurper looped in the sky and wheeled back around, speeding at The Paladin. It roared a mystic sentence in its hellish language and black fires sprung to life in all four hands.

Navarro eyed the brute carefully, his sword spinning in his palm.

The usurper cocked one arm back then pitched one sphere of the black flames, the sorcery whizzing at Navarro with dizzying velocity. Then it threw another and another then the last.

The brutes nearest the battle cheered on their usurper commander.

Invinitor slashed across, ripping into the first sphere of flames, but the impact sent Navarro stumbling several steps to the side.

The second sphere spiraled directly for him. Navarro's sliced across again, the blade driving through the attack, the fires being consumed suddenly. But the impact pushed him back several steps and nearly dislocated his shoulder. Invinitor sparked and vibrated, and Navarro struggled to hold it tight.

The third zoomed down at him swiftly, but reacting out of pure warrior instinct, The Paladin's sword arced overhead and chopped down viciously, ripping into the sphere mere feet from his skull.

From the corner of his eye, he spotted the last one diving diagonally at him, and The Paladin had time only to hack across in a desperate single-armed backhand chop. His aim was true dissolving the black flames just as they were about to dive into his side. When the blade collided against the sorcery, Navarro heard a loud snap. A sharp jab of pain made him cry out. The sword fell from his hand, his grip too weak to hold it.

His arm had been yanked out of the socket.

The usurper rocketed at him.

Navarro snatched up his sword with his good hand, feeling its violent vibrations, black sparks electrifying and flying from his blade. This was ten times worse than the first time. The Paladin feared the weapon had absorbed so much of the sorcery that it might explode and shatter into dozens of deadly shards. But he had no time to worry. The usurper swooped in, two of its wide hands slashing.

With great determination, biting back the severe pain in his shoulder, Navarro drove Invinitor at the lead hand. As he dove away, the blade cleaved one talon off at the wrist. The other talons lashed, raking Navarro's back, ripping into his armor, and tearing through his skin. Navarro crashed onto his hurt shoulder. Waves of pain rolled down his arm and across his back. The agonizing intensity nearly made him nauseous.

The demonspawn swept past, its shrill scream piercing the air.

"Navarro!" cried several concerned warriors around the battlefield.

He pushed himself to his feet, hair drenched from perspiration, fresh blood oozing down his back, his face grim.

The usurper touched down a dozen yards away, igniting black flames in one talon, and touching it to his bleeding stump. The brute screeched in pain, then dissolved the fire, the flow of its black blood staunched.

From every area of the battlefield was the weight of watching eyes. Monsters and warriors alike stared at the colossal fray.

"Lord, you said in your Bible, if God is on my side, who can prevail against me," Navarro said with a weak laugh. "Your Word is about to be put to the test. It looks like the winner of this determines the victory of the battle."

The violent shaking of his sword sobered him.

Hissing, the usurper noticed it as well. "Your sssword may have been able to consssume the sssingle blow before and remain intact. But absssorbing the energy of four evil blassstsss isss going to ssshred your holy weapon to piecccesss!"

The terrible trembling and humming from the sword and the energetic black sparks erupting on the blade made The Paladin believe. The vibrations grew more violent. Invinitor would splinter soon. With his one good hand, he held on tightly, determined.

"You could not imagine what you are up againsssst, warmblood," the usurper sibilated. "The forcccesss of hell are risssing to razzze all godlinessss from the world. Your God will flee. And wickedness will reign forever.

And I will parade your corpse asss evidenccce of Chrissst'sss weaknesssss!"

Ignoring the violent vibrating of his sword, Navarro looked the hideous monster squarely in the face.

"I don't think you know who you are dealing with, Ugly One. You stand against a man empowered by Christ Jesus, the King of kings and the Lord of lords! And He alone shall reign forever and ever!"

The usurper shrieked in absolute rage at the proclamation, leaped into the air and rocketed at The Paladin. Navarro raced full speed at the usurper as jeers from the monsters filled his ears. But the warriors' cheers encouraged him and strengthened his weakening resolve.

This would be the final blow, The Paladin knew. One of them would perish!

The usurper soared at him, jaws open, talons outstretched, closing ground swiftly. Navarro didn't slow his pace toward the speeding demonspawn. With the usurper's jaws tearing and talons ripping, the two collided. Invinitor thrust.

Two taloned claws ripped into his side, shredding muscle and hooking a rib excruciatingly. Navarro felt Invinitor make impact, but the usurper slammed into The Paladin hard, taking him off his feet and sending him flying through the air. His grip on the sword was torn away, and he landed in a bouncing, tumbling heap across the ground, as the usurper passed over him. His eyes went black, agony screaming from his dislocated arm and his ripped side and back.

He heard a muffled explosion and wondered if the usurper had heaved and missed with a black fire spheres.

Slowly, painfully, The Paladin pushed himself up, weaponless and wary that the usurper would wheel about to strafe him again. This time he would be defenseless.

But a second later, a violent crash behind turned him. He saw the usurper tumble and slam into a gawking mob of brutes. They were bowled over and scattered by the violent impact.

Fearlessly, Navarro raced at the demonspawn, fighting against the tremendous pain of his savage wounds. The Paladin leaped on the fallen monster before he could arise, fist reared back to slam into the back of the usurper's skull, but...

His skull was gone! All that was left was a blackened stump that used to be his neck. But with the sound of battle all around Navarro, where was his weapon? He recalled the blade slammed between the creature's mandibles and apparently had struck into the usurper's gaping jaws. *Had the sorcery which had caused his sword to violently reverberate disintegrated his magnificent blade, destroying the usurper?   Was Invinitor, the indestructible one, no more? Had it disintegrated with the mighty usurper's skull?*

He had no time to mourn the tremendous loss of his blade. Candace needed him.

He turned to her, and started her way. But to his horror, a masnevire had discovered Candace lying helpless on the field. The brute's lips curled in a feral sneer as he lifted his spear overhead to run her through.

A metallic glimmer caught Navarro's eye, the first rays of morning light seeping over the mountains reflecting off a blade to his left. He grabbed it and recognized the majestic, glistening sword. "Invinitor!" he confirmed. "Still unscathed and still beyond destruction."

"Hey! Dogbreath!" Navarro yelled, turning the brute's head. "Catch!"

With a mighty throw, the sword looped through the air. Before the brute could understand its doom, the sword pierced his midsection and drove into his backbone.

Although the noise of battle was all around him, the only thing Navarro could hear was his own heartbeat as he slowly, painfully made his way to Candace.

"The ugly, flying thing's down!" Zakili roared from somewhere in the din of battle. "The monsters are scattering! Take 'em down! Take 'em down now!"

Finally, Navarro reached Candace.

Steadily, The Paladin lowered himself to one knee, denying the terrible throbbing from his shoulder and the biting pain of his back and ribs. Looking on the woman, bruised and bloodied, tears welled in his eyes again. He could barely see her chest moving with the tell-tale signs of respiration, and he grew frightened, moving his ear close to her lips to hear any evidence of breathing. He held her hand. It was cool to his touch.

Hot tears streamed down his cheeks as he held her close. "Fight the power of death, Candace! You've gone through too much to fall now at the end. You mighty woman of God, you can't die!

"You asked me to defeat this evil. And I did. For you."

Candace, very still, did not respond.

* 25 *
VICTORY?

"Drive them back toward the wall!" Zakili ordered his mounted elves, and the archers let loose a rain of arrows at the leading front of the monster gang. Many were cut down and the others were effectively herded from the open ground to the towering wall surrounding the castle. Kelt's closest warriors joined in the fray, driving the brutes back with blade and arrow.

Angry fires burned in Zakili's gold-flecked eyes as he glanced around and saw the slain and mutilated men and elves. Dead and injured littered the ground. He gripped his ivory-colored bow and pulled back on the silvery string. A sizzling lightning arrow formed from the air, and he took a mark at the middle of the pack of brutes.

"Exterminate them all!" he roared, releasing his arrow and firing again and again.

Everywhere in the long courtyard between the protecting wall and the castle proper, goblins and masnevires scattered. Their usurper commander had been destroyed, black flames engulfed his head after The Paladin rammed Invinitor down his throat. The fighting men and elves had been reinforced by a score of mounted archers and the entire tide of the battle had changed.

None of the craven brutes desired to be martyrs for a losing cause, their heart for battle waned when they realized there'd be no victory. The lines and the fronts disintegrated into confused, self-destructive blobs of monster warriors. Those not fighting independently against the organized warriors, more often than not, found themselves breaking out into skirmishes among themselves, collapsing any semblance of a cohesive war machine.

Zakili organized the warriors into effective exterminating contingents, elves and men fighting side by side against the faltering brutes.

Looking across the field and seeing The Paladin kneeling next to a fallen warrior, Kelt moved in closer. He remembered how Navarro had healed one of his Elite Guards just moments from death after battling a cave ravager. Silently, he thanked God the holy warrior was here. The baron comforted many of the fallen, some grievously injured, and promised them help would come soon. He didn't doubt the Lord through Navarro's touch could heal all those wounded.

Drawing near, Kelt heard the fervent prayer of The Paladin as he placed a hand gingerly on the warrior's leg, the other on the ribs. Navarro's body blocked his view of the warrior, but from what he could see, the person was hurt terribly. His heart dropped for the tragedy his warriors had endured this night. He walked around to the side to get an unobstructed view of the warrior's face.

As he circled The Paladin, he saw the fallen warrior's long, golden tresses and smooth, feminine face.

"Candace!" he cried, his breath stolen.

Kelt rushed to her, falling on his knees beside his daughter, his expression horrified, his eyes blurred with sudden tears. He wanted to demand what had happened to her and what her condition was, but he heard The Paladin still praying.

"...Lord, You said that by Your wounds we are healed. Please, release Your powerful healing flow through me exceedingly more than you ever have before. King Jesus, rip the jaws of death open and snatch Candace from its vicious teeth!"

Kelt watched desperately as The Paladin's fingers clenched tighter onto Candace's leg and side, brow furrowing. The baron didn't know what was happening, but he sensed something beyond anything he'd ever experienced in the natural realm. Something supernatural. *It is the power of God,* he decided.

"Lord Jesus, I have strayed away from you for so long," Kelt confessed as he stared at Candace. "Please don't take my only girl from me. Spare her life. Spare my soul from a grief too heavy for me to bear. Forgive me, Lord, and save her life. Please!"

He looked to unmoving Candace, his heart heavy. As he glanced at The Paladin, he noticed that every muscle seemed taut, Navarro's face a mask of determination. It appeared as if he waged an unseen, spiritual war.

"How is she doing?" someone asked. Kelt looked back to see Zakili rushing over.

Looking at the pale hue of Candace's skin, the determined expression of Navarro's countenance and her motionless form on the ground, Kelt was speechless. How could he respond? She looked as if she was about to plunge over the precipice of death.

The Elf Prince stared sadly at the scene before him. Baron Kelt knelt despondently, helpless to do anything for Candace's situation. The elf's heart ached for Kelt. Then he turned to bloodied Navarro. Still praying fervently, The Paladin's tears washed lines through the red and black blood on his face. The elf groaned sadly when he looked onto Candace's still visage, but he quickly had to turn away. This wasn't the Candace he remembered from Verdant Wood. There, she was lively and vivacious, happy and giggling around his sisters, but now...

The crushing weight of guilt crashed down on him. She was in this terrible state because she'd turned to help him when the monster horde swarmed him. Using her power of prayer, she eliminated the whole front line of monsters, dropping scores of vile creatures all around the elf to buy him more time. The aid had cost her dearly, for the giant's club swept in, smashed her, and sent her spiraling. She sacrificed herself to save him. His gaze fell to the ground, as did a lone tear.

"Lord Jesus, unleash your virtue fully through me like never before!" Navarro cried, feeling the power of God already course through his arms and down his fingers into Candace's still form.

Kelt stared.

Zakili looked up hopefully. "Christ of Navarro, do what only you can do," he heard himself pray.

With a look of determination on his face, Navarro reared his head back, holding on tight, looking like a conduit of power from Heaven to earth.

Kelt, who was closest, gawked incredulously when he heard the sharp snap in Navarro's shoulder. The Paladin winced and held on. More amazingly, the gashes on his back and ribs began to close, scab and heal so quickly that before Kelt could fully take in what was happening, The Paladin's wounds were closed.

Looking down to his dear Candace, Kelt noticed her color return, a rosy tint flushing her cheeks. Her crushed legs straightened.

Then Navarro collapsed, cognizant enough to push himself off to the side instead of falling onto Candace's lying form.

Kelt went straight for his daughter as the elf helped Navarro back to his feet. Looking weary but victorious, The Paladin stepped forward and knelt beside the baron.

"How is she?" Navarro asked.

Candace took in a deep gasp before Kelt could respond. Her eyes opened briefly, and she looked to her father, then Navarro then Zakili, and back to The Paladin, a weak smile raising her lips. Slowly, her eyelids closed, and she lay very still again.

"What's happening?" Kelt demanded, his words edged with concern.

"I don't know," Navarro admitted, bending low and stroking the woman's long beautiful hair. "Candace," he pleaded. "Fight on! We have gained the victory over the horde. Don't let death have victory over you now! The Lord has too much He wants to accomplish through you. In Jesus' name, death will not defeat you."

Tears began to well in his eyes again, racing hot down his cheeks. He held her head close to his chest, stroking her hair ever so carefully. "You cannot die," he said resolutely through his tears. "We have won the day. This will not be a victory if you too are not here to rejoice with us!"

Candace remained motionless, although Navarro could feel the rhythmic motions of her chest as she inhaled and exhaled. Carefully he laid her down, removing his torn leather vesture to place under her head as a pillow. He saw a tear streak from the corner of her eye.

"I don't understand why she isn't conscious. I've never had the healing power of the Lord pour through me like it did when it poured into Candace."

Kelt knelt near, inspecting her closely.

Navarro turned away, refusing to imagine he was given power to heal her wounds only for her to slip into a coma. Zakili gripped The Paladin's strong shoulder, lending comfort to his friend.

"Navarro, act quickly," he heard Kelt calling. "I will loosen her belt. You remove her boots."

"What?" Zakili questioned.

"Remove her boots?" The Paladin queried.

"Quickly. We have no time to waste."

Navarro shrugged, and moved to her feet, slipping off one leather boot and then the other as Kelt unstrapped the belt holding her sword's sheath.

"This is going to bring her from her coma?" the elf asked, his words mixed with a combination of doubt and hope. "What now?"

Kelt winked to the elf and bent over and whispered something to Navarro after he motioned The Paladin his direction.

Navarro smiled, but when he looked to Candace's still form his face turned grim.

"Trust me," the baron encouraged.

Navarro nodded and rose.

"What do you have in mind, Baron Veldercrantz?" the elf inquired, the situation too serious for him to toss out one of his usual quips.

"Just watch," he said smiling.

Navarro bent down at her feet and gently grasped her slender ankle. His fingers danced lightly across the arch of her foot and onto her toes, tickling her.

Candace sat upright immediately, jerking her foot away from The Paladin's loose hold, giggling.

"Welcome back," Navarro said, beaming.

"How did you know?" she demanded, still laughing, returning The Paladin's contagious smile. Navarro nodded toward Kelt.

"I've raised you all my life..." the baron explained, reiterating his words from when she'd pretended to have fallen asleep early to avoid a self-absorbed prince.

"I knew you had to have some kind of weakness, you mighty warrior," Zakili bantered in deference to the brave woman.

Candace tittered and rolled her eyes, embarrassed. Then she looked back to Navarro. "I was enjoying the attention too much to just simply spring back to my feet. I have barely been able to get you this close."

Rising, she motioned Navarro forward. When he came, she embraced him tightly.

He returned her hug gratefully. "I thank God you're alive."

"I praise the Lord for you, Navarro," she said when she pulled back a little and looked into his eyes.

"Thank you for coming to our rescue," she said, turning from Navarro to Zakili.

The Elf Prince waved off the comment as if unnecessary. "We didn't have anything else more exciting to do if those monsters hadn't shown up."

She joined in laughter with Navarro and her father at the elf's response, hugging The Paladin close again. Her eyes went wide at a sudden recollection. "About what I said, when I was lying on the field..." she started. Her voice sounded a little panicked when she considered her dying statement.

"You shared what you thought were your last words to the last person you thought you'd ever see. There's no need to explain."

"How can I ever repay you?"

"Really," Navarro said, smiling. There is no need--"

Candace grabbed him with both hands and kissed him.

Stunned, Navarro's eyes opened wide. Swiftly though, he relaxed, embracing her gently, and returning a long kiss.

"I knew it!" Zakili cried. "I knew you had it in you!"

Kelt stood, mouth open, not sure what to say.

"Give me a shovel, I'll dig my own grave!" the friends heard a distant call, followed by more victorious shouts.

"That would be my youngest sister," Zakili said proudly. "The brutes are in complete disarray. The destruction of this throng is imminent." The elf's daggers leapt into his hands and begun their dangerous spin. "I don't want to miss out on the last of the fun!" He bowed courteously to his friends and raced toward the fighting.

"I, too, have much work to be done," Navarro said, holding Candace out at arm's length. "I would wish to finish off this evil beside you and Zakili, but there are needs far greater." He turned to Kelt. "Help me to locate the wounded and dying. They need the touch of the Lord."

"Go to them," Candace encouraged as she reached for her belt and boots. "I will fight beside Zakili to finish off the remaining horde."

* * * * *

The rest of the morning was consumed as Navarro went from one terribly wounded warrior to another, rejuvenating them and healing their wounds as the Lord poured His healing virtue through The Paladin. Each renewed warrior sprung up excitedly, thanking Navarro, grabbing a weapon, and rejoining the battle.

By early afternoon, Navarro had healed the wounds of the remaining warriors and elf fighters, going to the least injured last.

The scattered masnevires and goblins were on the run, trailed and shot down by the pursuing elf riders.

Navarro sat down for a moment and leaned against the castle wall, completely drained. Closing his eyes, he felt himself begin to finally relax after the long night of fighting and the demanding morning of healing.

A disturbance caught his attention, yelling and venomous shouts exchanged somewhere close by.

Rubbing his hand across his bloody face, Navarro pushed himself from the wall and investigated. As he rounded a bend in the courtyard, he saw Castle Veldercrantz's warriors up against an equally irritated band of elves.

"...you humans, are the lesser race!" one of the elves flouted. Looking closer, he noticed who said it, and he wasn't surprised.

It was Maengh.

"The lesser race?" one of Kelt's warriors echoed incredulously. "We fought together, and we fought valiantly to defeat this horde."

"You could've done nothing if not for us," Maengh accused.

"What?" came protests from several human warriors. The ringing of drawn weapons sounded from both mobs as the elves and Kelt's men drew closer, all with grim expressions.

"Is this how you want to repay your rescuers, you ungrateful warriors?" Maengh blurted, stirring ire and promoting prejudice between the two races. "Silver Elf blades await you," he challenged. "If you're brave enough."

"I'll take your venomous tongue out myself," threatened Baracus, the general of Kelt's forces.

"Get yourself back!" Navarro commanded in a strong voice, halting the advance of both groups. "What's going on here?"

"This is none of your concern, human," Maengh spat.

"This is definitely my concern," Navarro corrected. "What's happening?"

Maengh stood tight-lipped.

"Would anybody *else* care to tell me why the elves and men who worked so well together to defeat this monster horde are now at each other's throats?"

Several of the elves and men answered up, but Navarro had already suspected Maengh was behind the sudden contention. His senses warned of danger whenever he was around that one, but he couldn't understand why. Zakili had often referred to Maengh as a kindred spirit he had known longtime. The Paladin didn't know what to think of this elf.

Kelt and Zakili were at the disturbance shortly, dividing the groups and pressing them far away from each other.

"If the elves hadn't come to your rescue, you all would be corpses scattered across the castle grounds!" Maengh insulted.

"I think it is best you leave," Baron Kelt demanded tersely.

"With pleasure," Maengh spat snidely.

Zakili's punch drove him to the ground.

"Get up and get out of here," the Elf Prince commanded. "And not another word."

The jothenac started to rise up against Zakili, but the Elf Prince's stern gaze reminded him it would be best to deal with this elf on a battlefield of his choosing. Maengh turned away, hiding his sudden fangs.

"Forgive us for the loose tongue of my lesser," Zakili apologized and bowed before the baron.

"Blood is still hot from battle," Kelt responded. "We all come down from the rush in our own ways. No offense taken."

"Then you know we're not your betters. We're not your lessers. And we're not your enemies," Zakili said. "We are your friends."

"I do understand that now. And we're forever indebted to you for returning even after my ill treatment of you."

"Friendship debts don't need to be repaid. Neither of us would be standing here now unless we all worked together to vanquish this evil," Navarro added.

Candace walked up, beaming, and hugged Navarro from behind.

"We've won," she said.

Cheers exploded and the mood lightened on both sides.

"We emerged champions," Jorab cheered. "The monster horde is defeated. Now all that remains is the giant clan hiding in the valley of Lunumdra."

"We triumphed today against overwhelming odds. The Lord has given us the victory today. This is a time to celebrate," Navarro said, but he knew the danger was far from finished. Although they won a great battle, they destroyed only a contingent of a bigger throng hiding somewhere in Avundar.

When he and Zakili battled the giants in the valley, he learned that the horde was being led by a creature called Krylothon. They didn't face him today. Navarro had never seen a monster like the powerful winged creature commanding this contingent, but he knew it wasn't Krylothon. He feared they had yet to face a creature more formidable than the winged field commander. And beside the giants, there were also the threat of those troll-like slilitroks.

Our struggles are far from over. I believe they have only just begun.

The Paladin looked to the excited warriors. Elves and men mingled and congratulated each other with rugged hugs and the friendly banging of weapons. They'd seized the victory, and rejoicing was due. The challenges lying ahead they'd tackle on a different day.

But an ominous warning rumbled in his mind. He remembered the fire on the beach. He recalled the blind men he saw upon his arrival back on Avundar's shores. He relived the warning.

But recently, through dark magic, with communication brief
those who seek evil have communed with their chief,
and the demonic have spoken of a powerful key
that will unleash Diabolicus and set his army of demons free.
And with their anger having boiled for several thousands of years,
mankind will be hopeless if on earth they appear.
The fiends hunger to destroy!
And they will if this key can be found and then deployed.
Forces of evil in this world long for it to be found,
seeking feverishly this power to make the demons unbound.
Beware warrior, the wicked will burst from their caves and their dens,
earnestly seeking this power to bring mankind to an end.

Navarro cast the disparaging words and the emotions they evoked from his mind. "When darkness overtakes the godly, You have promised light will come bursting through, Oh, Lord. You are unassailable, unbeatable, and undefeated. You alone can crush the arrogant plans of the powers of darkness.

"Christ Jesus, You are King, and You are God. And I'm trusting You to empower us to prevail over this formidable wickedness!"

Candace turned his direction, and their gazes met. Navarro flashed a contagious smile. She grinned wide.